Enough Time

By J. Edwin Buja

Published by Crystal Lake Publishing—Where Stories Come Alive!

Website: www.crystallakepub.com

As always, this one is for Dianne.

I would like to thank the amazing Bruce Wozny for allowing me to use his song "Enough Time." Every time I hear it, I get choked up, so you can see why I was inspired to write a gory horror novel. Bruce is an incredible songwriter, player, and all-around friend. Thank you, Bruce.

Also, a shoutout to Stephen Cords who was there at the beginning and encouraged me to change the opening because it was boring. Besides being a great critic, Stephen is also a superb writer and, more importantly, a great and supportive friend.

Introduction:
"Have we got enough time?"

Benjamin Kenton, January 18, 1945

Ben Kenton shivered against the frigid Atlantic wind, the threadbare greatcoat, his last keepsake from the Great War, doing little to protect him from the cold. He'd wanted to wait in the cave, but they'd given him strict orders, accompanied by the cold steel of a Luger pressed against his forehead, to stay outside. The Germans had always been spiteful pricks. Since Ben wanted—no, needed—to get paid, he'd grudgingly obeyed.

He moved closer to the cliff face and turned away from the wind. With shaking hands, he dug a crumpled pack from deep within a pocket and withdrew a cigarette, his last one until he got some cash. Struggling to keep his cold hands still, he struck a match and lit the cigarette. To hell with the blackout. No one would notice the flare of a match and the burning end of his smoke. This wasn't like the trenches in France where any light could attract a sniper's bullet. People here weren't afraid of snipers. It was impossible for the bombers to cross over from Europe. The submarine menace had been destroyed, or so they thought. Now, there was a much more imminent danger lurking in the waters off the Jersey shore.

Relishing the slight warmth afforded by the cigarette, Ben looked out to sea, trying to spot his employers. They were out in the black somewhere, no doubt plotting the destruction of his homeland. Bastards with their black uniforms and jackboots. He'd stopped caring about his country after the way it treated him upon his return from the war all those years ago. No hero's welcome for Ben, just lack of work and, worse, lack of respect. Maybe his war record wasn't the most distinguished, but he had fought hard, when he couldn't avoid it, and deserved something for it.

Through angry tears, all Ben could see was the occasional whitecap on the waves rolling in and crashing against the rocks below. He couldn't avoid the freezing salt spray that made the narrow, rocky path even more slippery. A massive shiver ran through his body, and he almost lost his balance. He steadied himself against the cliff face. If he wasn't careful, there was little chance of survival if he slipped into the water. But Ben believed he would survive, because that's what he was—a survivor.

In France, he'd lived through Belleau Wood and the Argonne Forest, avoided the firing squad—the French bitches *had* been asking for it—thanks to a lucky Hun shell that destroyed all evidence of his crime, and the squad. Damn, he'd managed to avoid the flu epidemic, too. Even the communists hadn't been able to hurt him when he had been fighting them in Russia after the war. His zealousness when killing the Reds had earned him accolades from his commander, but that approbation had soon turned to condemnation when he engaged in the wholesale slaughter of anyone suspected of being the enemy, especially women. And children. There was that talk of less savory practices. Ben did have unusual tastes, but he'd been able to hide the tell-tale bite marks.

Turning away from the wind, Ben's gaze swept up the cliff

face. Far above, a black line separated the cliff's edge and the night sky. Of the inn, he could see no sign. The inn that had drawn him here like a beacon for reasons he didn't know. There was no glow from lights, but he knew it was up there, full of people who wanted nothing to do with his kind of lowlife. Then he remembered the bitch waiting by the trash, and he felt a stirring in his loins. He'd been lusting after her for days and the opportunity had been too good to pass up. The look of recognition and disdain when she saw him had sealed her fate. When Ben had taken her, he'd felt detached, almost as if it were someone else using the knife. Her look of resignation while she died had intensified his pleasure. Before her life drained away, though, she had stared deep into his eyes and seen something. He knew they were connected, but not how or why.

The same feeling had troubled him when he'd tossed that soldier off the cliff.

Ben knew he'd be long gone before anyone found her. Inhuman trash, only good for satisfying his needs.

But those swaggering swine from Germany would do right by him. Life would be good for Ben Kenton soon enough. With the gold they'd promised him, he'd be able to buy the inn and have his pick of women. Old Ben'd show them a thing or two about pleasure, just like he had to those French girls. He thought about what he had done, the fun he'd had, the screams, the blood, and felt a rising stiffness in his trousers.

A noise from behind him jarred Ben from his carnal thoughts. His mind snapped back to the present, and he again felt the wind bite through his shabby clothes. Whatever it was made him nervous. He stood still and listened hard, trying to filter out the sounds of wind and waves.

There it was again. Screams? But not of pleasure. Fear?

Someone must have stumbled on the party of sailors who had come ashore half an hour ago. You'd think trained men, especially Germans, would be able to kill someone quietly. Ben waited for more screams, or whatever they were. Now there was only the echo of the crashing waves coming from the cave.

"It must have been my imagination," he muttered, happy to hear the sound of his own voice. "I was remembering those girls." He could feel the stirring down below again and slid a hand in his coat pocket to touch himself. "Soon," he whispered. "Soon."

Flicking the butt at the water, Ben turned away from the wind to light another cigarette and swore when he remembered he'd already smoked his last. He regretted not checking the bitch's pockets. She'd had a pack hidden somewhere. Ben wanted to lash out and hit something but felt impotent in his rage. At least in the army he could shoot and stab things. When he had been hooked up with the mobs in Chicago as an enforcer, he'd been able to use his fists freely. The government spoiled his fun there, too. It wasn't fair that he should be reduced to this: begging for food and money, sleeping in alleys, and scrounging through garbage cans for whatever he could use. And now he was being forced to work with his country's enemies to stay alive.

Maybe after he got his payment, he could sell out the Germans to the FBI. Those bastards were always ready to go after someone no matter how flimsy the charge. There might even be a reward, and he would be hailed as a hero. It would be easy to provoke them into resisting arrest. They were arrogant Germans, after all. If they were killed in a shootout, he could get away with it scot-free.

"Yeah," he said. "Ben Kenton, hero of the nation. I like the sound of that."

More noise coming from deep within the cave distracted him. Running. Someone running toward him. More than one person. Panicked, Ben looked for somewhere to hide—he couldn't let the authorities find him, not here, not now—but there was nowhere.

The rocky path was only a couple of feet wide and led round the headland to a small stony beach. The beach couldn't be seen from above and was a favorite summer picnic place for lovers, like the bitch and her soldier. There was a small cleft in the cliff above the beach with just enough space to hide a man. Ben had hidden there several times last summer watching lovebirds, pleasuring himself while waiting for them to leave so he could check for forgotten coins or abandoned bits of food.

The cave provided the only open route to the path. If he could make it around the headland, he'd be safe. Otherwise, the only place for him to hide would be down amongst the rocks near the water, but he'd freeze to death in minutes. Ben had no choice, he'd have to brazen his way out of the situation. He'd done it enough times with the railroad bulls when they'd rousted him from a cozy boxcar.

When the thumping of the boots on the cave floor grew louder, Ben realized he had no time to run. He stepped back along the path a few feet and crouched so he would have a clear look at whoever it was coming at him and waited. The sound of running got closer. Heavy boots with hobnails. It had to be the German sailors. But why would they be running? Were there FBI agents after them? Ben felt momentary anger at the G-men for spoiling his plans.

Without warning, the first figure burst from the mouth of the cave. It was the *oberleutnant* or whatever he called himself. All blond hair and blue eyes, epitome of the master race. He'd treated Ben with contempt, as if the American was something to be scraped off the bottom of his boot. They were showing the world that they were not so high and mighty now. The look on the young officer's face told Ben everything. He'd seen it enough during the war on the fresh faces of officers who'd never seen combat or the dead: mind-numbing fear. The Nazi raced past Ben without so much as a glance of acknowledgement, all the time mouthing silent screams.

Immediately behind the *oberleutnant* came the four sailors. They looked terrified. Before Ben could ask what the hell was happening, the first sailor crashed into him, knocking him against the cliff face. Sharp rock dug into Ben's back, and he felt a sudden numbness there. He tried to regain his balance, but the three other sailors collided with him, and they all went down in a heap. Ben was on the bottom of the pile and, as the weight of the men bore down on him, he heard something snap and a searing pain rush up his left arm.

Ben struggled to free himself from the pile, but the pain from his wrist—broken, he was sure—prevented him from getting anywhere. He watched the sailor who had knocked him down slowly slide off the path and down the rocks. All the while, the sailor stared wide-eyed at the cave. Without a word, the sailor went into the water. As the others scrambled to untangle themselves from Ben, he smelled the familiar odor of urine. One of the sailors had pissed himself.

"Christ, get off me, you pigs," Ben yelled.

The sailors silently freed themselves from Ben. For the first time, he noticed the odd patch sewn on the right sleeve of their uniforms. It had a submarine with a bunch of circles around it and some letters in that fancy German script: DVA. They quickly got up and ran along the path after their leader. A look down at the rocks showed Ben that the sailor who had slid into the frigid water was not trying to climb out; instead, he was swimming out to sea—out to certain death.

Trying not to put any pressure on his wrist, Ben crawled along the path after the fleeing sailors. Still, they made no sounds, and it made him nervous. When he got to where the dinghy had been tied up, he almost burst out laughing. The *oberleutnant,* having untied the tiny craft, now frantically paddled it out to sea, toward the safety of the submarine. Obviously, the officer cared nothing for his men. For a fleeting moment, Ben felt disgusted with his employers. At least when he'd been in the army, some of the officers had looked after the men, especially in battle. The three sailors who'd been left behind stood stiffly looking out to sea.

One of the men, not much more than a boy, really, with close-cropped blond hair, turned to look back along the path. Ben could see the unbridled panic on the boy's face. The boy's eyes popped open, his jaw moving in a silent scream. The other two also turned, tears streaming down their faces. Quietly and without hesitation, the three turned back then ran into the water. The waves pushed back at them, causing the blond boy to stumble and go under. The others ignored him and continued to wade out to sea. The blond boy surfaced and began to swim, buffeted by the waves. His companions followed. In less than a minute, Ben lost sight of them in the swirling waters and darkness. He shivered at the thought of how cold that water must be.

Ben sat up, nursing his broken wrist. The cold eased the pain somewhat, and all he could think about was the money the Germans owed him. He couldn't very well swim out after them and demand his cash. And he couldn't call a cop. How would that sound? "Officer, I was a German spy and they didn't pay me for services rendered. Could you do something about it?" He'd be shot for sure. And where was that captain, the tall one who was in charge? Captain Weinz? He had at least been a little courteous toward Ben, perhaps recognizing the old soldier in him. Why hadn't the captain come running out of the cave?

Leaning against the cliff face, Ben felt lost. He closed his eyes and thought about what he was going to do. He had to get to a hospital and get his wrist seen to; there was a charity place a few miles down the road that would take care of him with no questions asked. A sudden shower of frigid Atlantic water woke Ben from his thoughts. Shaking his head, sorry for himself, he tried to get up. The slippery path and his broken wrist made this a difficult task. When he tried to stand, the smooth soles of his worn-out shoes slipped on the ice. Ben fell hard on his backside, smacked his injured wrist against the cliff face. He screamed, shutting his eyes hard against the pain. Tears froze on his face.

Ben opened his eyes, determined to get the hell out of there and find help. All he wanted now was to get his arm fixed, find a warm bed, and get something to eat.

Something flickered in the cave. There was a light steadily coming toward him, white and luminous. He tried to move away, but the pain and ice stopped him. Through tear-blurred eyes, Ben thought he could see people emerging from the cave entrance. But he wasn't seeing people, only shadows cast by a weird ball of white light. There appeared to be something or someone within the light.

The light moved toward the water. The shadows passed over Ben, and he shuddered from the intensity of the cold. It looked like there was a single person in the light, but he couldn't see for sure. Whomever it was, he seemed sure-footed, never once slipping on the icy rocks. In fact, it looked to Ben as if he was gliding down the rocks to the water. That was impossible, but he didn't want to wait and ask what was going on. When the light reached the edge of the water where the dinghy had been tied, it paused. Inside his head, Ben heard, *I'll deal with you later, traitor. Though this won't be the last time.* He didn't have a clue what that was about. Then the light moved out into the water.

No, that was wrong. It wasn't moving into the water; it was moving on the water. The first thing that came to Ben's mind was an angel. He was seeing an angel walking on water. He shook his head, trying to clear away the fuzz in his head brought on by cold and pain. When he looked out to sea again, the angel had gone. He knew he was in bad shape, in need of a doctor and a drink. Maybe he could get a shot of something at the hospital, to kill the pain, of course.

Ben's efforts to get up were stopped again by a distraction, this time a noise from out to sea. Through the sounds of the waves on the rocks and the howling wind, he heard screams. Blood-curdling screams. The Germans? He distinctly heard, "*Nein.*" No. Ben sat staring into the darkness, oblivious to the pain and cold.

The screams stopped.

There was a low rumble. Ben realized he wasn't hearing anything. He was feeling it through the solid rock. He placed his good hand flat on the icy path and felt vibrations that seemed to get stronger with every passing second. Looking out to where he imagined the submarine waited, Ben saw that the water had flattened out. Waves were no longer pounding the rocks. Even the wind had died down.

Ben scrambled to his feet, not caring about the damage he may have been doing to his broken wrist. All he could think about was escape. Something was happening and he didn't want to be around for it. Moving cautiously toward the cave, movement at the corner of his eye made him face the sea again. Out in the darkness, he had no way of knowing how far, there was a light rising into the sky. It wasn't the same as the one he'd seen earlier; this was orange like a fire. What he saw on the surface of the sea around the glow made him lose control of his bladder. Hot urine flowed down his legs. Ben stood transfixed watching a wall of water approach the shore; the wave emanated from the orange fire like the ripple on a pond from a tossed stone.

When the wave was about a hundred feet from shore, Ben's survival instincts kicked in. He ran slipping into the cave then raced away from the roar of the water closing in on the cliff. Trying to run faster, Ben hit his wrist on an outcropping, yelped in pain, twisted his foot on some loose rocks, and crashed to the ground. A sharp rock dug into his flesh causing more mind-numbing pain. He rolled over in time to see the wall of water hit the cliff, completely blocking the entrance with water. Ben also thought he could see the body of one of the sailors being smashed against the cliff. As he watched, the water came churning up the cave toward him. He frantically crawled over to where some large rocks had fallen from the cave ceiling and wedged his body between them.

Frigid water washed over Ben causing him to cry out in shock. Immediately, his mouth filled with unbearable cold, and he knew he was drowning. At the same time, there was warmth, his mind obviously playing tricks. The rocks moved from the pressure of the water trying to drag him out to sea. In an instant, the cave emptied as the sea water receded, the force of the wave exhausted on the cliff wall.

Ben sputtered, trying to breathe normally. His lungs burned from the cold salty water he had inhaled, and he sent a stream of projectile vomit splattering against the other side of the cave. His whole body was frozen, and he started to shiver.

"I'll never get out of this."

A warm wind, as fierce as the frigid water and as loud as a pre-dawn barrage, swept over him. It grew hotter, almost too hot to stand. It burned.

As quickly as the wind appeared, it stopped. Now there was only the sound of water gently slapping the rocks below.

Despair overtook his mind. Ben saw light from a spot near where a branch of the cave led to a secret door in the inn's cellar. He had discovered this a few weeks before when he had tried to find a way to sneak into the inn, and it had been this knowledge that had, for some reason known only to them, been so valuable to the Germans.

As the light neared, he could see that within it was a single blurred figure. This time there were no shadows. Relieved, Ben knew it must be Captain Weinz who would surely help him.

The figure came closer, and Ben began to have his doubts. The light seemed to be pushing a frigid wave before it, a cold far more intense than anything caused by the seawater. He shivered violently, his teeth chattering. His wrist throbbed; his heart pounded. He tried to back away from the approaching figure, but the wave had wedged him between the rocks. There was nowhere for him to go.

He glanced toward the cave entrance and thought for a moment he might be able to escape that way. But his hopes were dashed when he saw the ball of light returning, the shadows it cast moving steadily toward him. Whatever it had been doing out at sea was finished, and he was sure it was coming back for him.

The glow engulfed him. Extreme cold, making his fingers hurt almost immediately. He hadn't experienced anything like this since the Russian winter, when it had been more than forty below for days on end.

Ben saw the figure looming over him more clearly. Was that a smile he saw on the face of his tormenter? Yes, it was a smile, absolutely beautiful and somehow familiar, but there was no warmth in it, only anger. Anger and hatred so deep Ben knew without doubt that he was doomed.

The voice returned to his head, but that of a woman this time. He recognized it, but knew it was impossible. She was dead, but still spoke. *You killed me again. And my love.* A pause. *No, you're gone from him now.*

His mind wracked with confusion, Ben's heart beat faster and harder like it was trying to escape from his body. The figure bent down, touched his chest. Like a belt tightening around him, it cut off his breath. There was sudden warmth down below as Ben's bowels let loose, and he was overwhelmed with shame that when his corpse was found he would be ridiculed for lack of control.

Unfamiliar regret flooded through him for all the harm he had caused, especially to all those girls. Then fear took hold, a fear he hadn't known since the first time he had huddled in a trench in France during a Hun barrage.

Ben's mind snapped at the same time his heart burst. All went black and as he drifted away, he finally recognized her, his killer. His last thought was it would be warm in Hell.

Until he returned.

Chapter 1:
"Ain't it plain as January on your face" (1)

Peter Dawson, January 15, 2020

Distracted by the incessant drone inside the car, Peter Dawson didn't see that he had entered the inn parking lot until the snow squall cleared for a moment. He slammed on the brakes, but they didn't stop the car's steady movement toward the blackness ahead. A flash of light revealed the far away rough surface and whitecaps of the bay, which meant…

"Fuck!"

In a panic, Peter pumped the brakes and twisted the steering wheel to the right. It felt like the car was being pulled toward the edge. The car skidded, skewed right then left and at last slid to a jarring stop in a low snowbank. Beyond the bank, the car's headlights showed nothing but night. Another burst of light told him he was looking out across the bay to the lighthouse above the old gun battery.

The headlights also revealed a low stone wall that ran along the edge of the cliff. There was a gap directly in front of the car. But for the snowbank, in a few more feet the car would have gone through the gap and over the cliff into the icy waters below. Peter shuddered at the thought and felt a moment of vertigo when the image of the drop from the cliff flashed across his mind. Closing his eyes and taking a deep breath, Peter forced down the panic. He'd always had an immense fear of heights, but cliffs were especially disturbing. More often than not, he broke out in a cold sweat and had trouble breathing.

The nightmares were the worst.

Patrick Dawes, January 18, 1905

He felt dizzy and there was an ache in his chest, just below his sternum.

"Open the window and look out at the headland," said someone he knew but couldn't see.

Patrick did as instructed, wrestling with the rusty window latch. With the latch released, he managed to push the window up. When he shoved the shutters away, his momentum carried him part way through the opening. Panicked, Patrick grabbed the windowsill.

An icy blast of salt wind hit his face as he looked down at the sheer cliff. Incredible fear gripped Patrick, paralyzing him.

Behind him, he heard the unmistakable sound of a sword being drawn from its scabbard.

"Turn around, sodomite," said a gravelly voice.

Patrick turned, intense pain in his chest. The speaker, standing but two feet away, had a mad smile on his face. Patrick lowered his eyes to the sabre piercing his chest where the ache had been moments ago. A premonition?

"She's mine and I will do with her as I please. Neither you nor your sissy friend can stop me. Goodbye, sodomite."

The speaker shoved Patrick. The sabre exited his chest followed by a gush of blood as he fell back through the window.

For the brief span that was the rest of his life, Patrick regretted that he could not save the life of the woman he loved. Again.

Peter Dawson, January 15, 2020

"Were you trying to get us killed? We should have flown down then taken a cab from the airport, but, no, you're too cheap." Back in the real world, Peter realized the shrill voice of his distraction had never ceased in spite of his near-death experience. "Instead, you risk my life in this ancient bucket of rust."

Because you expected me to pay for your ticket as if I'm still some lovestruck fool. How can you be so damned clueless?

During the last hour of the three-hour drive, when the weather and road conditions had worsened, she had not shut up.

Peter rubbed at an ache in his chest. This was the last thing he needed right now.

A light came on near the front of the inn, revealing the main parking lot. Someone inside must have heard the car. He backed the car away from the seawall and into the lot. There were no other cars, so Peter parked as close to the main entrance as he could. Ice caught the wheels again and the car slid into another snowbank.

Don't say a word. Not a word. Beverly—never Bev upon pain of death—merely huffed in disgust.

Calm again, he winced and hoped there wasn't too much

damage to his beloved car. *Must distract myself. Calm down.* He'd spent far too much time fixing up this old beast for it to be scratched or dented because of his carelessness. His uncle had driven a '65 Falcon for ten years, and Peter had promised himself that, when he had enough cash, he'd get a car just like it. Eventually, he did. It wasn't glamorous, but it felt solid. A bonus was the bench seat in the front which was great for making out. He chuckled quietly, remembering…not much.

Peter turned off the motor, shut off the headlights, then closed his eyes a moment. He resisted the urge to say something smart to his travelling companion. That's all she was, and nothing more. He turned to face the irresistibly hot Beverly, once his girlfriend, almost his fiancée, though she'd insisted no one could know—department protocol and all that—despite the fact that she had pursued him. As unhappy as he was at the time, Peter now felt nothing but relief at having dodged a lifetime of nagging, dissatisfaction, and inadequacy.

Months after the breakup, they had become friends again, able to have the occasional dinner without her going off about something he'd said. Even so, he had to tread lightly, especially if his opinion differed significantly from Beverly's—something that was becoming more frequent.

Still, Peter couldn't shake those persistent, deep-down feelings whenever Beverly was nearby. But it was getting easier.

Beverly was just a colleague—*nothing more, remember that*—with no sense of humor. Sometimes, she treated him like a personal servant. He couldn't be her fella, but he sure as shit better treat her like a queen. In the dark interior of the car, he could feel her glaring, her eyes boring into him, drilling home the message that he had better be on his best behavior.

Or else.

She leaned forward and stared through the windshield. "This place looks like a hovel. It had better be a five-star inside or you're taking me somewhere else."

"I'm sure it's just fine inside. Maybe they're doing some renovations to the exterior." Though, why they would do them in the winter, he couldn't fathom.

"And don't forget, we're getting two rooms. Two rooms. Right?"

"You don't have to remind me," he answered softly. "I got the message the first time, even though I never suggested anything else."

I just hoped it might come true. Maybe you'll come to me in the middle of the night. Probably not. Still, one can have fantasies no matter how unrealistic.

Peter opened the car door and stepped out into the cold. "And I remembered the fourth time. And the tenth. So just fuck off," he said, letting the wind that tore through his heavy overcoat take his complaints away. But that wasn't what made him shiver. No, he was annoyed that he was allowing her mood to spoil what should have been an exciting time. Beverly would be waiting for him to open her car door, so he lingered a little, sweeping some snow from the windshield then the driver's-side windows. More concerned about the car than the woman, Peter checked the front and was relieved to see the solid steel bumper unharmed by the icy snowbank. He was careful not to look over the snowbank to the cliff and the waiting rocks and water below.

Knocking at the windshield brought him back to the real world. It was Beverly, impatient as usual. He walked to the back of the car, opened the trunk. The heavy thud of the passenger-side door let him know Beverly had given up on waiting. He looked over the trunk lid in time to see her stumble her way toward the front door of the inn. As usual, she had left him to do all the heavy lifting.

Peter nodded. "Not your fella anymore, but I can still be your dogsbody."

He grunted getting Beverly's bag out of the trunk, his neck and shoulders straining at the effort. Beverly's commentary had only added to the tension brought on by driving in such horrible conditions. *I need a massage.* Peter hesitated before extending the bag's handle so he could wheel it into the inn. The parking lot was an uneven mess of salty slush, gravel, and sand. Beverly would have a fit if he got her luggage dirty. The wheels would be useless anyway. Holding the bag up and away from the mess, Peter lifted his own much lighter bag out and hefted it on his shoulder, ignoring the pain. He closed the trunk with his elbow; he'd have to come back later for the rest.

Beverly was nowhere to be seen. As usual, she was not waiting to hold the door open for him. When he held the door open for her, which she expected, she didn't even acknowledge him, as if it was his job to be a doorman. He was not allowed to do something because he was trying to be nice to Beverly. No, whatever he did, it was because *she* wanted it, and he had to provide it. Because of her, he felt silly holding the door for anyone, even going to different doors to avoid the situation of having to be polite.

Thanks, bitch.

He huffed, disgusted with himself for still letting Beverly twist him up inside like this.

I'm not even going to think about the thing with the phones. But he couldn't help remembering how unpleasant she had been whenever he called to ask her out. And that, despite the fact that she would not allow him to ask her out on campus lest some busybody know her business.

Peter paused to look up at the inn. It was hard to see anything in the starless night and blowing snow. Then there was the briefest lull in the storm, and he had a momentary glimpse of the façade. The Inn on the Cliff had a long and dubious history going back at least to the 1820s when it had a different name. Something strange had happened around here in 1945, and he was determined to get to the bottom of it. In preparation for his visit, Peter had done extensive research about the place. He mentally kicked himself for mentioning it within earshot of Beverly at a faculty meeting last November. When she told him she wanted to accompany him, he was flabbergasted, even momentarily excited at the thought of doing something with her. She quickly explained about her search for an ancestor, killing any thoughts he'd had of reconciliation. In fact, she had come right out and told him not to expect anything.

For a moment, standing in the cold, Peter felt that old familiar heartache. *Why can't I just let go?* He closed his eyes and willed himself to get over it. As usual, he didn't listen.

Back in November, after he'd finished typing up his notes and made his plans, Peter had happily shared them with Beverly. He also shared some things he had discovered about her ancestor, Beauregard Kensington. She was overjoyed when she discovered he had made all the arrangements. Joy turned to anger when, misinterpreting her happiness, yet again, Peter had asked if she wanted to have dinner to discuss things. Beverly, naturally, assumed he wanted to talk about them. She went ballistic, quietly since they were in his office at the university, as was her way whenever they were in public together—public for Beverly being anywhere that wasn't the privacy of their homes. He winced remembering the vitriol she had spewed forth as she made it clear there was nothing to discuss. Peter had stood there taking it, knowing that to argue was fruitless.

And now, thinking about her, he sensed excitement down below. "Damn it, control yourself, you idiot. She's not that hot." *Yes, she is.* The flush of shame burned even in the cold. Three hours stuck in close proximity to her, surrounded by her scent, getting the occasional flash of a nylon-clad leg, those amazing lips, and remembering how she looked in the summer in shorts and sandals, didn't help.

Stop being a dick led by your dick. Jerk off and get over it.

Still, he had kept some of what he had found about Kensington to himself. Beverly would have to do some of her own work. There was some satisfaction in that.

"Crap," he said, knowing he was being petty. Peter took a deep breath and decided to stop feeling sorry for himself. *Imagine what life with her could have been like.*

To take his mind off his misery, he looked around the outside of the inn to familiarize himself with the place. The heavy snowfall still obscured most details, though he spotted a few construction vehicles parked on the west side of the inn next to a temporary office and a pair of porta-potties. A large, dark building loomed from the east side. He thought he saw a light up near the top, but it quickly winked out.

Peter chuckled, remembering the stories he'd read, the hints of the debauchery. There was supposedly a brothel here before the war and all kinds of nasty things were rumored to have happened. The society pages were always a hotbed of delicious gossip, some of which might actually be true.

While he pondered the goings on at the inn, he heard a knock. Beverly's pinched face glared at him through a window. She motioned at him to get inside. Now! He'd better get a move on, or he'd get another earful. He trudged up the steps and had to struggle to get the door open with one hand. The latch stuck, probably iced up from the cold, and he strained his thumb when he tried to press it down. No one helped, but he got it open and entered the inn.

The warmth enveloped him. Pausing, Peter realized it wasn't just the temperature inside the inn. There was a feeling, a sensation, nothing he could put his finger on, but it reminded him of staying at his grandparents' house at Christmas, sleeping in their bed while the adults partied downstairs.

I'm cautiously safe. I belong.

But there is something else. Something…dangerous.

And something… A shiver of arousal ran through him. He shook it off.

I'm just tired. It's probably Beverly.

Peter wiped his boots on the large mat in the foyer then walked over to reception where he set down the bags. A tall, thin man, dressed in a double-breasted suit, a shirt with a wing collar and bow tie, stood behind the reception desk. With his short black hair and a salt and pepper goatee, he looked a few years older than Peter. He appeared agitated but relieved that someone else was here to help deal with her. Peter closed his eyes and tried not to smile. Beverly could do that to you when she wanted something done.

"I have to get your small cases and our laptops," Peter said, turning to leave.

"Never mind," Beverly said, giving him the look that said she would brook no argument. "I want to get to my room and have a shower. I need to get sorted after that horrendous journey from the college. You can get the rest of the stuff after."

I can, can I? Peter thought with bitterness spiced with a dash of resignation.

She turned back to the man at the desk whose nostrils flared for an instant. A brass name plate on the desk read: Owen O'Dale - Manager. "Now, we want two rooms," she said in her sweetest voice, the one she used to manipulate people, make them think she actually cared. Peter leaned against the desk, interested to see how this would play out. "I know they're available. He checked your web site." Peter sniffed at being referred to only as 'he.' "Two rooms. And they absolutely must not be adjoining."

Peter's blood began to boil, especially when the man gave

him a quick look with a raised eyebrow. The heat rose from his chest and up his neck. There was sweat behind his ears, which were probably beet red by now. Did the bitch really have to rub it in that much? Was she expecting him to break into her room at night and try something? She'd made it perfectly clear while they were going out that she wasn't interested in anything of that sort. Being a gentleman, Peter had never tried, never suggested, nor even hinted. Beverly was masterful at the pre-emptive strike.

Then he felt guilty for thinking so badly of her. She must have her reasons. *If only you shared them.*

Owen O'Dale couldn't miss the discomfort on Peter's face, but his expression remained neutral, except for his flaring nostrils. For the first time, Peter noticed a violent red scar that ran from the man's right ear, down his neck, and under his collar. *Ouch.*

"That won't be a problem, madam," O'Dale said in a quiet voice. "We don't have many guests this time of year, and with the repairs and renovations…well—"

"I really don't care about that," Beverly interrupted, "just give me the key, please." Peter could hardly believe it—she'd batted her eyelashes. She really did.

She's playing you, O'Dale. You're in for a world of pain now.

He couldn't help himself. He grunted. Beverly turned to him for a moment, a smile still plastered across her face. Her eyes told a different story. Peter pretended to be choking so she wouldn't think he was criticizing her.

O'Dale passed her a registration card which she promptly

handed to Peter with the instruction, "You fill this out." She waited for the key. O'Dale glanced between his two guests, not quite sure which of them to address. Obviously deciding on caution, he turned and retrieved a key from the rack of hooks behind him. Almost all the hooks held keys. When he passed the key to Beverly, she said, "I want a high-speed internet connection in my room."

O'Dale set the key on the counter and thought for a moment then replied, "I'm sorry, madam, but we don't have any…connections."

Beverly's eyes widened. Her jaw stiffened. Any minute now, she would peak and launch into a tirade. Peter knew it would be ugly. Teeth clenched, she said, "According to your web site, all the rooms have high speed connections."

O'Dale shook his head, nostrils flaring, and said, "That's unfortunate. You see, what with the renovations and all…well." He paused and pursed his lips. "We haven't gotten around to having the …connections…installed. I'll have to see about the…website. Our man has probably gotten ahead of himself. I'm sure you know how it is, dealing with incompetence." His eyes darted to Peter then back to Beverly.

You bastard.

Beverly glared at O'Dale then turned to Peter. "Why didn't you check first, you idiot?" She stormed off toward the stairs.

"I'll have your bag brought up in a moment, madam," said O'Dale.

Beverly paused at the bottom of the stairs, turned to face the men, and said, smiling and pointing a finger at Peter, "He can bring them up." She went up three stairs then stopped.

"Top of the stairs, fourth floor, turn right, it's at the far end. Number forty-seven. That's four seven," said O'Dale. Beverly glared down at the manager. "No, madam, this is an old establishment. There is no elevator." His smile looked painful, as if he was pulling a muscle or two trying to maintain it.

Beverly inhaled sharply then proceeded up the stairs and out of sight. The lobby was instantly friendlier.

Emma Ranahan, January 15, 2020

The midwinter storm blew in from the sea sending huge waves crashing against the cliffs below. Some of the spray startled Emma when it reached her fourth-floor bedroom window. What power there was behind the wind and water. Was it this power that had destroyed a mystery submarine? Caused the walkway between the inn and the library to collapse? It was no wonder people had drowned below the cliffs or been swept from the footpath out to sea. Emma stared out the window and shuddered.

It was like this every January. Had been for as long as she could remember. With each passing year, it got worse.

Sometime around the fifteenth, she'd start to feel anxious, restless. There was something coming, but Emma had no clue what it could be. The dreams were the first sign. She'd wake in a cold sweat, shivering and scared half to death by the horrific visons that invaded her sleeping mind. The dreams were so real, she could remember every feeling, every moment of pain.

Every cut.

The coppery stink of blood.

Emma would be afraid to go to sleep. The first time it happened, just after her thirteenth birthday, her parents hadn't believed her. But it didn't take many screams and cries in the night for them to be convinced something was wrong with their daughter. Years of therapy had done nothing to solve the problem. Emma lived a happy life, loved her parents, had lots of friends. She was simply a lovely young girl who had bad dreams. The psychiatrists called her problems confabulations—fantastic fantasies that couldn't possibly be real.

In her later teens, Emma had tried regression therapy. It was an utter failure. Despite being in a deep trance, no memories had surfaced. No past lives had revealed themselves. The therapist flat out told Emma she was blocking any progress. It was Emma herself who refused to cooperate, who wouldn't let the therapist do her job.

She had even considered voodoo. There were rumors her ancestors had dabbled with it in New Orleans. Emma had never been able to pin anything down. The history of her family was vague to say the least. When she'd asked her parents outright, they'd looked at her in horror and quickly changed the subject. She later discovered she had been adopted.

What a load of bullshit.

Emma thought it might have been that the therapy had never occurred during the height of her trauma—mid January. It was as if, every year, the previous year's events had never happened and new trauma always came as a surprise.

A surprise to everyone but Emma.

Later, she'd tried to stay awake reading, watching movies, even taking stimulants. Nothing helped. She'd be wide awake one moment, then screaming her head off about whatever torture had been performed on her in her dreams the next. There were no friends to rescue her.

Friends? Give me a break. After the first time, I had a reputation for being nuts.

The other kids gave her the side-eye after she had a breakdown at school that first January. Even the teachers were wary. That was fine by Emma. She could concentrate on her studies without having to be bothered by trivial things like team sports, parties, or dates.

Saved a lot of money, didn't I?

As much as she told herself there was nothing intrinsically wrong, she simply suffered from "episodes," Emma had trouble believing in herself. Her self-esteem took a terrible hit and by the time she graduated from high school, she fostered the idea that she was a whacko as a means of self defense. No one could hurt you if you didn't let them get close enough.

At university, where she had hoped to get a fresh start, Emma would not allow anyone near her while the dreams ran their course. She couldn't explain why. No one would have believed her. She could scarcely believe it herself.

Anyway, none of her few friends, men or women, could stand being around her in January, or even December. It got to the point where she anticipated the night terrors to come and grew edgy and had a perpetual foul mood while she awaited the arrival of her dreams. And for two weeks after, she would walk around in a daze with haunted eyes, seemingly scared of her own shadow. After the dreams, when she was twenty, Emma never got out of her funk. Fear of what was to come cluttered her mind almost year-round.

If she was being honest, Emma never had much of a desire to have a relationship anyway. She'd yet to meet anyone who stirred any kind of emotion within her or could make her forget her burden. Now that she was twenty-five, Emma decided there was nothing for it but to endure. Though she knew what was coming, tried to prepare for the horrors, every one of them felt fresh.

She had been blessed when the Wycliffe Point library committee had hired her as the new librarian. A perk of the job was an apartment above the library. The building was an old warehouse. The library occupied the first three floors with the fourth floor used mostly for storage. The old offices had been converted to living quarters. The fact that the fourth floor was supposed to be haunted had never bothered Emma. Her dreams already haunted her. What would a few spectres be able to do that was worse than what her own mind put her through?

The bonus was that, when Emma did have her nightmares, no one could hear her scream. Anyone who did would put it down to the ghosts having a rant.

The grandfather clock in the living room chimed eight o'clock. Time for bed.

"I need plenty of rest for tomorrow," she said to her reflection in the window. "Remember, we're expecting visitors."

In the bathroom, Emma ran her hand over her belly. The keloids still stood out from her skin. The one around her neck always seemed to last longer than the others, but she would wear a turtleneck sweater to make sure no one would see it.

That was another dividend that came with her dreams. In addition to the solitude, keloids appeared on her body when she grew overly excited. Overly excited as in, having horrific nightmares. They'd started showing up in her teens. Fortunately, by then she was alone enough to not have to explain why no one was allowed to see her naked in January. No one knew about them. Emma had been careful not to schedule any doctor's appointments in January.

Not that there had really ever been anyone that wanted to see her naked—in January or any other time of the year.

Two professors from the University of North Massachusetts were coming to Wycliffe Point to do some kind of historical research. The next few days would be more interesting than most of her days at the library. There would be at least two patrons rather than the normal none. Emma laughed. It was amazing that she even had a job considering just how many of the locals visited the library. She'd heard that there was a rich benefactor, someone connected with the old inn next door, that had endowed the library with the stipulation that there must always be a live-in librarian. It was as if the job had been created specifically for her.

Emma had tried to find out about this Dawson fellow.

He'd managed to avoid being photographed for any of the university yearbooks and hadn't published anything that came with an author photo. *Why so elusive, Professor?* There was something about the name Dawson that stirred feelings deep inside her. Perhaps they had met in a past life. She laughed at the ridiculous idea.

The other professor, Kent, was more photogenic. Emma thought she was incredibly beautiful, but there was a hardness in her eyes. She'd taken an instant dislike to the woman even though she'd never met her. *This one might be trouble.*

Emma pulled on fresh panties and an old, extra-long tee shirt. The material was soft and would not irritate the keloids while she slept. She crawled into bed, took one of her sleeping pills, and hoped she'd have a peaceful night's sleep.

There was little chance of that.

Millie Ranahan, January 15, 1985

Millie placed the boxes on the front desk for Oliver to inspect. He picked up a snow globe from one box and shook it. She smiled as he watched the little white particles float around the building in the globe like the storm raging outside right now. The 'snow' settled and Oliver shook it again. He seemed to take great pleasure in the object.

"I don't know where it came from," said Millie. "It showed up a couple of weeks ago when a courier dropped off a package."

"I remember," said Oliver, shaking the globe yet again. He

giggled. "What's with this thing? It's delightful."

"According to the note in the package, that and the two broken globes are family heirlooms that date back to the turn of the century," said Millie. "The weird thing is, I didn't know I had any family. I mean, I must have relatives somewhere, but there was no record of them at the orphanage."

"So how did they figure out a way to get these heirlooms to you? And why send broken ones?"

Millie shook her head. These "family heirlooms" were as big a mystery to her as were the terrible scars that had appeared on her body last week. They itched something fierce, and the doctor had been skeptical when Millie told him they weren't old. She had become almost hysterical in the doctor's office when he kept repeating that the scars had to be at least five years old, probably older. Millie knew they were no more than five days old, but the doctor was adamant. The doctor had threatened to commit her for observation if she didn't calm down. Before he could do anything, Millie had stormed out of his office, her blouse wide open so all the patients in the waiting room could see her disfigurement as she left. No one had paid her any attention.

When she had returned to the inn, Oliver had seen the daggers in her eyes and known to steer clear of her until her temper calmed. He'd asked her if there was something wrong when he caught her scratching. She'd blustered and said something about a rash. She wasn't sure if he believed her, so she decided not to mention the scars. Ollie would have wanted to examine them and, though she knew she had nothing to worry about from him in that regard, her vanity would not allow her to expose herself.

Millie shrugged. "Not much of an heirloom, anyway. Seems a silly thing to hand down. Can you see the little people in the windows?"

Oliver looked closely at the globe then shook his head.

"Must have been my imagination," said Millie. "The broken ones have little inns as well."

"What's that thing in the other box? Is it glass?" They peered into the small box.

Inside, a pile of glass shards rested on a bed of cotton wool. "I haven't a clue," said Millie.

"It's a *Schusterkugel.* It's supposed to be filled with water and used to focus light," said Oliver. "They've been around for hundreds of years. That's where the idea for snow globes originated."

"Thanks for the history lesson, professor." She picked up the box and stared at its contents. "Dumb." She shivered when a gust of Atlantic wind caused an open door somewhere to slam shut. "I hate this time of year, Ollie."

"Don't we all," said Oliver. "My father is supposed to be here sometime in the next few days. He says something is going to happen, but he wouldn't tell me what."

"He's always been a little mysterious," said Millie. She stopped speaking as if surprised by what she had just said.

Oliver stared at her. "You've never met him, Millie. And I've rarely spoken about him."

"I don't know, Ollie," she said. "Something's got me stirred up. I've been having bad dreams again. They'd stopped for so many years. I thought they were gone for good. Now it's getting to where I'm afraid to go to sleep."

Oliver placed a hand on Millie's shoulder and gently squeezed. "I've got some pills that might help you sleep. I got them last year after I had my appendix out."

"Thanks, but I'd rather not. I don't like drugs of any kind. They messed me up something fierce when I was a kid. The doctors thought my nightmares were just 'girl problems.' You know, puberty and all."

"I'm sorry, Millie," said Oliver. "I wish there was something I could do."

Millie leaned her head down and kissed her friend's hand. It wasn't a romantic gesture, just one of affection. She looked up the stairs. "When I'm up there in the halls, it feels like someone's following me or watching from the rooms. It's worst up on the fourth floor, especially around number forty-seven. And it's always so cold there, even in the summer."

"The special suite for dignitaries. Some nasty people have stayed there. Bad karma?"

Millie scratched her belly again. When Ollie noticed, she stopped before he could ask any questions.

Millie closed her eyes and thought about the purchase she had made earlier that day. It was hidden in her room where a nosy maid like her would be unlikely to find it. The moment she had seen it, she knew she needed it to break the cycle. She had no idea what that cycle was or how a pistol would help.

Chapter 2:
"The love we have may never live again"

Peter Dawson, January 15, 2020

Heat rose from Peter's collar and hit his face. He'd had to mollify too many people because of Beverly's rudeness. For a second, he tried to remember why he had fallen so hard for her then remembered her smile and sweet disposition when they'd first met at the student-faculty meeting. And her body…oh, that body. He'd been played.

The man at reception hummed.

"Sorry," said Peter. "I'm Peter Dawson. This place is gorgeous." He held out his hand. Why be angry with the manager. After all, Beverly always brought out the worst in people.

With a huge smile that revealed perfect white teeth, O'Dale said, "I'm Owen O'Dale. Pleased to meet you, Professor Dawson. Welcome to the Inn on the Cliff." He shook Peter's hand vigorously with a firm grip. "I'm so glad you could come early."

"Peter. Professor makes me feel like some old fart with a tweed jacket and patches. And a pipe. Early for what?"

"Owen. And, if I'm not mistaken, under that overcoat, you're wearing a tweed jacket. Does it have patches on the elbows? A reunion of sorts."

"Yes, but I'm not an old fart. I'm confused."

"I'm sure you're not," said Owen. "Old, maybe," he added with a grin. "You'll figure it out."

"That was Beverly Kent. Don't ever call her Bev," said Peter, pointing in the direction of the stairs with his chin. "We're history professors at the University of North Massachusetts. We're here to do some research. I got a tip about a submarine, and she's looking for a relative." Owen's face registered no expression. "Sorry, I'm blustering," said Peter. He looked toward the stairs. "She makes me..." He stopped before he said anything offensive.

"That pill? I know," said Owen, nodding. "I'm surprised no one's killed her yet. How is it she's still alive?"

"She reduces her enemies to quivering lumps. Even her friends are afraid of her. Not that she has many."

"I'll pretend to be her friend then," said Owen.

"She always manages to get her way, though." Peter handed over his credit card.

"Maybe not this time," said Owen. He stared at the credit card, turned it over, then shrugged. "Sorry to bust your chops with that incompetent remark, but I needed to deflect her attention. My testicles were starting to withdraw into my body."

"Been there. Mine are just beginning to drop back down." Peter unconsciously scratched his crotch.

Owen looked up from the ancient credit card machine. "You and me both."

Peter decided he liked Owen and that the man would make his stay much more pleasant. "Do you know anything about the history of this area?" He signed the credit slip and returned it to Owen.

"I know all there is to know about the inn and most of the

county. I was trustee for the local historical society. The truth is, I ran the thing. If there's anything I can do to help, don't hesitate to ask."

"Haunted, I suppose," said Peter.

Owen nodded. "Completely. Mostly harmless. Waiting." He glanced to his left and right. "Just watch for the heartless parlor maid."

Peter's eyes popped open, and Owen laughed. Peter grinned then said, "I suppose the brothel is real, though."

Owen's nostrils flared, and he shook his head. "A mere rumor to act as a distraction from the murders." He smiled. "That's all in the past. I try to inhabit the now."

"Right," said Peter. "Murders." So, Owen was a joker and not to be taken too seriously. "I suppose you have to deal with lots of rude people. How do you remain so calm?" he asked, trying to be sarcastic. "The now?"

Owen's nostrils flared again, and he looked serious. "In the face of rudeness and humorlessness, I can be a rock." He looked toward the stairs. "She needs a good…um, I believe the term is…um, fucking off. She's your ex, isn't she?"

Taken aback by Owen's boldness, all Peter could do was frown and nod his head.

"You're better off," said Owen. "She'll suck the life out of you." When Peter sighed, he said, "Ah, fresh wounds. I'd say it's only been a couple of months, and the pain is still there. You still love her, don't you?"

Peter didn't answer but knew deep down that he didn't.

"Can't figure out why," Owen said. "That's what got you so dizzy."

Can't figure out why I let her get to me. Bitch.

Before Peter could respond, Owen added, "She'd do it with just about anyone, but she never let you screw her. Not even a hand under her skirt or a squeeze of a boob. Shame. She's got the most amazing caboose." He glanced at Peter. "Ah, but you're a gentleman so you risked blindness after every meeting."

Peter wanted to crawl under a rock. "Is it that obvious?"

"Don't worry, you'll get over it. True love is just around the corner. Trust me. There should be enough time this time." He pointed at a side door. "And everyone does it."

Amazed at the accuracy of what Owen had said, Peter asked, "How?"

Owen raised his hand in a fist then smiled. "Oh, you mean," he glanced toward the stairs. "Many years of experience with love and tragedy." He sighed. "Far too many years."

They remained silent for a few moments. Peter tried to figure out what the hell Owen was talking about. *Enough time for what?* He shrugged and reached for a pen to fill out the registration cards.

Owen grabbed the cards and said, "We'd better get you checked in. I'll fill these out. You're Peter Dawson and she's..." He looked up at Peter.

"Beverly Kent."

Owen's nostrils flared. "That's C U..."

"No. Kent. With a K E. Apparently, she has an ancestor from around here."

Owen looked at Peter with narrowed eyes. "Ancestor?" He

glanced over Peter's shoulder. Peter looked back. Three dust-covered snow globes and a pile of glass sat on a shelf in an alcove by the stairs. They appeared to be broken. He couldn't make out the scenes inside.

Peter turned back and said, "Kensington. Benjamin, Barney, something like that."

While Owen filled out the cards, his hand shook. When he wrote down Beverly's name, he muttered something. Peter could just make out, "Beauregard. Damnation." He set down the pen then seemed to gather his thoughts. "That explains a lot. Not what I was expecting," he said quietly. "Now, *where* am I?" Owen tapped the desk nervously and looked around the room as if trying to remember something.

Peter cleared his throat.

Startled, Owen said, "I'll give you a hand with the baggage. Perhaps I'll take madam's bag to her. Spare you a telling off. I'm suddenly feeling particularly brave."

Peter said, "Too bad about the internet. I need to do some research online."

"Of course," said Owen, grinning. "It's…high speed and is accessible in every room."

Peter smiled and decided he liked Owen even more.

After Peter had gone to retrieve the remaining bags from the car, Owen led him up the wide staircase. At the second-floor landing, Owen said, "You've got number two. It's down the hall that way, around the corner. On the southwest side. It's as far away from forty-seven and the northeast side as you can get. Near the old servant's quarters. Where she stayed." He went up a few steps then stopped and turned. "Breakfast is served between seven and nine. Comes with the room. How do you like your eggs?"

"Over easy, bacon not too crisp," Peter said.

Owen nodded with a smile and continued on his way, lurching from the weight of Beverly's bags.

Walking along the hall toward his room, Peter felt relieved to be alone. The drive down from Massachusetts had been miserable. Beverly had barely spoken to him, except for the last hour to complain, and had insisted they listen to Enya and Sarah McLachlan. It had been pure agony. He liked silence or loud rock. Trying to ignore the music had given him the chance to formulate his plan of attack for the coming week: local library, police headquarters, and the coroner's office. And add historical society, thanks to Owen.

Odd bird, that one. I'll have to sit and have a beer with him, get him to tell me lurid tales of the brothel that didn't exist. And murders. And waiting ghosts.

At that, Peter remembered what had first attracted him to Beverly besides her coy smile and sunny demeanor. Her tee shirt had been rather tight. He really should have listened to Paul, the old medievalist. He'd warned Peter there was more to Beverly than anyone cared to know. But Peter had been too love-struck and horny to listen. Poor Paul; shame about the frying pan incident. It wasn't all bad: the doctors *had* been able to remove it.

A few steps from his room, Peter passed a narrow staircase. He glanced up the stairs where he saw a woman crossing at the top. It was darker up there and he had trouble seeing details. She seemed to be wearing a long dress, maybe a nightgown, with a large wet-looking stain from her chest to the floor. She carried a bucket. He sensed she was not just sad, but lost, empty.

Why would I think that?

She must have sensed him staring because she paused to look down. Curly black hair poked out from a kerchief tied around her head and ringed her dark face. Despite the darkness, Peter saw her eyes were the most piercing green he had ever seen. Her sadness evaporated and she tilted her head slightly and smiled. She mouthed a silent hello. Then, as if embarrassed, she quickly moved a hand to cover the stain. With a slight nod to him, she continued on her way.

Patrick Dawes, January 18, 1905

Patrick stared at the photograph of Emelia Renihan. It was small and easily fit in the palm of his hand or its usual place—his billfold, which he kept close to his heart. Despite its size, the beauty of the subject was clear as day. Her perfect dark skin, that lovely yet shy smile, the long hair, uncharacteristically hanging loose about her shoulders. He sighed and closed his eyes to remember his first, and only, meeting with the fair Miss Renihan.

It had taken him several months to settle his affairs after leaving the cavalry. Then there was the inconvenience of the court of inquiry into an incident during the Spanish War. An officer, Bartholomew Kensington, had been accused of the unlawful killing of prisoners. Though he had been in close proximity to the alleged incident, and had first-hand accounts from some troopers who had witnessed the killing, the court had found his testimony of little use. The witnessing troopers had been killed shortly before the war's end, and there were no survivors among the prisoners to tell the tale.

Kensington had sat smugly and self-assured throughout the proceedings. When Patrick had entered the courtroom, Kensington had guffawed and let slip a word that, under different circumstances, would have caused Patrick to punch him in the jaw. Several times, if that was possible. It still angered him that Kensington had put about rumors concerning Patrick and his friend Oscar O'Dale. Whatever Oscar's leanings, they harmed no one and were no one's business but his own. Patrick chuckled when he remembered how Oscar had blustered and flailed trying to explain what he had meant when he had suggested some activity to Patrick. The poor man had been humiliated and feared he would be exposed. Patrick calmed him, assured Oscar he had no animosity toward his friend. Nothing would change between them. In fact, if the truth be known, and it never would, he regretted not having experimented.

But that was far in the past and Patrick and Oscar had served in the 9th together as boon companions. They always had each other's back, and one or the other had saved his friend's life on several occasions. Now Patrick was about to see his friend again for the first time since Oscar was mustered out due to his wounds in Cuba. It was unfortunate they had not crossed paths last summer in St. Louis. It would have been an excellent time to reminisce. It would also have been an opportunity to spend more time with the lovely Emelia.

Did she still have the snow globe he had won for her? The memory of the smile on her face when he presented the prize to her warmed his heart.

How fantastic that Patrick's best friend should be the manager at the inn at which the love of his life was employed.

But would Bartholomew be there as well? If there was any justice in the world, the evil swine would have been swinging from a rope or facing the firing squad. Or perhaps he could fry in that new machine, the electric chair. Kensington deserved it far more than that poor elephant.

The conductor came though the car to announce that they had arrived at their destination. A quick check of his pocket watch told Patrick that the train had arrived on time. It was two o'clock. There would be time to get settled in his room before he sought out Emelia. Had Oscar told her he was coming?

Did I mention Emelia in my letter? Damnation! I don't think I did. What if she's not there?

Feeling a little panicked and waiting for the train to come to a complete stop, Patrick looked through the window for his first sight of Wycliffe Point, but was disappointed to see nothing but snow. He slipped the photograph of Emelia back in his billfold which he then placed in a pocket inside his coat. Patrick kept patting the pocket to make sure his billfold, and the photograph, were still there.

He suddenly felt nervous. His immediate plans were to go to the inn and get to his room. A week ago, he had telegraphed Oscar to let him know he was coming and to book a room.

Oscar had assured him that a room was available. However, Oscar insisted Patrick would not be paying for his accommodation. But what about Emelia?

Will she remember me? Will she be happy to see me?

Patrick began to doubt himself. They'd spoken for what, five, maybe ten minutes at the fair. Was that enough time for him to have made an impression?

"Of course you did, you clod," he said to his reflection in the coach window.

Patrick wondered if there was a jeweler somewhere in town. He was thinking about getting a ring for Emelia.

Am I being presumptuous? Perhaps.

"Stop asking so many questions, damnit." His reflection didn't look too sure of himself, either.

However, if Patrick could face the hostiles out west or the Spanish in Cuba, he could certainly face a young woman when he asked her to marry him.

Pulling his valise from the rack above his seat, Patrick made his way to the end of the coach then stepped down to the platform. It was bitterly cold, but he had a thick overcoat that kept him sufficiently warm. Checking at the ticket booth, he found the inn was only about a mile from the train station. A brisk walk, but nothing compared to the endless western plains or the slog up the mountains in Cuba.

Patrick lit a cigar then set out for the inn.

He had been walking for about fifteen minutes and knew he was on the correct street to locate the inn. There was a sharp prod in his back. Stopping, he waited for whomever it was to walk in front of him. When he saw who it was, his heart sank.

Peter Dawson, January 15, 2020

Peter was transfixed, his heart raced, and there was an ache in his throat. "Wow," he said quietly. He felt a tickle start at his feet and move up his body until it reached his head and disappeared. The tension in his neck evaporated.

And just like that, he was completely free of Beverly. He'd be taking no more crap from her.

With that thought, he opened the door to his room and went inside. After a quick shower, he pulled on his sleeping boxers and a fresh tee shirt, then settled down on the bed to read over the notes he'd made last summer in Germany. It was best to refresh his mind before setting out to work. He didn't feel at all tired; excited, wired, distracted, but no longer tense from the drive with Beverly.

Damn, she was back in his head. Yet now it was different. He pitied the woman who proudly proclaimed she couldn't understand how anyone could be in love and had thoroughly rejected him. He was released from wallowing in the emptiness and desolation. He knew she wasn't worth it.

All this from a strange woman's brief smile at the top of the stairs. Impossible. I can think clearly again.

Peter stared into space trying to remember the woman's face. All he could see were her piercing green eyes.

He giggled and poured himself a generous portion of scotch from the bottle he'd hidden in his briefcase. The first sip was hot, burning his throat as it went down. The second, much smoother.

He went over his notes.

"I'm glad I typed these up," he said, embarrassed by the effort it took to decipher his own scrawl. The room was so warm and cozy. He had only read two or three pages, and taken a few more sips of scotch, when fatigue overtook him. His eyes fluttered then closed.

Peter was aware that he was above the sheets and blankets, now cold and unable to move. He knew he had to get under the covers, but in his half-sleepy state, couldn't get his limbs to obey. Something soft and light touched his feet. It tickled slightly as it moved up to his ankles then his calves. At his feet again. Hands? Yet so cold, as if they were only in his imagination. They moved up his legs and Peter felt a growing excitement. He loved being touched, caressed, tickled, but had not known such attention for so long. He groaned, still unable to wake, but now not wanting to spoil the dream.

The hands reached his inner thighs and the light touches of that other—hair, maybe—was now on his belly. He grew hard and popped out of his drawers. He stirred enough to move a hand closer to touch himself.

Something—those hands?—held him back, ever so gently. In his head, he heard, " *Wait.*"

And then the softest kiss, so light it might have been a cool breeze. His erection grew and Peter arched his back to push himself closer to whomever, whatever was there. Was that someone's cold breath? Peter's throat constricted with the pain of longing, so familiar and hated until this moment.

He couldn't open his eyes and was glad.

The lips returned for a last kiss then traveled up his stomach to his chest and neck. Someone was on top of him, but there was no weight, only a cold that burned him to his core. The lips brushed his. A tear of happiness slid down his cheek. It was quickly kissed away.

No tears. Not words, just an impression deep within his mind.

Something settled over his hardness as if a hundred icy feathers had fallen from above. He rose to meet it and was engulfed in a cold so exquisite he stopped breathing for a moment. He raised his hands and when the air changed from cool to icy, he knew he was touching his phantom lover.

Cold kisses covered his face while he slowly moved his hips.

There was sudden heat as something hot dripped on his chest and trickled down.

Far too soon, he knew release. Peter cried out and his arms fell to the bed, drained of strength by the intensity of his pleasure.

He was sure a hand reached into his chest and cupped his heart.

In his mind he heard, *Mine at last. This time.* He could feel again.

"Always," he said. "Every time."

The cold moved back down his body and when the last touches of ice left his toes, Peter fell into a deep sleep.

His dreams alternated between dark, curly hair and steep cliffs.

Emma Ranahan, January 15, 2020

She felt cold, the blankets and comforter that were supposed to cover her having fallen away. Half asleep but aware of her discomfort, Emma couldn't move. She sensed she was sleeping on her belly. Her subconscious knew this was bad. The pressure on the keloids would irritate them and, if it went on for too long, they might rupture. It had never happened because she had trained herself to sleep on her back.

A scent, familiar yet new, filled her nostrils. A man? And beneath her was not the smoothness of a sheet, but something hard and soft, warm and cold.

There was a heart—not hers—beating faster. Her own heartbeat caught up. Excitement coursed through her, a thrill deep down where no man had ever touched her. She had wanted this for what seemed an eternity, but it had always eluded her, torn away by something…evil and cruel.

Was there enough time this time?

Now deep in her dream, Emma knew there was a chance to fulfil her desires. He was with her at last. They would be together, and nothing could come between them. He penetrated her, and the pain and surprise were welcome. Soon, all feeling was replaced by a love that had always been there, hers at last, offered freely and without hesitation, always, every time.

As release came, Emma experienced horrendous pain in her chest as if something was tearing out her heart. Hot blood poured from the wound.

There was a cry from afar and a blinding light obscured everything.

Emma woke, shivering. In a daze, she rolled over, fulfilled but cheated. Her nightmares had always left her sweating and shaking with fear. She nearly always screamed until she became fully awake and aware it was all a dream. Her nightmares had never been this…pleasant?

But there had been the horribly familiar pain in her chest, and the unfamiliar yet satisfying pain between her legs.

Pushing herself up from the mattress, she sensed the wetness down below, but also all over. Gently, she brought a hand under the hem of her tee shirt and found that her panties were soaked. *That was some dream.* But there was more. Her tee was also wet. How much pleasure could she have had?

She reached for the bedside light and snapped it on.

When she saw the blood still oozing through her shirt, she screamed.

As Emma slowly lost consciousness, a face, full of malice filled her vision. That evil smile and look of satisfaction never changed.

Emmeline Ronaghan, January 18, 1865

Emmeline shivered. She hated the cold this far north. Back in Louisiana, the weather was always warm, maybe with a bit of a chill on a December night. But it was never cold enough to freeze your toes off if you stayed outside for too long. It also never snowed, though the hurricane winds could be fearsome. Emmeline pulled the cloak tighter around her body and attempted to pull open the inn door. It was crusted with ice from the sea spray and refused to move. If she was out here much longer, she feared she would freeze to death.

Another wave crashed against the rocks below. The spray covered Emmeline from head to toe. Panic rose within her. Bad enough to be cold, but to be wet now was far worse.

I'm going to die.

The wood she carried fell from her arms and clattered over the frozen ground. Why had no one refilled the firewood box in the cave? At least the cave was safe from the wind and sea spray. It was still cold, but Emmeline could bear that for a time.

No, the firewood box was empty, so she'd had to go to the wood pile out by the shed near the cliff edge. Instead of a few minutes to perform the task, it had taken Emmeline almost an hour to free enough wood from the frozen pile to have a sufficient amount for a decent fire. As it was, the ice-crusted wood needed to defrost.

Let him get the damned wood himself next time. I'm not a slave anymore, damn it.

Thinking about that swine gave Emmeline the strength she needed, and the frozen door burst open with a loud crack. She quickly grabbed a bucket that sat just inside and set it in the jamb to prevent the door from closing on her. Ignoring the angry shouts from inside, she blew on her frozen hands. As quickly as her cold body would allow, she gathered up the dropped wood and scooted inside.

The heat from the bread oven was a relief. Emmeline stood for a moment trying to get some warmth back into her shivering body. The smell of the baking bread helped take her mind from her discomfort. However, the smell also reminded her of her mama, dead now for two years.

Who killed you, Mama? What animal did that horrible thing to you?

She had her suspicions but kept them to herself. Even that nice Captain Daweson couldn't know what she suspected. He had tried to shield her from the unwanted attention of his commanding officer, and paid the price in extra duties and, worse, more dangerous assignments on the battlefield.

Dear Philip. If only...

Emmeline shook that silly idea out of her head. No self-respecting officer in the Union Army would ever allow himself to be associated with a lowly former slave. But, still, Philip had been so friendly and helpful to her after she was hired on by the army as a washerwoman. He'd even been able to get her some extra money by recommending her seamstress skills to his fellow officers.

He made her laugh, something that had been rare before her escape from the plantation.

She thought about that strange glass bottle he had given her last week—some kind of liquid filled it and the floating particles inside reflected light in the most beautiful way. What did he call it? *Shoostersomething.* Whatever it was, Emmeline treasured it because Philip had been so excited to give it to her.

Emmeline let herself imagine what life would be like with Philip, out west on that farm he always talked about.

She smiled. He did go on about that farm. Emmeline let a little laugh slip out when she thought about the way Philip fumbled with his words when he tried to explain his plans. She let herself think that he really meant to take her with him after he left the army when the war ended. If the war ever ended. Silly girl. Those kinds of fantasies were for the white ladies of the better classes, not for a…

She refused to allow herself to give thought to that word. The masters used it all the time, especially when they were wielding their whips and cudgels. Philip had said it once, jokingly, when they were talking in the laundry back in the Virginia camp. When he'd seen the look on her face, he went out of his way to apologize. Emmeline smiled at the memory. The poor man had almost come to tears. He felt so terrible, even if he was trying to be funny. She hadn't let him get away with that one. There were a lot of things she could forgive, but calling her that was not one of them.

Except for Philip.

Emmeline would do anything for Philip.

"You! Where's the goddammed wood?"

Emmeline froze. Colonel Kensington here in the kitchen? Why? She shuddered and kept her eyes glued to the floor.

"Well, answer me, animal." She heard the heavy stamp of his boots approaching. The kitchen had gone silent. The cooks and waiters knew better than to speak when Kensington was in a mood. "You're in for a damned good whipping, bitch."

A sharp pain in her thigh sent Emmeline to the floor. The bastard had kicked her. She looked up at her tormentor but refused to allow the pain to show on her face.

"The door was stuck with ice, sir," said Emmeline quietly. "And the wood box was empty." *Always be polite. Always. Better to say something than remain silent and suffer his wrath.* "The wood is there…"—she pointed at the pile next to the bread oven—"waiting for the snow to melt off. I'll bring it to the lobby fire in but a moment, sir."

Kensington stepped forward, planting his boot on one of Emmeline's hands. He slowly pressed down. She bit the inside of her cheek to keep from screaming. "I don't care about your excuses. Take it to the hearth in my quarters instead. Start a fire. I wish to sleep in comfort tonight." He leaned down, foot still on her hand, and grasped her chin. His strong fingers pressed into her neck, making it hard to breathe. Forcing her head up at an awkward angle to look at him, he said, so that only she could hear, "I've had enough of you and that fool captain. No more, do you hear me?" His anger had turned his face almost as red as his hair.

He let go of her chin. As he turned to leave the kitchen, he applied a little more pressure with his boot and Emmeline heard a crack. Pain shot up her arm and she was unable to stop a whimper from escaping her lips.

No one in the kitchen moved until Kensington had gone and they could hear the sound of his boots fading in the direction of the lobby.

Emmeline lifted her hand. Her little finger rested at an odd angle. Using her other hand, she held the broken digit tightly then jerked it straight. She nearly fainted from the pain.

The cook rushed over and knelt in front of Emmeline. She took hold of the wounded hand and quickly wrapped a piece of cloth around the finger to keep it straight. "What did you do to make him treat you so?" asked the cook.

Emmeline looked into the kindly eyes of the old white woman and said, "I live. That's all that is needed for people like him."

"You must have done something," said the cook, as if Emmeline had brought the torment upon herself.

I suppose I had by refusing to submit to his disgusting advances. No. Why should I be to blame for his actions?

Because that is my station in life, despite what that proclamation said.

Placing a hand on the cook's shoulder to steady herself, Emmeline got to her feet. Not looking at any of the others in the kitchen, she put the dried wood in a bucket and left. It was heavy, but after hauling huge laundry bags around for three years, Emmeline's muscles were strong. She winced and almost dropped the bucket when she tried to use her injured hand to carry some of the weight.

Rather than tote the wood through the lobby, where all the party attendees would see her, Emmeline took a back hallway that led to a set of servant's stairs. She passed a door to the lobby and paused. Her heartbeat quickened.

Philip stood by the fireplace talking to Major O'Dale. The major was another good man who had always treated Emmeline like a human being. Philip looked so handsome in his dress uniform with the high, stiff collar and all the braid. She felt a moment of pride at the thought that such a fine man might want to have some kind of life with her.

Never in a hundred years could that come true.

Emmeline sighed then continued on her way to the colonel's rooms. She couldn't escape the feeling that something was about to happen that would change her life forever.

Something bad.

Chapter 3:
"I know strictly speaking I can be replaced"

Beverly Kent, January 15, 2020

On the fourth-floor landing, Beverly paused when she heard a noise down the hall. She was sure she had heard a door closing, but there had been no one on the stairs ahead of her, and the hall felt completely dead. There was a large wooden door at the end, securely locked judging by the gigantic padlock. If someone had entered a room, it had to be one of the two near that door. A maid, maybe, turning down the sheets in her room. Beverly smiled when she thought about the chocolate that might be waiting for her on the pillow. If there was one thing that could break through her hard shell, it was chocolate.

Dawson constantly gave her chocolates, and he always had a bowl on his office desk brimming with those Halloween-sized bars. Beverly never failed to grab all the Snickers before someone else had the chance.

I hope she's good-looking. She thought about the housekeeper in Mexico last year. She had been something else. Free food for the whole week and some amazing sex with the expectation of a reward before Beverly checked out. *Maybe I should have left her a tip, but she had me for six days and that was tip enough.*

Beverly shrugged and said, "Whatever," to no one.

A loud clang behind her nearly made Beverly scream. Turning quickly, she caught sight of a woman in a long dress going down a flight of narrow stairs. The woman seemed to be carrying a bucket. The kerchief on the woman's head confirmed that she must be a maid. She probably banged the bucket into a wall. Careless idiot.

The inn appeared to have a decent-sized staff to take care of all of Beverly's needs. Now, if only she could get one of them to set Dawson straight.

Perhaps that Owen fellow would help. He was obviously attracted to her. How could he possibly resist? He was a man, after all. If she offered up the chance for a bit of fun in the sack, she'd be able to manipulate him into getting her what she wanted. It never hurt to curry favor with at least one of the locals.

Her charms had never failed her.

Continuing down the hall to her room, the air got cooler. She thought there might be cold air seeping through the big door. When she reached it and checked, there was nothing— not the slightest breeze. Curious, she took hold of the padlock and gave it a tug.

Buster Kenyon, January 18, 1985

Groggy and confused, cold and wet, he had a painful erection. When Buster opened his eyes, he saw his breath when he exhaled. There was also steam rising from something close by. Twisting his head to see better, Buster came nose to nose with… Who was she now? The mother. That's right, the mother. Just her head.

Buster remembered the family stopping to pick him up out

on the highway. His car had broken down, so he decided to walk the remaining three or four miles to the inn despite the storm and send a tow truck back later. His small case, the only piece of luggage he had bothered to bring, held everything he needed for his work.

He'd been walking for about five minutes when a converted school bus pulled up alongside him. A man leaned out from the driver's seat, a—what do people call them now?—Black. Yes, a Black man.

"You look cold, sir. Do you need a lift into town? I saw a car parked at the side of the road back there. Was that yours?"

Would the man never shut up? Why all the questions?

"Thank you," said Buster. He walked around the front of the bus then climbed the steps. Standing next to the driver, his heart soared. Looking back at him was a small family: mother, two very young females, grandparents. The father must be the driver. A pair of heads appeared from a small door near the back of the bus. Males! Twins! What a bonus!

It was clear the father or someone had put in a lot of work converting the old bus to some kind of motor home. With most of the side windows blocked off or removed, the vehicle would provide a cozy place for Buster to enjoy himself.

The bus lurched when the father put it back into gear and set off on his final journey.

"Maggie, get our guest a cup of coffee. He looks chilled to the bone," said the grandmother.

The mother nodded and went to a small hotplate on a counter at the side of the bus where a coffee pot percolated. She poured Buster a cup which she then passed to him. As soon as Buster had the cup in his hand, he stood then flung the boiling liquid at the mother. She screamed and went down, hands covering her scalded face. Buster kicked hard at her head, breaking her fingers as his steel-toed boot connected then drove them into her skull.

Before the stunned grandfather could react, Buster smashed the cup against the counter, grabbed the man's head, and ground the jagged edge into his throat. Arterial blood splattered against Buster's trousers.

The two females screamed. The grandmother tried to put herself between them and Buster. He punched her in the side of her head. Going down hard, her head connected with the edge of a counter. Hearing her skull crack, Buster figured she probably died instantly, which was a shame because that was one less bit of amusement for Buster.

It had all taken about ten seconds.

The bus grinding to a halt threw Buster off his feet. The father unbuckled his seat belt and climbed out of the driver's seat, yelling, "What the hell's going on back there?"

Stunned by the sight in front of him, the father did nothing while Buster pulled a knife from his coat pocket and stood. The man grunted when the knife entered his belly just above his belt. In shock, the father stared down while Buster sawed up until the blade stopped at the sternum. Dropping the weapon, Buster used both hands to reach into the open gut then pulled out whatever he could. With a grin, Buster held the steaming mess in front of the man's face before tossing them aside. Staring into the father's dying eyes, Buster smiled at the growing tightness in his trousers.

Turning his attention to the two females who were clutching each other, unable to move away from the corpses of their family, Buster shoved them toward the room at the back of the bus. Inside what turned out to be a small bedroom, he was pleased to see the two boys cowered in a corner, paralyzed with fear.

"Stay quiet, you vermin," said Buster as he closed the door, shutting them in for later. He checked on his first victims. The grandmother was indeed dead. Blood flowed from her ear. Buster stomped on her head sending blood and brains splattering over the floor just to be sure. The grandfather was still bleeding out. These animals were remarkably strong. Buster plunged his knife through the old man's temple to finish him off. The mother was on her knees crying. Buster grasped a handful of greasy hair and tilted her head back. Her skin had blistered and one eye looked like it might have been boiled. She wouldn't cause him any trouble. This was something to save for a bit of fun later.

Buster went to the driver's seat.

Ten minutes later, Buster pulled into the Inn on the Cliff's parking lot. There was some space between the inn and the large building on its right so Buster drove the bus there and parked it as close to the low wall as he could. From his high vantage point, he looked out over the cliff at the partially obscured bay. The storm had not let up.

Buster waited about half an hour to see if anyone from the inn would come outside to investigate the bus. No one came.

There was silence at the back of the bus. On his way, he retrieved his small case then checked the bodies of the adults.

The mother still lived but was unconscious.

Buster opened the door to the small bedroom. The four young were huddled together on the bed as far from the door as they could get. They had been crying and there was a familiar stink in the air. Closing the door behind him, Buster set the case down on the bed. He took out a roll of leather tied with a string. When the young saw what the roll held, they whimpered.

The interior of the room was still warm thanks to an electric heater, so Buster quietly removed his clothes. He picked up a boning knife then lost himself in a frenzy of blood and lust.

Two hours later, he woke. How or when he had left the bedroom to come to the front of the bus and play with the mother, he could not remember.

The heater no longer worked due, no doubt, to the battery losing its charge.

Buster sat up and saw the source of the rising steam—the torso of one of females. Standing, Buster scraped some of the gore from his arms and legs then used a dish cloth to wipe blood from his chest. Walking to the back of the bus through a mess of limbs, heads, and bodies, he was pleased to discover that none of the family had survived his pleasure in one piece.

A small bathroom midway along the length of the bus gave Buster the opportunity to take a cold shower. Much as he hated to wear the apparel of one of those mongrels, he donned some of the father's clothes. His own were soaked with blood and would be incredibly uncomfortable to wear when he entered the inn. A small bottle of cologne helped cover any residual smell from his fun and games.

It took only fifteen minutes for Buster to deal with the idiot at the front desk and get his room. Along the way, he encountered the one who was supposed to stop him, whatever that meant, and the one he had come to kill, for whatever reason. He didn't *need* a reason to kill, but he wanted to know to satisfy his curiosity.

In his room, number 47, Buster set his small case down on the bed. Something drew him to the wardrobe. Inside, there was only a pile of burlap. When Buster picked it up, his hand found something hard inside. Pulling aside the covering, he was overjoyed to see he now held an old cavalry sabre.

It felt familiar and would be perfect for what was coming.

Beverly Kent, January 15, 2020

Beverly shook the cobwebs from her head. In her room, she sat on the edge of the bed fuming. Tears of anger, frustration, and sadness flowed freely down her cheeks. She couldn't believe how stupid that man was.

What had ever possessed me to have anything to do with him? Why was I so strongly attracted to him?

Sure, he had seemed nice at first—quick to laugh, witty, and quite good-looking. Peter was one of the most decent men she'd ever met. He never said anything inappropriate, except, maybe, for the occasional double entendre. Being a man, she knew he only wanted to get her in bed, and that was fine by her. But for some reason, the very thought of being intimate with Peter repulsed her. Up until Peter, if a man, or woman for that matter, attracted Beverly, she would have happily bed him or her.

If Peter had thought he was going to get lucky, she had nipped that in the bud the very first time he took her out. When he dropped her at her apartment, there had been no goodnight kiss on the first date. Had it even been a first date? He *had* paid for the movie and dinner. A movie and dinner did not entitle a man to any kind of reward, particularly the physical kind.

Still, he was kind and made her laugh. She had been sorely tempted to let down her guard.

So why do I treat you like you're dirt?

Peter never even tried. There was that one time he brushed his hand along her breast. It was a complete accident. She *had* moved unexpectedly. From the expression on his face, anyone would have thought Peter had just committed the worst crime imaginable. Beverly chuckled at the memory.

Why was he so thick? How much abuse did she have to heap on him before he gave up on her? She'd flat out told him there was no future for them, but still, he persisted. Sure, it was nice to have someone fawn all over you. It was *all* men were good for. Peter *did* treat her like a queen.

At first, it had been fun. Fun until he started dropping hints that he loved her.

Love! What did that even mean? People were there for her to use in any way she wished.

To his credit, no one at the university had any idea that they had "dated" for seven months. As Beverly had made clear the day after their first "date," when he had eagerly approached her near her office, Peter was never to ask her out on campus or within earshot of any member of the faculty. Not only that, but he was not allowed to comment on anything that would even hint that something was going on. And he'd gone along with it. What a fool.

All their liaisons had been discreet on pain of death.

For Beverly, violation of her privacy was the worst thing that could happen. She guarded her privacy like a cornered rat; she simply would not tolerate any threats to it.

If he had anything to say to Beverly that was not work-related, Peter had to phone her at home after work hours. A few times, Peter had dared to complain because she wasn't overly friendly when he called. She soon put him in his place, even if he did have some justification.

No matter how she treated him, and she knew she was especially harsh with Peter, he simply would not go away.

Beverly went into the bathroom. Standing in front of the mirror over the sink, she stared at the person looking back at her. In the harsh bathroom light, the lines on her face stood out clearly. Every worry, moment of anger, and crack in her confidence was etched into her pale skin.

"Christ, the way my hair just hangs there, I look like a sick Morticia Addams." Closing her eyes, she tried to imagine a kinder, gentler, more open Beverly Kent. One who could treat Peter like a decent human being. When she opened her eyes, she saw the same old Beverly.

"Fuck."

Beverly stripped and took a long, hot shower. After, with a

towel wrapped around her hair but stark naked, she caught a glimpse of her body. Stopping to look, she said, "Not an ounce of fat. I look damned good." She turned. "And my butt *is* spectacular." Beverly smiled. "No wonder every man and woman I meet is attracted to me. I just wish you weren't all so boring. Peter, at least, is a little interesting."

And why am I suddenly so concerned about Peter and his feelings?

Throwing on a silky pajama top and clean panties, Beverly curled up on the bed to read the notes Peter had typed up for her. In his eagerness to please, he had done some research into her ancestor and saved her loads of initial research time.

You are a good guy, Peter. Find yourself someone else. Please.

"Research! Ha!" she said. "Damnit, you're the laughingstock of the university, Peter. You've got such little credibility thanks to your so-called theory." As if the Nazis had atomic submarines. Pure science fiction. It was all she could do to bite her tongue whenever she heard the barbs and snide remarks colleagues made behind his back. His idiocy was bringing down the reputation of everyone who came near him. At least, that's what most of the faculty thought.

Still...I hope you find your Holy Grail, Peter. Really, I do.

The room grew colder. These old inns were full of drafts that could kill a person. It was a good thing it was Peter footing the bill for the room. Beverly would have demanded a refund for such inhospitable conditions, but he was too nice to complain. She'd have a word with that O'Dale person in the morning. He'd do anything for her.

She was about to reach for a blanket when she felt something cold brush her shoulder. She shivered and jumped to her feet, scattering the notes, terrified it might be a bat. Filthy creatures. The front desk would be finding her new accommodations if there were bats in her room.

There was nothing—no flying creatures, nor even shadows of creatures.

It's just my imagination. She shook her head. *But I have no imagination.*

The cold touched Beverly again, this time across the back of her neck. She pulled a bathrobe from the chair next to the bathroom door and wrapped it around her shoulders. She almost turned off the light, but left it on, still a little nervous about the possibility of bats. The bedsheets were cold when she slid under the covers. Pillows were piled against the headboard so she could read, but her research notes were all over the floor. Before she could make a move to get them, Beverly's eyes grew heavy and closed.

The light fluttered then blinked out.

Half asleep, the cold brushed the back of her neck again—impossible since she was on her back—but this time it moved around her neck to her throat, hesitated a moment, then traveled down. She was unable to rouse herself as a chill slid between her breasts then reached out to cup them. She sighed and shivered. The soft silk of her pajama top excited her as it rubbed against her erect nipples. She breathed deeply savoring the icy caress though the touch was unwelcome. No one could be allowed to touch her like this unless she initiated it. Yet she couldn't resist.

As she yielded to the delight of the caresses, Beverly's half-conscious mind filled with confusion. Something was inside her head, both welcome and intrusive.

She sighed when the sensation traveled down her belly and easily slipped under the elastic of her panties. She gasped with anticipation. It slid through her neatly trimmed hair and tentatively entered her most private place.

"What's happening," she muttered/thought. "I won't do this." Unable to stop it, something parted her legs.

The cold engulfed Beverly. Her breasts felt the barest pressure as phantom hands stroked and squeezed them. Deep down, something penetrated farther than any man ever had. Its delicate massage stirred feelings within that she had never experienced. Different. Almost pleasurable.

This is so wrong. This is what I need. Beverly's mind roiled with the mixed messages. It was her, yet not her.

Her breathing grew more rapid. The cold inside her intensified, building a strange excitement and anticipation. She tried to close her legs to stop it, but she exploded and cried out.

"No! Yes!"

Immediately the cold withdrew. Beverly lay there in the throes of ecstasy, luxuriating in the pulsing. Tears poured down her face and she gasped for air.

"What was that?"

She heard laughter…from inside her head or somewhere further away? It was unpleasant, evil, familiar.

"Come back. Don't leave me," she said to the dark, full of despair and hope, but mostly confusion.

Then, she remembered…something.

Bartholomew Kensington, January 17, 1905

He returned to the inn unannounced. Not that anyone would have expected him or been happy to see him after all these years. Bartholomew was always "welcome" at the inn because he was, after all, a Kensington and Wycliffe Point belonged to the Kensingtons. His father had been mayor since before Bartholomew was born. The Kensington Land & Revenue Company owned most of the land in and around the town, and had a stake in anything else available. Rumor had it, back before Bartholomew left for war, that the family had even tried to purchase the fort and blockhouse on the headland across the bay. However, the Army refused to sell, but still had to pay a toll to use the single road which provided access to the headland. Most businesses in Wycliffe Point had a Kensington on the board, paid rent to KL&R Co., or had a mortgage with the Kensington Bank and Trust Company.

It was so good to be home.

Rather than go directly to his suite on the fourth floor, Bartholomew made his way to his secret room in the warehouse. If he was going to play, he needed to ensure the room was still secure and had adequate provisions for his pleasure.

When he stepped up to the fourth floor of the warehouse, he halted before exiting the stairwell. There were voices. It was late, winter, and there were no ships in the harbor at this time. No one should have been up here. To make matters worse, when he passed through the door from the stairwell, he perceived light emanating from the open door of his room.

Who? No one should be in my room. No one should even know it's there.

Anger built up inside Bartholomew at the violation of his privacy. No one could be allowed to trespass upon his killing domain.

Using the stealth he had learned while stalking his prey, Bartholomew crept to the room's entrance. The smell of cooking reached his nose, and he realized he was hungry.

Perhaps there's some tender young meat in there.

Smiling, Bartholomew drew his revolver then stepped into the room. He quickly observed eight of them sitting on stools around a potbellied stove. That was new. There were four adults and four young.

Good.

No one had noticed him. Yet. Keeping the revolver aimed at the small gathering, he reached back and slid the door closed. It rattled a little, causing one of the young ones—a small female that couldn't have been more than four or five years old—to turn and face him. She surprised him by smiling.

So sweet. So foolish

"Papa, there's a man with a gun," said the small female. "He looks cold and hungry."

The brood all turned to face Bartholomew. All had plates of food in their hands. He could see now that two of the adults were the parents of the children. The older pair must be the grandparents. Seeing them stirred deep memories Bartholomew couldn't dredge to the surface. No matter. He had other business that needed his attention.

The young adult male stood and said, "Sir, there's no need for the weapon. We're friendly and harmless. Please, join us for our evening meal." He motioned toward a pot sitting atop the stove. Bartholomew surmised it was stew of some sort. It certainly smelled enticing, missing only the most necessary ingredient.

"What are you doing here?" Bartholomew tried to keep his voice steady. No reason to spook the brood before he had them in his control. "Who allowed you into my room?"

The male that had spoken bowed. "I work for the owner of the warehouse, sir, and act as caretaker. The kind owner allows me and my family to live in this room for a small token rent."

"How long have you been here?" Bartholomew could feel the anger rising in him. What idiot relative had permitted this violation?

"I've been here a year, sir. My parents, wife, and children arrived on a steamer from Liverpool a few weeks ago."

Bartholomew turned and locked the door. He faced the brood, some of whom looked nervous now, and said, "You, the father, line the young up along that wall. Bind their hands. There's rope hanging from the peg." He pointed with his revolver.

"Sir!" The male took a step closer to Bartholomew but immediately retreated when he saw the weapon cocked and aimed at his face. "There's no need for this, sir."

"In my room, I decide what's needed, you pig. Now bind the hands of those small ones." The male obeyed. The other three adults stood frozen in place.

When the young were secured, their father quickly picked up a hammer that hung from the wall behind them. He swivelled and took one step toward his captor before he thumped to the floor with a bullet through his right eye. The bullet exited his skull and hit one of the young, a male—no loss, in the throat. The thing went down gurgling in a shower of blood.

Everyone in the room screamed. The remaining young cried and tried to run to their mother, but all they did was collide with each other and fall in a heap. The mother ran to her babies, but flew back against the stove when Bartholomew lashed out with the revolver and smashed her across the face.

"Stay there!"

Bartholomew gave the young his most menacing look, the one that had made prisoners soil themselves. They didn't move, shivering with fear, tears running down their dirty faces.

"On your knees. Now!" The old female had difficulty getting down, so the old male helped her. Then he helped the mother get to her knees. Blood flowed down her swollen face, but she remained silent.

"Please, sir," said the old male.

Cowards. And no sport at all.

Bartholomew walked to the stove and set his revolver down on one of the stools. Throwing off his overcoat, he revealed a sabre in a scabbard attached to his belt. Drawing the sabre, he raised it above his head then brought it down on the mother in a frenzy. He hacked at her so fast, her head was nothing but shredded bone and brain before she fell to the floor.

The old male tried to rise, but he went down with a sabre cut across his throat that almost took off his head. The old female collapsed in a heap, whimpering. Bartholomew kicked her over so she could see him then finished her off with countless swipes until she was little more than a mass of bloody clothing and flesh that might once have been alive.

The three young were in absolute panic, crying their eyes out, screaming for their parents. Bartholomew calmly walked over to them. He grabbed the little female who had seen him first by her hair and tossed her in the direction of the stove. She hit her head and lost consciousness. Then he finished off the last two young with his sabre.

Pulling a small table over to the stove, Bartholomew picked up the little female and laid her out. He quickly tore off her dress and leggings.

Bartholomew smiled then, using his sabre, he cut portions of the best ingredient of all and added them to the stew bubbling on the stove.

Beverly Kent, 15 January, 2020

Beverly sat up and screamed. She screamed until she couldn't breathe. Before she passed out, she realized two things: she felt very hungry, and her hand was moving furiously between her legs.

Chapter 4:
"But I'd love to stay together, more than friends"

Peter Dawson, January 16, 2020

Peter woke completely refreshed, as though he had slept for years and washed away all his burdensome anxieties. During his shower, the image of something dark waving in his face permeated his every thought. He had no idea what it was or what it meant and, to be quite honest, this morning he didn't care.

There was also that ache in his loins. "That was some dream," he said to the vaguely familiar grinning man in the fogged mirror. "Holy cow, I've never had one that felt that real. At least I didn't get any on the sheets." Looking down at his erection, he asked it, "When was the last time we had a wet dream? Twenty years?" He shook his head and tried to think of something that would kill his arousal. It would not go away. As if to mock him, his penis moved like it was waving to him.

Peter got dressed and solved his arousal problem when the elastic of his underpants slipped from his fingers and smacked his scrotum. He felt lucky his head missed the bed post when he involuntarily bent forward in pain.

"Smooth, Dawson," he said. "No wonder the ladies are lined up."

Outside his window the sky was clear. It was probably well below zero. Walking over, he peered out and saw the waves and spray of the ocean crashing on the rocky shore of the promontory across the bay. It reminded him that there was a steep cliff on the other side of this wall. He concentrated to tamp down the panic before it could rear its ugly head.

Across the bay, the old fort, occupied during World War II as a defense against a feared German invasion, squatted clearly visible at the cliff's edge. For a moment, he thought he saw someone moving about through the black slits of its gun ports.

No way, my eyesight isn't that good.

"I'll be visiting you soon enough," he said. "It's only a twenty-minute walk."

How did I know that?

"Is there anyone still alive who served in you during the war? There has to be. I'm feeling optimistic today."

He checked his pocket watch, a family heirloom that never left his side. It had survived wars, disasters, being lost several times, but it always found its way home. Beverly thought it an affectation. Beverly could get stuffed.

That felt good.

Seven o'clock on the dot. Peter, always an early riser, found it easy to get loads of work done before most people were even at their jobs. He always arrived first at the history department building and, since the mess with Beverly, often left last. The silence in the building was his friend.

He sighed deeply, regretting the time he had wasted pining for her when it was clear she would never take him back.

Did she ever really want me in the first place? Anyway, I don't want to go back.

Peter pulled on a heavy sweater then took a quick look in the mirror to make sure his hair hadn't gone insane. "Who knew falling in love with someone could be an unpardonable sin?" Peter shook his head. Once this research trip was over, he would get his life back together; he'd forget about the woman he saw every day at work and move on, find a new position somewhere else.

Nuts. Why wait?

"It starts today," he said with confidence. "No more being treated like a loser by a loser." There was a flutter of anxiety in his stomach as he anticipated today's first encounter with Beverly. She could be overpowering, but he was determined to stand his ground. He hoped.

When Peter stepped out of his room, the irresistible aroma of bacon and toast enveloped him. With his mouth watering as if he hadn't eaten in days, he followed the scent to the dining room.

He paused on the second-floor landing. Through the large window, he saw the glow of the sun over the eastern horizon. He turned to gaze up the stairs.

There's something about this window and those stairs. What is it?

Nothing came rushing to answer so he shrugged it off and walked briskly downstairs.

His nose led him straight to the dining room where he found Owen talking to an old Black couple. A younger Black couple joined them. It looked to Peter like a TV show where the scene had started slightly too soon and the actors hadn't begun to move. It was obviously a setup.

When Owen saw Peter enter, he said a few words to the diners, who looked over at Peter and smiled. Owen walked over. "Sleep well?"

Peter remembered his wet dream, unable to stop the embarrassment showing on his face

Owen grinned. "Crisp, clean, white sheets will do that to you. Should I have the maid make up your room while you eat?"

Peter shook his head. "Not necessary. I made the bed and cleaned up. No need to bother her. Or him."

"Her," said Owen. "Always her."

He guided Peter to a table for two over by a window. Four young Black children—two teenaged boys and two preteen girls—sat quietly at a table by another window. None of them were eating. They watched Peter walk to his table then turned away and talked amongst themselves. Something had excited them. Peter sat and waited while his host poured him a cup of steaming coffee.

"Two eggs, over easy, bacon not too crisp. Toast," Owen said. "Whole wheat or white?"

"White. Are there hash browns?" Peter asked. "I love hash browns."

Owen nodded. "Of course. Or you can have corned beef hash with a side of baked beans."

"Both?" Peter asked, hoping he didn't sound like a pig.

Owen simply smiled, tilted his head and left the room. He hadn't asked about Beverly. Something told Peter their host didn't much like her. Peter felt sudden panic. He hadn't made sure Beverly was up and ready for breakfast. If she missed eating because of him, she'd... What? Get angry?

"Fuck her," he said quietly.

The old man at the other table looked his way and nodded with a smile as if he had heard Peter and agreed with him. Peter smiled back, sure that he hadn't been heard. The children giggled.

A copy of the local paper, the *Wycliffe Point Democrat*, sat on the table, so Peter picked it up. The news was all local: no mention of war, politics, or the economy. There was, however, extensive coverage of the New Jersey Devils game against Boston from last night. There was something about the Calgary Flames-Hartford Whalers game that didn't seem right, but Peter didn't follow any sports enough to care about it. To make things even better, wonder of wonders, there were two–count 'em, two!–full pages of daily comics. They had even reprinted some of the classics, like *Peanuts*, *Steve Canyon*, and *Captain Easy*. This was amazing, and Peter briefly considered moving to Wycliffe Point just for the paper. His own hometown paper had completely dumped comic strips a couple of decades ago.

Immersed in the funnies, Peter didn't notice Owen arrive with his breakfast. Sure enough, next to the eggs and bacon were mounds of hash browns, corned beef hash, and baked beans. For a moment, Peter was nervous; he hadn't eaten a breakfast this large since the last time he visited his sister, the gourmet chef. That had been more than a couple of years ago, while he was trying to get up the nerve to ask Beverly out for dinner.

Why does she have to invade my every thought?

"Why, indeed? It should be someone else," said Owen before he returned to the kitchen.

Did I say that out loud?

A faint voice from the direction of the kitchen said, "No."

Peter shook his head to clear away the morning fuzziness.

With the funnies propped up on the windowsill, Peter tucked in. Everything was cooked to perfection; and the raspberry preserves that came with the toast were heaven. Maybe he *would* move here permanently. When he was finished, Owen came over, refilled his coffee, and cleared away the dirty dishes. A minute later, he returned with his own cup of coffee and a fresh pot and sat in the chair across from Peter.

"So," said Owen, "history. You're looking for a submarine. Tell me all."

Peter took a sip of coffee. "My field is World War II, particularly the German navy. I'm especially interested in submarines."

"Didn't they find one around here a few years ago?"

"Right, a few miles up the coast, but that's not what I'm looking for. Let me start at the beginning. I have a colleague in France who knows I'm interested in anything naval. Two years ago, he sent me copies of some documents he discovered in a cave not far from St. Nazaire. It was a German U-boat base during the war."

"There was a commando raid there, wasn't there?" asked Owen. "Twenty-eighth of March, nineteen forty-two."

"That's right," Peter said. "I'm impressed."

"I read the papers," said Owen.

"Right," said Peter. "Anyway, the documents had been

damaged by fire and water, but a lot was still legible. They mentioned a German naval commander named Gerhard Weinz, a Class Eighteen submarine called the U-10000, the winter of 1945, and Wycliffe Point."

"Wycliffe Point?" Owen leaned in, brow furrowed. "And you think that what happened in Wycliffe Point on January eighteenth, 1945 had something to do with German submarines?"

"That's rather specific, Owen," said Peter.

Owen seemed to get lost in thought for a moment. "So that's what it was." He smiled then said, "Lucky guess. So, there's no other reason you're here? Just the submarine?"

"That's right. Why? What did you think I was here for?"

"Wait a moment." Owen scratched the scar at the side of his neck. Peter realized that most of the times he had spoken to Owen, he stared at the scar as if it was a homing beacon. Now he found he couldn't take his eyes off the thing. The jagged scar ran from below the man's right ear and down his neck where it disappeared beneath his starched shirt collar. He wondered how he'd got it.

Owen said, "As far as I know, there's nothing in the Historical Society's archives. Do you suppose...?" He trailed off when there was a slight cough from behind Peter.

Peter turned to look into the face of Owen, except now he was dressed in a white chef's outfit. From behind, he heard, "Peter, meet my...brother, Oliver. He's our cook."

Oliver held out his hand to Peter, who took it limply. He couldn't take his eyes off the violent red scar that ran along the left side of Oliver's neck. Peter did a quick double take. The men were obviously twins, but the scar was a mystery.

Maybe they were Siamese twins, joined at the neck.

As if to answer the question, Owen quickly said, "It's from our days in professional tiddlywinks. Our last tournament ended in a brawl. It was quite horrible, and Oliver prefers not to speak of it." Peter thought he was kidding, trying to talk up some mundane truth.

The chef smiled and said, "I'm about to clean up. Will there be anything else?" Peter wanted more coffee. "Besides more coffee for our guest."

Cleaning up? How long have I been here? Peter checked his pocket watch. It was almost nine. He realized he'd missed seeing the four people at the other table leave. And the kids.

"Regulars," said Owen. "Here about the same time every time."

For half a second, Peter thought about Beverly and decided she must not want breakfast today. She didn't eat much anyway and if she wanted something…well, there was a doughnut shop down the road. It wasn't snowing yet. He turned back to Owen and asked, "Do you think I could get a look at your archives sometime this week? Maybe I can spot something useful."

"Not a problem. How's the day after tomorrow?"

"Fine."

"So, what's so special about this submarine of yours?" Oliver returned with a fresh pot of coffee and topped up Peter's cup. Owen's still looked full.

Peter organized his thoughts.

Careful, Peter, old boy. We don't want to rile the locals with crazy ideas.

Whenever he tried to explain his theory, he often messed it up. The skeptical looks on the faces of his audience didn't help. Neither did the snickers from Beverly—he'd overheard her in her office laughing at him to one of the other professors—and she liked to debunk his theory in front of anyone who would listen. Since her field was the Civil War, it made her comments all the more annoying. Why was she always showing up at his lectures? It wasn't to be supportive, and she had no interest in the subject matter.

I have the weirdest stalker ever—one that doesn't want me. Typical.

"Okay, bear with me for a few minutes. It was well-known that the Germans were doing atomic research during the war. You know, Werner von Braun and his bunch. Their heavy water plants had been bombed and the program went nowhere."

Owen nodded and prompted Peter to continue.

"I think I've found evidence that they were more successful that anyone thought. After I'd received those documents from France, I went to Germany to look through whatever naval records I could find. All I could uncover about Weinz, the German commander, was that he was attached to something called the *Deutsche Versuchsanstalt für Atomartig Forschung.* The German Experimental Institute for Atomic Research."

He waited for his listener's reaction. There was only a nod.

"There were only fourteen classes of German U-boat and none of them were numbered eighteen."

"What about U-boat records? The Germans were fanatical about keeping records, weren't they?"

Oliver appeared with yet another pot of coffee which he set on the table between them. Owen immediately topped off Peter's.

"Yes, but the assigned numbers for recorded U-boats don't go higher than the five thousands."

"So, you're stuck then?"

"I was for a year. By chance, an old German U-boat captain named Helmut Lintz published his memoirs. I would have missed it if not for another friend who keeps an eye out for neo-Nazi publications. It seems the captain is still a fervent Nazi and wanted to set the record straight about what he had done during the war. It's full of justification for what the U-boats did: sinking everything in sight, shooting sailors in the water, that kind of thing. The man seems to think Hitler was a saint."

Owen snorted. "Some fools over here thought so as well. We had a couple in town. I'll give you their names and show you photos. They won't be much help, though. They were eliminated during the war."

"Thanks," said Peter. "Eliminated how, exactly?"

"You'd be surprised. Let's just say, they saw the light," said Owen. "Now, back to the submarine."

"Yes," said Peter. "What caught my attention was a throwaway comment buried in the middle of Lintz's book. He mentions an experimental submarine called the 'Adolf Hitler' that was being built at a secret base somewhere along the French coast. The sub was numbered the U-10000 in honor of the ten-thousand-year Reich that Hitler was creating.”

Owen filled Peter’s coffee cup again. Peter felt the caffeine buzz and some pressure on his bladder. Owen appeared unaffected by the coffee. *Was he even drinking it?*

“So maybe there’s some truth to your theory after all.”

“There might just be. Critics have dismissed Lintz as a crackpot. They especially slam him for his wild assertions about what the Germans were planning to do in 1945. Lintz claims they had developed a new missile based on the V-2. It was supposed to have atomic warheads and was going to be used against the United States.”

Owen scratched his scar. His eyes were dark. To Peter, it seemed like Owen was getting angry. His nostrils flared, and he said, “I hate those evil swine. And traitors. Traitors are the worst. Even the worst of people hate the traitors.” Owen’s breathing got faster. He shook his head, then said, “Now is not the time. My apologies, Peter. You think this atomic submarine may have been in Wycliffe Point sometime in January 1945.”

The need to go to the bathroom grew more intense. Peter should have known better than to drink this much coffee first thing in the morning. It always upset his stomach and gave him violent cramps. He’d have to pay a visit to his room where he could sit in privacy. Maybe he should light a candle as well to absorb the smell. There was no point in offending the staff.

“Yes,” said Peter. “Last fall, I received a letter telling me that someone in Wycliffe Point had some information that might interest me. The writer didn’t tell me what that information was, or, for that matter, who the writer was. But it was imperative that I come down here in January."

"An anonymous benefactor?" said Owen with a smile. "How curious."

Peter had the feeling that Owen knew more than he was letting on about the letter. Could he have sent it?

"So," said Owen. "You're here to gather evidence so your colleagues don't all think you're a loon. And, furthermore, you want to prove yourself to that woman up in forty-seven. You know you'll never get back together with her, not that you were really together in the first place. But you want to show her that it's her loss not yours. Am I right or am I right?"

Peter sighed heavily, depressed at how easily the man read him. "It's always about the woman, isn't it? But you know, it's not about her anymore." He felt great relief being able to say that out loud.

Just then, a woman passed by the dining room door. Dressed in a dull blue dress that fell far below her knees, almost to the floor, she carried a bucket. The white apron tied around her waist seemed to have some very dark stains on it. She turned to look in the dining room. Peter forgot how to breathe. When she saw Peter, she smiled. She was the woman with dark curly hair from the stairs last night.

She must be a maid. Damned pretty, too.

Captain Philip Daweson, January 18, 1865

Philip drained the last of his Guinness then set the glass down on a sideboard. He quietly burped into his hand and scanned the room for Emmeline, but she was nowhere to be seen. *Damn!* Had Kensington interfered again and sent her off to perform some menial task elsewhere in the inn?

He pulled at the stiff collar of his dress uniform. Though it was freezing outside, the various fires in the inn blazed to the point Philip felt uncomfortable. But here, next to the fire by the front desk, was the best place to observe the gathering and see what Kensington might be doing.

"These fires are rather too much, don't you think, Captain?" Major O'Dale appeared beside Philip without a sound. The Major took a sip of wine.

"I was just thinking about New Orleans, sir. The incessant heat and humidity. At least here I can step outside and get some relief," said Philip.

"And freeze your tackle off," said the major. He finished his wine and signalled one of the waiters for another. If Philip wanted more Guinness, he'd have to go to the kitchen and tap his private keg. At the moment, he was more concerned about Emmeline. As if sensing his captain's concern, the major said, "I haven't seen her, Philip. You don't think Kensington's stalking her again, do you?"

"That's what worries me, Obadiah. He's had his eye on her ever since he caught us talking at the laundry last year. Despite his best efforts, I'm still around."

The major laughed. "Always positioning your company at the front of the lines and having you personally lead the charges should have gotten you killed Some angel must be looking out for you."

That angel is Emmeline.

There was a kerfuffle over by the main staircase. The guest of honor had arrived. Colonel Beauregard Kensington—"Bloody Beau" to his men because of his ruthlessness toward Confederate prisoners—was peacocking about, holding court. Wycliffe Point's dignitaries seemed eager to meet the returning soldier, hero of the Army of the James, even if he had led from the rear. And poor old Major General Butler had taken the blame for the fiasco at Fort Fisher. So much for the military advice of Kensington.

"Bastard," said Philip.

"Careful, Captain," said Obadiah. "He is, after all, our commanding officer. The war's not over yet."

Philip spat into the spittoon next to the fire. "He's corrupt, a liar, and a blowhard."

"True," said Obadiah. "But, like him, you benefitted from Butler's patronage in New Orleans and Virginia." Obadiah smiled. "We all did to some extent."

"But I only did it for Emmeline," said Philip. "I wanted to get a nest egg so we could head west and start a farm after the war." He sighed. "I know that's no excuse for what I did."

Obadiah nodded. "You should go north to the Canadas. They don't care so much about mixing the races there, my friend. I have relatives up that way. Near Detroit." He emptied another glass of wine and signalled for more.

"You're going to get drunk."

"I have to. It's the only way I can tolerate that maniac." When Obadiah said this, Kensington looked over at the two men as if he'd heard the insult. He smiled that insincere smile of his and nodded his head. "He knows."

"Humbug," said Philip. "How can he? Even Emmeline doesn't know my plans."

"You mean, you still haven't told her how you feel? It's been a year. Though she may be a lowly washerwoman and seamstress, she's also a woman. She has to be told. Has she shown no affection for you?"

"Some," said Philip. "We can talk freely now, and she laughs and smiles if I say something witty. She did accept the gift I gave her last week. But she holds back, as if she's afraid to speak out. She still thinks of herself as a slave. Remember, she lived that way for almost thirty years. If Butler hadn't allowed her to be hired by the army, she might still be foraging somewhere in Louisiana for her next meal."

"Ladies and gentlemen, may I have your attention, please." It was Samuel Kensington, the Mayor of Wycliffe Point, owner of the Kensington Inn, and uncle of tonight's guest of honor.

The room went silent. All eyes focused on the mayor.

"I'd like to read a telegram from the President of the United States, Abraham Lincoln."

The place erupted in cheers. It was a good five minutes before the mayor could continue. "The President wishes to convey his congratulations to Colonel Beauregard Kensington of the glorious 45th New Jersey Volunteer Infantry Regiment for his stellar war record and his efforts to keep our great nation united. In recognition of this, the president wishes the colonel to proceed to Washington, where he will be presented with the Congressional Medal of Honor."

There were more cheers and lots of back slapping and congratulations. Several men called for a speech. The elite of

Wycliffe Point all wanted to be associated with the war hero.

Philip and Obadiah looked at each other with sour faces.

"Lord Almighty," said Obadiah. "I'll give credit to Kensington for his patriotism, but a medal? No." He shook his head in disgust. "How many prisoners did he hang? And for what? Because he couldn't be bothered finding a place to house them? He seemed to take great delight in watching them die, always standing right in front of the gallows. He wouldn't even grant them the dignity of a hood."

"I have to find Emmeline now," said Philip, ignoring his friend's comments. He had more important things to do than discuss Kensington's war record. "There's no telling what he'll do. If he gets her to Washington, I'll never see her again." His voice cracked and he had a hard time keeping back the tears.

"Watch it,' said Obadiah.

Philip watched Kensington walk away from some plump woman and go into the dining room. A few moments later, the man returned and hurried up the stairs.

"What do you suppose that's all about?" Obadiah nodded at Kensington's back.

"No idea," said Philip. "I'm going to look for Emmeline."

Peter Dawson, January 16, 2020

"Pretty maids all in a row," Peter said quietly. He felt a rush of emotion and, for some reason, got an erection.

Owen smiled, then quietly said, "Told you so." He poured the last of the coffee into Peter's cup. "Speaking of pretty maids, what about your companion? She's quite lovely in a mean sort of way. Why's she here? You mentioned something yesterday about a relative. Kensington? Truly?"

"I did, didn't I?" said Peter. "She's looking for someone on her mother's side. He was supposed to have served for a time around here during the Civil War. Colonel Beauregard Kensington."

Owen's face went white making the scar stand out even more. "Bloody Beauregard? That bastard? Now?" His eyes darted about then settled on something beyond the dining room door. "Damnation."

Trying to be subtle, Peter glanced across the dining room to see what caught Owen's attention. It was the shelf with the snow globes. Owen's reaction to the name piqued Peter's curiosity. Perhaps what he'd found out about Kensington was true. "What do you know about him?"

Peter was aware of a thundering silence. The atmosphere in the room had changed. It felt colder and less welcoming. Owen looked sad. "Major O'Dale's diaries are in the archives."

"Who?"

Owen bit his lower lip, opened his mouth to say something, then shut it. Peter wondered why he would be reluctant to talk about this O'Dale person. A relative? Or maybe it was Kensington. From what Peter had discovered about the colonel's career, the soldier wasn't the type of man to inspire loyalty or compassion from those who knew him. What really happened to him in 1865?

Lost in thought, Peter missed what Owen said.

Seeing the confusion on Peter's face, Owen repeated himself. "Major Obadiah O'Dale was Kensington's second in command during the war. I read the diary and the events it describes are rather nasty, though, I haven't found any other sources to back up O'Dale's accusations. But I believe him."

Owen turned to look out into the lobby, perhaps checking to see if Beverly was around.

"What O'Dale describes is not something a relative would want to know about. And there's that other thing about him. Maybe it's best Miss Kent not find out about it."

Peter shook his head. "No, she needs to know everything. She an historian. She must have all the facts. She insists."

"Even if they may cause her pain?"

Especially if they cause her pain. No, that's cruel. He said, "She can take it. Nothing can be that bad."

"Oh, yes it can," said Owen.

Peter smiled. "Tell her anyway."

Owen shrugged. "It may take me a while to find it. It's in amongst some material I haven't catalogued yet. There are quite a few boxes."

"I understand," said Peter. But he didn't. To him, it felt like Owen was trying to put him off, delay things. No matter, it was Beverly's problem, not his.

Beverly entered the dining room. She had that pinched look on her face, the one she got whenever she was truly annoyed and ready to kill. Peter had seen it many times. "Shit."

Owen turned to face in the direction Peter was looking. He turned back quickly, and said, "Must make tracks. See how the kitchen is doing. Must do work. Anything." He practically leapt out of his seat and, keeping his face averted from Beverly, raced out to the kitchen.

Peter thought he heard a lock being engaged on the door and almost chuckled. But he didn't. Now was not the time for humor.

Beverly was here.

Emma Ranahan, January 16, 2020

Dressing quickly, Emma decided to be daring and wore a skirt to go with her leather boots. Somehow, this felt like the day for a skirt and boots. She also dabbed on some of her favorite scent—vanilla.

"I hope you appreciate the effort, Professor Dawson," she said as she locked her apartment door. As if the door needed locking. No one came up here. One could only gain access through the library, past her desk.

The moment Emma stepped into the library lobby, there was a knock at the front door. She smiled and went over to open it. A blast of frigid air and a short whirlwind blew through. Shutting out the cold, Emma turned to see the smiling face of the whirlwind—Oona Conroy, owner of the Clifftop Pub next door.

"I brought you your usual," said Oona holding up a paper bag. "Coffee, two creams. Two fresh Danish pastries—one apple, one raspberry." She handed the bag to Emma. "Are you set for lunch?"

"Yes, Oona," said Emma, taking the bag. "Are you ever

going to let me pay for breakfast?"

Oona huffed. "Not a chance, young lady. You're family, and family doesn't pay. Ever. And don't argue, madam."

Emma smiled at her friend. Oona had taken her under her wing shortly after Emma had been hired as librarian. Oona claimed she was the spitting image of her sister, Clara, though how that was possible, since Oona was white, eluded Emma. Every day for the last three years, Oona had been at the library front door with breakfast for her. More often than not, she would also come by at lunch with a sandwich or a bowl of chowder.

Oona was the only family Emma had now.

"Big day today, eh? People coming to visit." Oona laughed. "I told you someone would eventually show up to use the library."

Emma had a sip of coffee. "Truly, Oona, if it wasn't for you and the rest of your family borrowing books every week, I'd go stir crazy in here. Does no one in Wycliffe Point read?"

"They've got the internet and, to be honest, if those rich folks want to spend money maintaining something no one uses, let 'em. At least you get a job and lodgings."

"I can't argue with that," said Emma. "It does give me lots of time to read, though today I have to get materials ready for the professors."

"Is either of them a hunk?" Oona raised an eyebrow.

Emma lightly swatted Oona's arm. She was always trying to set Emma up with some man. Oona knew Emma wasn't interested. The woman had even said she could tell Emma was waiting for someone—her Prince Charming, to come rescue her from the prison that is the Wycliffe Point library.

"I don't know, Oona," said Emma. Something tingled in her stomach. For the last three years, she'd been aware of a growing anticipation, in addition to apprehension about whatever disaster was on its way. In her dreams, there was now someone, vague and always in the shadows, who tried to help her. Whoever it was always failed, but with each passing dream, the failure seemed less complete.

So, she was hopeful. *And isn't that an odd feeling, girl?*

"Should I reserve your usual table, my dear? You never know."

"That's just..." Emma hesitated. For some reason, she thought, what...? Who knew? "Why not, Oona. I might get lucky. Have you got any trifle?"

"No, but I can make a fresh one if you want."

Emma grinned. "I want." A shiver ran down from her head to her toes.

"Emma Ranahan!" said Oona. "What's gotten into you?"

Trying to suppress a giggle, Emma said, "I don't know what it is, but it I sense something good is going to happen for a change. And I want to be...rude."

Oona's face turned red. Emma laughed. "That's the Emma I like to see. Later." She left Emma alone in the library.

Emma went to her office where she set her breakfast on her desk. The clock in the lobby chimed nine. The professors could be here at any time. Leaving her coffee and Danish pastries, Emma rushed down to the basement to sort out the materials the professors had requested.

The moment her foot hit the basement floor, all the

happiness and joy she had experienced being with Oona evaporated.

Trying not to think about the foreboding that had just overwhelmed her, Emma quickly set about sorting resources for the professors. She had piled everything on a table yesterday. Two books and a pair of files on the Civil War for Professor Kent, along with a single reel of microfilm for the local paper from 1865.

For Professor Dawson, Emma had a stack of books. Next to the books, she stacked the reels of microfilm he had requested: July to December 1944 and January to June 1945. She also retrieved the same months for 1905 and 1985. He'd have to get the 1865 reel from the other professor when she was finished.

Emma left to go back to her office to wait for the professors when she stopped and turned to look back at the reels. Professor Dawson had only asked for 1944 and 1945.

What possessed me to leave the other reels?

"Oh, shit," she said, stepping slowly away from the microfilm drawers. "This one's going to be bad."

Emelia Renihan, January 17, 1905

Emelia jerked awake, sweat dripping from her forehead. There was that damned itch again. She slipped her hand under her nightgown and found the offending spot. For a moment, the soft mass that met her fingers surprised her, but then she realized it was another of those strange scars. Since she was about twelve, whenever she became anxious, or agitated, or in any way aroused, these horrible scars grew on her body. But only in January, as if they were a gift to welcome the new year.

The one around her neck wasn't so bad, though it forced her to wear high-necked dresses and blouses all the time, even when not on duty. Emelia felt lucky that she was not burdened by the scars during the summer when keeping her neck covered would have been agony in the heat and humidity. It was the ones that ran across her lower belly and down from her sternum to her crotch that caused the most discomfort. No amount of salve could relieve the itch, and Emelia had resorted to wearing multiple layers of blouses under her uniform to absorb the blood when she scratched too much.

If the things had simply stayed, Emelia could have dealt with them. But no, they had to appear and disappear, seemingly at will.

It wasn't the itching that had awoken Emelia this time. It was the dream. For the second night in a row, she'd dreamt of a strange, yet somehow familiar, man in an odd automobile. It didn't look like any of the vehicles she had seen in Wycliffe Point or on her recent travels to the Midwest. This one was jet black and all closed in. The seats weren't set high behind the front like a normal auto. It looked more like a low box than a carriage. And there was something about a bird of prey—a falcon, perhaps.

The man—the memory of him gave her a flutter in a most unusual place—was handsome, and Emelia wished she could remember where they might have met. St. Louis, maybe? He wasn't alone, but she couldn't see his traveling companion.

The person remained inside the auto, hidden in shadows. All Emelia knew was that whomever the person was, there was nothing but grief and malice there.

Realizing she wouldn't be able to get back to sleep, Emelia climbed out of bed, lit one of the gas lamps, then put on a thick robe. The room was terribly cold, she could see her breath. The fire had gone out. It must be hellishly cold outside because that had never happened before, even in the depths of the worst winters she could recall.

Emelia could just make out the tinny sound of the piano from the distant reception room. Someone, probably Oscar, was playing some of that ragtime music she'd first heard back in August at the St. Louis World's Fair. She smiled at the memory, still amazed that the inn's owners had taken her with them for their month-long sojourn to the event of the year.

Emelia concentrated on the sights she had seen at the fair to distract her from the terrible itching. The flying cigars—dirigibles, they had been called, the gigantic blue whale that hung in the animal exhibit, the electric streetcars. She smiled when she remembered that French organist who had put on a concert, such beautiful music and so different from the tune Oscar played. The Kensington's had allowed her to accompany them to the show, though she had to make sure she stayed in the shadows at the back of the box. She frowned when the phantom taste of that Jack Daniels whiskey filled her mouth. Horrible stuff, even if it did win a gold medal. Give her some decent beer any day of the week.

Closing her eyes, Emelia tried to recall any place or event where she may have encountered her dream visitor. He hadn't been at the anthropological exhibits, the human zoos. She had fled from there as quickly as she could when she realized what they were. Disgusting displays of people in their supposed natural habitats. The Asian displays were horrible, but the worst were the ones from Africa. Emelia almost screamed when she saw the first one. People who looked like her, wearing native garb and performing unusual dances. One of the men had noticed her and smiled, but it was a melancholy smile, as if he knew her family's sad history.

No, she had definitely not met him during the summer. Perhaps in Wycliffe Point on one of her shopping trips, or on one of her rare days off when she sat in the clifftop park and watched the waves roll in.

Who are you, strange man of my dreams? Will we have enough time this time?

Emelia shook her head in confusion. What did that mean? Enough time this time?

With a shrug, she reached for the book on her night table. Opening *The Virginian*, Emelia quietly thanked Oscar again for teaching her to read. Though she was a lowly chamber maid, and not one expected to receive much of an education, the inn's manager had taken an interest in her and shared what he had learned in his adventurous past. Emelia especially liked his tales of life as a cavalry officer out west and during the recent Spanish war.

When she asked him why he helped her, he had looked off wistfully and said, "Do you remember my uncle Obadiah? He visited the inn shortly after I became the manager. One day, he saw you and it was as if he knew you."

Emelia nodded. "He seemed so nice, Oscar. Yet there was a haunted look behind his eyes, as though he had seen something terrible that would not let him go."

"He's always like that, lost in thought, wary and looking behind him as if expecting someone to be there. It seemed to get worse when he visited the inn that time."

"He's never been back?"

"Once, last year, while you and the Kensington's were off galivanting about St. Louis. He was very interested in you and how you were doing. Kept asking if you had any suitors."

Emelia had laughed at that. Who could possibly want to court a chamber maid? There weren't that many people of her type in Wycliffe Point, and they were all spoken for anyway.

"That first time, Uncle Obadiah told me to help you and watch out for you. Whatever the reason, I enjoy it."

After reading for a few minutes, Emelia yawned. She realized the piano music from downstairs had stopped. Most likely someone staying at the inn who required Oscar's help.

She placed her book on a side table and picked up the snow globe. She shook it and watched while the "snow" inside swirled around the tiny little inn. If she looked closely, she imagined she could see tiny people in the windows. One of them even had dark skin like hers.

Patrick!

Now she remembered. There had been an area at the fair with games of chance and skill. Emelia had been walking through, listening to the people having fun while playing. Children yelled at their parents for money to go on the rides or purchase some sweet treat. Emelia had no money of her own, so she was forced to enjoy the sights and sounds vicariously through the others.

While she stood at one of the booths, something reflected sunlight into her eyes. Getting closer, but being sure not to touch or bump any of the gentlemen and ladies gathered around, she saw the most amazing thing. A small, glass globe on a stand shone in the bright sun. Inside the globe was the smallest building Emelia had ever seen. Moving as close as she dared, she was able to see it was a tiny inn that looked remarkably like the Kensington. Emelia felt a flutter in her stomach, which she could have dismissed as a sign of hunger, but knew it as a desire to have the thing. There was no chance of her having it as she was not permitted to participate in the activity, being a person of color in servitude. Besides, to win the prize, one had to fire a rifle at a very small target at the back of the booth. She had never held, nor even been near, a gun in her entire life.

Someone picked up the globe and shook it. Particles of something swirled in a liquid that made it appear as if the inn was in the middle of a blizzard. Emelia couldn't help herself and laughed out loud. This earned her a few stern looks from the people close by.

"I see you admire this small bauble," said a deep voice from her side.

Emelia turned and looked into the face of the most handsome man she had ever seen. Only slightly taller than her, he had incredibly kind eyes. She did not notice, nor later remember, what he was wearing.

"Did you address me, sir?" She couldn't believe anyone would speak to her here.

He gave her a small salute and said, "Yes, ma'am. I saw you staring at it and by the look on your face, I knew you had to have it."

Emelia blushed. The man smiled.

He held out his hand. "Colonel Patrick Dawes, late of the United States 9th Cavalry. And you are?"

Emelia took his hand and immediately a tingle run up her arm. Very quietly, she said, "Emelia Renihan, sir. Currently of the Kensington Inn, Wycliffe Point, New Jersey."

"Lovely, and a sense of humor," said Dawes. "The name's Irish, is it not?"

"I do not know, sir," she said. "My people… Well, I do not know the history of my people except that some were slaves. Our name no doubt comes from one of our former masters."

"Young lady, you have no master. Though I must confess, you could be mine." Dawes face flushed. "Pardon my manners, Miss Renihan. That was far too bold of me."

"There is nothing to pardon, sir."

"Please. Stop this sir bunk. I'm just plain old Patrick." Emelia thought there was nothing plain about Patrick Dawes. "Now, would you like me to win this bauble for you, Miss Renihan? Emelia, if I may."

Emelia couldn't take her eyes from his. "Yes, you may. Anything…Patrick."

Patrick smiled and walked up to the barker. He set down the snow globe and said, "I'm winning this for the lady. What do I do?"

The barker handed Patrick a rifle then pointed at the targets. "Hit the target five times."

Before the man could say another word, Patrick raised the rifle, hardly aimed, and fired five times. The barker retrieved the target and let out a sigh.

"Sir!" He handed Patrick the target. Emelia saw five holes, all within the central bullseye.

Patrick picked up the snow globe and handed it to Emelia. "My lady, please allow me to present you with this."

She could barely speak, but managed to say, "Thank you, Patrick. I shall treasure it."

From afar, someone called her name. It was one of the Kensington children. Emelia said, "I am so sorry, but I must return to the family. They require my services."

Patrick bowed and took her hand.

"Emelia, may I call on you in Wycliff Point?"

Emelia heard her name being called again. This time, there was an edge to it. Whichever child it was, the little beast was not happy.

"Yes. Soon. Please. Goodbye."

She had run off to meet the scruffy little creature who had been calling her. Impossible as it seemed, by the time the Kensington family returned to Wycliffe Point, Emelia had all but forgotten Patrick. There were too many duties to perform to permit her many thoughts of her own.

"Patrick," she said. A tear slipped down her cheek. She picked up the snow globe from her night table and shook it. The snow swirled around the little inn. Looking closely,

Emelia saw something had changed. A tiny woman who reminded her of herself stood on a balcony looking out at something far away. Just behind the little woman, a man appeared to be coming out to join the little lady. He was dressed all in blue, like a uniform.

She smiled. *Patrick? And Me?*

Then her heart did a flip, and all her joy vanished. At the front door of the miniature inn stood a man dressed in a long, black coat. He emanated an air of evil. Emelia shivered when the man turned his head to look up at her.

Impossible.

Emelia's sadness was compounded when she placed the snow globe back on the night table upon a small wooden box. The box contained the remains of her beloved *Schusterkugel.*

There was a gentle knock at her door.

"Who?" No one ever visited her room, especially in the evening. The servant's quarters were strictly off limits. Emelia sighed. No doubt a guest needed an extra blanket or had made a mess. Only the chamber maid could solve problems like that.

When Emelia opened the door, she was shocked to see Oscar. He looked distraught and pushed his way past her. Men were not allowed in a maid's room! Stunned by his boldness, she pulled her robe tighter around her waist.

"Close the door," he said. She did. "He's come back. He walked in about fifteen minutes ago."

"Who?" Emelia asked, confused.

"Bartholomew Kensington."

Chapter 5:
"Here we are together in a lonesome place"

Beverly Kent, January 16, 2020

In the chair vacated by O'Dale, Beverly sat glowering at Peter. He didn't shrink back the way he usually did under her angry gaze. "Well, Peter? Do you have an explanation?"

Look at you, sitting there all smug as if you don't care. I know you better than you think.

When Peter remained silent, Beverly said, "Thank you for waking me so I could have something to eat."

"You have an alarm. I thought you wanted to rest." He sounded…bored. How? With the love of his life sitting in front of him?

"My alarm is broken. Someone knocked it on the floor during the night."

My visitor? No, that was a dream.

"It's a wonder I got up at all. Something kept me awake most of the night."

Peter said, "You don't usually eat breakfast. Just a muffin and a cup of coffee I used bring you from the cafeteria." This was new; he never spoke back.

She noted his use of the past tense. "Maybe today, I wanted more," she said, trying to control her temper. Did that mean something? There was no one else in the room, but she was in discreet mode anyway. She could feel the anger building within, but this time it was different. There seemed to be a touch of frustration in there.

But what am I frustrated about?

"How was I supposed to know?" he asked, clearly annoyed. "You barely spoke to me last night." Beverly grew angrier at his audacity. "Perhaps if you treated me as anything other than your lackey, I would be more mindful of *your* needs, Bev."

You're annoyed by me? Wait. What did you call me?

"If you ever thought about anyone besides yourself, Peter, things would go much more smoothly. God, you're so selfish."

Before Peter could speak, O'Dale returned.

Beverly's face softened. In her sweetest voice, she said, "Good morning. Do you think I could get a cup of coffee, please?"

O'Dale smiled, showing those perfect white teeth. "Why, of course." He could barely look her in the eye. He seemed nervous, almost shy.

You're smitten. I've got you now.

"The kitchen is closed, but I'm sure I could rustle up some toast if you'd like it." His voice remained monotone, as if he was only going through the motions. And behind the smile, Beverly could see…nothing.

No, not shy. Hostile. What have I ever done to you to deserve that?

"That would be fine," Beverly said through gritted teeth. "I don't usually eat much." She smiled back at O'Dale, dropped her gaze then looked back with her head still tilted forward. A little flirting often got her what she wanted.

She got no reaction from O'Dale. He stared at her with no emotion showing on his face. She shivered. He smiled, but there was no warmth there. It had been a very long time since her flirting had failed to get her what she wanted.

What's the matter with you?

Peter got up and said, "Going to drop a load. I'll see you at the front desk in half an hour." He looked at O'Dale, smiled, and said, "See you later, Owen, old friend."

Old friend?

Beverly sat there, her mouth hanging open in surprise. Peter had never left her sitting alone before. Usually, he waited there like a puppy, taking it until she deigned to let him go. And he was never so crude. She watched him ascend the stairs.

What's gotten into you? Did you finally get the message? And why does that not make me happy? What's gotten into me?

She shook her head to clear the cobwebs. Looking at O'Dale, who hadn't moved, he still had that insincere smile on his face.

"I'm waiting for my coffee," she said with just a touch of annoyance. He should get the message.

O'Dale bowed then said, "Yes, of course you are, madam." He turned on his heel and went to the kitchen. He returned a minute later with a coffee pot and a mug. Setting the mug in front of Beverly, O'Dale filled it then turned to go back to the kitchen.

"No toast?" said Beverly, now even more annoyed. "And cream for my coffee."

O'Dale paused then continued into the kitchen. Beverly waited about five minutes, slowly sipping the worst coffee she had ever tasted, until she was ready to kill someone. Her stomach growled. She was about to stand and follow O'Dale into the kitchen to demand some food when the idiot came out of the kitchen with a plate of toast. He also had a dish with butter. These he placed on the table before Beverly, then produced several packets of preserves and a couple of creamers from his jacket pocket. He dropped those on the table next to the butter.

"That will be all, madam?" he asked, standing at attention, his face blank.

Beverly felt her blood boiling. "I don't appreciate your attitude, O'Dale." He didn't move or say anything. "I'm a customer and I expect to be treated with respect and have my needs seen to. Do you understand?"

O'Dale's face didn't change. There didn't appear to be the slightest hint that he knew he'd been put in his place. Hostility practically radiated from him. "Yes, madam. You're a customer and I will treat you as such. Breakfast is from seven until nine. If you miss the appointed time, you are out of luck because the kitchen closes and our chef…leaves until lunch. I provided you with some toast out of courtesy and consideration because Mr. Dawson is such a decent joe."

Beverly's eyes widened at O'Dale's brazen disrespect. "How dare— "

"I dare because I run the place, madam. If madam doesn't like it, madam can find other accommodation."

O'Dale's response stunned Beverly. No one, absolutely no one, had ever treated her that way. She'd be speaking to the owners to demand this creature be terminated at once. "Get me the owners, you piece of trash," she said as calmly as possible. "I demand to speak to the owners."

"Of course, madam," said O'Dale. He turned away, took a step then turned and came back to the table. Beverly glared at him, but all he did was point a finger at his chest and say, "Madam wished to speak to the owner? Is madam unhappy with the service? Dissatisfied with the breakfast? Annoyed that she's not being fawned upon?"

Shit, he owns the place. Just my luck. Dawson is in for it now.

"By the way, I shall require madam's…credit card…for a deposit on the room." This time, O'Dale grinned. "Madam can bring it to the front desk at madam's convenience before madam leaves the inn this morning."

"Dawson's paying for both rooms," she said, trying to hold in her anger. Beverly's heart beat faster, her hands shook. She clenched her fists, ready to lash out and destroy something. When she got like this, it was not unusual for someone to suffer. Usually, that someone was Dawson.

"No, madam, he is not. You had him all dizzy, but I think he's past that now." O'Dale stepped back. "I'll be at the front desk. I'm on duty at all times."

Beverly tried to say something, but her tongue seemed to be tied. She felt confused.

Why am I being treated this way? I deserve better than this, you insufferable toad.

"Will there be anything else, madam?" He didn't let her answer. "No, there won't. Then I shall return to the front desk and resume my work." He gave her the slightest bow and turned away.

Beverly watched O'Dale leave the room. She held on tightly to the edge of the table in her anger. The last time this happened, something wanted to rise up from her subconscious, but it couldn't seem to escape. That was the second time she'd almost remembered whatever it was. Now she was even more frustrated.

She tried to open one of the creamers, but it exploded all over her hand. "Fuck!" The second one opened properly so she poured herself another cup of the rancid coffee. It was better than nothing. Dawson could stop at a Starbuck's and get her something decent. As she raised the cup to her lips, she noticed the curdled lumps of cream floated atop the coffee. "Fuck!"

When she went to butter her toast, she realized Owen had not brought her a knife. Looking around the room, the tables had been cleared of all cutlery. There was no sideboard with plates and utensils. Angry and frustrated at the world, Beverly swept the toast, butter plate, and preserves off the table and watched them smash and bounce all over the floor. The cup of so-called coffee followed and spread a large brown stain across the carpet.

"I'll get someone to clean that up, madam," came O'Dale's voice from somewhere outside the dining room.

Beverly rose, shaking. Her face was on fire; she needed to hit something. "You fucking asshole," she said so no one could hear. It was obvious O'Dale was, in fact, immune to her charms, so she would get no satisfaction in that direction.

"Dawson, you're a dead man," she said, staring up toward where she thought his room might be.

Beverly turned to leave the dining room and almost

collided with a maid dressed in a dull blue dress and a filthy white apron. Long, black hair stuck out from under a dirty kerchief tied around her head. She stank. The maid had a bucket, but no mop or cloth.

"Stupid bitch," said Beverly. "How do you expect to clean up this mess? Are all you people this ignorant?" She looked in the bucket. It contained something red and slimy. Beverly recoiled when the stench of raw meat assailed her nose. She couldn't stop herself from gagging. The maid must have been coming from cleaning a mess in the kitchen.

When the maid's piercing green eyes met Beverly's, it looked as if the woman recognized her. That was impossible. Then Beverly felt an overwhelming wave of hate engulf her. She whimpered and peed a little. Beverly turned and hurried away.

"Damnit," she said, aware of the dampness. A tear slipped down her cheek, but she was already near the stairs so no one would see the wet patch at her crotch.

Beverly ran up to her room to change her clothes, determined to make the rest of the day a living hell for anyone who crossed her and did not do exactly as she demanded.

When she got close to her room, a cold breeze made Beverly shiver. She paused to see where it was coming from, but the only place was the large door at the end of the hall. Examining it more thoroughly, she touched the rough wood and heavy iron hinges. They were cold. This door definitely did not look like it belonged in a hotel. For a moment, Beverly wondered where it led. She thought she heard a sound from the other side.

It had better not be bats.

There was no chance she would go anywhere where those furry little monsters were waiting to swoop.

Safe in her room, Beverly quickly stripped out of her soiled trousers and panties then rinsed them in the sink. When she had cleaned herself, she opened her suitcase to get fresh clothes. She realized then she had not packed an extra pair of slacks. There were plenty of blouses, a couple of sweaters, several bras, and lots of panties. *Why?* All she had was a thin skirt. She'd have to wear pantyhose and her boots to keep warm. At least she wouldn't have to endure too much cold because Dawson would be driving to the library.

Beverly slammed her case shut and got dressed. A toenail caught in her pantyhose and caused a run. *No! Stop this!* Fortunately, it would be hidden by her boots.

She stood for a few moments with her hands pressed against her eyes. *I will not cry. I will not cry.* After a few deep breaths, she had composed herself enough to leave her room.

When she stepped back into the hall, there was a thump from behind the mysterious door, as if something lightly hit it. As Beverly walked up to it, the sound grew louder. When she pressed her ear to the wood, she thought she could hear a heartbeat.

Impossible. I must be hearing my own heart.

She gently placed a hand on the door. It opened toward her. Beverly took a step back while it soundlessly opened all the way.

There was nothing but darkness beyond the door. Beverly couldn't make out any details on the walls. Hell, she couldn't even see the walls, or floor.

Unable to move, Beverly stared into the black. Far away—it seemed like miles—a pinpoint of light appeared and steadily grew larger. Beverly wanted to step away, but her feet were glued to the floor. Now she really could hear her beating heart. She placed her hands over her ears, as if that would shut out sound coming from within her.

The point of light became a ball when it looked like it might be a hundred feet away. *Just how long is this damned hallway?* Within the ball was a figure.

Her?

Eyes wide with fear, Beverly prayed she wouldn't pee herself again.

The ball of light hovered a few feet in front of Beverly. The figure resolved itself into that idiot maid from downstairs. She still held the bucket, and Beverly smelled that awful muck inside. Beverly's fear vanished to be replaced by anger.

"Who the fuck do you…" Beverly stopped when she saw the malice on the woman's face. Her throat was slit and blood flowed freely from the wound. Blood also oozed through the front of the maid's blouse and soaked her filthy apron. *How much blood did she have left inside?* For the briefest moment, Beverly felt pity for the poor woman, but this quickly evaporated when the maid put the bucket down and reached inside.

With a loud, squelching sound, the maid lifted something red from the bucket and extended her hand toward Beverly. Her arm penetrated the edge of the ball of light and kept moving closer.

"Get away!" Beverly stepped back when she saw what was

in the maid's hand—a still-beating heart. Blood pumped out of the torn arteries and splattered on the hall floor.

The maid smiled and said, "See what you did?" Her voice was hollow, as if it came from a great distance.

"It wasn't me!" Beverly screamed and tried to run away, but something held her in place.

"Not you now, the you before," said the maid. "But not this time."

Beverly felt the hall spin and everything went dark. The floor rushed up to meet her face.

Colonel Beauregard Kensington, January 18, 1865

Beau loved this room.

Back in 1831, when his uncle had hired him to train as a clerk in the family import/export business, one of the first things he did was give young Beauregard a tour of the warehouse. Beau hadn't told the old man that he'd already spent many a happy hour in various parts of the building engaging in his favorite pastime: murder. There was always a quiet place where he could tie down some unfortunate animal and torture it to death. By the fourth or fifth dog, Beau had learned to look into their eyes at the moment of demise. There was always a glint, a sudden spark, that told him the beast knew it was about to die.

Seeing that spark provided a far more satisfying result than simple onanism. Self-pollution had never bothered Beau, no matter what the doctors claimed. If he suffered from the dreaded lethargy that was one of the unfortunate consequences of achieving release, it was only because it bored him and required so much effort despite the overwhelming need to do it. An accident with a slave girl while visiting a cousin down in New Orleans when he was a lad of fifteen had proved to be the turning point. Once he had seen that dying spark…oh, the joys Beau had discovered.

Dumb animals had never shown the same depth of fear as the slave girl. Up here in New Jersey, it was so much harder to find human animals that wouldn't be missed. Hence, Beau's special room.

As a clerk, and close relative of the warehouse owner, Beau carefully directed where goods were placed and who placed them. Over the course of a few months, he had managed to secure a room on the fourth floor on the seaward side. It was a good size, with a large window that opened over the sheer drop to the water below. It was incredibly handy for getting rid of his broken, dead playthings.

Beau had made sure many bales of cotton, easily made to disappear from the inventory with a little creative bookkeeping, had been diverted to his room to aid with sound proofing. That was another thing he owed his late cousin. It was him, the not sadly lamented Bartholomew, that had shown Beau how it was easy to have your way with a slave girl amidst the stacked cotton bales that deadened the sound of screams.

The screams were an important part of the sport.

Bartholomew had been shown just how effective the cotton was on Beau's final visit to New Jersey a short time before the war broke out.

The sound of rattling chains and muffled moans and whimpers woke him from his reverie. Ah, the brood from Virginia.

Beau walked over to his captives. The four young were wide-eyed with terror. They'd already pissed themselves and at least one had lost control of its bowels. Filthy animals. The mother wept silently over the gutted body of her mate. That would have to go out the window soon. Despite the cold, the smell had grown almost intolerable. The grandparents sat silently, watching Beau while he checked his toys. He could see the hatred in their eyes, all the better for when they died.

He stood over the old ones and smiled. "You'd like to see *me* die, wouldn't you?" He laughed then spat on them. "You're mine, you animals. I'm going to kill each one of you slowly. I'm going to see the fear in your eyes and watch the life flow out of you. And I'm going to enjoy watching the anticipation of your impending deaths growing within you. Who will be next?"

Neither of the old ones showed any kind of reaction. Years of poor treatment at the hands of their masters had numbed them. Or perhaps it was their pride that would not allow them to cower before him. He'd soon take care of that.

Walking over to the sobbing female, he drew his sabre. With a quick slash, he removed its nose. It screamed, causing Beau to grow excited with anticipation. He picked up the severed nose, tossed it at the old ones. Beau then went to one of the young and grabbed it by its dirty hair. It yelped like one of Beau's puppies. Holding its head back, he placed the edge of the sabre against its throat.

"Eat that," he said to the old female, indicating the severed nose. The thing didn't move. He carefully sawed across the exposed throat, drawing blood. The creature squirmed against the pain, but Beau was too strong for it to get away. It made no sound other than a choking gurgle. He must have cut too deeply and severed its vocal cords. A shame. "Eat that or I'll kill this one now."

The other young whimpered when the noseless one thudded to the floor unconscious.

Shaking its head in the negative, the old one said, "Take me. Leave the young ones. Please, sir."

Beau shrugged. "Have it your own way." He hoisted the thing he held to its feet then looked directly into its brown eyes. As slowly as he could, he sawed the blade across its throat. Blood flowed freely. He tried to watch the life drain from the tiny body, but the old female screamed something at him, and he was momentarily distracted. When he looked back, the young one was dead.

He'd missed the most glorious part of his game.

Bellowing his rage at being cheated of his satisfaction, Beau whipped around. The mother had regained consciousness and stared at him with angry eyes. However, the lack of nose on the face made Beau laugh. Still laughing, he casually walked over to it and removed its head with a single sweep of his sabre. The head rolled away and bumped up against the legs of the old female. A single tear slid down its cheek.

He'd return later to finish the rest.

After securely locking the room door, Beau waited a few moments to see if any noise was evident. As always, the room held its secrets in silence.

Crossing the walkway from the warehouse to the inn, Beau entered his room, cleaned himself, then put on his dress uniform.

Half an hour later, Colonel Beauregard Kensington, commanding officer of the 45th New Jersey Volunteer Infantry Regiment, stood with a glass of whisky in one hand and his other hand resting on the pommel of his sabre. He desperately wanted to draw his weapon and put it to use amongst these fat pigs and idiots who knew nothing of the horrors of battle and the joys of killing.

"Tell me, Colonel, what are your plans for after the war?" This was the wife of the mayor of Wycliffe Point. She stank of gin and sweat poured down her bloated face.

"That depends, madam, on how much longer the conflict will last," he said. *I will gut you like the heifer you are.* "Though all signs show that the Confederacy is on its last legs and shall surrender soon."

"So, you will be going back to the fighting, sir?" Now, who was *this* woman? No matter. She was the wife of someone here and, to be honest, Beau couldn't have cared less.

"Naturally, madam," said Beau with a slight bow.

"And free the poor slaves from their lives of torment," she said.

"It is my duty and my honor to defend this great nation. It is my pleasure to defeat the enemies of our wonderful republic," said Beau. *And watch them die on the gallows or by the blade of my sabre.* "I care not one whit for the mongrel coloreds."

Across the lobby, standing by the fire, Beau spied his second in command, Major O'Dale. He couldn't stop from smiling. The major was deep in conversation with that fool, Daweson. Poor Captain Daweson. Entranced by an animal into thinking it could be treated like a white woman. Led by the nose to his own doom. Or so Beau had thought. The captain had proven to be blessed by the most incredible luck. Minie balls had killed those around him, but left him unscathed. Cannon fire had slaughtered many in Daweson's company while doing nothing but dirtying the man's uniform. *That* had given him an excuse to fraternize with that washerwoman creature.

As soon as Beau had realized his Captain was enamored of the former slave, he had decided that he must have her for himself. It amused him that he could almost regard her as a human being despite her origins and nature. He had to admit that she did have a certain appeal, and he would have liked to use her in…less fatal ways. Much as he had tried to get her away from his subordinate, he had failed. The creature continually rebuffed his advances. Her position forced her to be respectful to a white man who could easily order her death, and Beau was sure there was some fear in there somewhere. However, she refused to co-operate.

Beau stiffened. These new feelings of arousal, caused by a living being rather than a dying one, had at first confused and appalled Beau. But he found himself curious as to where these unusual urges would lead him.

"Oh, my word, Colonel." It was that pig of a mayor's wife. "I didn't think I could interest you in such a way."

He stared at her and realized she was staring down at his crotch where there was an obvious bulge.

The woman looked around quickly to make sure no one else was close, then leaned in to whisper, "We needn't tell my husband. He wouldn't care, anyway. I can't remember the last time he was between my legs. Your quarters in half an hour, Colonel?"

Beau blinked his eyes. What in the blazes? "Please excuse me, madam," he said to her. "I must repair to my room to vomit."

Without another word, he turned away from the sputtering woman and proceeded into the inn's dining room. On his way, the object of his desire emerged from a side door. She halted abruptly when she saw him and cast her eyes to the floor.

Good. You know your place.

"You," he said to her. He pushed her arm and felt a thrill in his loins at the contact. "Stay far away from Captain Daweson, animal. His station is far above yours. All you will do is drag him into the gutter and taint his reputation."

As if I care about his reputation.

"Go outside and bring in more firewood. Later this evening, when all these guests have departed, you will come to my rooms. I will have duties for you there."

How could she possibly refuse? Subservience was bred into her.

She—what was her name? He had never bothered to find out—looked up at him then. There was unacceptable defiance in her eyes. She would need to be shown her place.

There was more there, in those eyes. Hatred? No! He

wanted… What?

For the first time in his life, Beauregard Kensington was at a loss. He had always had whatever he desired. If it was not his, he took it, consequences be damned. For him, holding the power of life and death in his hands was the ultimate satisfaction.

But now. This…woman. She made him want something different. His breathing quickened and his face flushed. Sweat poured down his forehead and he was uncomfortable in his uniform. Worse, he thought of her as something other than an animal—a woman of all things.

She grinned as if she knew there was confusion in his head. The bitch.

Now she smiled. How could she possibly know?

The anger welled up from deep within. He balled his hands into fists to keep them from shaking. It would not be good to lose control here, in front of the elite of Wycliffe Point. In front of his subordinates.

In front of her.

He turned abruptly. The warehouse. His room. Something had to die.

Beau needed release.

Beverly Kent, January 16, 2020

Instantly, Beverly's eyes opened and were stung by the bright light in the hall. The heavy door was closed again. Spitting out some dust and fuzz from the carpet, she got to her feet. Though she didn't want to do it, she pushed on the door. No movement at all. It was securely shut.

Beverly tried to clear her head.

"I'm tired. I'm upset. I haven't eaten. I'm seeing things." She almost believed herself. Leaning against the wall, she waited until her heartbeat steadied. Looking about quickly to see if anyone was around, Beverly slipped a hand under her skirt and felt her crotch. Dry, thank God.

"This fucking place," she said to the walls. "No more."

Taking a deep breath, Beverly made her way to the stairs and then the lobby. That fool O'Dale was in for it now. Nobody messed with Beverly Kent and got away with it.

At the bottom of the stairs, Beverly paused to gather her thoughts. She closed her eyes for a moment, imagining the look on O'Dale's face when she threw the full force of her anger at him.

When Beverly opened her eyes, the first thing she saw was that idiot of a maid passing through the dining room. The creature gave her a smile so full of defiance and hatred, Beverly took a step back and almost fell over an armchair. She sat, never taking her eyes from the maid. The maid stared back. Now there was a grin on her face.

"Who is she?"

"You'll find out soon enough," said O'Dale.

Beverly turned to glare at him, but he wasn't there. Instead, there was a vaguely familiar man in an old uniform. It looked like it came from the Civil War. He appeared hazy.

When she looked back at the dining room, the maid had disappeared. She wiped her eyes then glanced toward the front desk. O'Dale was there, stock still, but with the slightest grin on his face.

I've had about enough of this asshole.

Beverly leapt to her feet and strode briskly to the desk. O'Dale didn't move or even flinch when she gave him her sternest "you'd better not fuck with me" look.

O'Dale now sat behind the front desk writing something. She walked closer and, simply to annoy the man, slammed her hand down on the bell several times. He looked up at Beverly and flared his nostrils, his eyes dark, and that phony smile plastered across his face again.

"Yes, madam?" he said. "You brought your…credit card?"

"Where's that stupid maid? The one with the bucket." Beverly's face got hot with anger. "The bitch attacked me from the hallway on the other side of the door upstairs. I just saw her in the dining room."

"What door?"

"Don't play innocent with me, O'Dale. You know perfectly well that there's a door at the end of the hall next to my room. It opened and she came at me with a bucket."

"A bucket?" O'Dale tried to suppress a smile. How dare he. "That door does not open."

"Of course it does, you fool. I was there. I saw the hall and her coming at me."

O'Dale shook his head. "Impossible, madam. That door is nailed shut. On the other side is nothing but a brick wall."

"What do you mean, nothing. I saw the hall." Beverly wanted to punch him.

"On the other side of that wall is air. There used to be a

connecting walkway to the warehouse next door. It collapsed in 1905. There's nothing there." He crossed his arms. "Have you been drinking? It's rather early, don't you think?"

The audacity!

Beverly slammed her hand down on the counter. O'Dale didn't react. "I have not fucking been drinking, you asshole."

"Madam, do not use that tone with me, nor that language. I will not tolerate it."

"You'll tolerate whatever I fucking give you," said Beverly.

"No, madam, I will not." O'Dale pointed behind her. "Go out that door and look up. I'll wait."

Beverly stormed to the door and went outside. The howling wind immediately cut through her thin winter coat. As if to piss her off even more, a sudden gust blew up under her skirt. She looked up and saw nothing but the wall of the inn. On the fourth floor, there was the outline of an opening that had been filled in with brick. Directly across from the inn, a large building loomed, with a matching bricked up opening.

She returned to the lobby.

O'Dale said, "Well?" Beverly said nothing. "Then do you have your…credit card? You need to pay for your room."

Beverly stood there feeling defeated. No one came to her rescue. No one came to help her.

For the first time in forever, Beverly was utterly alone.

Chapter 6:
"Trying to make the best of who we are"

Peter Dawson, January 16, 2020

Stopping on the second-floor landing, Peter listened to the heated exchange.

Whatever was buzzing around in Beverly's bonnet, it must be serious for her to raise her voice like this. She valued her privacy so much, she rarely made an audible fuss lest strangers learn something they shouldn't. Peter felt sure he was in for a blast of anger, but, for the first time in far too long, he didn't care.

Adding to his curiosity was the fact that Beverly was even in the lobby before him. Usually, she made him wait. However, she wasn't waiting for him now. Rather, she stood at the front desk, shaking with anger and seemingly ready to leap the counter and murder Owen.

Peter slowed his approach, not wanting to miss a thing. Owen acknowledged him with a slight raising of an eyebrow. It was obvious to Peter that he was trying to suppress a grin.

"But why should I have to pay? This is supposed to be billed to the faculty," said Beverly. She looked shaken.

Odd.

Now he knew what was going on. When Owen had run Peter's credit card for a room deposit, he must not have included Beverly's room.

Oops.

He didn't remember saying anything to anyone about the

faculty picking up the tab for the inn. His research was, as some described it, out there, and he would never have had the gall to ask the university to fund him. There may have been a vague expectation on Beverly's part that he was going to pay for her room, but he chose to forget that idea.

"Be that as it may, madam," said Owen calmly, "I still require your...credit card. You can seek reimbursement from your faculty upon your return to the university." He smiled. "My hands are tied."

Beverly let out a long breath. "Didn't Dawson give you his card when we checked in? Can't you use his card?"

Peter winced.

"I was only authorized to use Mr. Dawson's...credit card...for Mr. Dawson's room. There was no mention of you, madam."

Peter grinned.

Now for some fun.

He walked up to the front desk and said, "Hello, all. How's everything going?" When Beverly gave him a withering look which, for once, didn't wither him, he asked, "Is there a problem?"

Beverly's nostrils flared.

Uh, oh. She's gonna blow.

"You know damn well what the problem is." Peter shook his head, held his hands open, and shrugged. "Give him your credit card for the room deposit and do it now."

"No," he said.

"No? What do you mean, no?" Her cheeks were crimson.

"No. It's a negative," said Peter. "No, as in I'm not doing

what you want, or no, as in you can't have what you want. Do you need a dictionary? I'm sure there's one around here somewhere." Owen reached under the desk and produced an Oxford which he gently placed on the counter.

Peter's heart thumped and his legs felt weak. He hadn't spoken back to Beverly…ever. It felt really good to stand up to her, but it was scary as well. Behind Beverly, Owen covered his mouth to stifle a laugh.

Beverly spun to face Owen, who quickly got busy checking some papers on the counter in front of him. Without looking up, he pushed the dictionary a little closer toward her. Facing Peter again, Beverly said, "Give him your fucking credit card and pay for my fucking room or else." Her hands were on her hips. She meant business.

When you stand that way, one can really see just how incredible your legs are. Those boots! Damn, you're beautiful. Silly to be wearing a skirt in this weather, though.

Peter smiled. "Or else what, Bev? You'll stop being nice to me? Oh, no, you have to start being nice before you can stop." He scratched his chin. "What else? You'll stop putting out? No, that's crude and I apologize. I meant that you'll withhold your affections. No, wait, you've never shown me your affections, so how would I know if you were withholding them?" He shrugged again and stared at the woman he had loved until last night. "Well, I'm stumped."

Beverly stood there fuming for a full minute before she tore open her jacket pocket and pulled out her wallet. She opened it too fast and spilled its contents, assorted cards and a few coins, on the floor. He noticed a small photo of him. That was a surprise as Beverly had never given him her photo. *I wonder where she got it.* Peter didn't move to help pick up the scattered items. Beverly got on her knees, retrieved her things, then stood. She brushed a stray strand of hair from her face then threw her credit card at Owen.

He caught it, moved it through his fingers like a magician with a playing card, then ran it through the card machine. "Madam," he said and held the receipt out for Beverly to sign.

"How fucking ancient is this place?" said Beverly. When she signed the receipt, she tore the thin paper top copy.

Yes, how ancient is this place? How did I miss that last night?

"All set now," said Owen. He handed Beverly her copy of the receipt. Peter stared at him. "I hope you have a stellar day, madam." He bowed his head slightly to Beverly. "You, too, Mr. Dawson. Good luck with your hunt. I'm sure you'll find far more than you expect at the library."

Peter thought that was a curious thing to say, but it reminded him that he didn't know the location of the library.

Owen smiled and said, "Out the side door over there, down the path to the cliff wall, then turn right onto the street. It's next door. The entrance is about a hundred yards along. Can't miss it. Big red building full of books. Says *'Carnegie Library'* above the door."

"That's wonderful," said Peter. "Well, Bev, ready for a brisk morning walk? There's no point driving a couple of hundred yards."

Owen said, "The path does go along the cliff edge. There's a fence, but, Mr. Dawson, please stay as far from there as possible."

"Is it dangerous?" *Damned cliffs. Maybe I should drive.*

"Not usually," said Owen. "But at last count, four good people and a bad one have fallen or been pushed from there. Let's not make it five."

Peter laughed. "I don't think I have anything to worry about, Owen, old friend."

Owen looked worried. "Please, Peter, do it for an old friend."

Confused by Owen's concern, Peter said, "Sure thing."

Beverly glared at him. "We're taking the fucking car. I'm not freezing my ass off for anyone."

"You'd only be freezing your ass off for yourself. That's unfortunate," he said and made his way to the side door without waiting for Beverly. By the time he reached the door, she was right behind him. She pushed her way past when he opened the door. "You're welcome," he said under his breath. "Bitch."

The short walk was brutal, with icy winds blowing in off the Atlantic, but Peter felt warm inside. Beverly complained the whole way. Her winter jacket was inadequate for this type of cold. The boots probably kept her lovely feet warm, but the skirt and pantyhose would do nothing to stop the wind from reaching her core.

Peter stayed close to the curb, as far as possible from the short wall at the edge of the cliff. He didn't need Owen to tell him to stay clear. His terror of heights would do that for him.

Besides, walking on the outside of the sidewalk was the courteous thing to do when walking with a lady. Even if that lady was a miserable Kent.

When they stepped into the Wycliffe Point Carnegie Library, a young, Black woman stood at the front desk waiting for them. Peter stopped short. She was, without doubt, the most beautiful woman he had ever seen.

"Welcome to the library, Professors Kent and Dawson," she said with an incredible and open smile. "I'm Miss Ranahan, the librarian."

Yes, you are.

Peter had written to her several weeks ago to enquire about library opening times and the availability of materials. Something about her stirred feelings deep within him. He didn't know why. She was about five feet six inches tall and slim. Her wavy black hair was tied back in a ponytail. Like Beverly, the librarian wore boots and a skirt. Unlike Beverly, Miss Ranahan's quite lovely legs were bare. *I guess the cold doesn't affect you.* Her blazer was open and the tight turtleneck sweater she wore revealed a not-at-all ample bosom.

But her most unbelievable and, to Peter, unusual feature was her piercing green eyes. They looked…haunted.

He couldn't for the life of him recall why he recognized her. Maybe a TV show or movie.

"I knew you'd be here about now, Professor," she said, addressing Peter and ignoring Beverly.

"Call me Peter."

Beverly looked furious. She didn't like it when he was nice to other women in her presence. She couldn't understand the concept of love, but she knew all about jealousy and not being the center of attention. Somehow, though, this didn't seem like simple jealousy. If Beverly had a weapon, Peter was sure she would have ripped the librarian wide open and torn out her heart.

What the fuck? Where'd that come from?

"Would you like some coffee?" the librarian asked. "I just brewed a fresh pot."

Beverly didn't reply. Peter politely declined and asked for directions to the bathroom. He'd better be careful because the effects of too much coffee for breakfast might make themselves known. The bathroom turned out to be quite acceptable: clean, private, and smelling of vanilla. He stood there for a few moments, waiting, then decided he didn't need the bathroom after all. The women were waiting when he returned ten minutes later. Beverly stood tapping her foot impatiently, her fists clenched.

"…it came down in 1905 and wasn't rebuilt. The library, oh, Professor Dawson, thank God," said Miss Ranahan, relief clearly showing on her face.

Peter had got there just in time. Beverly looked ready to snap—the librarian was lucky to be alive. There also seemed to be an underlying hostility.

"If you'd like to follow me, professors, I'll take you to what you need. It's in the basement." Miss Ranahan walked away.

They went down a wide, wood-paneled staircase that had recently been oiled, judging by the aroma on Peter's hand after he touched the banister. The librarian led them along a narrow aisle to an alcove where there was a carrel with a microfilm reader.

Miss Ranahan said, "The library doesn't have extensive holdings of local private papers and ephemera. You might want to try the local historical society archive. Perhaps you could ask the head of the society about getting access to them. I know he's very helpful. He's always eager to talk about local history. Sometimes it's hard to get him to stop." She laughed a sweet little laugh that made Peter's heart skip a beat.

"Owen mentioned that this morning at breakfast," said Peter.

Oh, crap. I've done it now. I know something she doesn't and didn't tell her and I reminded her about breakfast.

Beverly glared at him. "You didn't say anything about O'Dale to me, Peter." Before he could reply, she turned her attention back to Miss Ranahan, who looked confused. "Where are your Civil War records? I have *legitimate* research to do." Not giving Miss Ranahan a chance to answer, Beverly continued. "Besides relevant microfilm, I also want any papers, diaries, gazetteers, books on local history that cover the period I want, and anything else that's available."

Miss Ranahan stared at Beverly. The side of her mouth twitched a little, and Peter wasn't sure if she wanted to burst into tears or laughter. With Beverly, it could go either way.

In a steady voice that betrayed no emotion, the librarian said, "All that we have is laid out and waiting. If it is not sufficient, as I mentioned, you could ask the head of the local historical society. He *can* be very helpful *when* the mood strikes. If he likes you." The whole time she spoke, Miss

Ranahan did not take her eyes off Beverly. She also didn't blink.

"There," said the librarian. She pointed at the carrel. The instant she raised her hand, which almost touched her, Beverly flinched and looked afraid, but quickly recovered. Peter didn't think Miss Ranahan noticed. *What was that all about?*

On the table next to the microfilm reader were the materials they had requested: ten reels of microfilm, some files, and two stacks of books. Peter noted that the larger stack and several file folders dealt with his interests while the small stack—only two books and a couple of file folders, not so much a stack—were for Beverly. This gave him a small degree of satisfaction.

"As you can see," said Miss Ranahan, "there isn't much. You can always…"

Beverly broke in, "Check with the local historical blah, blah, blah. That is all." She waved the librarian away.

Confusion, surprise, hurt, anger, and contempt all quickly crossed the librarian's face. She stood with her hands clasped and glanced from Beverly to Peter and back. Peter quickly checked and saw no rings on her fingers.

"Thank you for being so helpful, Miss Ranahan," said Peter, trying to sound as sincere as possible. He was so angry with the way Beverly had spoken, his voice shook a little. "We both know how to use a microfilm reader. We can load it ourselves." He tried to smile, but it was difficult with Beverly around, so he took a step away then stared at the floor. Quietly, he said, "I'm not with her."

"Well?" said Beverly. Peter looked up and Beverly glared

daggers in his direction. Miss Ranahan nodded then left them to their work. He watched her walk away, feeling a sudden emptiness and need he couldn't explain.

Closing his eyes and taking a deep breath to clear his head, Peter looked at the materials in the carrel. He was eager to go through the microfilm records of the *Wycliffe Point Democrat*, the local paper for almost two hundred years. The reels containing the issues he had wanted, December 1944 to June 1945, were waiting for him. And that's when Peter knew he was in even more trouble. The Wycliffe Point library had a single microfilm reader and Beverly also wanted to go through microfilm.

Not unexpectedly, Beverly said, "I'll use the microfilm reader first. You can work on something else." Pushing aside the reels Peter needed, she set down her laptop bag, took out a notebook and pen, and waited.

He felt confident he could breeze through his reels in a couple of hours. His eyes had become accustomed to speed reading the contents of microfilm and finding the articles he needed for whatever research paper he was writing. Beverly, on the other hand, was deadly slow. She seemed to have trouble reading anything that wasn't on perfectly white paper in a clear typeface. He was certain he would get nothing done today.

Peter was surprised to see there were nine reels of microfilm for him. Strange. A year's-worth of microfilmed, small-town newspapers usually only took up two reels.

"I'll leave you to it," he said and picked up the books and microfilm left for him. Without waiting for Beverly to speak, he walked away. He knew perfectly well that she had trouble with any type of machine. Now she would have to rely on Peter's help.

Or not.

He heard Beverly curse him and fumble with the microfilm reader.

Peter found a small table in a far corner of the basement, out of sight of Beverly. He set down his books, film, and laptop bag, then took a deep breath. This trip was already a disaster, and it was only the second day and their first real day of work.

"Never again," he said quietly. *I'll not let her ruin my work again.*

He sat, flipped open one of the file folders to find several official-looking reports. They were dated for the middle of January 1945, exactly the period he needed. When he was in research mode, he could tune out even the most annoying noise. Right now, that noise was Beverly on the other side of the basement trying to load a reel of microfilm into the reader.

Peter started to read.

Police report on Mr. Owen O'Dale, Managerof the Kensington Inn, Wycliffe Point, January 15, 1945

Acting on an anonymous tip called in to the Wycliffe Point Police Department on January 14, 1945, Chief Winthrop and two officers proceeded to the Kensington Inn. It had been reported that the manager of the inn, Mr. Owen O'Dale, was running a brothel on the fourth floor.

Mr. O'Dale was questioned thoroughly by the Chief, after which Mr. O'Dale gave the Chief a tour of the entire inn. Nothing was found to indicate that there had been any illegal or immoral activities on the premises.

Complaint filed with the Wycliffe Point Police Department, January 15, 1945

This formal complaint is lodged by Mr. Owen O'Dale, manager of the Kensington Inn, against Mr. Benjamin Kenton of no fixed address.

For the past two weeks, Benjamin Kenton has made himself a nuisance at the Kensington Inn to such a degree that some staff are in fear for their safety. Kenton first approached Mr. O'Dale seeking employment as a laborer or any other position that might be available. Mr. O'Dale gave Kenton a few tasks to complete including removal of trash, some dishwashing, and errands to secure supplies from the wholesalers. Kenton proved to be incapable of performing the tasks properly or to completion. Money was reported missing from funds given for the supplies. Kenton denied any knowledge of said missing funds.

Kenton forced himself upon several female members of the inn staff. They rebuffed his advances, but he remained persistent. In particular, Miss Emily Renehan, the maid, reported that Kenton had cornered her in the pantry and, after groping her inappropriately, attempted to place his hand under her skirts. When she pushed him away, he struck her, at which time Miss Renehan hit him in the privates with a sack of potatoes. Miss Renehan reported that Kenton threatened retaliation.

His harassment was reported to Mr. O'Dale who then ordered Kenton from the property with the warning that the police would be contacted if he returned.

[Note: Mr. O'Dale mentioned that Kenton might have several facial bruises and small cuts, possible bruising to his abdomen and back, several missing teeth, and potential damage to his previously injured privates as a result of an accident on Kenton's part involving several pairs of heavy boots, a baseball bat, a skillet, three forks, and a broom handle.]

Confidential report on possible enemy activity in the vicinity of Wycliffe Point, in particular near the Kensington Inn, January 16, 1945

[Note: This report is unofficial and is a copy from the memory Chief Solomon Winthrop of the report written by Colonel Benjamin Macdonald, Commandant of the Army unit stationed at Fort Kensington.]

Following several sightings of strange things in Wycliffe Bay, Colonel Macdonald came to police headquarters to ~~request~~ demand the help of the department to interrogate witnesses. Several locals claim to have seen unusual movement out in the water of the bay. One citizen reported seeing what he interpreted to be a submarine periscope. This was immediately dismissed as impossible since no American submarines were in the area at the time, and no German or Japanese submarine could arrive at the Bay from Europe or the Pacific. Further sightings were also dismissed due to the unreliability of the witnesses who had been returning to their homes after a party to celebrate the return of several local men from the European theater.

[Note from Chief Winthrop: Several sightings of German submarines were reported off the east coast and at least one submarine was sunk. I believe the Colonel was trying to stifle any suggestion of German activity in the Wycliffe Point area because, in fact, there was.]

At least three people reported hearing strange talk coming from below the cliffs near the inn. One was sure the voices had spoken German. However, when quizzed by a German-speaking soldier, the witness could not verify that it was the language he heard. The Colonel put this down to hysteria caused by German propaganda.

A potential spy seen moving suspiciously along the shore was found to be one Benjamin Kenton, who was being sought in regard to allegations of harassment by staff members of the Kensington Inn. The Colonel was assured the dagger in the possession of Kenton was a souvenir from the Great War held purely for the purpose of self-defence. The dagger was of German manufacture, but held the crest of the late Kaiser and, therefore, was not believed to be from any recent visitor or spy from the Reich.

Chief Winthrop attempted to hold Kenton for further questioning regarding the allegations, but the Colonel interceded and allowed the man to leave. Kenton promptly disappeared.

The Colonel was satisfied that there was no activity by enemy aliens, be they German or Japanese. When it was pointed out that Japanese spies would be easy to spot in a small town on the east coast, the Colonel put forth the point that civilians and local law enforcement were not trained to expose spies and, therefore, should mind their own business.

The matter of spies in Wycliffe Point was dropped.

After reading the files, Peter spent an hour checking through the local history books searching for anything that might corroborate the police reports. There had to be something, or all his efforts had been wasted.

The whole time, he could hear Beverly slowly cranking the microfilm through the reader. It needed oil.

Miss Ranahan appeared noiselessly next to his table. Peter jumped when he realized she was standing there. She grinned as he tried to recover his dignity.

"You're stealthy," he said, trying to be witty and failing.

"It is a library," she said quietly. "I've learned to creep around without disturbing the patrons."

Peter found he couldn't stop staring at the librarian's eyes. They were the deepest green he had ever seen, and it was difficult to concentrate on what she was saying. He also couldn't help the wide grin on his face. He suddenly realized she had said something while he was lost in thought.

"My apologies, Miss Ranahan. I tuned out for a moment, lost in the green. You have eyes."

Miss Ranahan blushed. "Yes, Professor Dawson. I believe my people were slaves on a plantation owned by someone of Irish descent. They must have…intermingled. Hence my unusual eye color and name. Other than that, I don't know much about my ancestry."

Peter tried to think of something to say but came up blank.

"It's all right, Professor, or do you prefer Doctor? You don't have to say anything."

"Peter or Pete. I don't much care for titles and such."

"Neither do I. Please call me Emma, Peter. But never Emmeline or Millie or Emelia or Emily. They have…unfortunate associations for me."

"Ye gods, that's a beautiful name. Emma."

"Thank you." She smiled that wonderful smile again, but looked a little flustered. "Um, I was wondering if there's anything you need. Coffee, tea, water, shotgun."

Peter guffawed. This woman was amazing. A little flutter tickled his stomach.

Oh, no. She's too incredible to be around. I'm going to make an ass of myself.

"Tea would be lovely, Miss Ranahan. Emma. Despite a huge breakfast and too much coffee, I'm quite empty. I'll take a raincheck on the shotgun."

"I'll put the kettle on, and I have some cookies," she said. "I'll bring them down. There's a small office where we can have it. There's no food or drink allowed in the library proper."

Trying to be casual, he leaned back in his chair which promptly went over backward and sent him sprawling. To make matters worse, he farted a little.

I need the shotgun for myself.

When he had untangled his legs from those of the chair and regained his composure, Peter stood. Attempting to be cool, he leaned against a cabinet that turned out to have unlocked wheels. Standing up again, Peter didn't make a move. Emma rubbed her eyes with her left hand. Her shoulders shook. She looked at him and unsuccessfully tried not to giggle. Her face registered shock.

"I'm so sorry, Peter. But when you fell over..."—she looked at the floor then back at him— "did you toot?" She giggled some more. "And then you went over again." Her face took on a rosy glow. "This is a library. We must remain quiet so as not to disturb the other patrons."

"Are there any other patrons?" said Peter.

Emma shook her head and said, "Just you and..." she gestured toward the other side of the library.

"Yes, well, we must. You see... I think..." —he tried to say something intelligent—"Or even plain." —but failed.

"Yes, but this time I'm sincere," said Emma. "I'll let you

know when the kettle's boiled." She winked at him and turned away.

Peter watched her walk down the aisle then turn at the end toward Beverly's carrel.

"You have a wonderful behind, Emma," he said quietly. He sensed a tightness in his pants and looked down. "Oh, fuck. Did she notice?"

It was plain to see that he had an erection.

Emma's head popped around the corner. She looked at him with a smile, nodded her head in the affirmative, gave him a thumbs up sign, then promptly disappeared.

Emma Ranahan, January 16, 2020

She stopped to gather her thoughts. What on earth had just happened? She'd been speaking with that nice professor, Peter, and things had gone all…all what? They had remained professional until Peter mentioned her eyes. Emma couldn't remember the last time someone had commented on their unusual color. Unusual, that is, for a Black woman. Most of the men she had met couldn't seem to get past the color of her skin. If they did, they became focused on her chest or backside.

Peter had seemed to concentrate on her. And she loved every second of it. He'd even become aroused.

"Oh, no," she said quietly. "Why did I do that?" She'd heard his question. How did she even know that's what he was referring to? Emma hadn't been able to stop herself from letting him know what she saw.

What he must think of me!

Emma approached the carrel where Professor Kent struggled loudly with the microfilm reader. It was obvious the woman was clueless about the machine. The proper thing to do would be for Emma to offer help so the professor could get on with her work.

And get the hell out of my library, you bitch.

Emma gasped, astonished that she would think something like that. Normally, she could keep a cool head. Even in the privacy of her own apartment upstairs, she never swore. Yet, she found herself having a difficult time restraining her tongue. The horrible woman had been rude and hostile from the moment she entered the building. There was something else Emma couldn't put her finger on—a deep-seated hatred boiled within her when she looked at the bitch.

It was odd that she felt safe and warm with Peter but troubled with the other one.

As Emma approached the carrel where the shrew worked, she heard thumping and cursing. The woman looked over the top of the carrel and, when she saw Emma approaching, said, "What the fuck do you want?"

Before Emma could answer, she heard, "Fuck off."

"Not now," said Emma quietly. "I don't need her shit."

Emma made her way upstairs to her office. As usual, there was no one else in the library. It wasn't the weather's fault. They stayed away in droves even on the most pleasant of summer days.

Will we have a summer at last?

These strange thoughts were becoming more frequent. Bad

enough she was experiencing her normal—*normal?*—January blues, now Emma's head was filling with memories and hopes that weren't her own.

Emma put the kettle on and sat to wait for it to boil. She picked up her snow globe and shook it, watching the "snow" inside obscure the little inn. There appeared to be some movement in the inn, and when she brought the globe closer, there were little figures in the windows. They hadn't been there before. Had they?

Pulling a magnifying glass out of a drawer, Emma carefully examined the bauble.

Sure enough, there were little people in almost every tiny window, and some standing outside the front door. How could she have missed them before this? There were so many. Emma focused the magnifying glass on each figure.

In the windows, there were four who looked like soldiers—two in blue uniforms, one in brown, and one in green. They all had flaming red hair. She didn't like the look of them. Four more were also soldiers—two in blue and two in green. These tiny men had black hair.

She smiled at these fellows, feeling an odd warmth deep down when she looked at them.

Four were women in pale blue dresses with a splotch of red on the front. The women were Black like her. She quickly named them Emmeline, Emelia, Emily, and Millie. She didn't know why, but the names felt right. Three were men dressed in various types of suits, and one wore a blue uniform. These little men had brown hair.

The three at the front door of the inn were the oddest. A

tall man with brown hair carried a briefcase and was looking at a pocket watch. A woman carried a briefcase in one hand and a sword in the other. It was weird that she had red hair on one side of her head and black on the other. Another woman, Black, stood reading from a book. Emma knew these three, but didn't know how or why.

One more thing struck Emma as odd. On the wall of the inn's fourth floor, there was an outline of an opening filled with bricks of a slightly different color from the wall. This was just like the old inn next door with its bricked-up entrance to the long-fallen walkway to the library.

How was it possible she had never spotted these details before today?

Emma nearly dropped the snow globe when the kettle whistle startled her. She poured boiling water into the teapot and set it aside to steep.

Back at her desk, Emma pulled a small box from a drawer. She had found it while gathering materials for Peter and the bitch but had set it aside. Inside was an old journal and some letters. Something told her she shouldn't give this to Peter. Yet.

Letter from Obadiah O'Dale to Oscar O'Dale, January 13, 1905

[This letter was found tucked between the pages of the journal of Oscar O'Dale, manager of the Kensington Inn from 1899 to 1936. Obadiah O'Dale was the manager of the Kensington Inn from 1870 to 1899. As with other documents made available by Miss Ranahan, permission has not been granted for citation. Also, this letter is not to be seen by Professor Beverly Kent. Note: This letter was received on January 18, 1905. No explanation for the delay has been found.]

Oscar,

I hope this letter finds you in good health. I wish I could claim the same for myself. What you are about to read may seem fantastic, but I swear everything I write is the truth. Or at least, as close to the truth as I can get.

For several weeks, I have been troubled by horrific dreams that have caused me to use laudanum to acquire a modicum of sleep. I am haunted by events that occurred in January of 1865. The memory of these events, and the certainty that they are to be repeated, have forced me to reveal facts that, until now, were known only to me and several of the dead.

To save time, I have enclosed letters I wrote to my late Uncle Owen. I was able to reclaim them from his estate.

[Note: These letters are provided elsewhere in this narrative.]

As you can see, the name of Kensington is not one that earns much in the way of honor or respect if one is privy to the facts. While acting as manager of the Kensington Inn, I observed the growth and development of Bartholomew Kensington, nephew of the aforementioned Beauregard. In Bartholomew, I saw nothing but the spirit of his uncle and have believed since the sad day I met him that he is destined to repeat those despicable acts. As fantastic as this may sound, and I must confess to having difficulty believing myself. My dreams have warned me of dangers to come at the inn.

I have asked you to take Miss Renihan under your wing and protect her. This I know you have done admirably. However, I fear she is in the gravest danger. I sincerely believe that, using his nephew, Bartholomew, Beauregard Kensington seeks to harm her.

Please do not dismiss my fears out of hand. I have studied the works of Mr. Conan Doyle, Robert Owen, and Madame Blavatsky and her

Theosophical Society. On a side note, we may be related to Mr. Owen through his wife who was a Dale. This, I believe, gives great foundation to my experiences and fears.

You are aware of the kind of man—and I use that term loosely—Bartholomew Kensington has become. You have told me of your experiences with him whilst in the cavalry. Many of these experiences are similar to those I saw first-hand with Beauregard.

Whatever you do, whether you believe me or not, please be careful and safeguard Emelia. I let her down once before, and I have no intention of allowing that to happen again.

I have also been made aware, through psychic means, that an old friend is on his way to you. He has great interest in Emelia and, no doubt, will endeavor to do his utmost to destroy the evil that threatens her.

With Providence on my side, I shall be in Wycliffe Point by the 16th to assist you in preparation for our mission.

I remain Yr Humble and Obt Servt,

Uncle Obadiah

Telegram from Obadiah O'Dale to Oscar O'Dale, January 16, 1905

[This telegram was found clipped to the earlier letter from Obadiah O'Dale to Oscar O'Dale. Note: This telegram was received on January 18th. No explanation for the delay has been found.]

The Western Union Telegraph Company
Paid. Via Newark NJ
New York NY Jan 16
Oscar O'Dale
Kensington Inn

Unforeseen delays arriving morning eighteenth inst by train ### keep watch Emelia bart dangerous

Obadiah O'Dale ####

Chapter 7:
"I see disappointment on your pretty face"

Beverly Kent, January 16, 2020

"What the fuck do you want?"

Beverly was furious. The idiot librarian had broken her concentration. In a fit of pique, she slammed her notebook shut and tossed her pencil across the carrel. It bounced once, then rolled onto the floor and under the filing cabinet full of microfilm reels. "Fuck off," Beverly said.

Without a word, Ranahan turned tail and hurried away. Most people learned quickly to stay out of Beverly's way when things weren't going well.

If they would just do what I want, I wouldn't get so angry. Thinking that made her angrier. *And that…that…harlot isn't helping.*

Things were not going at all well today.

It had taken her almost half an hour to get the damned microfilm reader to work correctly. She could have asked Dawson for help, but she wasn't about to give him the satisfaction. And what had gotten into him recently? As much as she wanted him to keep his distance, his current behavior upset her—mouthing off to her, not groveling at her feet to please her. He'd even refused to pay for her room. Something had happened the previous night and she was determined to find out what. Dawson would pay for being so…independent.

That man at the inn, O'Dale, treating her as if she was just some random customer. She had a Ph.D. and was a renowned researcher in Civil War history. She deserved respect and consideration, not cold politeness and horrible coffee. It was irrelevant that he also owned the inn. Plus, she was fucking gorgeous and men, and most women, would and should feel lucky to do anything she demanded. Even being spoken to by Beverly was an honor for some of the lowlifes she encountered in her work.

Now, this…creature at the library, sneaking around like some dark phantom, interrupting her train of thought, ruining her concentration, all the while disrespecting her. To top it off, the colored bitch had shamelessly flirted with Dawson.

What the…? Where'd that come from? I may be nasty at times, but I have never been racist.

Beverly sat and put her face in her hands, fighting back tears. Something was terribly wrong with her. She simply wanted to be left alone to do her work. Was that too much to ask? Now she couldn't sleep because of the horrible dreams and hallucinating open doors that were bricked over. She was being attacked by people who weren't there, or people were tricking her into seeing things that were impossible. When the librarian had raised her hand to point the way to the stairs, she most definitely had *not* held a bloody heart in her hand that made Beverly flinch away.

"I do need to eat," she said, now more annoyed that Dawson was being so recalcitrant and would be unlikely to go find her something.

All these idiots were beneath her. Why did no one know their place?

"I need to hit something," she said. "Or worse."

The odd tingle in her stomach told her it would be much worse.

Beauregard Kensington, January 18, 1865

Angered by the idiotic sycophants at the party, he returned to his special room to take care of what remained of the Virginia brood. In an hour-long, frenzied haze of blood and hatred, he satisfied most of his needs. If only he could take an appetizer for later, to go with dinner.

Beau wiped his blade on a piece of cloth, making sure there was no blood remaining to tarnish the gleaming steel. Satisfied, he sheathed his weapon. A quick check of his pocket watch told him he'd best return to the party. It wouldn't do to have the locals miss him and wonder where he had been.

After securely locking the room door, Beau waited a few moments to see if any noise was evident. Nothing. As always, the room held its secrets in silence.

Beverly Kent, January 16, 2020

Beverly held in the scream. That was the third time she had envisioned someone committing an atrocity. It was the same red-haired man every time, though the clothes looked different. She thought she could still smell the stink of spilled blood.

She stared at the microfilm reader. The scratchy black and white image of an old newspaper still filled the screen. There had been a small article on the society page about a party being held in honor of a returning war hero—Colonel Beauregard Kensington. Beverly knew the name from somewhere. A photo of the colonel accompanied the article, but the quality of the old photo and microfilm made it all but impossible to see his features clearly.

"It's all your fault, Beau. *And* Dawson's. *And* that librarian bitch. *And* the moron at the inn. *And, and*—fuck."

Beverly picked up a box of microfilm and threw it at the filing cabinet where it broke open with a loud bang, unraveled, with the cracked reel bouncing off a door marked Private.

"Why?" she said quietly. She feared she might lash out at the next person to cross her. Beverly had never, ever, raised her hand to anyone—*try to forget the frying pan and that old fart Paul who got what he deserved*—and didn't want to start now. Should she ask Peter for help? He'd be there for her. She knew that without doubt.

Or did she? He'd flirted right along with that sow upstairs. He didn't care about her. He never had. Lying son of a bitch.

Beverly slammed her fist against the side of the carrel. The noise echoed through the basement.

Dawson must have heard her because his stupid face appeared over the carrel wall.

Great, just great. Now I'll have to listen to this idiot's commiserations. Just leave me the fuck alone, damn you. Unless you're coming to apologize.

He had that boyish grin on his face. "Any luck?" He

noticed the pile of microfilm then said, "Oh, I see."

See what, you tiresome piece of shit? See your death at my hands? See me kill your half-wit girlfriend? See me come out on top like I always do?

Just as she was about to bite Dawson's head off, a chill caressed Beverly's throat. Vague memories of intense pleasure crowded her mind. There was a stirring below. She shivered, wanted to be alone, but didn't know why.

Dawson stood there with a blank look on his face. No, it wasn't blank. It was…neutral, disinterested, distant. Beverly's eyes widened.

He really doesn't care. Why not?

Without warning, Beverly was overcome by the burden of sadness and loneliness she had borne since her childhood. She had never wanted for anything, except honesty. Her parents had spoiled her rotten, given her everything she wanted. However, she knew it was because they felt guilty for not paying her enough attention. They were always too busy with work or their fraternal organizations. Every year there was a huge birthday party for her, attended by all the children in her classes at school. They all had fun, but none of them had ever looked like they *wanted* to be there to celebrate with her. Beverly realized now the parents had forced their children to attend the parties to curry favor with her influential parents.

It wasn't about her. It never was.

She looked Dawson in the eyes and realized that she needed him. He was so useful, always there when she wanted anything. Always kind to her despite her horrific moods. A rock in her world of academic politics and back-stabbing, and her rush to be at the top. Peter didn't care about all that. He simply wanted to be happy, and he wanted those he cared about to be happy.

He wanted her to be happy. She smiled. There was a look of surprise on Peter's face. It amused her.

Quietly, she said, "Just a mention of a party in January of 1865. The mayor of Wycliffe Point threw a soiree. The article in the society column listed some of the notable guests, including a Colonel Beauregard Kensington and some Major O'Dale. The party was held in the dining room of the Kensington Inn, wherever that is. The colonel may have been a relative of the owner."

Being his usual positive self, Peter said, "Well, at least you know for sure he was here during the war. And the Inn on the Cliff was once the Kensington Inn. The name was changed for some reason."

She nodded. "The only other thing of interest for the whole month was the disappearance of one of the inn's maids. She apparently left the inn one evening on an errand and was never seen again. I still have the rest of the reel to check. I haven't even reached the end of the war yet."

Peter remained silent, waiting for her to finish.

"Oh, and on the same day, some unnamed soldier fell from the cliff outside the inn. Probably drunk." Beverly yawned. "My eyes hurt."

"Yes," said Peter, nodding. "Reading microfilm can be a *bitch* on the eyes."

Why would you say that?

Beverly's jaw set and she tilted her head slightly. She stared at the microfilm reader, unable to look Peter in the face.

"That doesn't help me much, does it?" she said. Quickly, she packed up her notebook and stood. "I'm going back to the inn. I'm hungry and I'm tired." Beverly waited for Peter to move. When he didn't, she said, "Well? Are we going or not?"

Peter said. "*We* aren't. I haven't had a chance to look at the microfilm yet, remember. I still have lots of work to do."

Instantly, all the warmth she had been feeling for Dawson evaporated. He could be such an asshole at times.

Beverly put her fists on her hips and hissed, "Fine. Just make sure you call me for dinner. I don't want to miss another meal because of you. And clean that up." She pointed at the pool of microfilm.

Dawson shrugged and said, "Sure, if I think of it." He walked away.

"What the?" Dawson was gone before Beverly could finish. She almost admired him. "It seems you've grown a few," she said quietly.

Gathering the rest of her belongings, Beverly walked toward the stairs. Halfway up, she noted that there was a bathroom.

The librarian rushed down and past with a muttered, "Excuse me." She was carrying a tray with two teacups and a pot of tea. There was also a plate of cookies. Beverly smiled and watched the woman descend the stairs then disappear around a corner.

Only two cups? One for him and one for me? Or one for him and one for you?

Her smile faded.

At the library's front door, Beverly paused to look around. Something caught her eye in the small office behind the main counter. An old book. Why would the librarian be reading an old book? Was she holding out? Was she deliberately messing with Beverly so her work would be inferior?

"Slattern." *What?*

Beverly crept back to the stairs and listened. The sound of muffled voices rose from the basement. The lovebirds were having a little social all by themselves.

"Fuck the pair of you," Beverly muttered.

Leaving her things on the counter, Beverly went around it and into the office. Picking up the old book, she discovered it was, in fact, a journal belonging to one Oscar O'Dale. *A relative of the obnoxious innkeeper?* It was dated for 1905.

When she thumbed through the journal, several pages fell out and onto the floor under the desk. Beverly ignored them.

Something caught her eye. A name. Bartholomew Kensington.

Finding the beginning of the entry, Beverly read what Oscar O'Dale had deemed important enough to record.

Oscar O'Dale, Journal entry for Tuesday, January 17, 1905

The celebration of the governor's birthday last evening was both enjoyable and exhausting. The Kensingtons hosted a large party that included most local dignitaries, their families, and several of the Governor's staff. The employees of the inn were rushed off their feet the whole time. However, they proved themselves capable of facing any difficulties or requests that arose due to the demands of the guests. I was pressed to play a few tunes I had learned last summer, much to the pleasure of the assembled company. Even the staff halted their duties for a few minutes to watch me perform.

I must confess that being the center of attention for this time was not something I would relish repeating. As manager of the Kensington Inn, I have enough exposure for my liking. Since retiring from the Army, all I seek is a quiet life and the chance to forget as many of the more unsavory and loathsome scenes it was my misfortune to witness.

The only dark note from last evening was the accidental destruction of a piece of glass by an inebriated guest. The object, referred to as a *Schusterkugel* by our Bavarian cook, was the possession of our maid, Emelia Renihan. A guest had mentioned something about one within earshot of the cook who then told the guest about Emelia's treasure. I had learned from Emelia that the bauble was a family heirloom, but no one in her family knew to whom it had originally belonged. She said it was simply there, on a shelf, one day and it was evident it belonged to her, though she could not explain why this was and how she could be so sure of such a strange thing.

Emelia had been summoned and she, being a kind and generous person, happily agreed to retrieve the item from her room to show the guest. Several other guests wished to see the glass thing and it was handed back and forth, rather carelessly, I must add. I could see the trepidation on Emelia's face, but these people were the local elite, and neither of us, Emelia in particular, could intervene or ask them to be more careful with someone else's possession. Inevitably, the *Schusterkugel* was dropped by one of the more drunken women.

Emelia held back her tears and then her anger when the woman refused to apologize or even hint at replacing the damaged item, though I fail to see how an heirloom such as that could be replaced. The woman dismissed Emelia's, and my own, concerns because we were "merely the staff and of no consequence, most especially someone of the colored race."

Very few guests remained, and the incident was quickly forgotten. As the majority of the staff had already retired by this time, I cleaned up the broken shards of glass myself. For reasons that elude me, rather than deposit the remains in the trash, I carefully placed them in a small box and set it aside to return to Emelia, who had gone away, deeply saddened, to her room. All I can say about the matter is that, at the time, it seemed the appropriate thing to do.

Oscar O'Dale, Journal entry for Wednesday, January 18, 1905

Late last night, the 17th, I was sitting in the lounge at the piano playing a little bit of ragtime. It's a new style of music I first heard while traveling with my employers last summer. It is a far cry from the Chopin I have played for most of my life. When I recall the horrors of my time with the 9th Cavalry at Pine Ridge and San Juan, I find it relaxing to play. It is as if the music is a tonic to relieve some of the anxiety and tension I hold within.

The day was fraught with trepidation. When I awoke yesterday morning, I had an overwhelming feeling that something malevolent hung over the inn. For the most part, I was able to keep my fears hidden. However, Emelia approached me in the afternoon to ask after my health. She explained that she sensed something was not quite right with me and was concerned. I thanked her for her concern and, I must confess, told her the white lie that I was suffering from indigestion after the birthday celebration. It was clear to me that she didn't believe my excuse, but, being the kind person she is, she did not press me further.

After I had been sitting at the piano for about half an hour, I realized the front door of the inn had opened and closed. I admit it was more than simply the rush of cold air that accompanied this event that made me shiver to my core.

Whoever the recently arrived person was, he made himself known by loudly banging on the bell at the front desk. There followed a few shouts demanding service. At first, I was not certain I recognized the voice. I hoped it was not the person I had in mind.

When I reached the lobby, I was horrified to see that my fears were not unfounded. Standing at the front desk, shaking snow from his heavy coat and kicking the desk to remove some clumps of slush, stood Bartholomew Kensington.

If anyone should read my journals, and I honestly can think of no reason why someone would wish to waste their time in such a pursuit, they will be familiar with Bartholomew Kensington. He is the nephew, and thus heir, of the current owners of the inn, they being without issue. Through my uncle

Obadiah, who for almost thirty years until my arrival served as the manager of the inn, I was told of the early exploits of Bartholomew.

As a youngster, he was a thug, a bully of the first order. The children, and many of the adults, of Wycliffe Point lived in fear of the boy. All knew to steer well clear of him, even when he was not in a foul mood. Many, myself included, suffered the wrath when Bartholomew believed he had been wronged. Truth told, he never needed an excuse to use his fists. He took great delight in bloodying the faces of all who came within reach. A particularly vicious deed he enjoyed was to hit boys in their privates then watch them writhe on the ground in agony. If the blow caused the victim to vomit, and in many instances it did, he would clap his hands in glee, and be sure to kick some of the resultant filth at the unfortunate he had chosen.

I will not write here what he was said to have done to the girls with both his fists and feet.

When I left the Point to join the army, I hoped I was done with the horrible fellow. However, it was my continued misfortune to cross paths with Bartholomew on several occasions. He had served in the 9th Cavalry and had been at Pine Ridge at the time of the massacre. Rumor had it that he had revelled in the killing and had been especially proficient with his sabre. It was with immense displeasure that I again encountered Bartholomew in Cuba during the war. Again, he was said to have treated prisoners poorly and taken pleasure in administering punishments to not just captured enemy combatants, but also his own men. Again, there were stories about girls, but I refused to listen to such disgusting tales.

I was relieved when, after I retired from the army due to wounds I suffered in Cuba, I learned Bartholomew had also left the army and gone to Europe. Word reached Wycliffe Point that he had become a mercenary and had been active in China against the Boxers, and in South Africa against the Boers. I had hoped he might not return.

Seeing him standing there shook me to my core. To make matters worse, the man appeared to be glowing with happiness, as if he had been given a great gift or, perhaps, had witnessed some joyous event. To add to my discomfiture, I thought I could detect about Bartholomew an unpleasant odor that reminded me of the battlefield: blood and rot.

Bartholomew greeted me with, "Do my eyes deceive me or is it my little sissy, O'Dale." He looked around the lobby as if searching for something, then said, "Where's that other sodomite friend of yours, O'Dale? Where's Dawes?"

It angered me that this animal referred to my friend Patrick in such a derogatory fashion. While it is true that I held a deep affection for Patrick, it was also true that he had never returned those feelings, except insofar as we remained very close. After a misunderstanding while getting drunk before deploying to the west, Patrick and I remained the best of friends. He never mentioned my indiscretion, and I never again allowed my deepest feelings for him to surface. Patrick is as good a man as I have ever met. Somehow, Bartholomew had viewed our friendship as something it was not and had taken great delight in taunting the pair of us. I felt especially bad for Patrick as he was the innocent in all this.

"Take my bags to my room, sissy. Now."

With that, he quickly went behind the desk to get the key to his room, then proceeded upstairs. The Kensingtons always have a suite of rooms reserved on the top floor of the inn for any visiting dignitaries. That usually means a Kensington relative. There haven't been any real—what do you call them? Celebrities?—here for as long as I have been manager.

I took Bartholomew's bags to his room. Before I left, he grabbed my arm and put his face close to mine. He then said something that I did not understand. "You won't get me this time, you worthless piece of trash. I'll be ready for you. And this time, the bitch is mine."

I knew not the woman to whom he referred to as "the bitch." However, something deep inside told me she was close.

Fearing the worst, I went to warn Emelia.

She was not altogether shocked by my news, but expressed a degree of hope that I found both unexpected and welcome.

Beverly Kent, January 16, 2020

Beverly closed the journal. "Is Bartholomew Kensington another relative? And what's all this weird shit O'Dale keeps babbling about?"

Are all the O'Dales out of their minds?

Looking down, Beverly saw a yellow scratch pad with some notes written in very neat cursive. She saw her name so bent to read it.

Is Professor Kent the one to worry about?

Who is Peter Dawson?

Do not, under any circumstances, let Kent see or know about the journals and other letters from the O'Dales. Provide her only with enough information to allow her to finish her research and get out of my library and my life.

Peter Dawson is cute.

Beverly's blood boiled. Who the hell did this stupid cunt think she was, keeping information from her? And…Dawson was cute?

"For fuck's sake."

A snow globe sat on the desk. It resembled the broken ones she had seen at the inn. Of course, it did. All fucking snow globes looked the same. She tapped it with her finger. Some of the "snow" swirled. She tapped it harder, and the globe moved a few millimeters. Tapping it again, Beverly moved the globe to the edge of the desk. Pausing to see if anyone would see, she gave the globe one more tap and sent it crashing to the floor.

The instant the globe shattered, Beverly felt like she had been punched in the stomach. The air left her lungs, and she thought she was suffocating. Her head pounded, and she could hear her own heartbeat. A pinpoint of pain at the center of her forehead slowly spread until it encompassed her whole skull.

She likened it to someone using a medieval torture device on her, trying to squeeze out a confession for some imagined sin.

Then the pain was gone. Beverly's head cleared and she could breathe.

Beverly Kent was back in control.

Staring down at the broken globe, Beverly relaxed and smiled. Amongst the shards of glass were very tiny people.

"Fucking bitch."

She placed the journal in her laptop bag then left the office.

At the library's front door, Beverly took a deep breath, savoring the fresh sea air. The sun had managed to get out from behind the clouds, but the wind still blew hard and cold. With a shiver, she stepped down to the sidewalk and turned in the direction of the inn. The open door of the library banged in the wind, but Beverly chose to ignore it. Not her problem.

When she arrived at the low wall and iron fence that provided some protection from the steep cliff, Beverly paused and looked out to sea. A few hundred yards away was the spot where that submarine thing had gone down. Beverly chuckled, remembering the terrified German sailors scrambling to escape the sinking vessel. Wouldn't Dawson just love to know what she knew?

How do I know what I know?

She laughed at the memory, strange as it was. Across the bay sat the old fort where, what was that one's name? Another Dawson, no, similar, not that it mattered one whit. He'd gone sailing off the cliff to meet a cold end in the sea. Just one more obstacle removed.

Stepping up on the wall and leaning over the fence, Beverly

looked down the cliff. She could just make out the path where the disappointment had died all those years ago. It was 1945, wasn't it? As useless and treacherous as that creature had been, the slave bitch had no right to eliminate him. There hadn't been any chance for revenge in '85, but there would be enough time this time for some extra cutting and slicing.

Gripping the fence, Beverly shook her head. She felt so lost and confused. These memories were not hers. She'd been born in 1985, but how could she remember something she couldn't possibly have witnessed?

There was one thing Beverly knew for certain: it was all the fault of that Ranahan bitch.

Further along the path, where it turned from the cliff to the side of the inn, Beverly slipped and fell against the iron fence atop the low wall that prevented people from falling off the cliff. *Not if someone gives you a helping hand or kick down.* While straightening herself, she noted a shadow on the ground. Looking up, she made out the vague profile of the walkway from the warehouse to the inn. It shimmered in the sunshine, taking form slowly. So, she had been right all along. There was a door near her room that led to a hallway. She must have imagined the bricked-up opening. Damned O'Dale must have been messing with her head.

Beverly arrived at the inn's side door in time to see a minivan pass along the road in the direction of the pub on the far side of the library. It turned into the pub's parking lot and eight figures piled out: the grandparents, the parents, and those luscious children. Despite them being tightly wrapped in warm coats and scarves, she recognized them for what they were: a warm-up before the main event. At least she knew where to find them. The pub had lodgings on the top floor.

But how to get them where she could play?

She chuckled.

The strong scent of vanilla met Beverly when she entered the inn. She walked quietly toward the front desk. There he was, as usual, as always. Obadiah O'Dale. Fucking turncoat.

No, not Obadiah. Owen.

O'Dale looked up when Beverly gave a slight cough. The look of recognition on the man's face gave her a thrill. She laughed and said, "Hello, old friend. You look a little different this time. Missing something?"

"You!" said O'Dale.

"Not altogether quite yet," said Beverly.

Beverly slipped to her knees, letting out a small scream. Looking down, she realized she had landed on a shard of glass from that ridiculous snow globe. How did it get here? Blood oozed from a cut on her kneecap. She blinked her eyes. They watered something fierce causing everything around her to be nothing but a blur.

"I feel confused," she said.

"Let me help you to your room, Professor Kent," said a familiar voice. Yes, one of the O'Dales, but which one.

"Thank you. I need a rest." Strong arms brought her to her feet. Her wounded knee throbbed. "I think I'm going to be sick. We should hurry."

Part way up the stairs, she stopped and looked into O'Dale's eyes. "Please, when Peter gets here, tell him I need him. Desperately. Please. Promise."

"I promise," said O'Dale.

"I was right you know," she said. "About the door upstairs."

"Damnation," he said.

The room whirled around her and a kaleidoscope of colors made her head hurt. Hot tears streamed down her cheeks.

"Oh, God. What have I done? What am I going to do?"

Chapter 8:
"But I believe that we could still go far"

Emma Ranahan, January 16, 2020

The Kent woman was coming up the stairs from the basement. It looked as if she had packed up her belongings and was leaving. Though it was obvious that she could see Emma carrying the tray with fragile cups on it, the woman did not get out of the way. Emma found herself hugging the wall as she twisted herself uncomfortably to avoid any sort of disaster with the tea.

"Excuse me," she said, not bothering to listen for a reply. She doubted she would get one anyway.

Emma took a few moments to compose herself at the bottom of the stairs. She hoped she wasn't being presumptuous with two teacups and the expectation that she and Peter would have a tea break together. If it was awkward, she could always say the second cup was for the other professor, although Peter no doubt knew she had left the library.

Walking as stealthily as possible so as not to disturb Peter at his work, Emma approached his carrell from behind. She thought for a second that he had fallen asleep since he wasn't moving a muscle. Then she heard a grunt and watched him write some notes.

Peter had his head completely inside the frame of the microfilm reader, taking notes without looking at what he was writing. It was obvious to Emma that this was a bad idea because his writing was barely comprehensible. She wanted to giggle when he wrote a line that went off the notepad and onto the surface of the table.

Peter made some more noises, as if talking to himself. He was completely oblivious to her presence, and she didn't have the heart or, at that moment, the courage to disturb him. Instead, she set the tray down on a table across the aisle from Peter's carrell in the hope that he would take a break and notice the tea and cookies. She fished a chocolate bar from a pocket in her skirt and gently placed it on the table where his hand might touch it if his writing strayed too far off the paper.

Emma stood watching Peter for a few minutes while he continued to write and talk to himself. It was difficult to understand what he was saying because the frame of the reader muffled his voice. He did seem to be having an argument with himself.

He's so much like me.

Quietly, Emma turned and went over to the microfilm drawers. There was a roll partially unravelled under the cabinet. She crouched to fish it out and was not surprised to see it was one of the reels that woman had been using. She nearly punched the cabinet when she discovered the reel had broken across one of the frames. The originals of the newspaper were nowhere to be found, and that meant it would be incredibly hard to repair the film.

Emma wanted to slap that ignorant bitch. Maybe the shotgun wasn't such a bad idea.

She returned to the main floor with clenched fists. Her anger grew when a blast of cold air coming from the open front door found her.

"She couldn't even be bothered to close the damned door!"

Emma shut it then spent a few minutes gathering up the papers that had been blown off their racks and torn. Fortunately, with so few people coming into the library, the damage would not be too inconvenient. She sighed when she realized the same could be said of the broken microfilm reel.

"I wish someone cared."

What broke Emma was what she found when she entered her office. Before she had stepped into the office, her nose told something was wrong. There was a sweet smell like antifreeze. Only one thing there contained anything that smelled like that. Her lovely snow globe lay shattered on the floor in a puddle of liquid. The little inn was in pieces, tiny people scattered across the floor.

She stood for a few seconds staring down at her lost treasure. She knew how it had broken. That bitch. But why would she be so malicious? Tears slid down Emma's cheeks while she picked up the pieces and placed them in a small box. The figures were so small, she needed tweezers to rescue them.

Curious, she got a magnifying glass and put one of the figures under it. It was a woman in a blue dress with a red splotch on the front. Looking closely, Emma caught her breath when she recognized the little lady.

It was her.

Millie Ranahan, January 15, 1985

Millie was covering for Oliver at the desk in the inn office when the phone rang. She didn't mind helping out because it was a lot better than cleaning rooms.

Perhaps it was someone calling to make a reservation. There weren't many at this time of year. Wycliffe Point wasn't exactly a winter wonderland. It was more of a frozen wasteland.

"The Inn on the Cliff, Wycliffe Point. Ms. Ranahan speaking. How may I help you?"

As soon as she heard the deep voice from the other end of the phone, Millie felt a quiver run through her. "Hello, Ms. Ranahan. My name is Prescott Davidson. I'm a travelling salesman from Michigan. I'm going to be in Wycliffe Point on Friday and was wondering if I could please reserve a room."

"Of course, Mr. Davidson." There was something familiar about the name, but Millie couldn't put her finger on it. "How long will you be with us?"

There was silence for a few moments, then Davidson said, "I don't know for sure, Ms. Ranahan. The truth is, I don't know why I'm coming there. I just feel compelled to be there on that specific date. The eighteenth. I suppose I'll be staying for as long as it takes."

"As long as it takes for what, Mr. Davidson?"

"Whatever business it is I'm supposed to handle, Ms. Ranahan. To be honest, I'm rather confused about it. However, I definitely wish to book a room. How about three nights for a start?"

"There's nothing special about those dates, sir," said Millie. But somewhere in the back of her mind, the eighteenth screamed out for recognition. "I don't see any problem with an open-ended reservation. We're not exactly overflowing with guests this time of year."

She took down Davidson's particulars.

"Ms.Ranahan, I do have a question," Davidson said. "Is there anyone there now, or anyone from before, who might have a connection to the army? Either directly as a member of the armed forces, or as a civilian worker attached to a unit in some way?"

That stunned Millie. She had worked part time in the laundry at the base across the bay. There was no telling what Davidson's motives might be, so she decided to keep quiet about it. "Not that I know of, sir." She was not about to put herself in any sort of precarious situation with a stranger. Instead, she referred Davidson to the library next door and, possibly, the local historical society.

Davidson thanked her and hung up. As soon as the receiver touched the cradle, the phone rang again.

Peter Dawson, January 16, 2020

Peter sat fuming about the way Beverly had acted. The swings between anger and kindness were dramatic and unpredictable. Never the easiest person to get along with, and that was being kind, today she seemed completely off the rails. Raking him over the coals for an imagined slight, or, for those rare times he stood up for himself, was fairly normal. He felt utterly confused by the erratic shift to quiet, almost friendly discussion. He may already have decided he was done with

Beverly romantically, but perhaps it would be smart to break with her completely.

He pondered the ramifications of that. It would definitely mean he would have to leave the university. He'd already given thought to that idea. Beverly had tenure and there was no way in hell she would ever leave to accommodate him. Peter couldn't stand the thought of them being at the same university. If he left, the odds of them crossing paths again would be slim. Their disciplines were very much unrelated. The problem was, there weren't a lot of jobs around for historians at the moment, teaching or otherwise.

Maybe he should simply run off with Emma and start anew somewhere far, far away.

What the hell? Where did that come from?

It was impossible for Peter to deny the instant attraction to the librarian, but to consider anything more would be both silly and presumptuous. He wasn't in high school anymore. What else could it be? Hormones? Did men have hormones? Could that weird sex dream last night have anything to do with his screwed-up thoughts today?

"Stop it, Pete, old boy. You're here to do work, not moon over someone you only met an hour ago." He quickly scanned the basement to see if anyone was around. "It wouldn't look good to be caught talking to yourself, would it? No, it wouldn't." He paused. "Okay, stop it." After about a minute staring at the microfilm reader, he said, "Good. Oh, fuck it. At least I don't argue with myself."

He loaded the reel of microfilm for July to December 1944 and prepared to scan it for any clues or warnings about the events in January.

"Yes, you do." Peter hung his head and quashed the urge to tell himself to fuck off.

Taking a deep breath, he began rolling through the *Wycliffe Point Democrat*. It took all of fifteen minutes to discover absolutely nothing.

Well, not absolutely nothing. Buried on the back page of a September paper was a small article about a gun battery moving in to the fort on the headland across the bay. It was the fort he had seen this morning. There wasn't much to the article that was of any use, except for the mention that the 12th New Jersey Artillery Regiment was the unit assigned to the battery. Perhaps later, he could check the names of the men stationed there during the war and see if any of them were still alive and would be willing to be interviewed. Maybe one of them might have seen something. It was a long shot since it had been seventy-five years ago.

Peter changed reels and prepared to read January to June 1945. He hadn't paid much attention when he picked up the microfilm boxes left by the librarian, simply noting that there was only a single reel for Beverly. Now that he thought about it, there seemed far too many for the period he wanted. Upon reading the box labels, he discovered that, in addition to December and January, 1944-45, he had been given reels for the same months in 1904-05 and 1984-85. He hadn't asked for these and was curious why Miss Ranahan would have thought he wanted them. That would have to wait for later. In the meantime, he had work to do.

The second reel proved much more interesting. Within minutes, Peter found something useful.

January 19, 1945

The body of a transient was discovered early this morning by a fisherman on the stone path below The Inn on the Cliff, formerly known as the notorious Kensington Inn. Police have identified the man as Benjamin Kenton, lately of Chicago, and said to have performed menial tasks at the Inn. The man was well-known to police, who suspected him of black marketeering, among other crimes. It is also believed by the police that he was involved with the Vincent Coll gang during Prohibition. The War Department confirms that Kenton served with distinction during the Great War and the campaign in Russia in 1919.

The county coroner, Mr. Campbell, declared, after his examination, that Kenton died from exposure probably due to intoxication. This is yet another example of the sad effects of alcohol and why the county should enact a policy banning its use. As we have stated many times in our editorials, Wycliffe Point should have remained, and should once again be, dry.

Mr. Campbell would not comment on the rumors that the man's face exhibited a horrific aspect, suggesting he had died of fright.

Also discovered was the body of Miss Emily Renehan, a maid at the Inn. Police have refused to speculate as to whether there is a connection between the two deaths. They have also refused, despite repeated request by your editor, to describe the cause of her death or the nature of the horrors perpetuated upon her person.

It wasn't much to go on, but it was an unusual event at about the right time.

I wonder if our Miss Ranahan is any relation to the maid who was found dead. The names are fairly close. Would she be offended if I asked?

During his studies, Peter had found an astonishing array of spellings for the same name, often within a single family. It seemed to depend upon the whims of whatever officials were taking names for a census, jury roll, or the local paper. Even his own name, Dawson, could cause confusion with variations including Dawes, David, and Davidson, though they had more to do with the origin of the name than the whim of census takers or government bureaucrats.

"Tread lightly, Peter, old chum," he said quietly. "You don't want to piss off another woman, especially one as..." He was at a loss for words.

In addition, what were these horrors perpetuated upon her person in 1945? And why was the Kensington Inn notorious?

He shook his head and returned to his reading.

A second article popped up a few minutes later.

January 21, 1945

Our representative at the police department reports that an unidentified man was discovered near the Wycliffe Point lighthouse late in the morning. The body was severely burned and the only distinguishing mark upon it was a strange tattoo of unknown meaning. A charred military style boot, the only clothing found on the body, suggests that he may have been a member of our armed forces. Several men have been reported missing by military authorities, and, though it pains us to report it in these patriotic times, it is believed they are deserters. No explanation has been offered for the burned condition of the body though some have suggested it may be related to the mysterious lights sighted offshore in the late hours of the 18th.

This was curious: a dead military man with an unusual tattoo. He made several notes to remind him to check with the county coroner's office to see if he could have a look at their records for this death. He might as well check out this Kenton character at the same time. And he definitely needed to find someone who may have witnessed these events. Maybe the coroner, Mr. Campbell, was still alive. There was also the local police chief or sheriff or whatever they have around here. And last, but by no means least, let's not forget the reporter. Owen's archive might have something as well.

"And what about Miss Ranahan?"

"Get real, Buddy," he said, talking to himself again. "First pretty woman you see, and you immediately get interested. Don't go there. Remember what happened last time." The image of Beverly as she looked the first time he saw her floated into his mind. She had been quite lovely. Not a classic beauty, but there was an air of confidence about her. That flaming red hair had been a major attraction. He wondered why she had decided to dye it black. For a fleeting moment, he wondered if she was a redhead everywhere.

Beverly had been very friendly when Peter had spoken to her at the faculty party. Witty, a great sense of humor, killer body, nice shoes, she was everything he wanted in a woman.

If only he had been able to see her true face before he got himself smitten and involved beyond control. Peter's ears heated up with embarrassment recalling the many ways he had made a fool of himself because of Beverly. He had wasted so much time and effort.

"Damnit. Stop being an idiot."

Putting Beverly out of his mind, which was the easiest it had been since he'd met her, Peter reread his notes. He got that excited feeling in his stomach, the feeling that told him he was on the verge of something big. He remained confident he would prove his theory.

Rereading the article, Peter took note of the date of the mysterious offshore lights. He went back over the papers from the fifteenth to the nineteenth to see if he had missed any articles, but there was nothing. For the paper to have noted the lights, someone must have reported them. They must have made some kind of impact in the town. He quickly went through the rest of the reel but found no further mention of weird lights. However, there was another dead man.

January 23, 1945

We are unhappy to report the discovery of yet another body in the bay. The unfortunate man was found wedged between the rocks at the bottom of the cliff below the local library. This person has been positively identified as a soldier from the battery on the Point who was reported missing some time on the morning of the 19th. His name has not been released pending notification of the family. The authorities assure us that

> this man was not a deserter, but a well-liked and respected member of the battery unit. We are all saddened by the loss of one of our brave soldiers.

Peter leaned back from the microfilm reader. Holy cow! Wycliffe Point had experienced a lot of death in January of 1945, at least one of which was a homicide. Could Owen's archive have any further information? Did anyone else die around this time?

Deciding that his eyes needed a rest from the microfilm reader, Peter picked up one of the unusual books left for him. *Weird and Wonderful New Jersey: Bizarre Happenings over the Last Century.* It had been published in the mid-seventies and when he had come upon it the first time, he had ignored it. Now it might prove useful.

Checking the table of contents, Peter found a chapter intriguingly titled "The First UFO Sightings in America?" Now that at least had the potential for being amusing. Peter had had a secret fascination with UFOs and ancient astronauts since he first saw Chariots of the Gods on late night TV.

Opening the book to the beginning of the chapter, he read.

> Not widely known among enthusiasts of the unusual are the New Jersey lights of the 18th of January 1945. Hushed up by the military at the time, the full story of the lights was only revealed to this writer in 1973. Though questioned by a reporter from the Wycliffe Point

Democrat, the commander of the artillery unit posted at the gun battery on the Wycliffe Point headland, Captain Benjamin Macdonald, denied that any of his men had reported strange offshore lights. None of the members of the battery were allowed to speak to the reporter and after the initial interest, the matter was forgotten. However, the incident came to my attention in the spring of 1969, and I began to search for the truth. I discovered one of the men stationed at the bunker, whose name I have been asked to keep confidential, was court-martialed shortly after the incident. I was able to track the man down and convince him to relate his story to me. His own story was not interesting, and had nothing to do with my research, but he did have a letter given to him by a fellow soldier stationed at the bunker, with instructions not to read it unless something happened to him. My source would not tell me what happened to his friend. For reasons he would not explain, he had never opened the letter. However, he allowed me to open it and copy its contents. He did not want to know what was written. In fact, he seemed afraid of the letter. I now pass on to my readers, the words of our mysterious soldier.

"It was about ten in the evening on the 18th of January [1945]. I was on guard duty in the bunker. There were usually two of us but my buddy, Private [name withheld], had some business he needed to take care of. He was stuck on this colored girl that worked over at the inn. Some bum was harassing her, so [name withheld] wanted to get over there and give the guy what for. I was covering for him. I don't know if he took care of the bum. He didn't come back, and I got transferred out the next day.

"Anyway, at about ten, I was looking out to sea, searching for any sign of Nazi U-boats or planes when I saw this ball of light. It was white and seemed to be floating along above the water. I think it came from the cliffs across the bay. I figured this because of what happened later.

"So, this ball of light goes out to sea, maybe three, four hundred yards then sinks. About five minutes later, this huge orange ball of light comes boiling out of the sea where the white light had sunk. It shoots straight up into the sky, hundreds of feet. There's a dull boom, like thunder that's miles away or like artillery fire over in another valley. Then the water starts to move. This huge wave comes right at the bunker. I near soiled my shorts when I saw it coming, thought it was going to wash away the whole place, solid concrete or not. But the wave just broke against the cliff.

"When the sea was calm again, and there was no sign of the orange ball of light. I saw the white light again. It came out of the water where I saw it sink and skimmed across the water back toward the cliffs on the other side of the bay. I watched it through my binoculars until it reached the cliff. Then it just vanished like the cliff swallowed it up. When I reported it to my commanding officer, he told me to shut up about it, that I was crazy and bucking for a Section Eight. I saw it. But no one believed me. You're the first person I've told since that morning.

"And I'll tell you the weirdest thing. Inside that ball of white light, I thought I saw a person."

My source flatly refused to answer any questions raised by the letter. He did concede that the writer disappeared sometime during the morning of the 19th of January. Could this be the same soldier whose body was discovered in the bay a few days later? I have not been able to find any further information.

And there you have it. The mysterious New Jersey lights. Was it a UFO? Did the only witness see people—aliens— inside their ship? Is there a secret UFO base somewhere under the water off the coast of Wycliffe Point? Perhaps...we'll never know.

Peter set the book down and furiously made notes. Something weird had happened in Wycliffe Point in January of 1945. Three men dead under unusual circumstances, a woman murdered, and strange lights in the night added up to something. He knew he had to figure out what all this meant. Could the soldier from the bunker still be alive? Or maybe the author of the book? He checked again and saw that it had been written by an Oliver O'Dale. Could this be Owen's brother?

Is everyone in this place related?

Peter made more notes, laid out his plan of attack.

After a few minutes, he heard footsteps and a cough. He looked up, pleased to see Emma standing at the edge of the alcove.

"I tried to make some noise so you wouldn't be startled again and toot," she said with a grin.

He smiled back at her, trying to suppress his embarrassment. "Not going to let me forget that, are you?"

"Um, no. Anyway, I'm sorry to bother you, Peter, but the library closes in five minutes."

Peter was confused. "Are you only open half the day today?" he asked.

Emma shook her head. "No, you've been down here all day. You were completely lost in your work when I came by to see if you still wanted a cup of tea and maybe some lunch. I didn't have the heart to disturb you."

He saw the table behind Emma where a tray sat with a teapot and two cups. There was also a plate of cookies. Bourbon creams! Had Emma wanted to have a cup of tea with him? Had he blown it yet again? When he looked back at Emma, she gave him a slight smile and nodded.

"Did you leave that chocolate bar on the table?" he asked. "I didn't think anything of it when I ate it. I guess I just assumed I had brought it, but didn't remember."

Emma blushed. "I wasn't sure if it was something you might like. It was all I had."

"It was perfect," said Peter. "And thank you very much. I appreciate it. Sorry about the waste of tea. So what time is it?" He could have checked his pocket watch, but the librarian's voice was so pleasant and answering would mean she'd have to stay a few seconds longer.

"It's almost five o'clock."

He had been completely absorbed in his research, and, as was usual for him, lost all track of time. Once, while working frantically on a paper for a scholarly magazine, by the time he had finished, Peter had missed not only dinner, but breakfast, two classes, and lunch. He loved his job. Emma came into the alcove to gather the boxes of microfilm. He inhaled her vanilla scent and felt the warmth radiating from her body. "Will you be needing these again?" she asked. Peter felt a sudden thrill when she smiled. "I can leave them here for you if you'd like. We don't get too many people down here."

"I don't think I'll be using the papers again," he said then paused. "On second thought, I might just want to check the papers, but not the ones I used today. I think it may be of value to widen my date parameters."

Emma smiled and said, "Nineteen oh five and nineteen eighty-five?"

Peter looked down at the boxes she had left him earlier. How did she know? He nodded then picked up *Weird and Wonderful New Jersey.* "I'd love to be able to read over this tonight. Can I apply for a library card even if I'm not from around here?"

"That won't be necessary. That book isn't particularly popular, so if it's gone for a day or two, it won't be missed. Plus, I know where you work so I can track you down like a dog if you don't return it." She smiled.

"It looks like my research will be going off in other

directions now," he said. "I'll have to talk to Owen, and Oliver, and see if I can find some of Wycliffe Point's residents from the nineteen forties. To be honest, I don't know for sure if I'll be back to the library or not."

Emma seemed a little disappointed at this. "Perhaps I can be of some help with the tracking, Peter?"

Peter smiled. "That would be wonderful, Emma. It would save me a lot of work since I don't have too much time here."

"I'm glad to help. It would be good to use my research skills for something other than genealogy. That's what most visitors here are after. Not that we get many visitors. You and...her are the first this week. Last week we had almost one, but he was just looking for a bathroom."

Distractedly, Peter gathered his notes and stuffed them in his laptop bag.

Emma. What a lovely name. What a lovely woman.

They left the basement in silence. Going up the stairs, they passed the bathroom and Peter felt a chill that made him shiver. He noticed Emma shivered at the same time.

Must be a crack in the wall somewhere letting in cold air.

When they reached the front door, Peter stood still for a moment while he mulled something over.

I don't want to leave.

Peter racked his brain trying to think of an excuse to stay longer even though Emma was no doubt anxious to get home for dinner. Then his stomach rumbled. He felt like he hadn't eaten anything all day. That gave him an idea.

Do I have the balls? She's not around to hobble me.

Emboldened, he turned and said, "There are some

questions I'd like to ask you. Would you like to have dinner with me, Emma?" His heart thumped in his chest, and he suddenly needed to pee something fierce. "Purely professional, of course. I'd completely understand if you already have plans or find the idea disgusting."

She smiled and blushed. "Of course, I would, Peter. Where?"

"You would? Really?"

"Yes, really," she said. "You're not all that disgusting." Very quietly, she added, "Perhaps a little smelly once in a while."

"Damnit! That was all the coffee."

Peter's knees felt shaky. He thought about the inn, but then remembered who might be waiting there. "Pick your favorite place, and I hope it isn't the inn, and we'll go there."

"The inn?" She laughed. "Do you like pub food? There's a wonderful place next door. I'll get my coat." She turned away from him, took a step then halted. Her shoulders appeared to sag, and he heard her sigh and perhaps catch her breath. Or was it a sob? She brushed a stray strand of hair from her face and continued on her way.

Peter's heart thumped even harder, and he felt a little light headed. Watching Emma walk to the office behind the front desk, he remembered where he had seen her. She was the spitting image of the maid at the inn. They could be twins.

Chapter 9:
"We've both made choices that were bad and good"

Peter Dawson, January 16, 2020

Emma returned from the office, shrugging on her coat. To Peter, she looked a little sad and confused, and that made him very unhappy. When she saw him waiting, anger flashed across her face and he immediately thought he had done something wrong.

"What'd I do?" It was his standard question when someone was mad at him, or at least seemed to be. He always assumed it was him that had caused the anger. Beverly was especially good at driving guilt deep into is head.

She smiled and Peter felt better. Whatever he did, it couldn't be that bad. "A little bit of wanton destruction and theft. Not you," she said. "I'll explain later. Let's enjoy dinner first."

He knew that Beverly had done something. She could be spiteful when crossed.

"I'm sorry I inflicted her upon you. If I could do it all over again, I'd never have told her about this place."

"Don't worry. You'll have a chance to make it right. Come on." She led him out the front door then locked it. Emma pulled at the door several times and twisted the knob vigorously as if making extra sure the door was secure. Peter recognized the paranoia.

By the time Peter and Emma stepped out of the library, the

wind had died down, but the air remained painfully cold. He could hear the deafening sound of the breakers hitting the cliffs below. Peter was surprised he hadn't noticed the sound on his way over from the inn, probably because Beverly had been complaining so much about missing breakfast and having to walk at all. To make matters worse, the sidewalk was slick with ice.

Peter's head swam a little when he imagined the drop from up here to the breakers.

Emma slipped and fell against Peter almost taking the pair of them down. Peter wrapped one arm around Emma's waist and held on to her while he grabbed for the iron railing in front of the library. His wrist twisted in a way that was wrong, but he stifled a yelp, not wanting to look weak in front of this angel. *Angel?* When it seemed like they were steady and not going to fall, Peter let go of Emma.

He held out his arm for Emma as they carefully made their way along the sidewalk to the pub. Though it was perfectly innocent, Peter felt a thrill having this woman holding on to him. There was something about her that warmed him inside despite the cold air.

His left wrist throbbed from the twist. He wanted to rub the soreness away, but didn't want to lose contact with Emma.

"Nuts. I left my laptop in the library. Maybe we should go get it." Already, Peter felt nervous about having dinner with Emma. He knew his self-destructive side wanted to sneak out.

Emma patted his arm. "That's way out of the way. There'll be enough time later. Let's not waste what little time we have now."

Peter smiled at her and said, "It's not that far, maybe five steps? But I like how you think." *And how you look, smell, speak, exist.*

It only took them five minutes to get to the pub, but that was enough for Peter to be frozen to his core. He couldn't stop the deep shivers. At least his teeth hadn't chattered. And he couldn't feel his wrist. Emma seemed unaffected by the cold.

When they entered the pub, which was delightfully warm and cozy and smelled of fish and chips, beer, and woodsmoke from the roaring fire across the way, a short woman with gray hair came up to them. Her face said she was in her late sixties, but her eyes made her look much younger. The smile on her face was so genuine, Peter instantly liked her and felt comfortable.

"Your usual table is ready, Emma," she said. Her name tag identified her as Oona. "Good thing you had me reserve it this morning. We just had a family arrive so we're expecting more customers than usual tonight."

Reserved this morning? Peter got the feeling something was going on here. He looked at Emma, who was blushing yet again.

"Who's the hunk? First date?"

Peter's face burned red. Considering this was supposed to be a business dinner and nothing had been said about romance, why would she assume he and Emma were on a date?

Emma laughed and said, "He's the new love of my life. Or he will be once we take care of some business. Professor Peter Dawson meet Oona Conroy, owner of the Clifftop Pub."

Oona held out her hand and Peter took it. Her grip was

quite firm. "Hurt her and I'll rip off your balls, sonny. Got it?" She stared at him for a moment then broke into a huge smile. "Just kidding." Serious again, she said, "But I mean it. Emma is like a daughter to me."

Peter's mind swirled with everything being said. *Love of my life? Take care of some business?* Beside him, Emma snorted, trying not to laugh.

"Trust me, Miss Conroy, hurting Emma is the farthest thing from my mind. She's just so damned..." Peter stopped when he realized he was being bold in that stupid and hopeful way you get when suddenly you don't care what anyone thinks and decide to tell the truth. He looked over at Emma. Her eyes were wide open and the smile on her face made Peter want to pick her up and run away with her. She looked like she was waiting for him to finish his sentence, but he suddenly felt foolish and couldn't.

What is happening to me?

Oona patted Peter's hand. "I know, sonny. She has that same effect on almost everyone. Come on."

Oona led them to a table in a quiet corner not far from the blazing fire. The light was dim, but not enough to make seeing a strain. Somehow, the location of the table muted the talk from the rest of the pub though there weren't too many other patrons. It was still a bit early for the dinner crowd. Peter took Emma's coat and hung it from a hook behind his seat. He waited for Emma to take her seat then sat across from her. He smiled at her and couldn't think of a single thing to say. No, that wasn't true. However, the things he wanted to say were ridiculous and silly and not fit to be uttered in the presence of someone he'd only met a few hours ago.

Besides, this was strictly business. Remember?

Before either could come up with a conversation starter, Oona returned with two steaming cups of hot chocolate. "To take the edge off," she said. "I'll be back with your drinks." She walked away.

"How does she know what I drink?" said Peter.

Emma closed her eyes, smiled, and said, "Guinness. Always Guinness."

Peter nodded. "Lucky guess."

"Not really."

They sat in silence and drank their hot chocolate. The moment they both finished, Oona appeared with a pint of Guinness for each of them.

"Perfect," said Peter. "Emma, you have wonderful taste in beer and movies, though I was surprised when you quoted dialogue from *Holiday Inn.* Odd choice."

She smiled. "I know. I should be, and am, offended by the *Abraham* scene, but the rest of the movie is so much fun. Besides, it was a product of its time, and as such serves to educate viewers on systemic racism."

"Wow. You must say that a lot. You have it down pat."

Emma narrowed her eyes. "Well, duh. What do you expect? You're an historian. You know what we've been through. What we've had to deal with."

Peter got hot with embarrassment. He wanted to say the right thing but went blank. In the end, he said, "I'm sorry Emma. I know all that. It's just that, I've never been this close to someone affected by that racist bullshit. It's never been this personal or meant this much to me. Sheltered life? You'd think after studying Nazis, I'd be more aware."

"You're a good man, Peter. You always have been. Always will be." Emma seemed a little confused by what she said. So was Peter. "Let's talk about something less depressing. Okay?"

Relieved, he picked up his pint and said, "Here's to a fruitful partnership. May we find all that we want."

Emma clinked her glass to his. "I think I have," she said quietly.

Peter nearly choked on his first swallow but quickly recovered.

"So, research into the lives of people who lived around here in 1945, and into the weird events around the inn," he said. "Where to start?"

Emma held up her hand and counted off. "Old phone books, gazetteers, county records at city hall, military records from the armory, church records, and the historical society's archive, which probably has more information than all the others combined. The former president was a packrat who never threw away a piece of paper. He even has all the receipts for the inn's purchases going back to its opening in 1825. Oh, and Solomon Winthrop. He was chief of police for the longest time and might know something. He's over a hundred, but still sharp. And I know a little bit about the history of Wycliffe Point. My people have been here since 1865."

Peter sat there with his mouth hanging open.

"I rambled on a bit, didn't I?" said Emma. "Sorry. That happens when I get excited."

"I know what you mean," said Peter. "I once spoke for

fifteen minutes non-stop to Beverly—Professor Kent, the bitch—about my submarine theory. Have I told you about it? If I haven't, I will, believe me. Anyway, it wasn't until she snored that I realized she wasn't paying attention. That should have been a hint right there, but I'm usually too dense to pick up on those kinds of signals." He stared down at the table. "Could've saved myself a lot of heartache," he said quietly. Emma snored and he looked back up at her. "I'm doing it now, aren't I?"

Emma smiled and Peter's heart did another flip.

"Will you for pity's sake stop doing that. It's starting to hurt."

Emma looked surprised. "What? I'm sorry. What did I do?"

Peter tried to say something, but he couldn't get the words out.

It's too soon, you fool. You'll make her run away screaming if you say anything. But it feels so right, like we're destined to be together. Asshole!

"Having an argument in your head?" said Emma. "Who's winning?"

Oona saved him from embarrassing himself when she set down two huge plates of fish and chips. The aroma overwhelmed Peter and he began to salivate. There were three large pieces of fish on each plate and a gigantic mound of fresh-cut chips. Between them sat a large bowl of mushy peas.

Peter looked up at Oona and said, "I love you. How did you know what I wanted?"

Oona laughed. "I saw how you reacted when you came in. You kept sniffing so I figured you must like fish and chips.

Enjoy." She turned to leave, but then turned back. "And it's not me you should be declaring your love to." She nodded her head toward Emma who blushed again, closed her eyes, and shook her head.

Peter couldn't think of a thing to say to that. *My mind surely is not earning its keep here. Come on wits.*

Oona left and they dug into their food. Both smothered their chips with malt vinegar—another point in Emma's favor. They ate silently for about five minutes then Peter had to take a break from stuffing his face before he got the hiccoughs from eating too fast. He'd already scoffed down most of his dinner, but still felt hungry. Setting down his knife and fork, he took a long drink of Guinness.

"Can I ask you a couple of personal questions, Emma?"

Emma stopped eating and said, "Fire away."

"Please tell me if this is too much. Are you related to the maid?"

Before he could finish, Emma said, "Yes. The one who was murdered in 1865. And 1905. And in 1945. Last but not least, 1985. That one was particularly sad—a suicide. Small wonder I don't work at the inn." She smiled. "Not that I could, anyway."

"Say what?" said Peter. "That many? But why?"

Emma shrugged. "Fate, a curse, destiny, the worst luck in the world, all of the above?"

"Thank you," he said, stunned by how casual she was about murdered relatives. "I didn't know if it would be something too painful to discuss. Or too private."

Emma shook her head. "No worries," she said. "It's

ancient history to me. I have a file at home that has all the details I could find about the killings. I'd be happy to show it to you." She paused to sip her drink. "That is, if you think it's relevant to your theory. And just what is your theory?"

"Oh, let me explain that later when there aren't as many people around to hear you laugh at how stupid it is."

"I don't think I would laugh, Peter. You don't strike me as the stupid kind."

"I went out with Beverly for far too many months."

"I stand corrected," said Emma. "You're a complete fucking tool. How could you? I mean, sure, she's beautiful, stunning even, and if I had inclinations that way, which I do sometimes, but, yuck. You deserve much better."

Peter stared at Emma. His heart pounded and the room spun. When he noticed his Guinness was empty, he realized that not eating since breakfast had made the alcohol go straight to his head.

Change the subject, old boy. You're heading into dangerous territory.

"Quite," he said. "Tell me, how are you related to the…four…maids?"

Emma blinked as if she expected him to say something else. "Oh, well, I don't know. I haven't been able to find out much about any of them. I do know the first maid, Emmeline Ronaghan, was a former slave brought to Wycliffe Point as a washerwoman and seamstress during the Civil War."

"Then how do you know you're related?"

She looked confused then said, "I just do."

Peter thought it best to let the matter drop for now. Then

he remembered the current maid at the inn. "What about the maid at the inn right now? I saw her last night and you two could be twins."

Emma looked confused. "I don't look anything like the maid, Peter. She's twice my age and also twice my size. Very nice lady, though. Mrs. Vaughan." She glanced around the pub. "She works here part-time, but she's probably gone now. Only works mornings."

"I didn't see *her*," said Peter. "This maid was up on the third floor. She had hair just like yours. At least it looked like the same color and it was long and wavy. I haven't seen your hair loose, so I don't know. I'd like to see it loose. And her eyes were the most incredible green. Like yours."

"It was dark, and you were tired from the drive and tension," said Emma. "That causes confusion sometimes. Trust me, I don't have a twin. I don't have any relatives. And the inn doesn't have a third floor."

There seemed to be a look of desperation in her eyes so this time Peter let it drop. "You're probably right, Emma." *No third floor? What?*

They finished their fish and chips in silence. At some point, Oona had returned and replaced their empty pints with fresh ones. She'd also dropped off a plate of fresh chips which were quickly devoured.

Peter sat back and patted his stomach. "Holy fu…cow, that was good. I'm so stuffed." He sipped his Guinness. The room spun a little more.

Pace yourself. No puking in front of the hot girl. Shut up and grow up!

"The food here is excellent," said Emma. "And you can swear if you want. I really don't mind and won't think less of you. I mean, you went out with that cunt professor, so anything you do now is a step up." Emma's eyes went wide and she gasped.

Peter laughed. "You have such a way with words, Miss Ranahan. In truth, I have to agree with your assessment." He had a small sip of Guinness. "Now, tell me why you were so upset before we left the library. What did she do?"

Emma took a deep breath. "Look, I don't know for sure it was her. But there was no one else in the library and she strikes me as the malicious type."

"You've got that right. Spiteful, too. So, what happened?"

"First, when she left, she didn't bother to close the door so there were papers blown all over the place. Then there was…" Emma choked, closed her eyes, relaxed. "I have…had a family heirloom—a snow globe. I've had it for as long as I can remember, and it's about the only thing I've got that links me to my family. I had left it on my desk."

"Oh, no."

She nodded. "When I went back upstairs, I found it had been knocked off the desk and smashed to pieces."

"No chance it was an accident?"

"None. It was in the middle of the desk. No way a breeze or misplaced elbow could have knocked it to the floor. It had to have been deliberate."

"Can it be replaced?"

"No. Neither can the journal."

"What journal?"

"It belonged to Oscar O'Dale. He was manager of the Kensington Inn at the turn of the last century. There were some…interesting entries to do with the murder in 1905. He also speculated about what happened in 1865. I was going to give it to you because that seemed the right thing to do. Now it's gone."

"And you think Beverly took it?"

"Who else. It wouldn't be of interest to anyone unless they wanted to investigate the inn's history. But it's extra bad that she has it."

"Why? What could be in it that could make trouble now?"

"I have a couple of letters from Obadiah O'Dale. They hint at what started this whole mess."

"What whole mess? You've got me a little confused. What has something that happened in 1905, or 1865, got to do with Beverly?"

"Haven't you felt it since you've been here? There's something happening. I've been having bad dreams. Actually, they're horrific nightmares. Been having them since I was little. Every now and then I have flashbacks to events I couldn't possibly have witnessed."

"Do these bad dreams involve anyone with red hair?" When Emma's eyes went wide, Peter said, "Yeah. Great. There's something about sabres and cliffs. A Black family getting butchered. What does it all mean?"

"I have no idea," said Emma. "But maybe if we dig into the history of this place, we can get some answers."

"We?" Peter liked the sound of that.

"Yes. We. There must be a reason I got all those microfilm

reels for you. 1865, 1905, 1945, and 1985. You didn't ask for them. Chief Winthrop was alive in '45 and '85. Maybe he remembers something that can help."

"I hope so." He drained his Guinness. "Did you by any chance have a dream that was…um…kind of…"

"Did I dream that I got screwed? Yes. Last night."

"Me, too. It was rather nice. I wish I could have seen her face."

When Emma smiled, Peter thought he knew whose face he would have seen. Impossible, but so was everything about this.

Emma's face went dark. "There's another thing." Her hand went to her belly then her neck. She thought for a moment, then said, "Never mind. Probably not linked."

"Dessert?" said Oona who had snuck up on them again.

Peter jumped and nearly tooted. Emma pinched her nose shut. He stuck out his tongue at her.

"Not a chance," said Peter, feeling a little childish. "I couldn't eat another bite."

"Fresh trifle," said Oona.

"You bitch," said Peter.

Oona laughed and said, "I'll bring two."

Peter checked his pocket watch. It was almost seven. They had been here for almost two hours. He kept losing time. Beverly had most likely discovered he wasn't at the inn and hadn't bothered to let her know about dinner. Had she eaten? Did he care? He hoped Owen was still alive.

"Worried about the time?" said Emma.

"Absolutely not," said Peter. "Just curious about what might be happening at the inn."

"Why do you care so much about the inn? To be honest, it's a little annoying," she said.

Oh, for fuck sakes, you moron. You've done it now.

The trifles arrived. They were large. A single serving could easily be shared by two people. Peter was not about to share his.

Peter tucked into his dessert. It was heavenly, perhaps the best trifle he'd ever eaten. Emma got some whipped cream on her nose, so Peter reached across the table and wiped it off with his index finger. He stuck the finger in his mouth and sucked off the cream. When he realized what he had done, he blushed and looked at Emma with sheer horror. What would she do?

Emma sat there smiling then quickly drained her Guinness. Oona had snuck up on them yet again and was chuckling. Emma said, "Another pint and you can lick whipped cream from wherever you want." She breathed deeply then closed her eyes for a couple of seconds and slowly exhaled.

Peter felt his pubic hair get pulled sharply as he quickly became aroused. He turned to Oona.

"Lovely lady," he said, trying not to slur his words. He felt quite tipsy now and his beating heart drowned out all other sounds in the pub. "I must apologize. I am no longer in love with you despite the amazing trifle. I am completely, helplessly, and unconditionally in love with the beautiful woman across the table from me. She is perfection personified, and I would die for her. I would like to order two more pints, but I am a gentleman."

Before Oona could say anything, Emma said, "Two more pints and a trifle to go, please, Oona."

"Extra whipped cream?"

"Oh, absolutely," said Emma.

She winked at Peter. Oona nodded then left.

The familiar butterflies started flapping their wings in Peter's guts. However, unlike most times when he got nervous, this almost hurt and he had to concentrate not to throw up. His hands shook.

Shut up. Shut up. Shut up. Don't say it. Don't say it.

He closed his eyes and shivered.

"Say it, Peter," said Emma. "You've wanted to since the beginning. I waited for so long to hear *you* say it. You never knew my side. I never had the chance to tell you. We always got interrupted."

Peter looked across the table at Emma. She shimmered and there seemed to be a glow around her, almost as if she was in a ball of light. Perhaps she was a projection from his weak and lonely mind.

A hand touched his. In the distance, a telephone rang.

Millie Ranahan, January 15, 1985

"The Inn on the Cliff, Wycliffe Point. Ms. Ranahan speaking. How may I help you?"

"Well don't you sound like the prettiest little girl in the whole wide world," said a gruff voice. "How old are you? Young, I hope." Millie said nothing. "I want a room. Preferably one with you in it."

Millie sighed. This was the kind of person she dreaded

encountering. Oliver would have known how to handle a pig like this. "We have plenty of rooms, sir. When will you be joining us?"

"Friday. You got a boyfriend?"

Trying to keep the irritation out of her voice, Millie said, "And the nature of your visit?"

"None of your fucking business. Who the fuck do you think you are nosing into my affairs?"

"My apologies, sir. It's a standard question." His tone rattled her. There was something about him that made her nervous. And it wasn't simply his rudeness.

"Good. You know your place. The name's Kenyon, Buster Kenyon."

At the sound of the name, Millie's heart raced and sweat broke out on her forehead. Images from her nightmares floated around her head and she became extremely uneasy.

"Now, I want the best suite in the inn, no matter what the cost, and no matter the inconvenience to anyone else who is either staying there currently or is expected to later." Kenyon spoke with a loud voice, and an assurance that indicated he expected everyone to jump when he wanted something done. That included Em.

Millie was tempted to tell the man to take his business elsewhere, but she was only a maid filling in for the manager. It was beyond her authority to do so, and she had no right to interfere with the owner's business. If, when Kenyon arrived, the owner wished to send him packing, that would be fine with her.

After taking down credit card information and a phone

number, Millie said, "Will there be anything else, sir?"

"I like a good, hard fuck. A bit of rough. No, a lot of rough. Know anyone available?" He laughed. "You, maybe?"

Before she could stop herself, Millie said, "I'm not into bestiality, Mr. Kenyon. There is a kennel up the road that may be more accommodating. Good day, sir." She hung up the phone then quickly took the receiver off the cradle so Kenyon couldn't get through if he called back.

She sat and shivered. This Friday would certainly be an interesting day. Millie wondered if she could get the weekend off.

Oliver would know what to do about Kenyon. As for Mr. Davidson, he seemed intriguing and might be worth the trouble of working this weekend.

She heard the front door open then felt a cold breeze. Oliver?

Oliver entered the office and hung up his coat. "Are we swamped with reservations, Millie?"

"Only two for this Friday, Ollie."

"I was kidding."

She told him about the two coming guests. Oliver was not happy about Kenyon.

"I'd better get back to cleaning the rooms," said Millie. "But first, I need something hot to drink. You?"

Oliver shook his head.

Millie was tying on her apron as she went through the kitchen door. It was her own fault for not paying attention, but when the cook collided with her, she lost it.

"Watch where you're going, you stupid idiot." Her apron

and the front of her dress were covered with blood. The cook, stunned and silent, the raw roast beef still in her hand. Millie held the dress up by the hem to keep the mess from dripping on the floor. Her face flushed.

Seeing the look of horror and fear on the cook's face, Millie said, "Oh my God, I'm so sorry. It's no excuse, but this guest on the phone was an absolute swine and rude and disgusting, and I should never have taken it out on you." A tear slid down her cheek.

"We've all had bad days, my dear," said the cook. "Don't you worry about it. The roast isn't hurt, and neither am I. Why don't you go and change into clean clothes. I'll have a nice cup of hot chocolate waiting for you when you're ready."

Millie turned to leave, and this time nearly bumped into Oliver.

"What the…" Oliver's face went pale, and he rushed from the kitchen. He had a particularly weak stomach when it came to blood, and he had seen the mess on Millie's clothes.

She took off her apron, folded it, then held it over the blood on her dress. When she reached the lobby, Oliver came around from the desk and approached her. He stopped short of Millie, gagged and wrinkled his nose, breathing through his mouth.

"Oliver," said Millie. "Forgive me. I'm so sorry. It's just a stain."

"It's all right. What exactly happened?" She explained. "I'm sure you can get the stain out." He gagged again.

Millie was a wizard with a sewing needle and with laundry, hence her part-time work at the army base. She was confident she could work her magic on the stained uniform. There wasn't a stain that could escape Millie's scrutiny. Whatever it was, by the time she had finished with it, the tablecloth or garment was as clean as the day it was purchased.

"It wasn't cook's fault. I wasn't watching where I was going."

"Go and change No need to get that mess all over the place." Oliver concentrated hard on Millie's face, determined not to look at the bloody mess. It was obvious his throat had begun to get that feeling of tightness that usually meant he was about to be sick.

"You're right, of course, Ollie," said Millie. "And from the looks of you, I'd better get this blood out of sight in a hurry."

She had reached the stairs to the second floor when Oliver called after her. "Millie, I think that Kenyon fellow might be a relative of the people who founded this place." She looked back at him. The look on his face told her he was worried.

"Now I understand," said Oliver, "why my father said he's coming."

"It's going to happen again, isn't it, Ollie?" Millie asked, now afraid.

Oliver nodded.

Millie was resigned to the fact that events had been set in motion and there was nothing she or Ollie, or anyone at all, could do to avert the approaching horror.

There was a low moan from deep within the inn as if it knew that something nasty was coming.

Peter Dawson, January 16, 2020

A hand squeezed his, instantly breaking the spell.

Peter jumped and the room spun. He wiped a tear from his cheek and shook his head. Emma still sat across from him, her hand holding his. The intensity of the feelings he experienced nearly overwhelmed him. The different perspective. Everything. He wanted to cry.

"You! It's you. You're Millie. The maid. I saw you. I was you. But how? It's usually some guy."

Chapter 10:
"Made mistakes along the way"

Beverly Kent, January 16, 2020

It was the most delicious of dreams. Like a kaleidoscope, images flashed of Peter being penetrated and killed. He didn't always look exactly the same, but it was him nonetheless. There was something off because she couldn't understand why *she* was penetrating *him*. It should have been the other way around, not that she would have let him anywhere near her.

There were also flashes of that harlot from the library. Her image never wavered: always the smug look of superiority and disdain, the horror when she realized her fate, and the anguish.

But there was confusion. The penetration was always by something hard and sharp. The climax that should have been clear or white was a red mist.

Adding to the confusion were the hands. Her hands. Masculine and hairy. The hair was red. Like hers.

Who am I? Am I me again? Who is the other?

"What's happening to me?"

Beverly slowly regained her senses. Her forehead rested on something cold and hard, so did her hip. The air stank of shit, urine, and vomit. She was wet and stiff.

When she opened her eyes, Beverly saw spots and floaters that made her dizzy. Then she saw the white of the porcelain toilet bowl, streaked with brown and orange, on which she rested her forehead.

"Oh, God…"

Lifting her head, only a little because her stiff neck wouldn't allow more movement, Beverly looked into the filthy bowl, full of vomit and—*no!*—her hair floating in the filth.

She sat back from the toilet and leaned against the bathtub, her long, muck-encrusted hair now slopping foulness onto her blouse. While the overpowering stench made her head spin, the muscles in her back screamed in protest. Her stomach lurched, but nothing came out. It was already spread all over the toilet bowl, the floor, and part way up the wall. Fearing what she would discover, Beverly looked down.

Her skirt was bunched up around her waist. A yellow puddle confirmed she'd done it for the second time in twenty-four hours. "It's worse than when I was little."

Adding to her discomfort was the brown mess that stained the gusset of her pantyhose and oozed out the sides of her panties. The pantyhose had kept most of the runny stuff from escaping onto the floor.

Sitting, shivering in her own filth, Beverly shook her head to try and clear her mind. Try as she might, she couldn't remember how she got into this situation. Something had happened at the library. Or was it on the way back to the inn?

Was I drunk?

There was something about a glass globe and a book. It was all so mixed up.

The hatred. It burned. She knew she was capable of intense dislike, especially if she didn't get her own way, but this hatred. It came from somewhere so deep within her, she feared for what it might make her do. Who was the hate for? Who could be so bad, so utterly detestable, that she had the overwhelming desire to kill? And kill in the most abominable way.

She pictured that librarian creature talking to Peter. That couldn't be right.

Beverly's body ached, her neck and back hurt, and her arms felt a little numb. How long had she been lying in that awkward position? Using the edge of the tub, Beverly heaved herself to her feet. Immediately, the mess contained by her pantyhose escaped and slid down her legs, dripping into her boots and the puddle at her feet. She rubbed her eyes then gagged, disgusted by the stink on her fingers.

The image that greeted Beverly when she looked in the mirror shocked and appalled her. Smeared makeup, swollen, red eyes, and—*can it get any worse?*—chunks of vomit in her sodden hair and stuck to her chin. She spat something into the sink, but didn't look to see what it was.

Needing to get herself sorted out, Beverly quickly stripped off her soiled clothes, leaving them in a pile next to the tub. She stepped in a puddle of mixed vomit and diarrhea. It squished up between her toes. Finally, ready to take a long hot shower, she thought about what would greet her when she finished.

When she tried to clean up, every step she took left a brown footprint, every move she made splashed something foul. A quick shower to rinse off the worst of it proved helpful.

For the next half hour, Beverly did what she could to get rid of the mess she had made. *If only I could remember making it.* The soiled clothes, including her boots, went into the tub to be thoroughly rinsed. She used a couple of the inn's towels to wipe up the mess on the floor, walls, and toilet bowl. The towels joined the clothes in the tub. In the cabinet under the sink, Beverly found a small container of cleanser that must have been forgotten by the maid. *I hate that fucking bitch.* Using all the remaining toilet paper, she cleaned the sink, toilet, and floor.

After rinsing her clothes, she found the skirt and boots were salvageable. She placed the boots over the radiator to dry, and the skirt over the shower curtain rod. The rest of her things were too damaged to keep.

There were extra bags in the garbage pail in which she deposited the used toilet paper—there was too much to flush—and her rinsed clothes. She'd be damned if anyone went through the trash and found her disgusting clothes. Fortunately, the bags were opaque so she would be able to dispose of them discreetly with no one being the wiser.

When the bathroom was cleaned to her satisfaction, Beverly decided a long, hot bath would be better than a shower.

While she relaxed in the tub, Beverly tried to drag forth memories of the day and whatever might have caused her distress. There was a vague recollection that someone had been nasty and rude to her. All she knew for certain was that she'd waited hours for Peter to come to her room. He hadn't appeared.

"I will kill that ungrateful son of a bitch," said Beverly to no one in particular. "No, worse. I'll expose him for the fraud that he is. His stupid theories and asinine research. Even worse, I'll tell everyone that he has a tiny cock."

She was unsure about that last thing. She'd never let Dawson anywhere near her, let alone actually seen what he was carrying. As much as she liked to get laid, the mere thought of doing it with Dawson made her ill.

"And that fucking librarian will pay for her disrespect."

Beverly took a deep breath. Plotting revenge on those who had wronged her had restored some of her dignity. No one had witnessed what happened in the bathroom. No one would ever know.

She was invulnerable again.

Climbing out of the now cold water, Beverly realized she had only left herself a small hand towel. "Fuck." Doing the best she could with what she had, she dried herself and as much of her hair as possible. When she tried to brush the tangles out of her hair, she saw that her natural red color was showing.

That dye was supposed to be permanent.

Thinking back on it, Beverly couldn't remember why she had used dye in the first place. Her flaming red hair was quite attractive; everyone told her so. It was about the time she met Dawson that Beverly had the overwhelming urge to change her hair color. Something about the flicker of recognition in his eyes as they were introduced set her off. It didn't matter much now. Dawson could jump off a cliff for all she cared. Maybe she'd give him a little poke to help.

The inn was chilly in spite of its warm appearance and that fire downstairs. The radiator in her room helped a little—enough to dry out her boots, she hoped. These old buildings were impossible to keep warm. Beverly went to her suitcase to get some fresh clothes. She always had plenty of underwear and socks, but she had neglected to pack extra pants. Checking the pants she had rinsed out the night before, after her first "accident," she was relieved to find they were dry. Picking up a bra, she shrugged and tossed it aside. Instead, she pulled on an extra tee shirt.

Warm and somewhat cozy now, Beverly wondered what to do next. The clock on the nightstand said it was after nine. How could so much time have passed? Her stomach growled and Beverly remembered she had missed lunch for some reason. Dawson could not have been relied upon to provide for her needs, especially since he had become stroppy with her. But why had she missed lunch? Beverly remembered packing up her belongings and walking up the library staircase intent on returning to the inn for something to eat. She had been sure the inn dining room would be open this time. But she'd had nothing, not even some hardtack.

What?

When Beverly saw her shadow on the wall, she realized that light was coming in the window. She pulled back the curtain to see bright sunshine. Damn! It was after nine in the morning. She'd been out all night. To make matters worse, she had missed breakfast again.

The next thing Beverly remembered was that idiot librarian rushing downstairs to the basement. The stupid slag was likely fawning over Dawson while he acted all smooth and cool. Bitch. Dawson was hers.

But I don't want him. I want...her? A momentary image of the woman spread-eagled and naked, tied to the bed in this very room, flashed across her mind. She was both repulsed and aroused. *What's the matter with me?*

Things became clearer. The walk back to the inn had been

treacherous and Beverly had slipped and seen something. What was it? Something blurry, like the image of a building through thick fog. That man downstairs had helped her to her room and had been ordered to send Dawson to her when he returned to the inn.

Where are you, you ungrateful idiot?

Leaving her room, the first thing that struck Beverly was the silence. There weren't that many people in the place to begin with, but this quiet was eerie. She expected to hear that cunt maid crashing around with her mop-less bucket. The memory of the bucket and what it contained—*what she thought it contained*—caused her to shudder.

No, there was some sound. Yelling, but muffled. Concentrating, Beverly couldn't make out any words, but she did pinpoint the origin of the argument: behind that wooden door. The one that didn't open, and when it did, there was nothing there but a dark hall. Unless she was outside where the wall was bricked up. Except, yesterday, on the walk from the library, Beverly had seen something above her. The outline of a walkway connecting the inn and the library. Hadn't that bitch bored her to death with stories about how it had come down in…when, 1905?

Best not ask O'Dale about it. He'd lie and claim there was nothing there. Beverly knew better. All these morons at the inn think they can pull one over on the great Beverly Kent. Well, she'd show them how wrong and misguided they were.

On the second-floor landing, Beverly paused and thought about checking Dawson's room. He had mentioned something about being on the second floor though he hadn't told her exactly which room. It shouldn't be hard to find.

Passing a large mirror, something caught Beverly's eye. When she looked into the mirror, she thought she was mistaken and that it was a painting. Staring back at her was an officer from the Union Army in the Civil War. A colonel in the 45th New Jersey Volunteer Infantry, if she read the insignia on his uniform correctly. Flaming curly red hair poked out from beneath his hat and thick muttonchop sideburns framed his stern face. Beverly found him to be quite handsome. His right hand was drawing his sabre from its scabbard. That was an odd thing to show in a portrait.

What struck Beverly the most were the eyes. Deep and dark, they seemed to peer into her soul. She became entranced with them, and everything went dark around her. Then he smiled and said, "What are you waiting for?"

Beverly screamed and ran for the stairs. Gripping the banister, she steadied her breathing. It couldn't have been real. Walking back slowly toward the painting, she peered around the edge as if hoping the man inside wouldn't notice her. Her own face looked back from the mirror.

Relief flooded through her. She hadn't gone crazy and seen a painting come to life. Something must have stirred her imagination and made her see a soldier rather than herself. She needed food and a good and comfortable night's sleep in a bed and not on a cold bathroom floor.

In the lobby, the only sound was the scratching of a pen on paper. That O'Dale creature sat behind the front desk writing something. She coughed to attract his attention. His eyes widened and he seemed to be examining her. Beverly approached him boldly. She had nothing to fear. The closer she got, the more O'Dale's face registered shock. He kept glancing at something behind her. Annoyed, she turned to see the shelf with the broken snow globes. There were three and that other broken thing.

Her hand automatically went to her knee where, yesterday, she had cut it open on a shard of glass. But that was in the lobby. She'd smashed the globe in the library. Now, there was nothing there but smooth, unbroken skin. Looking back at the shelf, something wasn't right about the globes. Had there been four yesterday?

Beverly leaned on the front desk, rang the bell, making O'Dale look genuinely frightened of her. Good. That's the way it should be.

"Yes, Professor…Kent," he said. "That is you, isn't it?"

"Of course it is, you no account pie eater. Who else would I be?" He shrugged. "Is Dawson here?"

"I do not know, madam," said O'Dale with a bit of a smile. "He did not return last night while I was still on duty. Perhaps he let himself in after I went to bed."

"You're lying and I don't know why. Probably trying to protect that snivelling fool. Is he sparking that uppity librarian? Ranahan?"

"It's none of my business, madam." O'Dale's smile grew wider.

"What's so goddammed funny, O'Dale?" Beverly could feel her anger building. Someone needed to be punished.

"I don't know what possessed me, madam. Perhaps it's the water. Or maybe a change in the weather. There does appear to be a big storm brewing."

"I don't care. I need food. Get me some."

"I'll see if there's anything left in the kitchen, madam. The cook has already gone until lunch."

"Whatever. Bring it to my room. And coffee. And not that rat's piss essence you fed me yesterday. Go to a Starbucks if you have to."

"Starbucks?"

"Where's your horse sense? There must be one in this hick fucking town. I'll be in my room. Sing out when you've got it." She turned to leave.

"One question before you go," said O'Dale. She looked over her shoulder at him. "Did you do that?" He pointed past her at the shelf of broken snow globes.

Beverly huffed. "What do you think?"

In her room, Beverly sat on the bed. Opening the journal she had taken from the library, she turned to the last entry she had read, January 17, 1905. She reread it then moved on to the next entry, January 19. When she saw the note clipped to the top of the page, she kicked herself for being careless. The letters must have been what slipped out when she picked up the journal in the library office. Damn. There might have been useful information in them.

Oscar O'Dale, Journal entry for Thursday, January 19, 1905

[Note from librarian B. Ranahan: both the referenced letter and telegram from Obadiah O'Dale are clipped to the entry for this date. The referenced letter from Patrick Dawes has not been found.]

Yesterday, the 18th, began on such a high note, but ended with horrors and sadness I can hardly comprehend. I shall endeavor to relate the events in the order that they occurred, leaving out nothing, not even my own culpability in the deaths of at least two people and my own inability to prevent the deaths of two more.

With the morning mail, I received two promising letters, closely followed by a telegram. First, my old friend from the cavalry, Patrick Dawes, stated he would be coming to Wycliffe Point and the inn to see Emelia. I had no idea they were acquainted, though I learned later in the day that they had met at the World's Fair last year. With the arrival the night before of Bartholomew Kensington, knowing an ally would soon be here made me more confident that the animal would be prevented from creating whatever mayhem he intended. In addition, Emelia could be either protected or taken away to safety.

The second letter and telegram were from my uncle, Obadiah. The first informed me that he, too, would be arriving to help protect Emelia. With the receipt of that letter, I had no more doubt that she was in peril from Bartholomew. The telegram was to let me know Obadiah had been delayed and would not be arriving until today.

I did not wish to frighten Emelia, so I sent her on a series of errands that, with luck, would keep her occupied until late into the day. This would allow enough time for the arrival of Uncle Obadiah and Patrick and keep her from Bartholomew's clutches.

Bartholomew, after receiving his breakfast in his rooms, left the inn and was not seen for the rest of the day. It was not until late into the evening that his activities for the day were discovered, unfortunately too late to be stopped.

Expecting the two o'clock train would be carrying my allies, I prepared to meet them at the station. However, the assistant cook did not arrive at her assigned time, and I was forced to remain at the inn until half past two. The missing assistant was new, having arrived with her family only a few weeks ago on a steamer from England. I was aware she had four children and assumed there had been an issue with one of them that caused her to miss work. Before I could enquire as to her whereabouts, there was a minor emergency in the kitchen that occupied me for a large portion of the afternoon.

By the time I arrived at the station, all passengers had left and no one I asked could remember seeing either Patrick or Uncle Obadiah.

I spent the rest of the afternoon and evening in a state of panic. Emelia had not returned from her errands by supper time. Uncle Obadiah and Patrick had not arrived at the inn. Worst of all, Bartholomew had virtually disappeared.

My duties at the inn forced me to remain at the front desk, though I did send out messages asking after the missing people. The local constable proved to be less than helpful and seemed interested only in receiving a free meal.

At exactly five minutes past nine, Bartholomew appeared from the upper floors and demanded my assistance with something unnamed. The time is correct because I checked the clock in the lobby a few moments before he arrived. He led me back upstairs then across the walkway to the warehouse. No amount of questioning garnered any information from him as to the purpose or nature of the required aid.

In the warehouse, we entered a room and I recoiled at the incredible stench of blood. Then I beheld a sight that will haunt me to my dying days. I had found Emelia, having failed in my task of protecting her.

Bartholomew knocked me out then tied me up. When I awoke, I tried not to look at poor Emelia, but could not pull my horrified gaze away. It was at this point that Bartholomew committed a gross indecency by urinating upon me. Disgusting as that might be, it was nothing compared to the indecencies he had perpetuated upon Emelia.

I ~~cannot~~ will not describe her wounds or the obscene things he did to her while I was helpless to do anything. Suffice to say, war did not prepare me for it, and I know deep in my soul that Bartholomew Kensington is burning in the lowest pits of Hell for his sins.

Salvation, for me at least, arrived in the form of Uncle Obadiah. He burst into the room, preventing Bartholomew from using his hammer on Emelia yet again. His rifle, steadily pointed at Bartholomew's head, was a welcome sight. He ordered Bartholomew to free me, at which point, I rushed over to Emelia in the slimmest of hopes that she might yet live. In retrospect, for her to have survived would have been a curse rather than a blessing.

I must admit to some confusion regarding the subsequent events. Bartholomew referred to Uncle Obadiah and the traitor. As Obadiah bound him with the rope, Bartholomew seemed to believe he was someone named Beau and that they had met before under similar circumstances. Obadiah claimed to have failed Emmeline a second time.

Obadiah passed me the rifle and took a stick of dynamite from inside his overcoat. He said it was his intention to destroy this killing room, and Bartholomew along with it. I had the distinct impression Obadiah was going to blow himself up as well.

At this point, while we were distracted, Bartholomew regained his feet, pushed past us, and ran out to the warehouse. Obadiah and I followed quickly, though I was several steps behind because I had slipped in some of Emelia's blood.

Bartholomew ran for the walkway, I assume under the belief that he could find aid at the inn. Obadiah surprised me with the speed with which he pursued Bartholomew. As he ran, he pulled an oil lamp from the wall and lit the stick of dynamite.

"Stay back, Oscar. If this doesn't end it, be ready to protect her again. Stay there!"

Obadiah sprinted and threw himself at Bartholomew who, still bound, had not been able to run as fast as he wished. The men fell in a heap about midway across the walkway.

Bartholomew screamed and attempted to get away from Obadiah, but could not. I saw the fuse on the dynamite was almost done, so I lurched back around a corner and fell to the ground.

The sound that followed deafened me. I feared I was in the midst of an earthquake and that the warehouse would collapse, taking me with it. It did not happen, as can be seen by my writing this journal entry.

I rose on shaky legs and went back around the corner. To my horror, the walkway was gone. Clinging to the door frame, I peered down at the chasm between the warehouse and the inn, but I could only see a small amount of rubble, some bricks, and a few timbers.

The rest of the walkway, blown to bits along with Obadiah and Bartholomew, had gone over the cliff and into the bay below.

Remarkably, the wooden door to the inn across the abyss was unharmed.

For a few minutes, I stood there wondering what I should do next. In the distance, I could hear the fire alarm bell ringing. That meant the local fire brigade would be on the scene within a short time.

I decided to protect the honor and dignity of Emelia. To me, that was more important than anything. I rushed back to the killing room, closed and locked the door, then ran back downstairs and across to the inn. In the panic resulting from the explosion, no one in the lobby noticed I was without a coat on a frigid night. Providence was on my side as they assumed I had already been outside and was returning.

The rest of the night was a blur of activity. Various people, including the local constable and the mayor, interviewed the staff and guests to ascertain if anyone knew what caused the collapse. A few mentioned hearing what they thought was an explosion. However, no evidence of such a thing was found. The few timbers and bricks on the path below showed no fire or explosive damage, the rest, I assume, having fallen into the sea. The authorities quickly dismissed the explosion theory and put it down to a structural failure.

I was interviewed for quite some time because it was assumed I had the earliest knowledge of the collapse due to me being witnessed returning shortly thereafter. I maintained that I had heard a loud noise and, when I ventured outside to investigate, discovered the walkway had gone. The events of the evening and the fates of those poor souls involved were not disclosed. I feared no one, particularly the Kensington family, would have believed Bartholomew was capable of such atrocities. More likely, they would find scapegoats elsewhere. Word has been spreading that the family from the warehouse, also missing, which included our assistant cook, may have been anarchists from Europe and had perpetrated the destruction as a political statement. I did not disabuse anyone of this misguided fantasy.

Chapter 11:
"We've been cleaning up the very best we could"

Peter Dawson, January 17, 2020

Peter's head throbbed and his mouth tasted like an old boot. He ached all over. Something furry tickled his nose. Very slowly, Peter opened his eyes. It was morning. The sun shone through a very large window he didn't recognize. Something blurred his vision. Focusing now, he discovered it was black hair. He leaned up on one elbow and saw the most beautiful sight he had ever encountered.

Emma Ranahan lay on her back next to him, snoring like a banshee. Her hair, previously tied in a ponytail, now fanned out from her head on the pillow. It was much curlier than he remembered. There was sweat on her face and her lipstick had smeared all over her mouth. White globs of something peppered her cheeks.

Her skin against his was hot and sticky, from his belly to his calves. Her feet, however, were ice cold.

Her feet! She was naked! So was he!

What have I done? He felt both terrified and excited.

Then he remembered—the pub, the third pint, trifle to go. And Emma.

Oh, lord, Emma.

So soft, smelling of vanilla. She tasted of salt and…cream? Peter looked over at the bedside table. An empty bowl sat there with the remains of a dessert. Trifle. Peter gasped when he remembered what they had done with the trifle. He gently lifted the sheet. Dried whipped cream and custard had been smeared on both of their bodies. That's what was on her cheeks. It appeared to be everywhere.

Even there!

Peter became erect again and poked Emma's side. She snorted then opened her eyes and rolled over to face him.

She grimaced and said, "Morning breath."

"Sorry," said Peter. He put his hand in front of his mouth so he could speak.

Emma pulled his hand away. "I don't care," she said and pulled him close so she could kiss him. "Is this what I think it is?"

Her warm hand grasped him. He nodded.

"Good," she said and rolled him onto his back. She climbed up and straddled his belly. Ever so gently, with her eyes closed and a huge smile on her face, Emma slid back and guided him into her.

Peter placed his hands on her hips. Her skin was smooth and hot and perfect. "Oh my..." said Peter then stopped.

What the hell?

He jerked back, almost knocking Emma off when he pulled his hands away from her. She opened her eyes. Peter saw fear and pain in them so deep it hurt him to think about it.

Shiny, thick, light brown scars stood out almost a quarter inch from Emma's abdomen. They looked puffy. One ran straight up from her pubic hair to her sternum. Another crossed from hip to hip below her belly. A third circled her throat. He must have been terribly drunk not to have noticed them last night.

Despite the vicious wounds, Emma remained the most beautiful woman he had ever met.

Forget that. What horrific injury must Emma have endured to get the scars. To Peter, it looked as if someone had tried to gut and behead her. Incredible anger and a deeper sorrow than he had ever experienced welled up in him. He gasped then couldn't stop the tears when something else forced its way to the forefront of his mind.

Guilt.

He knew the responsibility belonged to him. Emma was disfigured because he had failed her. Peter didn't know how, when, or why. That didn't matter. Emma had been hurt, and he hadn't stopped it.

"You can see them," said Emma quietly. It wasn't a question.

He tried to respond, but it caught in his throat. Tears now blurred his vision and ran down his face into his ears.

"Keloids," she said. Emma stared up at the ceiling. "Why? Why fucking now? I have a chance to be happy, and these goddammed things ruin it." She pressed the heels of her hands against her eyes and took a deep breath. "I'm not going to cry. I'm cried out." She looked down at her scars. "Fucking things." Now she held her hands in front of her abdomen. They were curled like claws and the nails looked like they could do some serious damage.

Peter reached up and grasped her wrists. "Don't," he said as gently as possible.

"Why the fuck not?" Emma's eyes pierced his. The green in her eyes intensified, almost glowing. Her face was hard and her snarl revealed perfect teeth, ready to tear out Peter's throat. She panted, waiting for him to make a move.

Peter had no idea how long they stayed like this, staring into each other's eyes. The whole time, he tried to show love in his eyes, but feared all she would see was the guilt.

Then, without warning, Emma's face softened. Her eyes returned to normal. She smiled and her breathing quietened. He released her wrists.

Stroking Peter's face, she said, "No guilt. Never."

"But…" A finger pressed against his lips stopped him. She leaned down to kiss him softly and all guilt drained away. "Thank you."

Tentatively, Peter reached out and touched the vertical scar—rubbery yet firm. Emma winced and he quickly pulled his hand away.

"Sorry," he said. It felt lame.

"It's all right," she said. "They sometimes sting when touched, but mostly they itch like crazy. Are you going to be sick?"

Peter shook his head. "No. I'm surprised is all. I must have missed them in the throes of passion last night."

This time Emma shook her head. "No, you didn't. They weren't there." She looked down and ran her finger along the side of the vertical keloid. Her eye spasmed when she did it and she winced again. "I can't help myself. I have to touch them."

"I don't understand," said Peter. "How?"

Emma sighed. "Every January, they spring up. It's as if

they're a reminder that I can never be happy. That I'm doomed to some terrible fate."

"So, what about last night?"

Emma shrugged her shoulders. "I don't know. They usually stay at least until the eighteenth. They begin to fade on the nineteenth or twentieth. Then they're just gone. This is the first time they've gone then come back. I was so hopeful that maybe you'd scared them away."

"But that's…"

"Silly? Weird? Bizarre? Completely and totally fucked up?" She stroked Peter's cheek. Her hand felt lovely, and he didn't want her to stop. "What do you remember?"

"Trifle? Too much Guinness?"

"No, I mean the other stuff. You know."

"Yeah, I know. Can we talk about it later? I need a clear head." He looked around the room. Nothing was familiar except the empty trifle bowl. "Where are we? This isn't the inn."

"You keep mentioning the inn. I don't know why. This is my room on the fourth floor of the library building. Back when it was a warehouse, there was a suite of offices up here. The board offered the rooms to me at a bargain rent when they hired me. How could I refuse?"

"How drunk were we last night? I barely remember a thing. And certainly not coming back to the library. And what about…" He nodded at the keloids.

"For once, I forgot about them. Didn't even notice they weren't there or didn't care." Emma chuckled. "It's a shame you don't remember. Licking up the whipped cream and custard? Burrowing for the mandarin orange segment because you don't like cherries? Those segments get squishy really fast."

Peter's erection returned. Emma wriggled on him, and he slipped back inside her. She was so hot, he thought he would catch fire.

"Fuck!"

"We are," said Emma.

"No," said Peter. He ran his hands over her smooth abdomen. The keloids were gone. "They've disappeared again, Emma."

"We must be doing something right. Now, shut up and concentrate." Emma leaned down and covered Peter's mouth with her own. As her tongue found his, he forgot about everything and lost himself in the woman he loved more than life itself.

Sometime later—it didn't matter when because time didn't matter around Emma—they lay side by side on sweaty sheets. Peter felt drained. Emma played with his pubic hair, twirling it around her index finger. He stroked her shoulder, admiring her smooth skin.

"You know," he said. "Whipped cream doesn't smell so good hours after it's been used inappropriately."

"Way to ruin the mood, killjoy." Emma pulled her hair-wrapped finger making Peter yelp at the sudden pain. "Still not as bad as morning breath," she said. "Morning after sex with trifle breath."

"Speaking of food, I am famished."

"We can go over to the pub. They do a wicked all-you-can-eat Sunday brunch."

"Tempting, but it's Friday. I think. Or maybe Saturday."

"It is. Regular breakfast then." Emma leaned back and looked at the empty trifle bowl then said. "No trifle left. All I can offer is cream pie."

Half an hour later, Peter said, "Shower?"

Emma stared into his eyes. To him it felt like she was looking at his soul. She placed a hand on his chest. "Mine at last. This time."

"Always," he said. "Every time."

Peter had an overwhelming sense of déjà vu.

Captain Philip Daweson, January 18, 1865

Philip returned to the lobby. Obadiah still stood there, though he swayed a little. There was another glass of wine in his hand.

"Well?" said Obadiah.

Philip shook his head. "Nothing, Obadiah. I asked all around and nobody has seen Emmeline for quite some time. Or, no one's admitting to seeing her. What's going on? Where's Kensington?"

Obadiah emptied his glass then burped. "Excuse me." His words were a little slurred. "He came back down a few minutes ago. His face was flushed and he was breathing heavily. If I had had less wine to drink, I'd have sworn he had blood on his boots. Anyway, he went out to the kitchen for a few minutes then came back in. He's over there." Obadiah pointed toward the lobby.

Kensington again basked in the attention of those who would have fled in fear and disgust had they known the real man. He seemed much happier and friendlier than he had earlier. Perhaps he'd had more to drink. *Or killed someone.* Something caught Kensington's attention, and he looked up the stairs then smiled. Philip followed his gaze but saw nothing except a passing shadow near the second-floor landing.

Philip looked back over toward Kensington to see him race up the stairs. Why would he leave his own celebration again?

"I'll be back," said Philip. He hurried after his nemesis.

Philip heard Kensington going up the stairs ahead of him. He decided the man was going to his room. There was a special suite reserved for dignitaries on the fourth floor near the walkway to the warehouse next door. Philip reached the fourth floor in time to see Kensington enter his room.

Trying to be silent, Philip crept along the hall until he stood outside the Colonel's door. Pressing his ear against the wood, he heard nothing. Moments later, there was a thump followed by muffled voices. He waited until there was silence. As carefully as he could, Philip opened the door. Fortunately, the hinges were well-oiled and made no sound.

The sight that greeted Philip nearly made his mind crumble.

Emmeline, laid out on the bed, hands and feet tied to the bedposts with heavy rope. Her apron had been torn off and lay in a heap next to the bed. The colonel had just finished using a bayonet to cut away her clothes. For a moment, Philip was taken aback by the sight of his lady love sprawled out, her most private areas open for all to see. He'd never seen a naked woman before. The removal of her clothes had been careless and there were many bloody cuts on her body.

The colonel stood next to the bed. "You won't rebuff me again, you animal," said Kensington as he undid the buttons on his fly and pulled out his pecker. It was hard and long. "You'll do what I want."

Emmeline screamed and cried, "Never, you bastard. My heart belongs to another." She yanked at her bonds, but they were secure.

"Swine!" Philip launched himself at the colonel.

"Philip!" said Emmeline when she saw her rescuer.

Faster than seemed possible, Kensington grabbed the bayonet from the nightstand and twisted to meet Philip. Before Philip could stop or evade the weapon, Kensington thrust it into his shoulder. The pain was incredible, but Philip would not let a mere wound prevent him from saving the woman he loved.

Kensington twisted the bayonet, and the pain was so intense that Philip cried out and fell to the floor.

He passed out.

When Philip regained consciousness, he found himself bound and lying on a straw-covered floor. The stench of death and decay filled the air, worse than anything Philip had experienced on the battlefield. He peered in the direction of the stench and made out a pile of...bodies. He counted at least six. There might have been more. Splashes of dried blood covered the floor. A woman's head lay not far from his knee. And was that…? Yes, there was a nose in a pool of blood.

He saw now that he was in a warehouse, probably the one attached to the inn. "Help!" It only came out as a croak.

"Don't bother, Daweson. No one can hear you here. We won't be interrupted while I play. Now, stand up."

Emmeline called out for Philip. A loud slap followed.

Philip's head felt fuzzy. He tried to focus on the voice of his captor. Kensington, standing over him, with his service revolver pointed at Emmeline. Completely naked now, she had been strung up by her arms from a roof beam. Her head hung forward and blood dripped from her mouth. She looked down at Philip through tear-filled eyes.

"Stand up or I'll shoot the whore."

Philip struggled to stand. The bayonet, which was still lodged in his shoulder, slid out and fell to the floor. "You son of a bitch," he said. He pulled against his bonds, but his wrists were secured with a heavy chain to a hook high up on a post.

Kensington laughed. "So, you think you love this thing, this animal. You're pathetic, Daweson. It's only good for one thing, and I intend to use it for that until it's dead."

The intense throbbing from his shoulder wound caused Philip to have trouble seeing as his vision clouded from pain and blood loss.

Emmeline screamed.

Kensington holstered his revolver and walked over to her. "To think I might have had feelings for you," he said. "I'm going to watch you die. I'm going to enjoy it. And no one can stop me."

He slapped her across the face then did something that

caused her to struggle frantically. Philip heard gurgling and a laugh from Kensington.

"That should shut it up," said Kensington. He threw something that landed at Philip's feet. Dear god, it was a tongue. Hers!

"You…" Before Philip could say more, Kensington rushed toward him and stuffed something woolen and foul-smelling in his mouth. He tried but could not spit it out. The stink made him want to vomit and he had to concentrate lest he lose control and choke himself to death.

"Watch, Daweson, you pathetic scum." As Kensington walked slowly toward Emmeline, he drew his sabre from its scabbard. Philip's heart sank. Kensington always kept his weapon razor sharp. The better to cut off the limbs of his enemies in battle. He slashed once sideways and then up. The sound of something heavy and wet hitting the floor followed. Kensington stood aside to let Philip see his handiwork.

Philip closed his eyes to blank out the horrific sight of the love of his life hanging from the beam with two wide gashes in her abdomen. He refused to look any lower.

"Look!" Kensington slapped Philip across the face, dislodging the gag. Philip spat it out then vomited. Kensington grabbed Philip by the chin then forced him to open his eyes. He tried to resist, but loss of blood from the bayonet wound had weakened him too much.

Steam rose from the bloody mass at his love's feet. It was still connected to her. Philip sobbed when Emmeline opened her eyes, and he realized she was still alive. He could scarcely imagine the pain she must be enduring.

Kensington released Philip's jaw and returned to Emmeline. This time, he held his sword against her throat. "Look at me, bitch. I want to feel you die."

"Please, don't," said Philip.

Emmeline spat a glob of bloody phlegm in her tormentor's face. Kensington's eyes lit up and he slowly sawed into her neck. Emmeline opened her eyes again for just a moment, enough time to look over at Philip. There was a hint of a smile upon her face, to be replaced by shock when the sabre sliced through her carotid artery. Blood spurted from the cut covering the front of Kensington's uniform. A last gasp of air escaped through the gash. The sawing motion grew faster and more frantic.

"No!" Kensington pushed hard on the hilt. There was a loud scrape as the sabre cut through her spine. "No!" Emmeline's head fell back, held to her body by a flap of skin.

"No! I didn't feel it." Kensington dropped his weapon and grabbed Emmeline's hair. He held her face close to his and stared intently into her dead eyes. "No!" He released her head and shoved his hand into her abdomen. Pulling hard, twisting and grunting, his hand came away with something large and red. He walked over to Philip and held out his prize. With an evil smile on his face, Kensington said, "You wanted to win her heart, Daweson." He laughed. "Now I have it."

Philip vomited again and felt his hopes and dreams drain from his mind. He had no more reason to live.

Kensington casually tossed Emmeline's heart aside then retrieved his sabre. He unhooked the chain holding Philip and gave it a pull. "Now you, Daweson. Move." Kensington motioned with the revolver toward a door on the far wall.

Philip tried not to look at Emmeline's corpse as he passed her.

"Open it." Kensington nodded toward the heavy wooden door.

Philip pushed it open to reveal a long, narrow hall. A cold breeze caressed his face.

"Go on."

On unsteady feet, Philip walked down the hall. Bright moonlight shone through a small window. Off in the distance, he could see the waves in the bay. At the other end of the hall stood another heavy wooden door. The men went through it into a large room full of bales of cotton and boxes of something Philip couldn't identify. Kensington prodded him with the sabre, and he fell against one of the boxes. The edge caught his wound forcing a gasp from his lips. The pain was almost unbearable.

"The stairs," said his captor.

A few feet along a wall, there was an opening to a staircase. With Kensington following, still pointing the sabre at him, Philip hobbled down three flights until they came to a landing where goods were loaded onto wagons.

"Out."

Philip pulled open one of the large doors and immediately felt the cold ocean wind. He smelled salt in the air and, strangely, a hint of vanilla. Kensington pushed him along until they came to a low wall overlooking the cliff. Far below, waves crashed against the rocks, sending salt spray almost all the way up to the cliff top.

"Jump," said Kensington.

"No," said Philip. He turned to face Kensington, realizing he did have a reason to live. "I'm going to kill you."

"Too late."

Before he could move, Kensington's sabre pierced Philip's chest. The pain was even worse than the stab wound. Unable to stop himself, Philip fell back, sliding off the blade. His calves hit the top of the low wall, and he went over.

The rocks and waves rushing up to meet him were clearly lit by the moonlight. In the few seconds he had to live, Philip Daweson thought about Emmeline.

"I lo…"

Emma Ranahan, January 17, 2020

Though it felt like an eternity, barely a few seconds had passed before Emma opened her eyes to behold Peter's smiling face. Her hand remained on his chest. When she removed it, for a fleeting moment, she saw a gaping wound over his heart.

"I failed," she said. "Not again." Her racing heartbeat thumped in her ears, drowning out the chimes of the wall clock. It was nine.

"What are you talking about?" Peter stroked her cheek. "You went cross-eyed there." She took his hand in hers and kissed it.

"I died. Horribly. He did it. Then he killed you."

"Who? What? Me? How?"

"Remember last night? You faded away for a moment.

When you came back, you said something about it being a woman this time, not some guy. This time, for me, it was you. Usually, I see a woman. I think I know what's happening."

"Tell me," said Peter. "I'm confused as all hell."

"Later. I need time to calm down. Regain my balance. You know, get my shit together. Come on." She climbed out of bed and waited for Peter to join her. He didn't move but laid there staring at her. "What?"

"I'm admiring you. You're so…perfect. From the top of your curly hair to the tips of your lovely feet."

Emma curtsied. "Thank you, sir."

The second he got out of bed, she grasped his hand, as if afraid to let go. It made using the toilet a bit awkward, especially for a thoroughly embarrassed Peter.

"After what we did last night, you're afraid to let me see you pee?"

"I need…" He was sheepish.

"Oh. Tough." Emma knelt next to him and waited. "Hurry up. I need to go."

She held his hand going into the shower, maintained some contact throughout, whether thigh, shoulder, bum, or lips. Dressing was fairly easy because she insisted they sit side by side on the bed. Peter had been squeamish about putting on the same clothes he wore yesterday. In the end, Emma loaned him a pair of her socks, a tee shirt, and, after a short debate, a clean pair of her plain white panties. She was surprised her things fit him so well.

"I've got some stockings," she said when they were both fully dressed.

Peter grinned. "Garter as well?" When she nodded, he shocked her when he said, "Later, when all this shit is over."

She still wouldn't let go of his hand. They sat next to each other in a booth in the pub, their food laid out before them. Emma had to eat with her right hand while Peter struggled to coordinate his left hand and a fork. In the end, Peter had her throw her left leg over his right leg, then he wrapped his left leg around hers. They were locked together and could hardly move. Eating became much easier, and Emma relaxed.

Oona hovered, trying to hear their conversation while constantly refilling their coffee mugs. Finally, Emma said, "Yes, Oona, Peter spent the night. We had wild, rampant sex and spread custard and whipped cream from the trifle all over each other then licked it off."

Peter looked at her wide-eyed and with his mouth hanging open. "What?"

Oona's face had turned bright red.

Peter faced Oona and said, "Sorry about that. TMI. By the way, are you making more trifle today?"

"Mandarin segments instead of cherries," said Emma.

"What about peach slices or pears?" Peter thought for a second then added, "What about a banana?"

"Perverts," said Oona. She walked away with a smile on her face.

"Thank you," said Emma. She leaned closer and kissed his cheek. "That's for taking my mind off…things…for a little while."

"Any time at all, my love," said Peter.

With breakfast finished, Oona cleared away the dishes.

Emma said, "Should we go back to my place and talk about it, or do you want to do it here?"

"I want to do it everywhere with you," said Peter. "But talking about it here might be better. Neutral territory and all."

"Okay." She signalled Oona for more coffee.

"You go first," said Peter.

"Okay. First, I get these damned keloids every January along with horrific dreams. I think I know about three women: Emmeline during the Civil War, Emelia sometime around the turn of the twentieth century, and Millie in the eighties."

Right," said Peter. "I've got Philip in January, 1865. He knows Emmeline. Patrick in January, 1905, knows Emelia."

"You seem precise about the dates," said Emma.

"In the dreams or visions, I recognize some of the references," said Peter. "I'm surprised I can pinpoint them. Usually with dreams, it's vague."

"I guess we can cross-reference my vague dreams with your precise dates," said Emma. "So, Millie takes a reservation from someone named Prescott Davidson, Emelia knows Patrick and is wary of Bart. Emmeline is assaulted by Beau."

Peter wrote everything down on a notepad, trying to keep it organized.

"Patrick is killed and tossed off a cliff by someone I didn't see clearly. Philip hates Beau and knows he's trouble for Emmeline."

They traded information for the next twenty minutes. Peter added the information he'd picked up about 1945 which neither of them had experienced.

When Peter finished, he presented the notepad to Emma.

He'd listed what few facts they knew:

> 1865 – Emmeline and Philip love each other and are killed by Beau.

> 1905 – Emelia and Patrick love each other. Someone named Bart is there to make trouble and probably kills Patrick.

> 1945 – Emily is assaulted by Ben then later found murdered. Ben is also killed.

> 1985 – Em has some kind of encounter with Prescott and Buster.

> 2020 – Emma and Peter love each other. There's trouble coming.

> Emelia, Millie, and Emma have bad dreams and keloids that seem to match the wounds inflicted on Emmeline. They also have snow globes that get broken. Except for Emma, they are maids at the inn.

"Damn," said Peter. "There's something missing. And 1945 seems incomplete, but I can read some things into those articles I found. The events sort of fit the pattern."

"Some pattern," said Emma. "Boy and girl love each other. Boy and girl get killed by evil boy."

"The woman's names are variations of the same name. So

are the last names of the man"

"What about the bad guy?" Emma looked concerned.

Peter listed them off. "Kensington twice, Kenton, Kenyon."

"Oh, shit," said Emma. "Kent."

"No way. First off, she's a woman. Second, she's not a killer." He stared at her. "Emma, I don't want you to get murdered. And I don't want to get murdered, either. What are we going to do?"

Emma registered surprise. Peter dealt with historical facts. This kind of thing was all speculation and guess work. Plus, it was fucking out there, almost supernatural. "You believe this stuff?"

"I don't know for sure, but if there's any danger to you, I can't afford to ignore it." He studied the notepad for a minute or so. "We're early."

"What do you mean?"

"1865, 1905, 1945, 1985. Every forty years. It's not due until 2025. What's going on?"

Emma smiled. "So, we've been given a chance to stop this thing way before it's supposed to happen. We know what's coming. We can avoid it."

"The dreams and all, the players seemed to know something was coming as well. Look how they fared."

"Yes, but we have an advantage. Like you said, we're early."

Emma squeezed Peter's hand. He smiled then leaned in to kiss her cheek. She decided not to mention another common element that ran throughout this whole weird mess—the O'Dales.

Chapter 12:
"And it matters what we say, every second, every day"

Bartholomew Kensington, January 18, 1905

He'd developed a taste for kaffir bitches while serving as a mercenary in South Africa. The Boers had been terrible people, but they knew how to treat the natives. So did the British. Those concentration camps where they kept their Boer prisoners, mostly women and children, and the colored natives had been a wonder to see. So much horror and privation in one small area. So many chances to view death up close. They had died in droves from starvation and disease.

A few had died at his hands while under private "interrogation." The females had been the most satisfying, especially the colored ones. And the young.

Now there was that haughty colored maid at the inn who had always treated him with veiled contempt. The look on the sissy's face when he saw Bartholomew at the reception desk last night was priceless.

I'm sure you shat your breeches, O'Dale.

No doubt O'Dale ran off to warn the bitch that her destiny had arrived and would be calling on her at the soonest possible moment.

Dreams of a tall man in a uniform doing unspeakable things in a dark room that smelled like a charnel house haunted Bartholomew's sleep. To anyone else, these would have been terrifying nightmares, but to him, they only caused him to soil the bed with his seed. He woke with a hunger he hadn't felt in years.

I need to kill something. I need to kill it slowly and painfully. I need to watch it suffer. I need to see the life drain out of its eyes.

Breakfast had been served in his suite of rooms, though to call it a suite was laughable. It earned that name simply because it had its own lavatory and the occupant was not forced to share the facilities down the hall with the lesser mortals who stayed at the inn. This privacy, and the suite's location next to the walkway to the warehouse, had served Bartholomew well during his previous stays when his sojourns into the night had provided playthings for his secret room.

There had been much work preparing the secret room in the warehouse. Something told him it had been built just for him. When he stepped inside the first time—what...twenty years ago?—it was as if he had come home. He belonged there. Bartholomew was certain he could hear the moans and screams of the many people and animals who had suffered and died in the room purely for the pleasure of...of...whom?

Bartholomew had stood there staring at the red-brown stains on the walls and floor. When he rattled the chains hanging from the ceiling, he felt a thrill run through his whole body. He became aroused with excitement by the memories of the joyous times spent here by...by...whom?

"Who are you? Tell me. I demand you tell me," he had said to the air, but no answer had come to him.

He had sensed a presence back then, and in subsequent visits it had always been there. However, he had never been able to learn anything.

Until last night. Before retiring, Bartholomew had gone over to the room to make sure it was still secure. There was no point in luring his target to her painful doom if his lair had been compromised. The moment he entered the room and saw the familiar chains and shackles, blood stains, and heard the howling wind outside the window, he knew. He had no clue as to the reason or the method. Bartholomew simply knew.

Beauregard Kensington had built this room. Beauregard had played his games here, killed here, spent some of the happiest times of his life in this very place. But Beauregard had also died here, murdered by a traitor who owed his life to his commanding officer. Shamelessly shot between the eyes by a coward who dared not face his better like a man.

O'Dale.

I'll avenge you, uncle.

When he had seen the mongrel family squatting here last night, it had been the final prompt he needed.

Bartholomew's time had come. It was his turn to play.

Beverly Kent, January 17, 2020

She woke with a scream. It wasn't as bad as the last time. She was ashamed of herself for showing such weakness. It was shock more than anything, finally realizing who she was and what she had to do.

When Beverly entered the bathroom to take a shower, she was not the least bit surprised when her reflection in the mirror showed her flaming red hair had returned in all its glory. No more hiding. It was part of what made her different from all those lesser creatures. It made her stand out in a crowd. She would bask in the adoration of those around her.

Beverly would also destroy that snivelling piece of shit who had treated her with such disrespect yesterday.

"Dawson, your time has come," she said to the stunning vision in the mirror. The smile on her face was unfamiliar, more, dare she think it, evil. Beverly chuckled. As if she could be evil. No, what she did was righteous. To hell with anyone who disagreed and stood in her way. When she felt a tingle in her loins, she said, "And I'm going to eviscerate that slut of yours as well. While you watch, helpless, you little sissy."

Unable to resist, Beverly pleasured herself while leaning on the sink. It was a little strange to be doing it this way, fingers sunk into wet and flashy folds. Her hand and fingers should have been around something rigid. No matter. Her eyes never left those of her reflection while she did it.

The longer she lasted, the more her vision blurred until the reflection staring back at her didn't look like her at all. She now seemed more masculine. Her hair looked shorter, neater, more controlled.

When *he* reached *his* peak, Beverly squeezed her eyes shut as visions flashed across their insides. Blood by the gallon, bodies hanging from nooses and chains, women and children cut to pieces and in some cases, partially devoured. All the men who were *his* eternal enemy—Dawson, Dawes, whatever—

would die. That betraying bent swine O'Dale, always in the background, always goading, always a coward. And last, her, the one *he'd* wanted from the beginning and the one *he* could never get. The one *he* would at last conquer and batter until she was unrecognizable. *He'd* feast on her heart tonight.

Beverly's orgasm was so powerful, she lost her grip on the sink and fell to the floor. She pulsed and grunted for a good five minutes before calming down enough to rise.

When she saw herself in the mirror again, she immediately picked up the huge hunting knife hanging in a sheath from the doorknob—*that wasn't there five minutes ago*—and roughly hacked at her hair until it was short enough to satisfy her new sense of style.

After a steaming hot shower, she went to dress but found her remaining clothes had been shredded. Who would do such a thing? That librarian bitch! Who else would hate Beverly enough to do something so petty? Was the stupid cow afraid Peter might return to his true love.

Me!

Not sure what to do without any clothes, Beverly went to the wardrobe. One never knew what a previous guest might have left. When she pulled open the door, she was pleased to see it had plenty of clothes on hangers. However, everything was for a man. Fuck! Worse, the things looked like something from a period movie—nothing from the twenty-first century. On the upside, they didn't smell musty or moldy and there was no evidence of moths.

She pulled out an undershirt that was made of soft cotton. It felt good against her bare skin. A regular man's shirt fit perfectly even though it hadn't been made for her. A pair of trousers looked to be from some old uniform. Civil War, perhaps? At least it wasn't made with that shoddy material from early in the war. These were properly tailored, no doubt for an officer. Like the shirt, they were a right as rain. A pair of wool socks completed her ensemble. Seeing herself in the mirror, Beverly thought she appeared quite dashing.

As luck would have it, there was an old army greatcoat that might have seen better days but would serve well in the inclement weather she saw through the window. A bad storm was brewing.

Her own boots had dried sufficiently on the radiator, so she slipped them on, tucking her trousers inside to keep them dry. She paused for a moment to wonder how it was that the trousers fit in the boots so well, as if cut especially for her footwear.

She made sure to put the journal in her bread bag. It might be useful later.

About to leave, something caught her eye reflecting light from deep in the wardrobe. Reaching in, she found an old cavalry sabre. When she unsheathed it, Beverly was overjoyed to see it had been well-maintained. The steel gleamed and the edge was razor sharp. She slung the scabbard over her neck so the weapon would be hidden under her greatcoat. No need to draw attention from the Grey Backs that infested this town.

Beverly went down to the lobby for some breakfast.

When that rat, O'Dale, spied her from behind the front desk, all the color drained from his already pale skin.

She laughed at his discomfort. "What's the matter, sissy?

Ready to wet yourself? Need to run off and find your sodomite friend?"

"You're all here," said O'Dale as if he didn't want to believe it.

"You bet your fucking ass I am," said Beverly. She looked into the empty dining room then said, "Enough of your phantom breakfasts. I need real food for the work ahead."

Turning toward the front door, she spied the broken snow globes on the shelf. Four now. *I'm free again. No one will capture me again.*

When Beverly stepped out into the cold, she took a deep breath. In spite of the icy wind, she felt refreshed, as if she'd been cooped up inside for far too long and any escape to the outside was a relief. She looked toward the library where, no doubt, Dawson and that slut were doing something depraved, and spotted the pub next door. Real food.

There was something else about the pub that drew her toward it. She didn't know what it was, but she'd find out soon enough.

When Beverly reached the spot where the cliff path turned toward the library, she heard a noise and paused. Stepping in a small niche by a door, she watched while Dawson and the slut exited the library. She'd been right! They had been engaging in debauchery like the animals they were. Scum!

Beverly's two worst enemies walked to the pub then entered.

So much for her getting breakfast. There was no way she would go in there while those two sat and laughed at her. On the other hand, what did she care what they thought? They'd be dead soon enough, anyway.

Walking past the library front door, Beverly glanced over and had an idea. Perhaps the stupid bitch had forgotten to lock the door. That would give Beverly the opportunity to do some exploration and maybe find more information that would be helpful.

Providence was on her side! When she tried the door handle, it turned. The moronic cow had indeed forgotten to lock the door. With that sort of incompetence, she and Dawson were perfect for each other.

Beverly quickly slipped into the library. She made sure to lock the door to stop anyone from interrupting her search. Then she made a beeline for the office. That whore might have something of value there.

Beverly ransacked the office. She pulled drawers from the desk and dumped the contents on the floor. For the most part, she didn't bother to see what came out. She began to feel pleasure in the destruction. When she'd emptied every possible drawer and cabinet, pushed everything off the desk and shelves, Beverly stood amongst the mess and thought. Something made her look up.

Yes. Upstairs, beyond where the filthy public was allowed to go.

She found the staircase to the next floor and proceeded up to the fourth. Here she found a large, sliding barn door. The wood looked ancient. There didn't appear to be a lock of any sort, so Beverly shoved it to the side. She pushed so hard, one of the door wheels popped off the rail. The weight of the wood dragged the door down until it bent the rail. It would be useless.

Beverly smiled.

Walking through the opening, Beverly had a choice of turning left or right. Her instinct told her to turn left, so she turned right to find out what might not be so important. It turned out to be very important. She'd found the slut's lair.

Not bothering to search for anything, Beverly walked through the apartment destroying anything not nailed down. Pictures were torn from the walls and flung across the room to shatter, books and knickknacks swept from shelves. In the kitchen, she opened a window and let in a cold Atlantic wind. She then threw the microwave, blender, toaster, dishware, and cutlery out into the crashing waves below.

In the bedroom, Beverly got a nasty surprise. The bed was rumpled, and she could almost taste the stench of their rutting. Using the sabre she had found in the wardrobe, she slashed the pillows and mattress, then she opened the closet and cut apart any clothes hanging up. A chest of drawers was upended, spilling out its contents. Feeling particularly nasty, Beverly stood in the middle of the pile of clothes, dropped her pants and underwear, and pissed and shit on that bitch's things. She grabbed a white cashmere sweater and used it to clean herself.

When she had destroyed as much of the slut's apartment as she could, Beverly went back out to the hall and went where her instinct had told her to go in the first place.

It was obvious this part of the floor had hardly been visited in the last few years. Dust lay thick on the floor and there was a musty odor like wet dog and rotting paper. Though the atmosphere was not welcoming, Beverly felt comfortable up here. She passed another barn door and had the urge to stop and check it out. However, she wanted to see what the rest of the floor held.

It turned out there wasn't much else to see. Some rotting boxes and bales of cotton were all she found. At the far end, there was yet another barn door, this one padlocked. Picking up a crowbar conveniently lying on the floor by a crate, Beverly worked on the lock until it snapped open. Sliding back the door, she met utter darkness. Waiting a short while, her eyes adapted, and she could pick out a few things. A staircase led down somewhere, and the stairwell turned left a few feet away from the door.

Curious, Beverly walked to the turn. She was stunned by what met her: a walkway to the inn. This was what she had seen on the other side of that heavy door by her room. That lying piece of garbage O'Dale had told her the structure didn't exist. Even the whore had suggested it had fallen down over a century ago.

Beverly laughed. Its depth surprised her. Normally her laughter was more high-pitched, but this was almost frightening in its intensity. She knew who would be making the crossing from the inn to the warehouse via the walkway.

Returning to the main area of the floor, Beverly went to the barn door that had tempted her earlier. The moment she touched the wood, it felt warm and welcoming, as if she was with an old friend. A key hung from the wall next to the door. It seemed like a stupid place to put a key if someone wanted the door kept closed. But Beverly had been dealing with idiots for most of her life, so this didn't surprise her.

She used the key on the lock. It turned smoothly and without noise as if it had been maintained with care. When she slid it open, her nose was assailed with a bizarre mix of smells. There was rot and decay, like something had died recently. She recognized the coppery scent of blood. It was very strong and seemed fresh, which made no sense. Underlying the stronger smells was the pleasant aroma of cooked meat. Pork. Beverly's mouth watered and she realized how hungry she was. She needed to find food quickly.

Across the room was the outline of a large window. Beverly walked to it, feeling like she was home. If she had ever experienced it for real, she thought this is what Christmas would be like. Warm and happy with a heightened sense of anticipation.

Beverly pulled open the shutters and was treated to a beautiful sight. Wycliffe Bay stretched out before her; rough waves pounded the cliffs below. The sound brought back pleasant memories of shoving people through the window to their deaths. No. They were already dead. By the time they went through the window, they were nothing more than offal. Beverly giggled and thought she could feel a growing erection. But that was impossible since she didn't have the right equipment.

Across the bay, she could see the old fort where Paul whatever had been stationed.

Who's he? Another Dawson?

Another victim, no doubt. They'd all gone over the cliff. Small wonder the current Dawson had such a fear of heights.

He'd practically wet himself if he got close to a cliff. Beverly looked forward to introducing him to her favorite garbage disposal.

Her stomach gurgled.

"I need something to eat. Now."

She remembered something she had seen yesterday, on her way back to the inn in the afternoon. A minivan full of animals waiting to be hunted. They had pulled in next door, at the pub where she had been going before her most fortuitous detour.

Beverly turned to leave but bumped into the table by the stove. Everything went black.

Bartholomew Kensington, January 18, 1905

He'd been furious that he couldn't find the slut. No doubt, that sissy O'Dale had secreted her somewhere within the inn, or, perhaps, had already sent her away. Whatever the case, O'Dale would pay for his audacity at interfering with Bartholomew's plans.

You'll watch me kill her, then I'll make you devour some part of her. No! I'll remove your pecker and feed it to her while you watch. Then I'll cut off something of hers.

He giggled, causing a passing couple to stare at him.

"What are you looking at? You want to confront me? You want to feel pain? Just say the word." Bartholomew's bloodlust was in high gear after disposing of that interloper Dawes. Thrusting his sabre through the man's guts hadn't been nearly as satisfying as it should have been. He needed some release. "Well?"

The woman cowered in fear. Her companion, hardly more than a boy, looked afraid, but stood his ground, attempting to be a man. "Sir," said the boy with a shaky voice. "You dishonor the lady. I shall demand an apology."

"Fuck off, you worthless piece of offal," said Bartholomew with his face mere inches from the boy's. "I know who you are, and I know who your father is. Say one more word and I shall see to it that he loses everything and your pathetic family goes to the poorhouse."

The boy stepped back, eyes wide in terror. Bartholomew almost smiled when he detected an aroma that informed him the boy had, indeed, shat himself.

"Remove yourself from my sight, worm, or I'll make you watch while I fuck your lady friend here in the ass. You'd like that, wouldn't you?"

"Sh...sh...she's my sister, sir. Please don't harm her." The boy shook so badly he could hardly stand.

"Even better, worm. I'll make you fuck her first." The girl attempted to scream, but only a squeak came out. Bartholomew gave the pair what he hoped was his most evil and fearsome smile. They stepped back. "Go! Now!"

The pair ran along the street and around the corner. The poor worm left a brown trail in his wake.

Bartholomew laughed then held his breath.

Walking toward him from the direction of the tavern next to the warehouse was the object of his murderous lust. Head down to avoid the freezing wind, it didn't notice him. He stepped back into a recess next to the warehouse door and waited for it to get closer. There were no other people on the street.

When the animal was opposite him, Bartholomew reached out, grabbed its shoulder, and spun it to face him. Shock registered on its face for a mere second before he punched with all his strength. There was a loud crack as its jaw broke. It fell into his arms. Treating it as nothing more than a sack of flesh, Bartholomew tossed it over his shoulder and strode to the side door of the warehouse.

Upon reaching his room, he tossed his prize to the floor. He picked up one of the tiny playthings from the night before. It was the female he had partially consumed. Bartholomew opened the window to the sea then tossed it out. The rest of the brood quickly followed.

Ten minutes later, with the trash disposed of, the animal was naked and trussed up like the pig he believed it to be. Bartholomew heaved on the pulley and watched while it rose up to hang with its feet a few inches above the straw-covered floor. He smiled when it woke and tried to speak, but the shattered jaw made anything other than a grunt impossible. Blood dripped from its smashed mouth. Several pearly white teeth pierced its lower lip.

"Don't worry, my pretty little pig. You'll have company soon enough." He punched it as hard as he could in the stomach. Bloody vomit spewed forth, narrowly missing Bartholomew's heavy coat.

Bartholomew pulled his sabre from its scabbard. Standing in front of it, he poked it with the point until its eyes opened and looked down at him.

"A little preparation, pig," he said. He lightly sawed the blade across its belly. Blood flowed freely. Then he ran the blade from its disgusting groin to just below the teats. For a final touch, he ran the blade around its neck creating a bloody necklace.

He left the room, but didn't bother with the padlock. It was a Saturday night and most of the minions who worked in the warehouse had already gone home. The few who were left had no reason at all to come up to the fourth floor. Besides, it wouldn't take him long to bring the sissy back here.

Bartholomew crossed the walkway over to the inn and entered the hall on the fourth floor near his rooms. The sound of a piano reached his ears. Good, O'Dale was here. He boldly walked to the staircase then down to the lobby. There was no one in sight. O'Dale sat at the piano playing that foul so-called music. He was completely unaware that his doom stood behind him.

"I need you, sissy. Now," said Bartholomew in his most authoritative voice.

O'Dale's military training kicked in and he immediately stood to attention at the sound of his commanding officer barking an order. "Sir," he said.

"With me." Bartholomew walked back to the stairs.

O'Dale followed without questioning the reason. When they reached the fourth floor, Bartholomew pointed at the door to the walkway. "There." O'Dale opened the heavy wooden door and entered the passage.

"What is this all about, Kensington?"

"So, the sissy has grown balls. Good. No questions, just keep moving. You'll find out soon enough. And show me the respect I deserve."

"I am," said O'Dale.

Bartholomew smiled.

This is going to be so much fun.

He guided O'Dale to the secret room then pushed him through the door. Before O'Dale could react to the sight that met him, Bartholomew drew his revolver from a pocket in his coat and brought the handle down on the back of O'Dale's head. He fell to the floor in a heap.

It didn't take very long to tie up the unconscious man.

Bartholomew waited for O'Dale to wake up. When he did, O'Dale's eyes focused on the thing hanging from the ceiling beam.

"Kensington! What have you done, you animal?" O'Dale struggled against his bonds, but they held him in place.

Never taking his eyes from his captive, Bartholomew walked over to O'Dale. He undid his fly and pulled out his pecker. "Big enough for you, sissy?" The fool's eyes were glued to the thing waving in front of his face. He looked anything but pleased. With a small laugh, Bartholomew urinated over O'Dale. When he finished, he returned to the trussed pig. On the way, he picked up a hammer and a barrel stave. The stave had been sharpened at one end.

Standing behind the pig, Bartholomew lined up the sharp end of the stave. "Watch, O'Dale." He swung the hammer.

The object of his pleasure grunted, but made no other sound.

"No!" O'Dale jumped to his feet and ran at Bartholomew. He managed to get within five feet of him before the chains went tight and yanked O'Dale back. There were tears in his eyes.

Bartholomew raised the hammer again. This time, he hoped the pig would do more than grunt.

"Stop, you swine." The voice came from the open door. Bartholomew hadn't noticed it opening because he had been so focused on his game.

Bartholomew swung the hammer again. This time, he achieved a little more than he expected when the cuts on the pig's abdomen split open. He'd cut too far, and it had emptied out.

"I said stop," he heard, this time with a shaky voice.

At first, he didn't recognize the intruder, he was very old, but Beauregard knew the man.

"The traitor," said Bartholomew. "The coward that shot me in the head all those years ago. What do you want?"

The intruder looked a little confused, then said, "That must be Beau speaking through you. I knew he'd come back." The traitor waved a rifle at Bartholomew. "Drop the hammer and step away from her." Bartholomew did as instructed. "Now, free Oscar."

When the chains fell from Oscar's wrists, he ran over to the pig. "Emelia?" The pig made no sound.

Damn, it's already dead.

"You've spoiled my fun," he said to the traitor.

"Oscar. How is she?"

"Dead, Uncle Obadiah. This piece of shit has killed her."

Bartholomew saw the rifle stock swing toward his head then saw nothing but black. When he opened his eyes, he was on the floor in his secret room with his wrists bound behind his back.

"Still a coward, O'Dale. Untie me and face me like a man."

"You're no man, Beau or Bart or whoever the hell you are today. Your time has come to an end. Get up."

Bartholomew stood on shaky legs. The rifle must have struck him harder than he realized. He felt a little dizzy. The traitor still pointed the rifle at Bartholomew's chest. The sissy stood behind his uncle with something in his hands.

The traitor said, "Get down on your knees."

"Make up your mind, traitor." Kneeling, Bartholomew watched while the sissy gave what he was holding to the traitor and took the rifle. His heart skipped a beat when he saw what the old man held: a stick of dynamite.

"You haven't got the guts," he said to the old man. The sissy looked scared, not a surprise, but also like he had no idea what was happening. "It does." He nodded his head toward the hanging carcass.

"Oscar," said the traitor. "I failed Emmeline again. I can't let her be found like this. I intend to give her some dignity."

"I don't understand," said the sissy. *Idiot.* "Emmeline?"

The traitor stared at him. Bartholomew wanted to bite off the little shit's finger.

"That creature has killed a good woman in the most heinous and dishonorable way," said the traitor. "Twice! And I failed to save her both times. I failed to save my friend as well.

Go, Oscar. Live your life."

The sissy didn't move. "What are you going to do, Uncle Obadiah?"

Laughing, Bartholomew roared and tried to leap at him, but couldn't get any leverage and fell on his side. He wriggled until he was back on his knees. The anger burned inside him. These two would die in the most painful way and for the longest time possible. Bartholomew had learned a few things from the savages out west and the heathens in China. The death of a thousand cuts, or skinning to make a hat or pouch for his tools.

"I've lived a good life. Time to finish this," said the traitor. "I'm going to destroy this killing room. I hope by doing that, this creature will also be destroyed for eternity."

"No!"

This time Bartholomew gained his feet. He rushed at the traitor, knocked him aside into the quivering form of the sissy. While the two fools tried to untangle themselves, Bartholomew ran out the door and over to the walkway. If he could make it across and get to his room, he'd be able to put an end to this farce.

He ran as if his life depended on it. Bartholomew Kensington had never run from anything in his life, but there was too much at stake now. He heard the idiots pursuing him. The traitor was yelling something at the sissy, but Bartholomew couldn't understand what it was.

Halfway across the walkway, he heard the thumping of running feet then felt something slam into his back. His face smashed into the floor and everything went black again.

Beverly Kent, January 17, 2020

It was so cold. Her eyes opened slowly; her lids were stuck together, causing a little pain when they parted. She raised herself off the floor, feeling wind at her back. Everything she could see was covered with frost.

She felt empty and shivered. There was an ache in her neck where the sabre hilt had dug in while she was unconscious. Her backside and fingers were completely numb. Blowing on them, Beverly surveyed her surroundings. She was still in the secret room. No wonder she was frozen: the window shutters had blown open letting in the cold Atlantic gale. She quickly pulled the shutters closed.

Leaning against the table, Beverly realized it had been dark outside. How long had she been out? Before everything went black, she'd been on her way to that pub next door to get something to eat. Forget that. After what she had just experienced, she needed to know more. Beverly reached for her bread bag where she'd placed the journal. It would tell her what had happened in 1905. The moment she had that thought, she realized she no longer had the bag.

Where did I leave it? Did I drop it?

"Fuck, Dawson!"

Beverly rushed out the door and made her way to the stairs. She had to get back to the inn to sort herself out. Dawson might be there. Before going down the stairs, something told her to check around the corner. When she looked, everything seemed as it should be.

Rushing across the walkway leading to the inn, Beverly had a momentary thought that something didn't quite add up. She dismissed the thought as befuddlement because of her current situation. A bit of rest, some coffee, and a better plan for dealing with her enemies would sort her out.

At the other end of the walkway, Beverly pushed open the heavy wood door and entered the inn. Her room was on her left, so she went in. She sat on the bed and immediately fell asleep.

Chapter 13:
"Ain't it plain as January on your face" (2)

Emma Ranahan, January 17, 2020

"So, what do you think we should do now?" Peter looked at Emma while he waited for her to answer. It appeared he had placed her in charge. Emma liked the idea, but it seemed a little strange Peter would so easily take a secondary role.

"Why are you asking me? You're the man who's supposed to keep me alive. You've got the historical background to know what's going on. Come up with a plan." Emma watched Peter's face. He was clearly mulling things over in his head. She wanted him to be more assertive.

"I don't know," he said. "I'm so used to being stuck in the background when it comes to Beverly. It's hard to think for myself right now."

"Come on. This is about stopping Beverly from doing us harm. There's no reason for you to be kowtowing to her or waiting for her to give you approval. You're not under her control anymore. Remember? Now, get a grip."

Emma knew speaking to him this way was bad. He'd been beaten down so much by that bitch that he was still feeling useless and inadequate. In the past, he'd been brave, running to her aid even if it meant he was killed—over and over again. That cycle had to stop, and she needed Peter to be strong.

"Bear with me. This isn't some departmental infighting or intrigue. We're talking about someone who's out for blood. This is serious stuff here, not academic bullshit. I've never had to deal with this kind of thing before."

Emma laughed.

Peter looked offended. "What's so damned funny?"

"I'm sorry, it's all just a little ridiculous when you think about it. Here we are, two people in the twenty-first century, talking about past lives and some reincarnated maniac who's out to get us." When he tried to move away, she put a hand on his wrist, still afraid to break contact. "What I mean is, it's all happening so fast. Yesterday, I didn't even know you, yet here we are, stuck with each other."

"I could never think of it as being stuck with you. I've been waiting my whole life for this opportunity. Now that I've found you, there's no way I'm letting you go." He paused for a moment, staring off as if deep in thought. "That is, as long as you're okay with it."

"For fuck's sake, of course I'm okay with it. Damn. Last night, I stuck a piece of fruit in my…" Her face got hot with embarrassment. "How could you possibly think I'm not okay with it?"

He smiled. "Is it too soon to run away and get married?"

"Yes." She saw disappointment in his face. "I mean, we have to make sure we don't get murdered first. If it wasn't for that, we'd be off on a honeymoon somewhere warm where we could…" She blushed again.

"What?"

"Sorry. My mind keeps going to the most disgusting places. I've never had these kinds of…dirty thoughts fill my head so much."

"Tell me about it. The moment I first laid eyes on you, I wanted to get in your pants. I never thought it would literally happen. I just wish they were…" It was Peter's turn to blush.

"Yesterday's?" He nodded, and Emma slapped his arm. "Pig." She let her hand drop to his lap and gripped his hardness. She squeezed and said, "They're back at my place, waiting for you." She felt him pulse.

Someone cleared their throat. She quickly yanked her hand away from Peter's lap and smacked it on the bottom of the table. Emma looked up to see Oona's smiling face.

"You two are filthy," she said. "But, please, could you speak up? I missed a couple of the juicier bits."

"Sorry, Oona," said Peter. "She's got me out of control."

"Of course she has, my boy. She's been waiting so long for you to show up, the excitement is clouding her judgement. Just warn me if you lose control. I'll clear the table so I don't lose any crockery."

"This is all getting a little out of hand," said Emma. As much fun as she was having, there was serious stuff to consider.

"I wanted to give you this," said Oona. She placed a shoulder bag on the table. "One of the kids from upstairs found it a little while ago in front of the library. She gave it to me in case I knew who it belonged to. When I looked inside, I knew it was yours."

Emma didn't recognize the bag.

"It's Beverly's," said Peter as if reading her mind.

She opened it and took out Oscar's 1905 journal. "That bitch. She did take it."

"Can I see that?" said Peter. The second his hand touched the cover, all Emma saw was black.

Patrick Dawes, January 18, 1905

"Sodomite!" said Bartholomew Kensington. "I knew it was you disembarking from the train."

"What do you want, Kensington?" said Patrick. He spat out the remains of his cigar.

"I want to know why you're in my town," said Kensington.

"Your town? Just because you have a wealthy family, it doesn't mean you own Wycliffe Point."

Kensington laughed. "Yes, it does, sodomite. We've owned it for over a hundred years. Now, what are you doing here?" He shoved the barrel of his revolver into Patrick's ribs.

"I'm going to the inn," said Patrick, reluctant to say anything else.

"Ah, planning some buggery with that sissy O'Dale. I thought as much." He prodded Patrick with the revolver. "Well, get going."

Ten minutes later, the pair stood near the front door to the inn.

"No, not in there," said Kensington. He motioned to the south side of the inn.

Around the corner, Patrick saw a walkway that connected the inn to a large warehouse. It looked to be about four stories up. When they got to a heavy wood door under the walkway, Kensington slid it open and pushed Patrick in. Using a lantern, he led Patrick up four flights of stairs.

"That door over there," said Kensington. About thirty feet

into the large room, there appeared to be a smaller section that was walled off, surrounded by large shipping crates. Once inside the room, Kensington shoved Patrick away and locked the door. "Welcome to my little hidey hole, sodomite."

The room stank of death and, oddly, stew. The floor was slippery with what could only be congealing blood. Patrick knew blood when he saw and smelled it. *What had happened in this room?*

"You can't keep me here, Kensington," said Patrick. "I'm expected."

Kensington laughed. "So, you never arrived. No one met you, except me, and no one will miss you. I've dealt with you before and I'll do it again."

"What the hell are you talking about?" Patrick said, unsure what Kensington was talking about. Though they had spent many years in the same cavalry troop, their paths had rarely crossed. Patrick managed to stay out of Kensington's way, and Kensington spent lots of time with the higher ups doing who knew what.

"I don't know, sodomite," said Kensington. He seemed confused. "It doesn't matter."

Emma Ranahan, January 17, 2020

"Did you see that?" Emma stared at Peter who shook his head. "Tell me you saw it."

Peter nodded. "I did. But how? How can we share the same hallucination?"

"I don't think it was an hallucination," said Emma. "I think it was a memory. And we shared it because I have a death grip on your wrist. Our flesh is touching."

"You mean, like we're one person now?" Peter chuckled. "That's ridiculous."

"Then explain it." Emma felt a building anger. It wasn't directed at Peter, but at whatever forces were doing this to them. Someone or something had a lot to answer for. "Well?"

Peter looked sheepish. "We're one person when we touch. Flesh to flesh, not just, you know, arm in arm. Imagine what it would be like if we were both naked and touching more."

Emma shivered. "I can and you know what it was like." She gave it some thought. "You know, if we were touching more when we had these…episodes or memories, maybe they wouldn't be so bad."

"You think we could control them?"

Emma shook her head. "I don't think so. They're memories. We can't change the past. We can just make it more bearable to remember."

"So, this journal…" Peter held it up. "Do you think it could help us?"

"Can't hurt," she said. "Let's start here." She opened the journal to the January 19. It seemed like the logical place to start because all the weirdness began around then.

"I'll leave you to it, then," said Oona.

"I'm so sorry, Oona," said Emma. "I forgot you were there."

"With this hunk, I'm not surprised. Coffee?"

"Please."

Emma and Peter read the journal in silence. When they had finished the entry for January 19, 1905, they sat back. Both were breathing heavily. Emma's eyes burned forcing her to hold back the tears. Peter looked like he was struggling, too.

"Bartholomew was some kind of evil bastard," said Peter. "I remember meeting Emelia at the World's Fair. That came to me the first night I was here. I also remember being killed by Bart." He rubbed his chest. "Do I always get stabbed in the chest and tossed off a cliff?"

"It would seem so," said Emma. "I'm glad I haven't had any memories of being murdered. I don't know how I would take it."

"Trust me," said Peter. "You don't want those. I've seen what he did." His face went pale. "I can't let her do that to you, I can't."

"I hope you don't have to die for me. Not again."

"I'll do what I can. Believe me, I don't want to die either."

"Shall we continue? Find out what happened after we were killed?" Emma laughed. "That sounds so messed up."

"Yeah." They both drained their coffees. She didn't remember Oona coming back with the pot.

"Okay," said Emma. "January the twentieth."

Oscar O'Dale, Journal entry for Friday, January 20, 1905

For the residents and employees of the inn, all has returned to normal. For myself, life can never be the same.

Workmen quickly cleared away what little rubble remained of the walkway. The doors in the inn and warehouse were secured to prevent some unfortunate from exiting one of the buildings and dropping to the cobbled path below. Plans were made to brick up the openings when the weather was more clement.

Claiming exhaustion from the previous day's events, I retired to my room. When sufficient time had passed, I was able to leave the inn and return to the killing room.

Emelia remained where I had laid her last night. The fire in the stove had gone out so the room was quite cold. This meant that corruption of her body had not taken its course. The room didn't reek of death, though I could still smell the stench of murder. I cleaned Emelia as best I could and used some fishing line to sew up her wounds. Prior to that, I had gone to her room at the inn and taken some clothing in which I dressed my dear friend. When she was fully clothed, and her dignity restored, she looked as though she was sleeping rather than dead. I tied a scarf about her neck to hide the gash there that her blouse collar did not reach.

With her body thus prepared, I placed Emelia in a canvas sack and sewed the opening shut. The ground was too hard to dig for a proper grave, so I waited until late afternoon when darkness fell and carried her down the cliff path to a small beach below the inn. It was beastly cold, but I ignored it while attempting to give my friend a decent burial. I knew if her body was discovered by the authorities, Emelia would have been consigned to a pauper's grave outside of the local cemetery. I also knew there would be no investigation into the death of a maid, particularly one of the negro race. It would be yet one more indignity thrust upon an innocent woman.

I managed to dig away a little bit of sand between some rocks at the base of the cliff. Into this slight depression, I lowered Emelia then covered her. To be sure no wild beast would ravage her grave, I placed rocks on top. She was far above the tide line, and it was unlikely that the sea water would uncover her even in the roughest weather.

With tears in my eyes and a lump in my throat, and though I had no religion of my own, I said a brief prayer over Emelia then returned to the killing room. I threw much of what the room contained out the window and down to the water. I wanted no evidence of any activity to remain. The belongings of the family who had been residing in the room went first. It saddened me when I discovered a small doll wedged behind the stove. The bastard must have killed the children. I could only hope they met their ends quickly.

The death of my friend Patrick was confirmed when I discovered his billfold in a crevice between the floorboards under the window. Upon opening it, I found his photograph of Emelia. She looked so happy. These days were compounding horror with never-ending sadness. The three people I cared about the most were gone, and I had to live with the knowledge that I was unable to prevent their deaths.

I still wonder at the final words of Uncle Obadiah: "If this doesn't end it, be ready to protect her again." Did he really believe that all we had endured had happened before and might be repeated at some future date?

I did not welcome this burden, but knew I had to be prepared. All I needed to know was how.

Peter Dawson, January 17, 2020

"We have to find her. She deserves a decent burial." Peter had difficulty speaking because of the huge lump in his throat. He wanted to be sick. The very idea that a previous incarnation of his beloved Emma could be lying somewhere close by made him want to scream. It also made him want to do serious damage to Beverly to stop her from causing any more harm.

Yet, what harm had Beverly caused? Besides treating people like cattle and only thinking of herself, what had Beverly really done to deserve such a horrible fate? A broken snow globe hardly constituted a major offense.

"Thank you," said Emma. "But I don't know if I can help search for her. What would happen if we were both there at the same time?"

Peter took Emma's hand in his. Their thighs were still touching, and no matter what Peter did, Emma maintained some sort of physical contact with him. He liked it and hoped it would continue.

"This isn't a time paradox like you see in movies. I don't think the world will end if the two of you are together. You're different incarnations, not the same person in a different time."

"Are you listening to yourself?" Emma had a small smile on her face. It instantly made Peter feel better. "We're talking as if all this reincarnation stuff is real."

"It feels real to me every time I have one of those memories or read something in a journal or book."

"I hear what you're saying. It still seems surreal."

"I wonder if Beverly is experiencing anything like this," said Peter. Though she was no longer someone he cared about, he couldn't help but be concerned about her. They did have some history, after all, even if it wasn't the most pleasant experience. And she was a fellow human being.

"Has she seemed different to you? I mean, I wouldn't know. She's been nothing but a complete bitch to me since the moment we met."

"Her mood swings are pretty severe," said Peter. "I can usually set her off just by thinking the wrong thing. But yesterday at the library, she was totally off. One second all friendly and quiet, the next nearly tearing off my head. To be honest, if these earlier incarnations of her—Beau, Bart, Buster, or Ben —are having any influence on her, I can't really tell."

"We need to be careful around her. If she is being influenced, she might be getting ready to do something nasty to us. Do you think she would go so far as to try and kill us?"

Peter thought then said, "I honestly don't know. I've seen

her do some pretty horrible stuff to people. And her vicious tongue can cause untold harm. But actual physical assault?" He shrugged.

"When's the last time you saw her?" Emma took a sip of coffee. Oona was in stealth mode again. "I passed her on the library stairs yesterday around noon."

"Yeah, it would have been shortly before that for me. I've been a little, shall we say, preoccupied with something since then."

Emma wrapped her arms around Peter's shoulders and gave him a peck on the cheek. "And what would that preoccupation be?"

"Sheer bloody perfection," said Peter. He looked into Emma's eyes and his heart missed a beat then melted. "I still have trouble saying it."

"I love you, Peter."

"I love you, Emma." They kissed.

Holding up Oscar's journal, Emma said, "We do need to fill in some gaps. They're 1945 and 1985."

"Any ideas?"

She nodded. "I know just the man. The old police chief, Sol Winthrop. He lives in a house on the cliff. It's up the road a little way. We can walk if the weather's not too harsh."

"Let's check."

Holding hands, Peter and Emma walked to the back of the pub where some windows overlooked the bay. Outside, the sun shone and the water looked fairly calm. It wouldn't be a bad walk.

Peter leaned closer to the window and saw the edge of the cliff under the sill. His head spun.

Prescott Davidson, January 18, 1985

Prescott had known from his earliest days that he wanted to be a writer. Discovering last year that his father, Reginald, had been a professional Tiddlywinks player had given him the push he needed to pursue his desired career. Thirty-five wasn't too late to start. It was unfortunate his father had died in a fall while Prescott was serving in Vietnam. As luck would have it, a distant relative at a family reunion mentioned that one of Reginald's old teammates was the manager of an inn in New Jersey.

Several letters and a train ride to Wycliffe Point later, Prescott stepped out of his cab in front of the Inn on the Cliff. The bright sun made the front of the inn shimmer. For a moment, Prescott thought he saw a covered walkway between the inn and the library next door, but he dismissed it as an afterimage of the façade of the inn.

Walking across the inn's parking lot, Prescott was struck by how familiar the place felt. He'd never been here before. Hell, he'd never been in New Jersey before. Yet he felt like he belonged here.

"I'm just tired from the trip," he said to the air. He pulled out his pocket watch and checked the time. Good. Not too early to check in.

Inside the inn, it was warm, cozy, and welcoming. He was

home. Prescott walked to the front desk where a tall, thin man with a goatee stood going through some papers. He knew the man, Oliver O'Dale—Manager according to the brass nameplate on the counter—but for the life of him, couldn't remember how.

O'Dale looked up when he heard Prescott and smiled. "May I be of service?"

Prescott held out his hand. "Prescott Davidson. I have a reservation."

O'Dale's eyes went wide. "Oh, yes. I should have recognized you. Welcome, Mr. Davidson. I hope your stay this time is longer and proves more…enjoyable."

"What?" said Prescott. "I've never been here before. And please, call me Prescott."

O'Dale studied Prescott's face. "Hmm, yes, my apologies, Prescott. You resemble someone from my past. I'm Oliver." He reached into a drawer and pulled out a registration card which he passed to his guest. "If you would be so kind as to fill out the card, I will have your bags taken to your room."

Prescott held up his briefcase and a small knapsack. "This is all I have. Thanks. Are there a lot of people staying here?" He took out a pen to fill in the card.

"The inn is practically empty, but that's not surprising given that January is not exactly the height of the tourist season in New Jersey," said Oliver. "Not many people are interested in the weird and wonderful of the state, including the mysterious lights of 1945. Add terrible winter storms and frigid Atlantic winds to the mix, and Wycliffe Point is *the* place to avoid."

"That's too bad," said Prescott. "But I'm not really here as a tourist. I'm doing some research for a book about professional Tiddlywinks. Perhaps you know who I'm looking for? You have the same last name. Owen O'Dale?"

"My uncle," said Oliver. "He'll probably be here soon. It's that time again."

"Say what?" said Prescott.

"Every forty years," said Oliver, "a snow globe gets broken and starts events rolling." He pointed toward a shelf across the lobby. It held two broken snow globes and a pile of glass.

As Prescott contemplated this, trying to figure out what the hell the man was talking about, he heard a thump from behind him. He turned quickly and spied what he assumed was a maid coming down the stairs. She carried a bucket, but no mop. There appeared to be a huge stain on the front of her unusually long dress and apron. To Prescott, she looked like something out of an old Western.

What made her appearance more unusual was the sunlight flooding in through the huge window on the landing. There was a halo around the woman, and she seemed a little blurry and slightly out of focus.

When the maid reached the bottom of the stairs and came toward him, Prescott gasped upon seeing her clearly. There was something familiar about her, and he had felt an instant warmth toward the young lady. No, it was more than simple warmth. It was a need to be protective, which startled him because he had never had the least interest in the company of the fairer sex, or even in the company of other men. There was another, unfamiliar feeling welling up within him. It tickled and made him want to laugh and be happy.

"My word, you're beautiful," said Prescott. When she smiled, he realized he had spoken a little too loudly. "I'm so sorry, miss."

"Ranahan. Millie Ranahan," she said.

"Is there anything I can do for you today, Miss Ranahan?" *What the hell does that mean? Why would I ask that?* Prescott felt like an idiot and wanted to run and hide.

"Perhaps it's because you are so reliable and ready to serve, Mr., um, it's Davidson this time, isn't it? Hasn't it been that way since the beginning?" she said. "And please, call me Em."

They stared at each other in silence. Prescott wasn't sure what to do now. *I'm so confused and I've only been here five minutes. And why do I sense impending doom?*

Millie shook her head and said, "I'm sorry, Mr. Davidson. I haven't a clue what that means or even what I'm thinking. I'm not usually this scatter-brained, but ever since I arrived at Wycliffe Point, I haven't been able to think clearly."

Oliver cleared his throat. "Millie has been with us for only a short time, Prescott. She hasn't quite got the feel of the place yet."

Prescott nodded, pretending he understood.

The front door burst open, and a man walked in.

Millie turned to face the new arrival. At the same time, she and Oliver said, "Fuck."

The stranger stopped and looked at the three people at the front desk. A smile spread across his face.

"It's so nice to be welcomed," he said as he set his suitcase down next to Millie. He nodded to her, then let his eyes drift over her, clearly assessing her. His smile grew wider, and he said, "Nice."

Millie shivered but said nothing.

"That's no way to speak to a lady," said Prescott, more offended than he expected.

The stranger looked over Prescott and huffed. "Another loser." He turned to Oliver and said, "Buster Kenyon. I have a reservation."

Momentarily flustered, Oliver retrieved a registration card and passed it to Kenyon. "Of course, Mister Kenyon. If you would be so kind as to fill this out, I'll have my man show you to your room."

As he signed, Kenyon said, "Not a negro, I assume. I won't have one of them touching my belongings." He looked at Millie and pointed. "For that, I'd make an exception."

Millie sighed then said, "Here we go again. Will this never end?" With downcast eyes, she turned and walked up the stairs.

The three men watched her go until she turned left at the second-floor landing and disappeared.

"Nice ass," said Kenyon. "I'm definitely going to have fun with her."

"We'll see about that, Kenyon," said Oliver. He came around the front desk and picked up Kenyon's suitcase. "Follow me," he said and proceeded up the stairs without waiting to see if his guest was behind him.

"I'll come, too," said Prescott. He suddenly felt protective of Oliver and didn't want to leave him alone with this pig of a man. *Buster! What an asshole name.*

Oliver walked up three flights of stairs, turned right at the top, and led Kenyon to his room. Handing Kenyon the room key, Oliver left without another word. Prescott followed.

When they were well away from Kenyon, Prescott said, "I feel like a bit of an idiot. I honestly don't know what I would have done if he'd tried anything with Millie."

"You would have stood up for her like the honorable man you have always been, Prescott," said Oliver. "You're down on the second floor."

Perhaps this time I can stop the killings. Prescott paused and tried to clear his head. "I keep having the most bizarre thoughts, Oliver. It's like I expect something to happen."

Oliver looked at him with a sad expression on his face. That told Prescott all he needed to know.

Damn. Can I endure this again?

They paused on the second-floor landing when they saw Millie approaching. She carried her bucket in her right hand. In her left was something he couldn't identify. She had been crying and it broke Prescott's heart to see her like this. She stood in front of them and held out her left hand. Prescott now recognized a shattered snow globe. Inside were the broken remains of a tiny inn. The sharp glass had cut Millie's fingers, but she didn't seem to notice.

"I knocked it off my table. Now it's my fault. I can't go through this again," she said. "We both know how it ends. The scars hardly ever go away now."

Oliver placed a hand on her elbow and said, "Please. Be patient. My uncle hasn't arrived yet. Perhaps this time he'll save you."

"I wish," she said. A tear slid down her cheek. "But we both know it's inevitable. He's too strong, and I'm too weak." Millie closed her eyes. "It hurts so much. I can't do it again."

"But there's no way to avoid it, Millie. It has to play out like it always does."

"Can I help?" Prescott looked from one to the other. It all still confused him, but he also knew he had a part in whatever was going on here.

She shook her head. "No, Prescott. Thank you. Oliver, I can change things this time. I have a gun."

Oliver gasped. "That won't stop him."

"It's not for him. I'm going to use it on myself. Deny him his pleasure."

"No you can't. I won't allow it."

"You can't stop me, Oliver, any more than you can stop him." She leaned forward and kissed Oliver's cheek. "Goodbye, my friend. Until the next time."

She looked Prescott in the eyes. "Is there nothing I can do?"

"Sweet, sweet Prescott. You always try to stop him, but he always bests you. Perhaps some other time."

Millie set the broken snow globe on the windowsill then reached into the bucket and pulled out a revolver. Something red dripped from it. Blood! Too much to be from the small cuts on Millie's fingers. He realized, too, that the stain on her clothes was blood. So much blood. Where could it have all come from? She dropped her bucket and walked away, the revolver at her side. Both men stood, rooted to the floor, unable to move.

"Oliver!" a shout came from somewhere downstairs.

Someone ran up the stairs.

The man running toward them was the mirror image of Oliver, but with grayer hair.

"Uncle!" said Oliver. "She's going to kill herself."

"We can't let that happen," said the man Prescott assumed was Owen O'Dale. He looked at Prescott. "Dawson? Are you Dawson this time around?"

Prescott nodded. "But it's Davidson now. Same thing, I suppose, just a variation."

A shot rang out. Immediately Prescott felt searing pain in his chest and an immense sense of loss.

From behind and above them was the crash of a door flung open. Seconds later, Kenyon came barrelling down the stairs waving a huge sabre. For a moment, Prescott wondered where the man had found the weapon. It was too large to conceal beneath a coat and Kenyon's suitcase had been fairly small.

"No!" screamed Kenyon at the top of his lungs. He ran down the third-floor hall, screamed again. There was a series of grunts and thuds. When Kenyon appeared again, he was covered in blood.

Oliver and Owen moved to block Kenyon's way. He slashed at them with the sabre and both men went down, blood spurting from wounds in their necks.

"What the fuck?" Prescott stopped wondering anything as the sabre pierced his stomach then tore through his back.

"You'll never stop me, you ridiculous little man," said Kenyon.

"Too late, asshole," said Prescott. He tried to ignore the searing pain in his guts, but Kenyon was moving the sword around, carving up his insides. He had the most evil grin on his face. "You've lost again."

Prescott reached out and got his hands around Kenyon's neck. He knew there was no way he could choke the man, not with two feet of steel run through him. But perhaps…

Kenyon's eyes widened as Prescott pushed forward, forcing him against the window. The glass gave way, and the two men went through and down amid screams and blood.

The last thing Prescott heard after he hit the rocks and the hilt of the sword wedged in his chest was the satisfying sound of Kenyon's neck snapping.

And still, nothing was resolved.

It would happen again.

Peter Dawson, January 17, 2020

He opened his eyes and looked up into the lovely face of…her.

"Who am I?"

She smiled. "Peter. You passed out. I'm Emma."

"That's a relief. Thanks for telling me. I didn't want to ask."

Emma helped Peter get to his feet.

"Did you see that?" he asked.

She nodded.

"I won't let you do that to yourself."

"I know," said Emma. "At least that time, you took care of the son of a bitch."

"Owen and Oliver."

Before Peter could say more, Emma pulled him toward the door. "Winthrop. Now. He might have some answers. We still have time to figure things out. We can't let Beau or Beverly or whoever it is get us this time around."

"What do you mean?"

"Everything bad happens on the eighteenth. Tomorrow."

Too stunned to say anything, Peter followed Emma out into the winter cold.

Chapter 14:
"And I would not expect you to pretend"

Peter Dawson, January 17, 2020

The storm had grown worse since they entered the pub. The wind seemed to be blowing from every direction and got in every little crevice or opening in Peter's clothes. He wished he had some long johns instead of a flimsy pair of lady's underclothes. He could have also used his heavy parka rather than the winter coat he had brought. Why did he always assume he wouldn't be outside very much on these trips? Tossing extra stuff, like warm clothes and snow boots, in the car wouldn't have taken up significant room. He could still get a few boxes of books in there.

Thank you, Beverly, for making preparations for the trip hectic and confusing. Now Peter didn't know if he was shivering because of the cold or Beverly. She had always been abrupt when angry, but the last time he encountered her, she was absolutely foul. He could see the change in her usually hard eyes; that time they seemed weirdly out of focus, as if she was trying to see something through a fog. Was it really only yesterday?

As if sensing his thoughts, Emma asked, "Do you think Beau's got her?" She gave voice to something Peter didn't want to face.

"You know, it's really difficult to tell with her. She's nasty on most days. What we encountered at the library could have been her on a regular day when someone crossed her or didn't answer a question quickly enough."

Emma huffed. "So, if Beverly is possessed by the spirit of one of the most vicious men ever, we won't necessarily notice. Damn."

Peter patted Emma's wrist. "We'll have to be more observant in the future. I suspect she's somewhere right now trying to figure out where I am so she can get her claws in me. No doubt, she'll check here once she thinks of it."

"Well, if she comes to the pub and gives Oona a hard time, she's in for it. Oona doesn't take any shit from anyone. I've seen her throw sailors out the door."

"Are sailors particularly rough and tough?" Peter was curious.

"No," said Emma. "I've just seen her toss out sailors."

"You know, for someone who is the most beautiful woman in the world, you sure are a goofball."

"I have to be. Think about what's going on and what we are believing in."

He nodded. "Mass murder, torture, ghosts, possession, reincarnation, sex. Is there more?"

"Isn't that enough, though why you included sex in there, I don't know."

"It's nothing to trifle with." Emma punched Peter's arm surprisingly hard. "Now, tell me about this Winthrop fellow. What's he like?"

She pointed to a house at the corner of the main road. In spite of the swirling snow, he could tell it was huge, like some of the stately homes Peter had seen in Newport. On the other side of the house, just barely visible through the increasingly heavy snowfall, was another inn, one Peter hadn't known about. The closer they got to the house, the easier it was for Peter to see where the rear garden ended at the edge of a cliff. He got a little wobbly, but Emma steadied him.

"Sol doesn't mince words, Peter. If he thinks you're an idiot, he'll tell you. He's also a product of his time." Emma sighed. "That means he'll make comments about my tits and ass. And he'll use those words, not something softer."

"Boobs? Hooters? Knockers? Shnubblies?"

Emma stopped and stared at Peter. He thought she would slap him. "I've told you before to be careful with your words. Remember? You called me a…I can't say it, but you were so apologetic, I had to forgive you, and you've never said anything bad since. Until now."

Peter felt confused. "I have a vague recollection of saying something stupid. But that was…oh, shit…that was a hundred and fifty years ago. You're remembering past events that happened to someone else as if they're your own memories. I think I am, too."

"When this is over, if we make it through this time, we need to go somewhere quiet where we can talk over all the crazy stuff." Peter nodded. "I can say those things, but that still doesn't excuse you for speaking out of turn."

"Look, I'm sorry, Emma. I can't help making jokes when things are getting awkward. I'll be more careful with what I say, but don't you think you're overreacting just a little bit?"

As the old saying goes, if looks could kill. "Overreacting? You fucking idiot. How should I react? I've had to put up with sexist, racist, and classist bullshit for so fucking long, I can barely hold myself back from putting my fist through your teeth."

Emma seemed on the verge of tears and Peter wanted to crawl under a rock. After all this time, he'd blown it because of his stupid sense of humor. There was a lump in his throat so large, he couldn't even get a squeak out.

Her face softened for an instant.

"Look, Peter, I love you beyond measure. I have for forever. I know you would never do anything at all to harm me or make me unhappy. You've given your life for me so many times. Please, bear with me. I've had to deal with this stuff and hold it in so much, I've hurt myself. I *need* to get it out. I *need* you to allow me to let it out. I *need* you to support me, even if it means you become my punching bag."

Peter couldn't think of a thing to say. Well, he could, but he wasn't about to take any chances. Emma's hands were balled into fists, and she was shaking like she wanted to use them.

"Just know that it's not you. But you're here, now. You're going to bear the brunt of it until we can get all the other garbage and that vicious bitch Beverly out of the way."

"Hit me."

Emma looked startled.

"Hit me. Now hard. Let some of it out. Go on."

Before he could say another word, Emma's fist connected with his nose. Peter went flying back and landed on his backside on a windrow from a plow then slid down to the sidewalk. His eyes were wide open in shock.

She'd actually done it. Peter gingerly touched his face. It throbbed, but his nose didn't feel broken. He could still breathe through it. There was blood that froze almost as soon as it reached his upper lip. His backside hurt as well because there had been a chunk of rough ice under the softer snow.

Emma had a look of horror on her face as if she couldn't believe what she'd done. She held out her hand and helped Peter up. He brushed snow off his coat then smiled at her. When she tried to speak, Peter held up his hand and shook his head.

"Let me say this. I have no idea what you've been through, what you've endured, what kind of shit you've had to take throughout your life. Or lives. I can surmise that you've had to keep quiet about it and haven't been able to stand up for yourself, and few of your friends have stood up for you, either. I will never know. You don't have to explain anything to me. I'm here for you in whatever capacity you need."

"But I punched you, Peter. You're bleeding." She wiped some blood from the corner of his mouth, causing him to wince. It stung.

"Nothing you can do will send me away, Emma. I'm here, with you, behind you, next to you, in front of you when there's danger."

"Thank you."

He held out his arm for Emma. "Now, shall we continue to the wonderful Chief Winthrop?" Once they had started walking again, Peter said, "I hope he can fill in the holes for 1945. Somehow, I don't feel complete."

"Me, either." Emma rested her head on his shoulder while they walked. "Shnubblies?"

"The smallest of the three breast sizes from an ancient high school joke." Emma looked down at her chest then back at him. He waited for another punch. When none came, he said, "My favorites."

They walked in silence until reaching their destination. At the chief's house, Emma raised her hand to knock on the front door, but before she could connect, it swung open.

"Hurry up, you two. I'm freezing my balls off in here. Don't let the snow in." The voice was gruff and deep. Peter guessed the old boy smoked heavily. There was also the reek of cigarettes and the yellowish tint to the wallpaper that clued him in. He slammed the door shut behind them. Peter thought the chief's manner did not bode well for getting information. He'd dealt with this kind of person before: old-fashioned, tight-lipped, and dismissive of young people who were prying into things best left undisturbed.

Though he had to be over a hundred years old, the chief was still a huge man. There didn't appear to be an ounce of fat on him and when he shook Peter's hand, the grip was firm. He also had a full head of wavy gray hair.

Peter noticed the chief check out Emma's backside when she passed him into the living room. He looked over at Peter and raised his eyebrows. The old man said, "Amazing," so quietly Peter could barely hear.

Okay, Petey, be on the lookout. You don't want your girlfriend to punch you in the face again.

He rubbed his nose gently. Now that they were inside, his

face was defrosting in the cozy warmth. There was a throbbing between his eyes. Two black eyes? Probably.

Winthrop noticed Peter's nose and said, "Your girlfriend clock you for saying something stupid?" Peter nodded. "I've got some cream stuff that will numb the pain."

Winthrop guided them to a pair of easy chairs then disappeared before returning with a small tube which he passed to Peter. "Rub a little of that into your face."

Peter did what he was told. "Thank you, Chief Winthrop," said Peter.

"Call me Sol. Forget all that formal shit, I'm too old for it." Peter smiled. It hurt.

Sol sat in a recliner and leaned back then lit up a cigarette. The room was already heavy with smoke and making it difficult at times for Peter to breathe. As long as he didn't consciously think about breathing, he had no problem. He choked for a moment.

"You ever going to give those things up?" Emma waved a hand in front of her face.

"My dear, I'm a hundred and five. What's the point?" He took a very long drag on the cigarette then butted it out. "I guess I know why you're here. I heard about the professor from the big university down here looking for fanciful Nazi subs. Probably want all the details about January of '45 as well. Right?"

"Yes, sir," said Peter. "Anything you can tell us."

"Good. I've been wanting to get this off my chest for decades. No one ever showed much interest, and I didn't want to attract the wrong kind of attention." Sol rubbed his chin.

"Where to start."

Peter wanted to jump for joy. He truly hadn't expected any cooperation from Sol.

"How about the brothel?" said Peter. Emma gave him a hard look. "What? It's legitimate research. I've read that there might have been one, but it seems like a myth. And there was some guy named Kenton that seemed to be stirring things up."

"Oh, it was real," said Sol. "We got a tip about it. It was that bum, Ben Kenton, that called it in. Kenton had it in for Owen O'Dale because he'd tried to find work at the inn and Owen turned him away. Owen told me he'd had a bad feeling about Kenton the moment he showed his face at the inn. He said there was something familiar about Kenton, but he couldn't place where he'd seen him. I learned much later, after the bodies had been found, that Owen finally figured out Kenton was a relative of the Kensingtons. He bore a remarkable resemblance to someone Owen's uncle Oscar knew in the army. Oscar had sent Owen an old photo of the guy, Beau or Bart Kensington; I forget which. Anyway, he said this Kenton guy looked enough like the photo that he could have been a nephew or cousin."

"We know about Beau and Bart, Sol," said Emma. "Bad news, the both of them."

Sol continued. "We didn't take it very seriously, the tip. I took a couple of officers along to make things look good. While I spoke to Owen and acted like I was investigating the tip, the boys stayed in the dining room having lunch on Owen."

Sol smiled then lit up another cigarette. Peter didn't say

anything in case it might discourage the old fella.

"Funny thing about it. I left this bit out of the report because…well, the Kensingtons were still bigwigs in Wycliffe Point and they wouldn't have appreciated any scandal coming their way. Especially if they weren't making any money out of it. High society, maybe, but they were money-grubbing pricks, every one of them.

"Anyway, I went upstairs with Owen, you know, to check out this supposed brothel on the fourth floor. Well, damned if the son of a bitch wasn't in fact running one." He laughed then went into a coughing fit.

Emma went over and held Sol's shoulders until he settled down. He stared at her backside when she returned to her seat.

"I need to cough more." Emma didn't react. "Now, where was I? Owen. He had about a dozen girls up there, each with her own room. Remember, at that time, there was the army unit over at the camp across the bay. Lots of lonely and horny young men ready to dip their wicks in anything that moved. Owen's little enterprise kept them happy. And clean, as well. If any of those boys had picked up a dose of the clap, they'd have been court martialled and given a dishonorable discharge. All because they needed to let off some steam."

"Seems reasonable," said Peter. He'd considered partaking of the services of a brothel when he was at his most frustrated with Beverly. He didn't have the nerve to go through with it.

"Damned good thing, too," said Emma, giving Peter the stink-eye. She was in his mind again.

Trying to distract Emma, Peter said, "What about the sub?"

"I'll get to the sub stuff in a moment. I want to finish about old Owen and the brothel. He was extremely discreet about it. The Kensingtons never found out a thing. Owen was able to get the girls some legit work in town—laundry, cooking, cleaning, even a few odd jobs over at the fort. The girls had a reason to be there other than fucking the boys in uniform.

"Right. So, I didn't figure Owen and his girls were doing any harm. Essential wartime work, if you ask me. Hell, once I knew about it, I took a few dips myself. On the house, of course."

"Sol! You devil," said Emma with a look of mock horror.

He shrugged. "Oh, and by the way." Sol looked around the room as if checking for anyone listening. Then, quietly, he said, "He had one room with a—what do you call them now—gays? One of those gays, you know, in case there were any that were bent and needed some. Because, you know, Owen was one."

Feeling a little uncomfortable about Sol's views, Peter cut in. "What, exactly, has the brothel to do with later events? Other than to clear up a couple of questions."

Sol thought for a moment. "In a way, it kicked off some of the events. That weasel, Kenton, couldn't get a free ride there, so he went sour. Then he went after the maid and all that other guff."

"I read about the possibility of German collaborators," said Peter.

"Maybe," said Sol. "Really, it was that miserable fucker in charge over at the fort at the time. What was his name—Macdonald? Ben fucking Macdonald. Shit, that bastard was a stickler for rules. Neckties on at all times. Standing at attention while on guard duty even if a storm wind was blowing off the Atlantic. Random inspections any time of the day or night. It's a wonder none of the men deserted or shot him and dumped him in the bay.

"And no, that fella we pulled out of the bay after the…incident…was not a deserter. Macdonald tried to make out the guy had been AWOL, but I talked to one of his buddies and he told me the guy had taken an hour to go propose to his girl and hadn't come back. He told me this guy, hey, his name was Paul something. Hold on."

Sol struggled to get out of his recliner then went into another room. When he returned, he handed some things to Peter. "Found these a couple of days after all the trouble. I don't know why I kept them. Dawson, that's his name. Any relation?"

Peter stared down at a pocket watch and a ring.

Paul Dawson, January 18, 1945

He was late. And Paul was never late. Except today, this evening, for possibly the most important event in his life. Today of all days, the ever-punctual Paul Dawson was late.

The wind carried away his cry of, "Fuck!"

Limping along the coast road, Paul shivered. The icy wind blowing off the water and through the clifftop park cut through his army greatcoat, and his boots didn't do much to keep out the cold despite three pairs of socks. He clapped and rubbed his hands together to try and get his blood circulating again. For the first time in…ever, Paul wished he was back in North Africa. The nights could get cold, almost down to freezing, but there was nothing like this. The noonday sun had been bearable, and you could find shade, even though the humidity drenched your clothes in a few minutes.

"I can't believe I'd rather be back in Tunisia," said Paul to the wind. "No, that's nuts."

His right leg ached where the white-hot shrapnel from a German eighty-eight shell had done its worst. That February back in '43 in Kasserine Pass had been a slaughterhouse, and Paul felt like the luckiest guy in the world for surviving it. A hunk of metal in your thigh, several months to heal, then reassignment Stateside because the Army didn't want limping soldiers to slow them down. What more could a guy ask?

"Some goddamn sunshine, maybe," said Paul. The person walking the other way along the road gave him an odd look, but when he saw Paul's uniform, he reached up and gave his fedora a pull in salute. Paul nodded back and decided to keep his mouth shut.

He didn't have time to mess about. Emily would be waiting for him in the tunnel below the inn.

Captain Macdonald wouldn't note Paul's absence because Harvey said he'd cover for him. Neither of them expected any action tonight. It was too damned cold, and the Germans weren't on this side of the Atlantic anyway. Of course, you couldn't tell the officers that. Strictly by the book, two men on watch at all times, eyes glued to the sea searching for Nazi subs or battleships or whatever the hell the Krauts were ready to send over.

And don't forget your goddamn neckties.

The officers didn't understand how important it was for Paul to see Emily tonight. He was going to propose, had used his last month's pay to buy a ring. He'd even splashed out extra to have it engraved—*Paul & Emily Always*. Harvey had already agreed to be his best man. Now all Paul needed was to get Emily to agree to marry him.

There was no doubt in Paul's mind that Emily would say yes. She'd been reluctant to have anything to do with him after they'd met back in June at that USO dance at the swanky Inn on the Cliff. Paul had fallen for Emily the moment he saw her serving food at the buffet table. He later learned she was employed as a maid at the inn, but they were short-handed that night, so Emily had been pressed into service.

He'd carried a torch for her ever since.

Before he'd even seen her, Paul had heard the rumble in the place about the colored woman serving whites. A lot of the soldiers and sailors were appalled that such a horror could be allowed to happen and wouldn't go near the food. It was jake for the inn to employ one of them as a maid. Even the US Army had used them for transport and general duties so that white soldiers could do what they did best: fight. Paul had even heard there was a unit of Negro pilots somewhere in Europe helping defend the bombers dumping their loads on Germany. Supposed to be incredible pilots, too.

But touch their food! Never. Paul had laughed. What about all the colored cooks in the army?

Paul hadn't cared about any of that color bunk. He'd wanted chow.

When he got to the buffet table, Paul had no trouble getting served. The most beautiful woman he had ever set eyes on was at one end, mostly alone, waiting to hand out sandwiches and cakes. Dressed in a dark maid's uniform with a white apron, she had her hair tied back with a bright red ribbon. Now that was bold, adding color where it didn't belong.

There was something about her that made Paul think he'd met her before, but he couldn't put a finger on it.

With a pounding heart, Paul had gone over and introduced himself. The look on her face was priceless. A white talking to a colored! What a sensation! Behind the shock, though, was a hint of recognition and happiness that warmed his heart.

She'd smiled and said her name was Emily, but Paul could call her whatever he liked.

Paul hung around Emily's buffet for the rest of the night. He'd never eaten so many sandwiches or so much cake. And he had practically drowned in the coffee. There was beer, but Paul had duty the next day and hated hangovers. Besides, he only drank Guinness.

A couple of Navy types came by and tried to stir up trouble, but Emily had held her own with insults that made Paul blush. The sailors had gone away with their tails between their legs. He kept an eye out to make sure they didn't return to cause Emily any trouble, not that she appeared to need his help.

Before returning to the barracks at the fort across the bay, Paul had asked Emily if he could come calling on her. You'd have thought he'd called her mother a foul name by the look on her face.

"Your type doesn't mix with my type," she'd said.

"Bullshit," said Paul. "I'm a man, you're a woman. Our types mix all the time. When's your next day off?"

Emily had resisted, but Paul had persisted, and Emily eventually agreed to meet him for a picnic at the park on the cliff about half way between the inn and the fort.

Since then, every moment of leave Paul had was spent with Emily, when she could get away from the inn. When she couldn't get away, Paul would sit at a picnic table on the inn grounds on the off chance he would catch a glimpse of her passing a window. When Emily heard about this, she made sure to open a window in whatever room she was cleaning so she could look out and wave at him. A few times, she'd managed to sneak out and meet him for a kiss and cuddle.

Paul felt a stirring when he remembered that time with Emily on the beach below the inn. It was a pebble beach, but there was enough room to lay out a blanket and catch some sun while having a picnic. The best thing about the beach was that it was only accessible through the cave below the inn or a blocked-off narrow path from the warehouse next door. Therefore, it was quite private and the two had no need to worry about intruders. Not that intruders would have had anything to see. They weren't married yet and Paul was a respectful gentleman. He chuckled at the image of Emily's face when he'd kissed her pretty little toes. Perhaps that was taking things a little too far, though Emily hadn't seemed to mind Paul's boldness.

Tonight, they were meeting in the cave below the inn used to store firewood, trash cans, and assorted other supplies. Emily and Paul had begun meeting there when the weather turned in the fall and the wind off the bay was too cold for comfort.

Paul slid his hand in his coat pocket for the hundredth time since he left the fort. He wanted to be absolutely sure the ring was still there. His pocket watch was there, too. He pulled it out then opened it to check the time. He knew he was late and still worried about getting back to the fort before the captain found out he was AWOL. Harvey could only cover so much. He knew he should let it go. There was nothing Paul could do about it now.

It would take him another ten minutes to reach the inn and rendezvous with Emily. Ten, fifteen minutes to do the deed, and he'd be back at the fort in about forty-five minutes. That was cutting it close. "Take care of yourself, Harv. Forget about me."

Engaged to the most incredible woman he'd ever met. Whatever difficulties they'd face because they were mixing the races, they could face together. The world was changing, and Paul was sure he and Emily would come out on top. Life was good.

About a hundred yards from the cave entrance, Paul came to an abrupt stop when he heard voices. Men. Several of them.

Paul knew he couldn't afford any more delays.

One of the men barked an order. In German. Paul gasped. He'd know that foul language anywhere. There'd been enough of it yelled about back at Kasserine when the Krauts were plowing through the American lines.

"Oh, God, Emily. I hope you're safe," said Paul as quietly as he could, thinking if he said it out loud, it would have to be true.

Paul reached into his greatcoat pocket—not the one with the ring, that was still safe and secure—the other. The one with his .45. Normally, away from the fort, he wouldn't have carried a weapon, but there was something about tonight that had made him grab one from the armory at the last minute. That creep Kenton might still be lurking about. If he saw him again, Kenton would get more than just a beating. No one, but no one, assaulted Paul Dawson's girl and got away with it, even if said girl was kind and let the guy off with a sack of potatoes to the nuts. He was thankful for his foresight now.

Treading as softly as he could on the icy path, Paul moved closer to the cave entrance. There was no one nearby, but he could see movement at the far end, where the path went down to the pebble beach.

All he could think was that Emily might be in danger.

When he reached the far end of the cave, there was no one there. He thought he heard someone take a step on the path across the way that led up to the warehouse.

Paul took a step to investigate when he heard, "Paul?" in a quiet, feminine voice.

Emily!

He turned quickly to go meet the love of his life then felt a searing pain in his back. The .45 dropped from his hand and clattered away down the path. Paul looked down to see the end of a sword, dripping blood, protruding from his chest.

Who uses a sword?

Rough hands grabbed Paul's shoulders and pulled him back. He tried to call out to Emily, but the pain was too much.

In a few moments, he was propped up at the edge of the cliff.

Paul put his hand in his coat pocket and wrapped it around the ring box. "I won't be late next time, Emily. I'm so sorry."

Someone shoved, letting Paul's body slide off the sword and plunge to the rocks and frigid Atlantic water below.

Peter Dawson, January 17, 2020

Oh, crap. Another me killed trying to save the girl?

Peter shook his head. The room spun. "Related? I don't think so. Just a coincidence. Or not. Probably. I don't know anymore." Emma prodded him in the side and when he looked at her, she gave him a smile.

Emma squeezed Peter's hand. "It's okay. It wasn't your fault. It never is."

"I need to try harder," he said. The butterflies in his stomach were doing double duty and Peter knew he'd have to find a bathroom quickly or risk embarrassing himself. Thinking about the soldier going over the cliff also gave him a brief attack of vertigo, which did nothing to calm his stomach.

"Are you two finished with whatever romantic shit you're doing?"

Peter tried to say something.

"Don't deny it, young fella. If I had Emma on my arm, I'd

be flustered, too. Shit, given the chance, I could still get my cock hard for her."

Emma slapped Sol's arm. "Sol! I've told you about that before. You can't go around saying those kinds of rude and sexist things. No, don't try to explain that you're old and set in your ways. Just stop it." She did not look like she was joking.

Sol butted out his cigarette and immediately lit another. "Sorry, Emma, but…I know, it's no excuse." Leaning in close to Peter, Sol added, "But she is fucking gorgeous."

"True," said Peter. "I can't deny it, Emma. You're just about the most beautiful woman I have ever met, seen, dreamed about, or imagined." *Holy shit! Did I just say that out loud in front of someone?*

"I'd better tell you about the sub, now," said Sol. Peter nodded. "Let me get a few papers and things in the room out back." Sol left the room.

"Are you all right, Peter?"

"I'm sorry," he said. "That flashback or memory or whatever it was…it threw me for a loop. Getting killed again. I should have said something to Sol."

"Don't worry about it. I think he got the message. Sol's never been quite that crude before, though."

"Must be the effects of trifle," said Peter.

"Don't you start, Mr. Dawson. Remember, we're trying not to get ourselves murdered here."

There was a loud thump from somewhere in the house and a distinct grunt of, "Fuck," then silence.

A couple of minutes later, Sol came thumping into the

room carrying a bankers box. It looked heavy so Peter rushed over to help the old man. When Peter tried to take the box, Sol yanked it away.

"I'm not dead yet and I've still got muscles. Go sit while I sort through this shit."

Peter rejoined Emma. They held hands while Sol emptied the box on the coffee table. He placed the empty box next to his recliner and waited.

"So, Sol, do you know anything about a submarine being around at the time? January, 1945?" Peter fidgeted, impatient. The brothel stories were interesting, but not entirely relevant to his research. On the other hand, he was getting more information about another of his…antecedents? *Past lives? This is getting very New Agey.*

"It's real," said Emma

"So, what do you want to know about the sub?"

"Was it really there?" said Peter. "I know there's nothing official, but I have some records from Germany that hint at the possibility."

"This should answer your question," said Sol. He picked up a biscuit tin. "I never showed any of it to those army types that came around investigating after the incident. Officious pricks with their Espionage Act and blatant threats. Fuck 'em. I let them run around chasing their tails while I kept that to myself."

Sol opened the tin and handed an object to Peter. His jaw dropped when he saw it was a cap that belonged to a U-boat commander. Some of the braid on the peak was gone and there were burn marks all over it.

"Found that lodged in the rocks a couple days after the government types left," said Sol. "I knew what it was right away. I'd seen some newsreels of those Nazi cocksuckers."

Next, Sol handed Peter a small patch, also with burn marks. It was black and had a submarine with several circles around it. In German script were the letters DVA under a small swastika. "*Deutsche Versuchsanstalt für Atomartig Forschung.* The German Experimental Institute for Atomic Research," said Peter quietly.

"What's that?" said Sol.

Peter shook his head to clear his thoughts. "It was a secret Nazi organization doing atomic research. Sort of their version of the Manhattan Project, but, luckily, theirs never got very far." Waving the patch, he added, "At least, we didn't think so."

"This is the last thing I found related to what you're asking," said Sol. He held up a small metal disk. "Does this help?"

Peter recognized it: a *Kreigsmarine* identity disk. When he examined it, he clearly saw the name Gerhard Weinz and a number. On the reverse side, the number U-10000 made Peter shiver. He giggled then broke out into a full laugh. Peter stood and paced around the living room, clapping his hands and mumbling, "I'm right. I'm right. Fuck you, Beverly."

"Peter! What is it?" Emma put her hand on his arm when he moved close to her.

He looked into Emma's green eyes and realized that nothing mattered except her. Still, he had not only found what he originally came to Wycliffe Point to find, but he'd found something better. He held up the disk. "This is the identity disk, dog tag, of a German U-boat captain named Weinz. It actually has the name of his boat on the reverse. Emma, this is proof that the submarine I've theorized about did in fact exist. It was here in Wycliffe Point in January of 1945. The weird lights that people reported? They weren't a UFO. It was a small nuclear explosion that destroyed the sub and everyone on it."

"So, what does this mean?" Emma looked worried. "Are you done now? Are you going to leave?"

Peter shrugged. "Well, I have to do some more research then write up my notes. After that, I'll need to write a paper about the sub. Or maybe I'll do a book. This is only the beginning, Emma. They won't laugh at me ever again. Especially that bitch Beverly."

"Oh." Emma stared at her feet.

Sol clapped his hands. "Good for you, boy."

"However," said Peter. "That's not important anymore." He knelt next to Emma and took her hand. "I have something I must do first that is far more important than any theory about German submarines. This time, I have to save the life of the woman I love."

"Okay, you lovebirds," said Sol. He'd moved over to the front window. "No one's going anywhere right now. It'd be too easy to take a wrong turn and end up at the bottom of a cliff and in the bay."

He pulled back the curtain to reveal nothing but white. Peter went over to see for himself. He tried to spot the pub and the library, but saw neither. The snow had become so heavy, it was impossible to see more than a couple of feet outside. The thought of going over a cliff in this weather was enough to convince Peter to stay put.

Sol let the curtain close. "It's getting close to dinner time. Why don't you let me fix us some supper? Later, if the storm's let up, you can head back to wherever you're staying."

"That sounds like a good idea, Sol," said Emma.

"If you can't leave later, I have a spare room. Only one bed. I don't think you'd mind sharing, would you?"

A hearty dinner later, the storm hadn't let up. In fact, it seemed to be getting worse.

Peter resigned himself to having to spend the night with Emma again.

"Is that so bad?" Emma smacked Peter's arm. "Well?"

"Emma, my dear, I look forward to spending every night from now on sharing a bed with you. At least Beverly won't be able to find us."

"The walls in this old place are fairly thick. And my room's at the other end of the hall. Make all the racket you need." Sol grinned.

Emma glared at the old boy. Peter couldn't help but smile. And get aroused.

"Maybe not. You'll need a good night's rest," said Sol. "Tomorrow's the eighteenth. *That's* always the date the shit seems to hit the fan."

Chapter 15:
"Speaking strictly as a member of the human race"

Beverly Kent: morning, January 18, 2020

Feeling refreshed after a strange night's sleep, Beverly went down to the lobby. O'Dale stood behind the front desk, unmoving. He stared at her with a look of sheer horror on his face.

You know what's coming, don't you, sodomite?

She smiled at him, gave him a quick wave. Then, to rub in just how helpless he was this time around, she opened her greatcoat to show him the sabre resting in its scabbard. The idiot's eyes flared open. Good. He knew exactly what was coming and that there was absolutely nothing he could do to interfere this time.

A door opened to her right and that other O'Dale swine came out of the kitchen. He stopped dead when he spied Beverly. *Dead. Funny.* His hand went to his neck. He rubbed at the scar there. As if they were the same person, the first O'Dale rubbed his own scar.

The memory of making those wounds pleased her. She anticipated being able to recreate them on someone else.

Beverly exited the inn. As she was about to cross the parking lot to the warehouse, she spied Dawson's vehicle under several inches of fresh snow. He had a ridiculous sentimental attachment to the hunk of steel. If you had to have a connection with a conveyance, at least make it a horse; their hooves could do significant injury to an exposed head. She stepped over to the car, looked about the lot then saw something that would be fun. She picked up a concrete block from a pile next to some gigantic yellow machine. The block was surprisingly light. Or Beverly was much stronger than she knew.

Standing next to Dawson's prize, she raised the block and flung it at the windshield. The glass shattered, and the block hit the steering wheel, bending it a little, and settled in the driver's seat. Pleased with the damage, Beverly put three more blocks through windows.

She walked away feeling very satisfied indeed.

Walking past the library, she noticed the front door still stood open, letting in snow and wind. Good. More destruction. Obviously, the bitch hadn't been back. Off somewhere fucking everything in sight. Whore. Killing her this time would be more fulfilling than usual.

Beverly arrived at the pub and walked in. She surveyed the room. No one else was there now, but she could hear someone in the back making a lot of noise. Taking a seat at a table by a window, she watched the storm over the bay. She preferred warmer weather, but a storm was always good for masking activities people might find…unusual.

"I'm sorry, we're about to close to get ready for the afternoon lunch rush."

Was there nowhere in this damned town she could get a decent meal when she wanted one? When Beverly saw who spoke, she nearly leapt out of her seat and strangled the bitch. Keeping calm so as not to cause a fuss before she was ready,

Beverly gave the bitch her best smile.

"I'm so sorry. I saw the pub was open, and then those two people just walked out. I assumed you were still serving." She fingered the hunting knife she had strapped to her belt. The urge to unsheathe it and stick it in this turncoat was hard to resist. A woman now! Well, since she had switched somehow, why shouldn't one of the others. That might explain why Dawson was such an insipid wimp. He could really be a she. That slut in the library was more of a man than Dawson could ever be. Beverly realized the turncoat had been speaking.

"Sorry again, my mind wandered. You were saying?"

The turncoat, the nametag said she was Oona, smiled. "I said, we're closing to get ready for the mid-day rush. It's always a madhouse here on a Saturday afternoon, so we like to take a little extra time to make sure everything is all set."

Oona stared at Beverly. Did she recognize her old nemesis? Did she know who she was?

"Do I know you?" Oona's eyes bore into Beverly, making her feel a little uncomfortable. She wasn't ready to act yet. And she really did need something to eat.

Beverly shook her head. "I don't think so…Oona. I'm from out of town. Just arrived the other day. Doing some research at the library next door."

"Oh, so you've met Miss Ranahan." Oona looked pleased.

"You mean the ni…nice woman in charge there. Yes. Quite helpful." Beverly realized she needed to be careful. There were things in this pub she wanted to get. Especially the young ones. "Stunningly beautiful, too."

Oona raised an eyebrow. "Yes, she is. Unfortunately, she's taken."

You bet she is.

Beverly's stomach gurgled.

"Maybe I can rustle up something," said Oona. "The cook's over getting supplies at the market, but we have some frozen waffles. And the coffee pot is still on."

"I hope the coffee's good and not that rancid garbage they serve next door."

Oona looked confused. "Right. I'll be back."

True to her word, Oona returned with some waffles, syrup, and coffee. Beverly was pleased the coffee tasted good. Not perfect, but better than that hot sewer water she'd been served before.

Beverly ate her breakfast quickly. Oona returned to refill her coffee but mostly kept busy behind the bar and in the kitchen.

When she had finished, Beverly pulled out her sabre, ready to go after her prey.

The turncoat, Oona, was behind the bar reading something. Once in a while, she'd glance up at Beverly, then read more. Her brow was furrowed, and she did not look happy.

Beverly rose and walked over to the bar, keeping the sabre hidden behind her back.

The closer Beverly got, the more Oona looked uncomfortable. But it was obvious she still didn't recognize Beverly.

"Something's off, O'Dale," said Beverly. "You don't know me? Your loss."

"Know you?" said Oona. "Why? And why are you using my maiden name?"

Beverly laughed. "Wouldn't you like to know. What's that you're reading?"

Oona tried to shove the papers under the bar, but Beverly was faster. She whipped out the sabre and brought it down on O'Dale's hand, severing it at the wrist. When Oona went to scream, Beverly punched her in the face, knocking her out. She stared at her fist.

"I *am* stronger than I thought."

Knowing she didn't have much time before the cook returned from the market, Beverly dragged the unconscious turncoat by the hair into the back of the pub leaving a bloody trail. She found some zip ties and bound her captive to the heavy butcher block table in the center of the kitchen.

"That'll be handy later."

She heard a noise at the back door. Quickly, Beverly hid beside a large pantry and waited.

"Oona?" No doubt it was the cook.

Watching the cook's reflection in the stainless-steel backsplash of the stove, she waited until he got closer.

"Oona!" The cook bent to help the unconscious turncoat.

Beverly raised the sabre and brought it down across the cook's neck. She was pleased it was sharp enough to go right through flesh and bone and separate the man's head from his body. She flexed her newfound muscles.

Needing time to sort out her next move, Beverly went and

locked the front and back doors. Curious about what had tipped off the turncoat, she retrieved the papers from the bar. They were letters.

Letter from Major Obadiah O'Dale, 45th New Jersey Volunteer Infantry, January 20, 1865

Dear Uncle Owen,

Now that the campaign to capture Fort Fisher is over, and Major General Butler has been forced to take the blame for its initial failure, I, along with the rest of the officers and men of the 45th New Jersey, have returned to Wycliffe Point. It was a long and miserable trip made all the more miserable by the absence of good friends and comrades lost along the way since we left our homes in October 1861.

Before I detail the events that occurred on the night of the celebration held by the mayor of Wycliffe Point, allow me to provide you with some context from my time as the Colonel's second-in-command during the war. However, I am not writing to you to tell of our exploits fighting the Rebs.

As you may remember, the Colonel and I were in command of an eleven-month volunteer regiment mustered in New Jersey in late 1861. When that unit was mustered out, most of the officers and men immediately reformed as the 45th for another eleven months. It shows the respect the men had for the Colonel that so many returned to service after they could have gone home. Alas, it also shows many of them, myself included, were willing to overlook the Colonel's zealousness when dealing with the enemy, whether real or imagined.

Let there be no doubt, Colonel Beauregard Kensington is an American patriot and staunch defender of the Union. Of that, there can be no question. In battle, he always led from the rear, like many officers I have encountered who are happy to send men to their deaths while observing from a distance.

It is, however, his methods that leave much to be desired.

The first assignment of the 45th was to support Major General Butler in his occupation of the city of New Orleans.

The place had fallen without much of a fight, and we settled in expecting a fairly easy time of it. Butler was a tyrant and kept the local populace under control and permitted his officers to, shall we say, liberate whatever they wanted under the name of contraband goods. I admit I procured a small savings during our short stay in the city.

As an aside, allow me to mention that, while we were in the city, there was a series of brutal murders in the French Quarter. Butler was unconcerned, having issued General Order #28 which made any woman who showed disrespect to an officer a virtual whore. I raise this only as a point of interest given subsequent events in Wycliffe Point. I will let you make whatever connections and conclusions you wish.

The first time I became aware that the Colonel was—shall we say, one to be watched—came about shortly after the 45th arrived in Virginia in 1863. One of the volunteers, a man named Gray, had been informed that his wife was gravely ill. When the Colonel refused the man's request to return home to care for her,

Gray simply left. Or, as the Colonel said, deserted his sacred duty. Gray was captured a few days later and returned to the 45th. The officers expected there to be a court martial, and that Gray would be sent to the stockade. The Colonel had other ideas. Feeling we were in a dire situation, about to go into battle, the Colonel believed Gray should be dealt with swiftly.

Standing before the Colonel and his officers, Gray was asked if he did, in fact, leave the regiment without permission. Gray couldn't deny it and said so. The Colonel then said Gray had deserted and therefore deserved immediate punishment. I can still clearly remember the moment it happened.

Colonel Kensington stood from his chair and approached Gray. He said, "Private Gray, you have admitted to desertion under fire. The sentence of this court is death." With those words, the Colonel pulled out his pistol, pressed the barrel to Gray's forehead, and fired. Those observing this were shocked, but when the Colonel asked if anyone had any objections to him carrying out the sentence, I must shamefully admit, no one said a word. Gray's body was thrown into a mass grave with dead rebels. The man has no marker.

A few days later, we were in the midst of battle. The rebels were coming at us from three sides, but we held them off. During that battle, we lost twenty good men. Another ten were wounded. That evening, while we were eating at the staff tent during a lull in the fighting, several pickets came to us with three rebels they had just captured and tied up. The rebels claimed they wanted to surrender because they were tired of fighting a losing battle. Without looking up from his supper, the Colonel said, "Hang them. Now."

The rebels looked shocked, as did our men. No one moved.

"Major O'Dale," said the Colonel, "carry out my orders, immediately."

"Sir," I said. "These men are prisoners of war. They should be treated as such."

The Colonel looked at the men for the first time. "I see no uniforms." It was true. By this time, many rebels no longer had uniforms, just tatters of whatever clothing they could throw together. "They are spies. Deal with them accordingly."

The rebels denied they were spies.

The Colonel said, "Major O'Dale, if I must leave my supper, you will be charged with insubordination and dealt with severely. Am I understood?"

I hesitated for a second, said, "Sir," then led the men and their prisoners away. The rebels were scared and one of them tried to run, but he fell and hit his head on a rock. The other two were untied and ordered to carry their unconscious comrade to a spot under some trees where we had tethered our wagon mules. The rebels were made to stand on a wagon while ropes were tossed over a low branch. The unconscious man was strung up as well.

Before I was able to give the order, I became aware of the presence of Colonel Kensington. He stood to my left and stared intently at the men awaiting their deaths. The Colonel stepped close to the end of the wagon and waited. If the men fell, they would be dangling within a foot or so of the Colonel.

"Give the order, Major," he said.

Hating every second of this, I ordered our men to move the wagon. The rebels took a long time to die because they didn't drop far enough or hard enough. A couple of our men were sick watching the struggles of the dying rebels. I still see their bloated faces in my dreams.

The Colonel did not move during the whole of the time the rebels died. From what I could see, he was staring intently at their dying faces. He had not permitted us to provide the men with hoods.

The last incident I will describe occurred as we were on our way back to New Jersey after the battle at Fort Fisher. We came upon a party of runaway slaves in a barn where we had hoped to bivouac for the night. Though there was room aplenty for all our men and the runaways, the Colonel ordered the runaways out of the barn. I will not repeat the words he used to describe them. When one of the other officers protested, the Colonel backhanded him so hard he flew into one of the stalls and landed in a pile of horse dung. Looking down at the filth-covered officer, Kensington said, "You wish to defend those things? Well, now you stink like one of them."

Nothing more was said, though from then on we were on the lookout for any other runaways. We wanted to be sure they stayed well clear of the Colonel and his abhorrent behavior.

It is the Colonel's disposition toward the coloreds that must be discussed now as it relates directly to the horrors to come.

Major General Butler had a policy of hiring runaway slaves as workers for the army. This policy proved useful, though it was terminated once there were too many people to hire.

In any case, one of those hired was a former slave by the name of Emmeline Ronaghan. She was taken on as a washerwoman and quickly became a valuable and hard worker. It was with Miss Ronaghan that things changed for the worse.

One of my fellow officers, and a close friend, Captain Philip Daweson, had taken an interest in Emmeline. You may remember Philip from our days at school. I fear he is lost to us, murdered for his misguided love. But I get ahead of myself.

Philip became enamored with Emmeline and spent every moment he could in her presence. She was reluctant at first, but soon warmed to him and they became, as far as I could tell, good friends.

There were two things I did not know at the time. First, Philip had fallen deeply in love with Emmeline and wished to marry her despite the problems a mixed-race marriage would have created. Second, Colonel Kensington took note of Philip's interest in Emmeline.

I regret I did not notice the subtle change in the Colonel's relationship with his captain. Philip was given extra duties, and his company became the vanguard for any actions we took against the rebels. Throughout all of this, despite the dangers he faced, Philip remained happy. I believe this was due to his affection for Emmeline.

The colonel, on the other hand, became increasingly enraged. His rancor toward Philip remained a mystery to both of us until a few days before the poorly planned move against Fort Fisher.

Philip and Emmeline were caught by the Colonel in, what he called, a compromising position. In fact, they were simply talking in the privacy of the laundry tent. I know this because I was witness to the occurrence.

The Colonel flew into a fit of apoplexy and ordered Philip to stay far away from Emmeline on pain of severe penalty. Emmeline was banished to another unit where it would have been difficult for Philip to see her.

Shortly after this, there occurred the fiasco at Fort Fisher, and the regiment's subsequent return to Wycliffe Point.

Now, I must relate to you the events of the last few days and my unwavering belief that my commanding officer, Colonel Beauregard Kensington, had to be put down in the swiftest and harshest manner possible.

I am sure you read in the local newspaper about the party held in honor of the returning heroes of the 45th. Of course, only the officers from the regiment were invited. The rest of the men were mustered out and returned home. The officers, myself included, had yet to determine if we wished to end our fighting days or rejoin for what was sure to be the last few months of the war.

Kensington would have been hard to miss with his loud voice, outgoing manner, and flaming red hair. He was bedecked with medals from his service in the Mexican war where, I have subsequently learned, he had come under suspicion for mistreatment of prisoners. I know you warned me to be wary of the man, but I disregarded you because, at the time, we needed men of his calibre to defeat the rebels.

The party was held at the Kensington Inn. You surely remember the inn from your previous visits. It sits upon a cliff overlooking the bay and is known as one of the finer establishments in New Jersey. I had been at the inn several times before the war for various reasons and had decided I would like to pursue employment there after the hostilities were concluded.

As I have mentioned, the Colonel is a man of short temper, patriotic fervor, high standards, and a seething hatred for the colored race. What I had not known was that the Colonel was also a misogynist of the highest order.

The party was quite the local affair. The mayor and the entire town council were in attendance, as well as leading local businessmen and their wives. A few of the officers also had wives present. Captain Daweson and I were the only unmarried officers present, apart from the Colonel.

Colonel Kensington was the center of attention, always surrounded by those wishing to hear stories of his exploits.

Seeking to avoid confrontation with the Colonel, we stayed well away as I, for one, would have been hard pressed not to contradict him on many of his facts. The wives were quite taken with the Colonel as he is a most striking man in appearance, seeming almost regal in his dress uniform. He is quite the raconteur and kept everyone amused.

Trouble did not begin until it was time to sit for our meal. The waitstaff at the inn were mostly freemen or runaways and this did not go unnoticed by the Colonel. He made a rather loud show of refusing to be served by any of the colored staff, being adamant that he would not touch food that had been soiled by their hands. The entire room went silent while he demanded to be served by someone white.

During the meal, few guests spoke to the Colonel. That was left to the unlucky ones who were seated at his table. These unfortunates included myself and Philip. Conversation was somewhat strained, though it soon became clear the guests were more uncomfortable with the loudness of the Colonel's protests, rather than their content. It seems that, though we of the Union are fighting to preserve the United States, the freeing of the slaves is not always met with much enthusiasm. There was great fear that hordes of freemen would travel north and steal the jobs waiting for the return of the serving soldiers.

After dinner, we returned to the lobby area for more drink. I freely admit, I drank far too much wine. However, the quantity I drank did not in any way interfere with my ability to understand what I was seeing and act upon it.

Philip had been frantic about Emmeline. I believe he had planned to take her away from Wycliffe Point that very evening. He had excused himself at one point and, I regret to say, I did not notice he was gone for far too long. When I did finally take note of my friend's absence, I also realized the Colonel was not present. When I made enquiries, no one seemed to know where either man was or had left.

I began a search of the inn. Naturally, the first places I tried were Philip's and the Colonel's rooms. Both were securely locked, though I did find what I concluded was blood outside of the Colonel's chamber.

Upon seeing the blood, I went to my own room to secure my service revolver. The Colonel was the only officer at the party who had carried his weapons—revolver and sabre. In my room, I thought I heard some conversation outside. Being as it was on the second floor, this did not seem unreasonable. I looked through my window in time to see Colonel Kensington impale some poor unfortunate with his sabre then kick his victim off the cliff below the inn.

I fear the individual may have been my friend, Philip, but as no body has been recovered, I cannot be absolutely certain.

Having witnessed what I was sure was murder, I rushed down the stairs and out of the inn. I had neglected to put on a coat. It was bitterly cold from the Atlantic wind. The roar of the waves crashing on the rocks was deafening. Upon looking over the cliff edge, I could see nothing but water and sea spray. No one was about.

I returned to Kensington's rooms and forced the door. There was blood on the carpet and rumpled bed linens. A search of his belongings gave me no clues as to where he might have fled. And I was sure that he had gone. It would have been insane for him to remain in the area.

More enquiries of the inn's staff yielded no results. It was as though no one cared that three people were missing. By this time, the party guests had all returned to their homes. Frustrated by my lack of success, I retired to my room to, I must admit, drown myself in wine.

I subsequently drank myself into oblivion.

The following day, my friends and the Colonel were still missing.

I beg that you, with your local connections as a member of Congress, inform the Sheriff of my concerns and have him look into the situation. I fear that the Colonel's connection to the mayor and some businessmen in the community will hinder any investigation I might seek to initiate.

I remain,
Yr Humble and Obt Servt,
Obadiah

Letter from Major Obadiah O'Dale, January 27, 1865

Dear Uncle Owen,

Let me preface this letter by telling you that it is my intention to atone for the crimes I have been forced to commit. I freely admit to the deeds and, if given a second chance, would do them again. You were correct in everything you surmised about Beauregard Kensington, Uncle Owen. The world has been rid of a great evil disguised as a man.

I must now apologize for my dissembling. I did not relate what truly happened on the night of the 18th inst. It was my hope the Sheriff might find my friend Philip's body, however that was a fanciful hope.

In the meantime, thank you for your

valiant efforts with the Sheriff. Unfortunately, the influence of the Kensingtons is very strong in Wycliffe Point and, after only a cursory investigation, and a free dinner at the inn, it was concluded the Colonel had already left for Washington to receive his Medal of Honor. Philip was counted as a deserter since he had not yet been officially mustered out of the 45th. As for Emmeline, she was a colored servant, and no one cared a whit about her.

As I stated in my previous missive, on the night of the 18th I found a bottle of wine and a glass. My intention was to sit by the window and stare out at the bay while slowly drinking myself into welcome oblivion. However, hardly had I been sitting, and having had but a single glass of wine, when I was distracted from my staring by a light off to the right of the inn. The light was not constant and seemed to flicker as if caused by someone walking past a window with a candle.

Standing close to my own window, I tried to spy the source of the light, but couldn't. Not caring about the cold outside, I opened the window and leaned out. I was met with a fierce and frigid wind blowing across the bay from out in the Atlantic. It was pitch black outside and I could see practically nothing. Across the bay was a promontory on which a stone fort had been constructed during the time of troubles with the British that resulted in the burning of the White House in Washington. At this time, the fort was nothing more than a black silhouette against the cloudless sky.

It appeared there was a building next to the inn, one I had apparently never noticed in all my visits there. It was from one of the upper windows that this flicker emanated. The rest of the building remained in darkness. I watched for a few moments, my curiosity piqued, but soon lost interest as nothing more seemed to occur. I was about to close the window when I saw the flicker again. This time there was definitely a visible shadow of movement.

While I cannot swear as to what I saw, I can say, based on my experience during the war, that it was a person slashing something with a sabre. This immediately sent a shiver down my spine far worse than anything caused by the winter wind. In my mind, that could only be one person: Beauregard Kensington. Perhaps I was obsessed with finding the killer. A shadow is a tenuous thing upon which to base a suspicion, but I was desperate to take some kind of action, even if it would prove to be fruitless.

I rushed down to the main desk to enquire about the building. The man at the desk informed me that it was a warehouse owned by the same people as those who had built the inn: the Kensingtons. When I asked if anyone from the inn had access to it, the clerk told me there was a walkway on the fourth floor that crossed over to the corresponding floor of the warehouse.

The door, however, was always kept locked.

It would have been madness for Kensington to have stayed at the inn, but I assumed he was mad. Could he have been hiding in the warehouse that belonged to his family?

Hurrying to the front door, I was stopped by the sudden realization that not only was I not armed, I was also only in my shirtsleeves and would surely freeze to death before I reached the warehouse. I rushed up to my room and retrieved my service revolver from my case. It was still loaded. As I pulled on my greatcoat, I pondered the value of taking my sabre with me. If Kensington was armed with more than just a sabre, my own weapon would be useless. However, based upon what I saw in the window, it did appear possible that he was carrying one. I strapped the scabbard to my belt then made sure my coat concealed it. The fewer questions I had to answer, the better.

There was a narrow path between the inn and the warehouse. It was covered with ice and snow and proved to be treacherous. Twice I slipped and only avoided landing on my backside by grabbing on to the iron fence that ran alongside the path.

I paused at the spot where I assumed Philip had been pushed to his death. My heart was heavy.

When I reached the warehouse, I had to pause to warm my hands. In my haste to leave I had forgotten gloves. I blew on my hands then reached for a door at the side of the warehouse. It was unlocked. This made me even more sure that my quarry was within.

The howling wind and crashing of the waves on the rocks below the cliff masked any sound the door might have made when I opened it. Once inside, I closed it gently then waited for my eyes to adjust to the darkness. All the windows wcrc blockcd by shipping crates and barrels. As I became accustomed to the dark, I perceived a small patch of black that appeared lighter than the rest. I approached the patch and found it to be a flight of wide stairs. The glow of light had come from somewhere up above.

I removed my greatcoat to give me freedom of motion and immediately felt the cold within the building. There was nothing I could do for it now. I withdrew my revolver and cautiously proceeded up the staircase. I held on to my scabbard lest it rattle and raise the alarm. With each step, I could feel the air around me getting staler. Something on one of the upper floors was rotting.

At the top of the stairs, I paused for I had heard something off in the distance. It sounded like a whimper. Trying to force my ears to hear, I concentrated then heard the sound again. It was definitely a whimper, but this time there were at least two people making the noises. Or they might have been animals, I couldn't be sure.

It was lucky for me that the old warehouse had been well-constructed. The floors were solid, and as I made my way along the corridor on the fourth floor, there were no squeaks or creaks from the floorboards.

I proceeded across the floor until I came to a small door. There was a thin band of light showing at the bottom. The source of the glow I had seen.

As quietly as I could, I opened the door.

The room was lit by several lanterns hanging from hooks in the roof beams. At the center of the room stood Kensington, his back to me. I could not see past him. He seemed to be making thrusting motions with his right arm. His sabre arm. Accompanying the motions, was a dull, wet sound I recognized as flesh being cut.

Kensington stepped aside and I was unable to stop myself from gasping.

During my service in the army, I have seen men torn asunder by artillery fire, watched limbs sawn off because of minie balls, heard the screams of horses and cavalrymen impaled on *chevaux-de-frise*. And I've seen the damage inflicted with a well-handled sabre. None of that carnage prepared me for what I saw in that room.

Emmeline hung by her arms from a roof beam. But Kensington, and I have no doubt he was the perpetrator, had violated her body in such a way as to doom him to perpetual torture in the deepest pits of Hell.

While I shall not go into detail, suffice to say, Kensington's sabre had been thrust up into Emmeline's body in such a way that the point protruded from her chest. Her head was impaled upon the point.

It was all I could do not to vomit. By happenstance, the wine I had consumed gave me the strength to confront Kensington.

The man had turned when I gasped, but had not come toward me. He was drenched in blood. When he grinned at me and nodded toward Emmeline, I could see there was no sanity behind those eyes.

"Want to play, O'Dale?" His voice was a quiet rasp. "You have your sabre. Good. It's far more pleasurable than your pecker. Believe me."

I raised my revolver and aimed it at Kensington's head. "Die, you son of a bitch," I said then fired.

His brains blasted out the back of his

skull and splattered across what I took to be bales of rancid cotton. Kensington's body hit the floor with a dull thud. Holstering my revolver, I drew my sabre. I approached the corpse, wary in case he might not yet be dead, despite the clear hole through his head I tried not to cry for Emmeline. My insides were in turmoil at the sight I beheld and the realization that Philip was, indeed, dead.

Standing over Kensington's body. I raised my sabre and brought it down upon his neck, severing his head from his body in a single slash. I then dropped my sabre and fell to my knees. Tears poured from my eyes. What this monster had done here brought me close to insanity. No human should be capable of such animalistic brutality.

Emmeline. Philip. I am sure those many women in New Orleans. The rebel prisoners. How many had died to satisfy this maniac's bloodlust?

Before leaving, I cut down Emmeline and laid her carefully upon the floor. To spare her further indignity, I removed

Kensington's sabre then carefully placed her head next to her torso. I covered her body with my greatcoat. Even in death, she was lovely.

Kensington, I left where he lay.

When I returned to the inn, the lobby was empty. I went straight to my room and drowned myself with wine.

The next morning, I donned my uniform and went to the lobby to wait. The horrific scene was sure to be found and I was fully prepared to face whatever punishment was deemed fitting. I fully expected to be found out as I had left my greatcoat behind.

The Sheriff arrived and conducted his cursory and quite useless investigation. After five hours, no alarm had been raised.

I returned to my room, gathered my belongings, and went to the Wycliffe Point armory. The 45th might be mustering in again. I wanted to return to the war where I might find peace in the arms of death.

I write this at the Wycliffe Point train station as I await transport with the 45th to wherever we are required.

I remain,
Yr Humble and Obt Servt,
Obadiah

Beverly Kent, morning, January 18.2020

Beverly tossed the letters aside. So that was where all this started—Beau in 1865. And he keeps coming back for more. She laughed.

That turncoat couldn't face Beau like a man. No, he had to commit murder from a distance. The woman O'Dale made a noise and rolled over. Blood poured from her nose and a couple of teeth were missing. She'd stuffed the stump of her arm into her shirt to stop some of the bleeding. It hadn't worked very well.

"I suppose you thought you could protect it," said Beverly.

Oona looked up at Beverly and spat. She spied her cook and gasped, but made no other sound. With a look of resignation, she said, "She's a human being, not an animal. He'll protect her this time. It's happening much earlier."

"So, you finally know what's going on. Too little, too late."

"Things can change."

"Like 1985 when the animal killed itself and robbed me of my pleasure?"

This time Oona laughed. "He got you, though. Took you with him off the cliff."

Beverly knelt next to Oona and took hold of her chin. "Maybe, but don't forget, everyone died that time. And it's your turn now."

The turncoat grunted when Beverly shoved her sabre into her belly. She watched her eyes while she sawed upward. "I love working with my sabre. It was supposed to be used on that bitch and her puppy. But I didn't know *you'd* be here. Lucky me."

"Fuck you, Kensington," said Oona through clenched teeth.

"Still alive? I'm a bit rusty." Beverly grabbed a handful of the woman's hair then held it up. Pulling her trusty sabre from the woman's guts, she used it to scalp the traitor. Oona coughed blood and died. "And that's the end of the fucking turncoat O'Dales." She tossed the scalp on the butcher block.

A squeak of the kitchen door alerted Beverly to someone entering the room behind her. Without thinking, she spun, leapt at the intruder, then slashed her sabre across its throat. It was one of the mongrel young. Checking the creature, Beverly was happy to note it wasn't the youngest. That would have been a terrible waste.

She looked up. Somewhere in this pub, on the upper floors, were the rest of the creatures she hunted. Beverly was glad she had her weapon of choice. It had served her well every other time.

Enough had changed this time around, that butchering the animals here instead of the killing room wouldn't throw her plans off course.

Whistling a tune that had been popular during the Civil War, Beverly wiped the mongrel blood from the blade. With a happy heart and the thrill of anticipation, she found the stairs and went up.

Now for some fun. And perhaps a bite to eat.

Chapter 16:
"I'd love to have the chance to start again"

Emma Ranahan, morning, January 18, 2020

"This could become a habit." Peter looked into Emma's eyes then leaned forward to kiss her. "I did miss the trifle, though."

Emma glared at him then threw back the covers to reveal her nakedness. She immediately pulled them back when she felt how cold the room had become. She cuddled into Peter. He jerked away.

"What the hell, Emma? Are your feet always that cold? They weren't like that yesterday."

"We were in my apartment, not the home of a pensioner who seems too cheap to keep the heat on overnight. Get closer. Warm me up."

They stayed like that for several minutes until they heard Sol in the bathroom.

"Does Sol have another bathroom?"

"I don't think so. Do you want to go looking for it without any clothes on?"

Peter laughed. "I think Sol would prefer it if you did. In fact, I'm sure of it."

There was a knock at the door. Sol's voice came through, "Wakey, wakey, young people. It's the 18th. Shit's about to hit the fan and there's more for you to learn. I'll be in the kitchen making breakfast."

They waited for the sound of his footsteps to fade, then both leapt out of the bed. Gathering their clothes from the day before, they made a beeline for the bathroom. It was hot and steamy from Sol taking a shower. On the hamper was a pile of clothes with a note. Emma picked it up and read.

> I figured you would want clean clothes.
> These are some of my late wife's. The
> things for Peter belonged to my son. I
> think everything will fit. And no, Peter,
> the underwear isn't used. He left some
> fresh packs before he moved out.

"Thoughtful of Sol." She picked up a pair of trousers. "Is it significant that these look like something from the forties?"

They stood and stared at each other for a while. The meaning of today had finally hit her and she guessed Peter was feeling the same—an overwhelming sense of dread.

Peter said. "Let's shower, eat, and figure out how we're going to avoid being murdered by a crazy history professor who's possessed by the spirit of a dead ancestor."

"When you put it that way, it still sounds fucking weird."

Emma climbed in the shower. She reached out and pulled Peter in with her.

After a surprisingly long shower, they dressed and went for breakfast. When Sol saw Emma, he stopped what he was doing. "If it wasn't for you being a little younger, Emma, you'd be the spitting image of my late Mary."

"Mary was Black?"

"Well, except for that part. And her hair was blonde. Her boobs were bigger. Sorry." He remained silent for a few seconds. "I miss her."

Emma went over and gave him a hug. She slapped his hand when he tried to grab a cheek.

"So, what have you got to show us?" asked Peter. "Is it more to do with the sub?"

"A little. Some police reports from the time. And I've got a few things from 1985 that you will find interesting. It'll explain why I haven't thrown you out on your ears for being loonies. But you still owe me some explaining."

"How much time do you think we have? Beverly's out there doing who knows what."

"I can start with the police reports, if you don't mind reading some gruesome stuff with breakfast." When Peter nodded, Sol left the table then returned with a folder. He passed it to Peter. "Coroner's reports."

Peter opened the folder and took out the first report. Emma shuffled closer so she could read at the same time as Peter.

Summary of the Coroner's reports on the bodies of Oscar O'Dale (male), Benjamin Kenton (male), Emily Renehan (female), January 19, 1945

[Provided to Peter Dawson by retired Police Chief Solomon Winthrop.]

> Oscar O'Dale, male, aged 75. The subject died as a result of a massive heart attack caused by a coronary occlusion. It is the opinion of the coroner that the

subject would have instantly succumbed to the heart attack and could not have been saved.

Benjamin Kenton, male, aged 40. The exact cause of the subject's death could not be found. There were several possibilities evidenced by the body. The lungs were filled with seawater. The heart had burst. The body exhibited numerous lacerations, broken bones, and internal injuries consistent with severe body trauma. The trauma may have been caused by the body's being pummelled against the cliff face by the rogue wave reported on the night of the subject's death. Finally, the face of the subject was frozen in a look of abject terror which suggests a fright may have led to the bursting of the heart. The subject was also suffering from an advanced case of syphilis.

Emily Renehan, negro, female, aged 30. The subject suffered a deep wound which bisected the abdomen from the pubis to the sternum. This wound cut through the stomach lining, the uterus, severed several sections of the small intestine, and the transverse colon of the large intestine. A lateral wound crossed the lower abdomen and also severed the small intestine and both the ascending and descending colon. The weapon nicked both iliac crests of the pelvis. Finally, a deep wound to the neck which resulted in the severing of the carotid artery and the jugular vein would have caused the subject to bleed to death in seconds. There was also evidence of post-mortem sexual interference.

When she read the description of the horror suffered by her previous self, Emma felt the room spin. She heard her head hit the table, then nothing.

Emily Renehan, January 18, 1945

She shook the snow globe then brought it close to her eyes so she could watch the white particles swirl around the inn. It amazed her that the building in the globe looked so much like the place she worked, right down to the blank door on the wall facing the old warehouse. If she concentrated hard enough, Emily could see the little people who lived in the inn. The light in the room was dim because of the heavy blackout curtains over the windows. Emily rubbed her eyes a couple of times as if that would help her focus. She wanted to see the couples again.

When she first received the snow globe—a gift from a distant aunt, one she didn't know she had, who said it had been in the family for decades—Emily had imagined she saw movement in the inn's windows. Sure enough, in a fourth-floor window, a couple stood arm in arm. The man, dressed in a cavalry uniform like one she had seen in a movie, looked vaguely familiar. The woman was dark skinned like her. There was another couple standing on a third-floor balcony. This man, also familiar, had a uniform, but it looked different from the other one. And the woman's clothes looked more modern, though still old compared to current fashion. She was also dark skinned.

Emily put down the globe before she saw that other, evil one. He gave her a bad feeling, lurking in the shadows of the little inn, seeming to wait for a chance to do something bad. She shivered when she thought about him and immediately remembered that man, Ben something, who had tried to assault her. She'd taken good care of him, and so had Paul and some of the men who worked at the inn. He hadn't shown his face at the inn for a few days, but Emily still felt nervous whenever she had to go outside with the trash or look for something in the pantry.

The grandfather clock downstairs chimed, and Emily quickly got her heavy coat from the wardrobe. Paul had asked her to meet him in the cave under the inn at eight o'clock. He'd be there in half an hour. Paul was never late.

She wondered why he was so anxious to see her. When he'd

called this afternoon, which almost got her in trouble with Mr. O'Dale, the manager, because staff were not allowed to use the inn's telephone, Paul seemed excited. He wouldn't tell Emily why he wanted to see her so badly, but she had a crazy idea that he might try something silly.

She thought, hoped, feared, prayed, doubted, he was going to propose. It was a ridiculous idea, even if New Jersey was one of the few states that didn't have anti-miscegenation laws. Where would they live? What would they do? She didn't care. Emily wanted to be with Paul.

Emily still had trouble believing Paul was a real person and not some dream that took form whenever she felt fanciful. When he approached her at the USO dance, she had been wary. White men had tried it on with her before, figuring she would be an easy mark because of her low station in life. She'd sent them packing with a few choice words, and the occasional kick to the groin.

But Paul's moxie and persistence had captured her heart. He seemed so sincere and open about his interest in her. Emily felt safe with Paul.

When Emily passed the hallway leading to the lobby, she heard Mr. O'Dale speaking to a guest. He seemed a little put off, as if the guest was making some unreasonable demand. Emily admired the way Mr. O'Dale could always calm irate guests and, oftentimes, send them away without whatever it was they were demanding, thinking they had won the argument.

"Miss Renehan!" It was Mr. O'Dale. Emily paused for a moment to consider whether or not to see what he wanted, but the grandfather clock began to chime eight o'clock. Paul would be waiting.

Emily ran through the kitchen to the door leading to the cave. She hoped Mr. O'Dale would forgive her for ignoring him this one time. Paul was far more important.

Though the cave was well-protected from the icy sea winds, it was still frightfully cold. She stepped back, next to the large enclosure built to store the trash cans. There was a can sitting near the wall, so Emily, knowing how Mr. O'Dale was fanatical about keeping everything, even the trash cans, spotlessly clean, took a seat to wait for Paul. The chill from the metal can lid penetrated the layers of her heavy coat, but her feet were sore from standing too much, and her knees ached from the hours spent scrubbing the bathroom floors. It was a relief to sit, even for a few moments. Perhaps Paul would massage her feet again. He seemed to take great pleasure in that small task. In fact, Emily had noticed that he became somewhat aroused while he rubbed her feet. He'd even jokingly kissed her toes once down on the small beach at the bottom of the cliff path. A thrill ran through her when she felt the softness of his lips.

Emily experienced that thrill now, but it quickly passed when she thought about her scars.

What would Paul say when she told him? They'd probably be gone by the end of the month, like they always were, but what about next January? How would Paul react when her body was suddenly marred by hideous scars that she couldn't explain? Fortunately, they hadn't been intimate. Yet.

With shaking hands, and nervous now because of the scars,

Emily pulled a packet of cigarettes from her coat pocket. Mr. O'Dale discouraged smoking and would not permit employees to indulge while on inn property. She thought it unlikely anyone would catch her in the few minutes it would take her to have one.

Before she could light up, a hand appeared before her holding a lighter. Transfixed by the dancing flame, Emily didn't feel the other hand cover her mouth until it was too late. The flame went out and she was dragged back behind the trash enclosure. She tried to scream, but was cut off by a foul-smelling rag stuffed into her mouth. Whoever it was assaulting her had her on the ground, straddling her waist. In the dim light, Emily could make out the ugly features of that horrible man who had been bothering her. Ben something.

He smiled down at her. "I've already taken care of that army asshole. Now it's your turn, bitch." Something cold and hard pressed against Emily's throat followed by a warmth as liquid flowed down her exposed neck. The maniac had cut her throat in the same place as that damned scar. Emily knew she was going to die and instantly wished Paul had been able to save her…this time.

The man tore open Emily's coat then pulled her skirt up. She tried to resist, but knew her strength was leaving her body with the blood from her neck. There was a tugging on her belly then unbelievable pain. She was sure he had just sliced along the scar below her belly.

At the last moment, as life faded from her, Emily looked into the eyes of her killer and recognized the other.

Peter Dawson, late morning, January 18, 2020

The moment she had fainted, Peter fell to his knees next to Emma and held her. She jerked and moaned for several minutes then opened her eyes. She looked afraid.

Rubbing her stomach, she said, "I saw him kill me, Peter." She tried to crawl further into Peter's arms, shivering. "I've not seen him in the other…dreams or memories. And then the report, with the details of the wounds."

"Your keloids," said Peter.

She nodded. "I wish I didn't know. He's an animal."

"Do you think she's going to be as bad?"

Emma let out a long breath. He figured she was as tired of all the crazy shit happening as he was. Peter wanted to go home, with Emma, and live a normal life without crazed killers stalking them, and nightmares about past incarnations.

He didn't say anything which was good because, what could he say? She knew he'd seen Beau or whoever he was at the time in his own memories. He'd also seen her killed. How had she been so lucky to avoid it all this time?

"Is she all right?" Sol stood next to them. Emma looked up at him and smiled. "I'll get you something to drink. I think I need one. Peter?"

"It's a bit early, but sure, why not? Thanks." Peter squeezed Emma again. "How are you now?"

She pulled away from Peter then leaned forward to kiss his cheek. "I'm okay now. It was such a shock. How have you been able to stand it?"

"Look, this has only been happening to me for a couple of days, since I arrived in Wycliffe Point. It's all new. Thanks." He took a shot glass from Sol who passed another to Emma.

"Highland Park 18," said Sol. He knocked back his own drink. When Peter and Emma had done the same, he said, "I could use another. You?"

Peter shook his head. "No. Later. I need to know more about 1945."

"There." Sol pointed to the file folder then passed it to Peter. "Read the other police report from the time. Then read the summary I wrote afterward. Might shed some light on things."

Emma didn't pull her chair away from Peter's. She could read the reports at the same time, but she had a death grip on his arm, still shaken.

Police report on the events that occurred at and below the Kensington Inn, Wycliffe Point, January 18, 1945

[Copy provided to Peter Dawson by retired Police Chief Solomon Winthrop.]

> The Chief of Police was called to the Kensington Inn at 11:00 p.m. by Mr. Owen O'Dale, manager of the inn. He

reported the discovery of two bodies, both of whom he suggested had died under mysterious circumstances. He also wished to report a further death, this due to natural causes.

Upon arrival at the inn, the Chief was shown to a room on the main floor where he was presented with the body of a man identified as Oscar O'Dale, formerly of Wycliffe Point, lately of Albany, New York, uncle of Mr. Owen O'Dale. Mr. O'Dale informed the Chief that his uncle had arrived at the inn at approximately nine pm in an agitated state. He told the manager he feared several persons at the inn might be in danger though he could not be specific as to the nature of the danger. The persons at risk were a maid, Miss Emily Renehan, and any guest whose name might be Dawson. The threat, he said, was coming from someone possibly named Kensington or something similar.

The manager immediately realized his uncle was referring to Paul Dawson, a soldier currently stationed at the fort, who was involved with Miss Renehan. Mr. O'Dale assumed that the threat was from a man named Ben Kenton, already known to police, and sought in regard to an assault on Miss Renehan.

Before any action could be taken on the part of the O'Dales, Mr. O'Dale said that his uncle cried out that it was too late, pointed at a light coming from the ocean side of the inn, then fell down dead of an apparent heart attack (This will be confirmed by the coroner.).

Mr. O'Dale then led the Chief to a cave below the inn where trash is stored. Behind some cans, he revealed the mutilated body of Miss Renehan. She had been dead for some time as the blood on her clothes was frozen solid and her body held no heat. The body was immediately covered with a tarpaulin due to the horrific nature of the mutilations (These will be described in detail by the coroner.).

Below the inn, at a point where the cave opens on to a path leading to a small pebble beach, Mr. O'Dale showed the body of the previously noted Ben Kenton. The man appeared to have drowned though the look of sheer terror on his face told a possible alternate story. Also found in the cave was a pocket watch with the name Paul Dawson inscribed within and a gold ring with the inscription, *Emily & Paul Always.* It is postulated that Mr. Dawson may have been another victim of the killer.

The three bodies were conveyed to the coroner's office for examination.

Summary of the coroner's reports on the bodies found in Wycliffe Bay on January 20 and 22, 1945

[Summary provided to Peter Dawson by retired Police Chief Solomon Winthrop.]

John Doe #1, male, aged approximately twenty-five years. The body was severely burnt though the cause of the burns could not be identified. The single distinguishing mark is a partially burned tattoo on the upper right arm. The letters D and V could be distinguished. A single boot was still on the body. It has been identified as the style of boot worn by members of the German Navy.

Paul Dawson, male, aged thirty-five. For security purposes, the identity of the subject is to remain confidential. The subject showed damage due to exposure to the cold water. The eyes and some soft tissues are missing due to the activity of crabs or fish. A wound on the subject's torso, probably made by a long sharp blade such as a sword, traversed the body from the center of the back, through the heart, then out the front puncturing the sternum. This wound, however, was not the cause of death, though it would have proved fatal. As the lungs were filled with sea water, the man had drowned.

Note: The bodies of a negro family consisting of four adults (presumable parents and grandparents), two teenaged boys, and two young girls which were discovered in a shack at the edge of the inn property are believed to have no connection to the events leading to the deaths of the aforementioned people.

"Why does he kill the family first every time?" Peter scratched the back of his head

"Because he can and because he likes it," said Emma.

Sol coughed. "Earlier you mentioned saving her life this time. I'm so damned confused and I know I'm not senile even if I am over a hundred years old. What the hell are you talking about?"

"You wouldn't believe us if we told you everything," said Emma.

"Does it have anything to do with the murders at the inn, the fire, what happened to Owen and Oliver in 1985?"

Emma nodded.

"Folks," said Peter. "I know about the murders, or at least some of them. There seem to be so many. I think. Or are they all the same, just repeated over and over?" Peter scratched his head. "And what fire? Where? And what about Owen and Oliver? They both seemed fine except for those nasty scars on their necks from Tiddlywinks."

Emma burst out laughing. Sol chuckled. He rose from his chair and shuffled out of the room. Over his shoulder, he said, "Emma, explain to the poor boy about the inn, will you? I'm off to get another box from the attic with some things that you both might find interesting. And perhaps enlightening."

When he heard Sol going into the other room, Peter took Emma's hand and said, "What the hell is going on? What is it about the inn? It seems fine to me."

"Peter, you keep saying you're staying there," she said. "Which inn? There's the one next door to this, where Mrs. Vaughan works. You saw it when we arrived here. The only other inn is the Inn on the Cliff, past the library. It's a ruin that's being renovated. It was gutted in the fire. You can't be staying there. It's not open yet, probably not for another year at least."

"The Inn on the Cliff. Beverly and I checked in a couple of days ago. I made the arrangements online. Owen is very friendly, if a little weird. His brother, Oliver, I haven't seen much. The rest of the guests seem friendly enough, but they keep to themselves. To be honest, I've only seen the Black family." He paused, thinking. "Damn. Four adults, four kids."

"Has anything strange happened?" Emma looked concerned.

Peter hesitated. *Should he tell her about that first night? Damn it.* With all this talk about multiple lives and murders, how could his experience seem any weirder?

"Okay, Emma. The first night I saw someone on the stairs. A maid. She looked just like you. The two of you could be twins. Later, in bed, I..." She squeezed his arm in encouragement. "I got laid. The thing is, I was half asleep and didn't see her. To be honest, I'm not even sure there was really someone there. But it sure felt amazing. And this will sound completely deranged... I thought it was the maid or maybe...well, you."

Emma blinked a lot as if processing what Peter had told her.

"I need a drink," she said. She poured them both another shot of whiskey.

She heard Sol thumping around.

Holding Peter's hand, Emma began her story. "First, the

inn burned down in 1985. Like I said, it's being renovated, but it's not open yet. When it burned down, Oliver O'Dale was the manager. Owen O'Dale was Oliver's uncle. They were both killed in the fire along with several guests and a maid. I think the maid was me and one of the guests was you. I assume the killer was in there somewhere, too."

"What exactly are you saying?"

"Are you deaf?" She smiled. "You can't be staying at the inn. It's not open. You can't be interacting with Owen and Oliver because they're both dead. There can't be any other guests, unless they're dead as well."

"But that's impossible. I mean, Beverly's staying there. She's had conversations with Owen. It just can't be true."

"After all this, that's what can't be true?"

Peter guffawed. "I stayed there. My stuff's there. My car is parked there. I had a meal." Peter stopped speaking, mulling over what Emma had said. "If it's not open, it might explain my appetite yesterday. Why I was so hungry despite a huge breakfast and at least a pot of coffee. Coffee usually makes me need to… Anyway, I didn't need. Could I have imagined all of it? Imagined such a great meal? All that detail?"

"I don't know."

"Look, Emma, all this stuff—the repeated murders, reincarnation, flashbacks, that's hard enough to get my head around, even though we've talked it through. But now you're telling me that what's happening now, this year, right here, to me, is a fantasy." Peter got up, grabbed his coat. "This is bullshit. I don't know what the fuck you're trying to do. Did someone slip some magic mushrooms into my breakfast?" He pulled on his coat and went to the front door. "Give Sol my apologies. I'll see you later. Maybe."

Emma sat, unmoving. As Peter left the house, he heard her say, "Can this situation get any stranger?"

"Oh, yes," said Sol. "Wait until you see this."

Peter yanked the door closed behind him.

Chapter 17:
"But have we got enough time?"

Peter Dawson, afternoon, January 18, 2020

Peter stormed out of the house, yanking the door closed behind him. The vibration caused snow on the roof to slide off, some landing on his head, a lot going down his collar. He shivered. The tears in his eyes froze as they slid down his cheeks.

Great. And now it's snowing harder than ever. Fuck!

He walked down the path then halted, uncertain about what to do. One thing was for sure: he needed time to think. It was enough to believe all the reincarnation stuff he and Emma had experienced, but to accept all that had happened at the inn was an illusion… That, perhaps, was a step too far.

"Fuck!" he screamed at the sky.

A passing crow screamed back at him. It sounded remarkably like, "fuck you."

Looking north along the road, Peter could just about see the pub and the library building. The inn was completely obscured, though the other buildings would probably have blocked his view anyway. Even now, he couldn't be certain the inn wasn't real. With a quick glance back at Sol's house, he decided to investigate. It would give him time to clear his head and calm down. Peter felt unreasonably angry with Emma and she deserved none of it.

"Messed it up again, Petey, old boy. Pick a maniac or alienate perfection."

At the end of the garden path, Peter opened the gate and stepped out onto where he assumed the sidewalk was located.

Immediately, his feet went out from under him landing him in a deep, but soft, snowbank. More snow went down his collar. Getting to his knees, he knew he was on the sidewalk when his kneecap found the edge of an uneven flagstone. He was tempted to admit defeat, turn around, and return to the warmth of the house. However, a previously unknown stubbornness overtook him, forcing him to get to his feet and hobble off in the vague direction of the pub.

Peter planned out his actions. First, he would check in at the pub. If the inn was an illusion, perhaps Beverly had gone there for a meal. If she was still there, he could confront her. That is, if he had the nerve. He had no idea what he would do or say if he did encounter his ex-flame. Beverly was scary enough as it is; possessed by a psychotic ancestor, she might be downright dangerous.

After the pub, there was the library where he could pick up his laptop. It would allow him to check his emails and see for himself, and maybe prove to Emma, that he had corresponded with the Inn on the Cliff and Owen O'Dale.

Then there would come the scariest part: the inn itself. Either he would find it to be perfectly normal, or it would be a ruin in the process of being renovated. Either way, within the hour, he would know the truth.

I just hope I can handle the truth. I hope it's real. Owen is too cool of a guy to be a ghost or whatever.

Peter found the front door of the pub locked. It was supposed to reopen for the lunch rush, but there was a crude and hastily written sign in the window stating it would be closed until further notice. That seemed odd. When he and

Emma had left, everything had been normal. Oona was happy and had said she would make more trifle.

Peering inside, Peter saw no movement and no sign that anyone was there. Deciding to make absolutely sure everything was okay, he followed a path around to the back of the pub. There was an open door letting in wind and snow. That was an unlikely thing for Oona to miss.

Cautiously, Peter entered, finding himself in the kitchen. He resisted the temptation to call out. If Beverly was here, there was no point in alerting her to his presence too soon. He could at least try to find a weapon first, maybe a shotgun or flamethrower.

The moment he pushed the door closed behind him, as soon as the fresh air was cut off, the stench reached his nose.

Blood and excrement.

"Fuck."

Taking one step further in, Peter's foot connected with something solid. He watched the cook's head roll across the tiles then come to a rest in the large pool of congealed blood that surrounded the cook's body.

Why am I not running away, screaming like a little child? I've just found a beheaded cook.

Given what he had seen in his…flashbacks… memories…hallucinations, this was nothing.

There was no point checking to see if the cook was still alive. Staying as far away from the corpse as possible, Peter made his way to the far side of the kitchen hoping to find Oona. He didn't think the chances were good given all that had already happened.

What little hope Peter had was dashed by the sight of Oona Conroy propped up against a chopping block.

Peter assumed it was Oona. The shredded clothes looked familiar. The poor woman had been gutted, her insides pulled out and strewn about the floor. Whoever had done it must have been ferociously angry because there were stab and slash wounds all over Oona's body. Even her hands and feet had been pierced then cut off. The maniac had taken the weapon, whatever it was, to Oona's head, carving up her neck and face until she was almost unrecognizable. Her scalp rested at the center of the chopping block.

Unable to take any more, Peter ran over to the sink and vomited. He stayed there until all that was left were dry heaves.

It was from here he noticed the boy lying by the door to the dining room. Someone had slashed his throat open, coating the walls and floor with arterial spray. From the look of surprise on the boy's face, he must have walked in on the murderer and paid the price.

"You wouldn't have been alone," said Peter. He looked up to where he knew there were rooms for guests. "Oh, fuck. No."

The dead boy was Black. The prelude to the murder of his past loves was the slaughter of a Black family. That might mean that there were more dead people in the pub.

"This is too much," said Peter.

He stumbled into the dining room to call the police but discovered the telephone behind the bar had been torn from its jack then smashed. "Shit." Peter never carried a cell phone because too often it went off while he was in the middle of doing some research and broke his train of thought. There was no sign of a cell belonging to the pub staff anywhere. While he was behind the bar, Peter spotted some papers covered with writing on the floor. Picking them up, he saw they were letters, so he stuffed them in his coat pocket for later.

Cautiously, Peter went up the narrow staircase to the guestrooms. All the doors were open, but the place was absolutely silent except for a steady drip. Unless the killer was lurking in some hiding spot waiting to kill him, Peter figured he was alone. Moving along the hall, he glanced in each room. That was enough to tell him the prelude had concluded. The dripping was blood from a head caught by the hair in a ceiling fan.

"How fast are you killing?" he asked, scanning the slaughtered remains, "And how do you know how to kill?"

The phones in the rooms had been trashed. Peter was isolated.

Returning to the main floor, Peter paused to note that he felt remarkably calm despite discovering ten eviscerated people. All his past lives had been military men, so maybe some of their experience and fortitude had rubbed off on Peter. He hoped some of their skill with weapons would rub off, too.

Though he was reluctant to see Oona's body again, Peter left the pub through the kitchen door. There would be too much to explain if someone caught him leaving through the front.

The storm had increased in its ferocity, making it almost impossible to see across the road due to the heavy, swirling snow. Only the sound of crashing waves behind the howling wind hinted at the presence of the bay.

Peter reached the front door of the library. It was securely locked, and he had no idea if there was a back entrance. He assumed there would be a side door leading to a flight of stairs. He walked along the sidewalk, slipping occasionally on the ice under the snow. His thighs ached from the tension it took to be careful.

When he reached the north end of the library building, the Inn on the Cliff loomed through the blowing snow. It was real. He could see the lump that was his precious Falcon buried under the snow. Strange indentations in the snow where the windshield should have been made him groan. Would she have been that petty? Would she really have taken the time to trash his beloved car?

There was no sign of life at the inn, no lights burned, the doors were closed.

Peter let out a small yelp when he felt a hand on his shoulder. Spinning quickly, prepared to fight, or try to fight, whoever was attacking, relief flowed through him when he saw Emma's beautiful face. She had tears in her eyes.

"Emma, I'm so sorry for what I said. I'm an idiot, a moron, a fool who doesn't deserve you. Can you forgive me? Please."

He longed for her to smile for him, but instead she said, "She destroyed everything, Peter. The bitch tore apart everything I own. And she literally shit on the remains." Emma's mouth kept moving, but nothing came out. She shook her head.

Taking her in his arms, Peter said, "I was in the pub. She's been there, too. You don't want to go in there."

Emma looked into his eyes. "Oona?"

Peter nodded. "Oona, the cook, the eight members of a Black family. It was Kensington. Or his surrogate."

"We have to get the police. Let's go back to Sol's and call."

"Is there a phone in the library? It's right here."

"I'm not thinking straight. Sorry. I just want to get out of this…" Emma stared over Peter's shoulder with her mouth hanging open. "Tell me you see it, too. Please." There was panic in her voice.

He turned to see what had alarmed her.

In four of the inn's windows, lights now shone. Clear as day, in each window stood a man in uniform. All had red hair, held a sabre, and smiled at the couple outside.

"No way," said Peter. "Impossible."

"We're both having the same hallucination. Come on. We have to get back to Sol's. There's something you have to read."

"I found some letters." He patted his pocket to make sure they were still there. "Oh, fuck."

As they both watched, a fifth light illuminated a window. Staring down at them, wielding a sabre, face haloed by flaming red hair, stood Beverly. She, too, wore a uniform.

"What the actual?"

Emma pulled on Peter's arm, but he was transfixed by the sight of Beverly up there. Very slowly, she raised something to her face and took a bite.

It was a small leg.

Emma Ranahan, afternoon, January 18, 2020

She led Peter around the side of the library and through a heavy door to the main floor.

"I don't think I can face going up to my rooms again," she said. "In the basement, there's an office. It should be safe. For now, I hope."

"Lead on," said Peter.

When they reached the basement, Emma pulled Peter along the main corridor. Again, she was afraid to let go of him in case he was taken away. Or worse, he disappeared and all this crap was an illusion. If he wasn't real, what was the point of fighting back?

Next to the carrel with the microfilm reader was the entrance to the old room where the money had been kept when the warehouse was a going concern. Inside was a vault, no longer in operation, but secure enough to keep them safe from Beverly or Beau or anyone wielding a sabre. Emma slammed the door then had Peter drag a heavy four-drawer file cabinet in front of it. For some reason, she didn't think the barrier would stop a lunatic determined to get through the door. But it would delay her.

A desk had been set up inside the old vault. Emma sat in one of the chairs, Peter took the other.

"We should be okay in here for a while," she said.

"Emma," said Peter. He seemed at a loss for words.

"It's all right, Peter. I understand. I'm not angry with you. This whole affair is confusing and unbelievable. If you had told me all that had happened, and I hadn't experienced any of it myself, I'd think you were nuts. And then there's this." She opened her coat then lifted her sweater. The keloids were back, itchier than ever. This time around, they felt like they were bigger, as well. One of them bled from her constant scratching.

Peter took her hand. "We'll get through this. I don't know how, but we will. Do you have any idea what to do?"

"Maybe. Sol gave me these." She took a folder out of her coat pocket and passed it to Peter. "It's a report he wrote in 1985. It explains a lot. Keep an open mind, Peter."

"Do we really have time for this?"

"It's important. We'll make time. Read."

Police report on the destruction of the Inn on the Cliff and the deaths of several employees and residents, Wycliffe Point, January 31, 1985

[Copy provided to Emma Ranahan and Peter Dawson by retired Police Chief Solomon Winthrop.]

> This report is not being filed with the rest of the documentation relating to the fire and deaths at the Inn on the Cliff.
>
> Having been present the last time the inn was the scene or tragedy (January 1945), I have been able to extrapolate and speculate regarding the events and participants involved. Were official

channels to read this, I, Solomon Winthrop, Chief of Police, would be out of a job and probably confined to a sanitorium.

For detailed background information on the events of January 1945, refer to official police records. These are in-depth and include information not released to the general public due to security measures imposed by the War Department during World War 2.

In summary, in 1945, a female employee of the inn (Emily Renehan) was brutally murdered in a cave below the inn. Also killed was a transient (Ben Kenton) whom authorities believe was involved in the woman's death. A relative of an employee (Oscar O'Dale) died of a heart attack under suspicious circumstances possibly related to the other two deaths. A soldier connected to the deceased woman (Paul Dawson) was found dead in the bay a few days later. I have linked his death to the woman's. Several unidentified bodies, later suspected of being German sailors, were found in the bay at the time.

The Inn on the Cliff burned on January 18th of this year. The Fire Marshall's investigation concluded the blaze was caused by a leaking propane tank at the back of the inn. The gas had seeped into the kitchen area of the inn where a short in the ancient electrical wiring ignited it. Due to the inn's old and dry wood. the fire was out of control before the Fire Department could save the building. All that remained was a shell.

Five people were caught in the blaze, later identified as:

- Oliver and Owen O'Dale, respectively manager and owner of the inn
- Em Ranahan, maid
- Prescott Davidson, salesman from Michigan
- Buster Kenyon, unknown

What's described above, however, is not what happened.

The afternoon of the blaze, I had received a call from the local tow truck company that they had retrieved an abandoned car a few miles out of town.

There was no note and nothing in the car to help identify the owner. As it turned out, the car was a rental. Something the truck driver had noticed was a set of footprints leading away from the car toward town. He said he followed the tracks in his truck for about a mile before they disappeared next to a set of bus tire tracks. The driver thought the car driver had been picked up by some good Samaritan.

Wrapping up warmly because, though the storm had passed, there was still a frigid wind blowing into town from the Atlantic, I climbed into my patrol car. It seemed a good idea to cruise around town to see if I could spot an unfamiliar bus. Or any bus, for that matter.

Barely had I gone a few blocks, when I spied a bus parked between the Inn on the Cliff and the library building next door. There used to be a walkway up on the fourth floor that connected the two buildings, but that had collapsed back in 1905. I pulled up behind the bus and noted that it had out-of-state plates.

There was no sound of activity inside the bus, which appeared to have been converted into a motor home. I found a set of tracks leading from the front door toward the inn's main entrance. I decided to check out the bus first, then pursue my enquiries at the inn.

The bus door was unlocked. I was able to get it open and was immediately assailed by an overpowering stench that was all too familiar. I had taken only a single step into the bus when I saw the first bloodstain. There was a splash of blood across the windshield that told me something awful had occurred here.

I reached the driver's seat and saw the interior, then had to run back outside where I vomited up my lunch, breakfast, and probably a few meals from the day before. I hadn't seen carnage like that since I had served in Korea. Regaining my composure, I returned to the interior of the bus. The only way to quickly assess the number of victims was to count the heads. Arms, legs, and entrails were tossed all about the place. There were four corpses—two female, two male. There was also a small torso which I immediately could tell was that of a little girl.

When I returned after vomiting yet again, I proceeded to the rear of the bus where I found the eviscerated bodies of three children, two boys, one girl. There was an extra girl's head which I concluded belonged to the torso I had found before. One of the smaller legs showed evidence of bites. I chose to attribute this to rats, though the bites were far too large to be caused by rodents. This allows me to sleep at night.

A further search of the bus revealed some blood-covered men's clothes that, at first glance, did not appear to fit either of the adult males. Upon checking the small bathroom, there was evidence someone had showered to remove large quantities of blood and viscera. I concluded that whoever had perpetuated this crime had left his own soiled clothes and stolen some belonging to one of the victims.

It seemed clear the killer (for some reason, I assumed there was only one) had gone to the inn. I wondered at the sanity of someone who would do this horrendous thing to a family then casually walk away with no effort to hide the crime. Or, perhaps, the killer simply didn't care about being caught.

Pulling my service revolver, I went to the front entrance. Upon entering, a strong wind rushed down the stairs. This was caused by the window at the second-floor landing being broken. I later concluded the break was due to two men going through it to their deaths on the rocks below.

On the stairs themselves, I found two men I had known for a long time. Oliver O'Dale, the current manager of the inn, had a deep wound to his neck. I determined it must have come from a long blade. He was quite dead as the blade had severed his carotid artery. There were blood sprays across the walls and a huge pool around his head.

The other victim was Owen O'Dale, Oliver's uncle and the current owner of the inn. He also had a gash at his neck, but this was not bleeding as he was clutching his neck and had stanched the flow of blood. When I checked for a pulse, I was shocked to find him still alive. His eyes fluttered open and he recognized me.

"Hold on, old friend," I said. "I'll go call for help."

He grabbed my wrist when I tried to leave. "No. Upstairs. Millie. Shot. Check her."

Millie Ranahan was the new maid at the inn. I had met her a few times. She was also someone I had recognized when she arrived.

I found a room on the second floor with its door standing wide open. Inside lay the body of Millie the maid. I was thankful I had already emptied my stomach. The sight that greeted me was of such bloody savagery, I could scarcely believe it could have been done by a human.

Her head lay in a wide pool of blood. She was on her back with a pistol still gripped in her hand. Blood oozed from a wound in her temple. She was dead, clearly a suicide. This was a small comfort. Her neck and torso were slashed open by something long and extremely sharp, possibly a sword. The cuts had gone cleanly through her clothing and into her body. The poor woman's head had practically been severed from her body. I immediately thought of a previous maid who had been murdered at the inn forty years prior to this. These wounds were almost identical to those of so long ago. For a moment, I wondered if both crimes had been committed by the same hand. Although the cuts were severe, there was no blood spatter from them. I concluded they were inflicted post-mortem.

The strangest thing about Millie was that there was a smile upon her face as if she was happy with what she had done. I couldn't imagine why.

I quickly returned to Owen, who had managed to sit himself up against the wall. He was still trying to hold the wound in his neck closed. From the paleness of his skin, I didn't think he would survive the wait for an ambulance.

As I knelt next to Owen, he opened his eyes. "Sol," he said. "Don't let it happen again."

"What do you mean, Owen?" I asked.

"1945. Remember." My mind immediately flashed back to the events of January 1945 and the deaths that had occurred then at the inn. I had been correct in my theory about the maid's wounds. "Must stop it. You know what I mean. They're the same ones."

I was confused by what he meant, and it must have shown on my face.

"Millie up there. Davidson and Kenyon went through the window. Remember before?"

The names came back to me. Emily Renehan. Paul Dawson. Ben Kenton.

Owen saw the recognition in my eyes. "Same ones. Every time. Dead family somewhere?"

I nodded. "Outside in a bus."

"Burn it down."

"What? Burn what?"

He clutched my arm with a strength I wouldn't have thought possible given the amount of blood he had lost.

"They'll come back in forty years. It'll happen again. Here. Burn the place down. Please."

With that, Owen let out a final breath and died.

I sat back, avoiding the pooled blood, and thought about what I had discovered and what Owen had said. It was fantastic, but I had been there in 1945. I remembered. The names were too similar. In fact, two of them were identical.

Deciding I needed more information, and that, since everyone here was dead, a few hours wouldn't make any difference, I left the scene. I carefully locked the front door and returned to my office. There, I pulled my files from the 1945 case. Owen had mentioned every forty years. The walkway had collapsed in 1905. I pulled any records I could find on events surrounding the inn for that year. Just to be thorough, I also checked for 1865.

Two hours later, I returned to the inn. Nothing had changed. No one had moved, not that I expected anyone to get up and walk away. But after what I had read, it would not have surprised me.

Before doing anything further, I made my way down to the bottom of the cliff. At a place below the second landing window, I discovered two bodies—Davidson and Kenyon. They were badly damaged from the fall and contact with the rocks. However, it was clear that Davidson had been run through with a sabre, which was still embedded in his chest. Kenyon showed evidence of having been throttled, though it was impossible to discern if this was the cause of death or the fall. In any case, I chose to carry the two bodies, one at a time, up to the inn and place them in the lobby.

Using knowledge I had gained from reading fire marshal reports, and experience gained as an engineer in Korea, I set about readying the inn for destruction. Within half an hour, the Inn on the Cliff was ablaze. I was sure there was no way the Fire Department would be able to arrive in time to save the building. I helped by not calling in an alarm until I was sure. There was no danger to the library next door.

I was able to guide the Fire Marshal to a satisfactory conclusion that did not indicate arson on my part.

The bodies were identified, including the Black family from the bus. I came up with a believable story about what happened and quickly closed the case. Fortunately, no one in authority in Wycliffe Point desired any scandal that might hurt the town's economy.

To my everlasting shame. I had compromised a crime scene and destroyed evidence. However, it is my firm belief, and something I can never relate to anyone, that by doing what I did, I have saved the lives of some people who may not yet have been born.

I am sure if ever anyone reads this report, I will either be charged with a crime or committed to an asylum.

Peter Dawson, afternoon, January 18, 2020

"I don't know what's more upsetting, the events this report describes, or the fact that Owen, who I thought of as a friend, isn't real. He's a ghost, I think."

"Peter, I think Owen has always been our friend. In everything we've read or remembered, an O'Dale has been there to help try and keep us alive. And after, he's cleaned up the mess."

"That makes sense in a weird way. He must have been the one who sent me the letter about the sub. When I was speaking to him…two days ago…he sort of hinted that he knew more than he was letting on. Son of a bitch!" Peter thumped the desk. "I thought he wasn't drinking any coffee at breakfast. I should have paid more attention."

"You didn't drink any coffee at breakfast, either," said Emma.

"Maybe, but I thought I was drinking. It was so good."

"What about Owen and Oliver? Even if they're ghosts, they're trying to help."

He thought about that. "I don't think they can leave the inn. Unless." He snapped his fingers. "That walkway. It connected this building to the inn. Maybe because of that, they can get over here."

"How's that going to help us? We can't get hold of them."

"Call them?"

Emma shrugged. "There's no phone in here. Besides, when Beverly trashed my place, she went to town on the library as well. The phones have been destroyed."

"We could just leave." When Emma didn't respond, he continued. "Why not? We can go back to Sol's, borrow a car, or get a rental, then get the hell away from here. Beverly can't get us if we run away."

"Listen to yourself, Peter. Run away? This is all five years early. It's not supposed to happen again until 2025."

"He did arrange for us to come to the inn. I don't think he expected Beverly to be there, too."

"Exactly. Owen has deliberately set things in motion to give us a chance. A head start. We can't simply abandon him."

"But Beau or whoever is also a ghost. He can't get to us."

"But Beverly can."

Peter sighed. "I know. That's why we can't leave. We have to take this to her. And that scares the living fuck out of me. She has a sabre. We've got nothing."

She grasped his hand and squeezed. "Yes, we do. We're together this time. We know what's going to happen and who's going to do it. We have enough time this time to stop it from happening one more time."

Chapter 18:
"Have we got time to make it happen one more time?"

Peter Dawson, January 18, 2020

"Ready, Emma, my love? We're about to try and not get murdered for the fifth time." Peter drew her in close for a tighter hug. She shook in his arms.

"I guess I'm as ready as I'll ever be. This is so fucked up, but we don't have a choice." Emma squeezed Peter's waist.

"Until now, it's never been up to us to decide what happens."

"I suppose not," she said then pulled away. "Now?"

He nodded and Emma moved closer to the library front door.

Peter wasn't completely confident about the plan, but it seemed like the best approach. That is, the best until he could think of something better…safer…saner. After all this time, to take the chance of losing Emma now, when they were so close, seemed utterly idiotic. Yet, they had to try to change their fate. As quietly as she could, Emma placed her key in the large lock and twisted. There was an audible click, and both held their breath in case someone else heard. The wind still howled outside and there was a small, frigid breeze streaming through the cracks around the door. Peter smiled at Emma then leaned in to give her a peck on the cheek. In truth, he wanted to pick her up and run as far away from Wycliffe Point as they could get. But Emma was right.

Things had been put into motion to give them the possibility to break the vicious cycle of murder. It wouldn't be right for them to throw that opportunity away because they were a little afraid. A little! Getting a sabre through the guts or being eviscerated was something that inspired more than a little fear. Peter was ready to soil his pants, and he was sure Emma felt the same.

Peter stuck his head out the door, looked both ways, and when he saw the coast was clear, gave Emma a little push. She barreled her way through the door then took off down the sidewalk toward Sol's place.

Let's hope he still has his service pistol and is willing to hand it over.

Scrunching his eyes closed for a second as if it would squeeze away the fear, Peter dashed out the door then pulled it shut behind him. There was no turning back now. Before him stood the inn, a dark shadow in the storm waiting to…do what? Devour him? Severely murder him? Trap him in an endless time loop from which there was no escape until the sun exploded and destroyed the earth? And even then, would the cycle stop?

What in the holy fuck was that all about?

He had a quick look, but Emma had already disappeared into the swirling snow.

There's nothing for it now, my lad. Onward, into the fray.

Peter made his way through the deepening snow. There was a layer of ice underneath that made the trip treacherous, but enough snow had fallen to stop him from slipping. When he reached the path between the library and the inn, he paused and looked to his right. The sound of the waves pounding the rocky shore rose though a white fog that completely blanked out any sign of the bay. He couldn't even see the low stone wall or the iron railing that topped it.

The thought of falling from the cliff gave Peter a shiver worse than anything caused by the cold. Four times he had gone down that cliff. He hoped there wouldn't be a fifth.

As he passed his snow-covered Falcon, it was even more obvious to Peter that someone had smashed in the windshield. Through the side door, he could just about make out the head rest on the driver's side. The rest of the interior was packed with snow like someone's practical joke with Styrofoam peanuts. The hurt became worse when he realized the rear window had also been destroyed. So much for all that work.

Fucking bitch.

Should he really blame Beverly? After all, she was possessed. Fuck that, she would have done it out of spite, possession or not.

When he reached the inn's side door, he saw that it was padlocked shut. In addition, there were a couple of planks nailed to the frame to block access. *I guess it really is closed. Damn.* Blown snow was piled almost halfway up the door. Moving to the front entrance, he found a heavy chain run through the double door handles, also held together with a heavy padlock. There appeared to be no light inside the inn. When he pressed his face against the glass window of the door, he could see nothing.

Do I try to find a tool to break in or wait for Emma with the gun?

Suddenly paralyzed with indecision, not knowing what to do, Peter decided to go to Sol's and hook up with Emma. He wasn't particularly anxious to get into the inn and face Beverly or whatever awaited him inside alone. Maybe Emma would have some ideas. He took a step down toward the parking lot when he heard the rattle of chains and a heavy thud.

Peter turned to see the chain in a pile on the concrete porch. The nailed boards were next to it. There was no snow. The porch wasn't even wet. Light shone from within the inn. As he stepped back up to the porch, careful to avoid the nails sticking up from the boards, one of the doors swung open. A blast of warm air hit him, welcoming him to the inn.

The moment Peter stepped inside, the door slammed shut behind him. The raging storm outside was muted and only the occasional rattle of a wind-blown shutter let him know how nasty the weather had become.

The fire burned brightly in the hearth, lighting the whole lobby. Behind the front desk stood Owen with a huge smile on his face.

"I wondered when you'd be back," he said. "We've been waiting." He came out from behind the desk and took Peter's arm. Unconsciously, Peter touched Owen's hand to make sure he was real and not a phantom.

You feel solid enough. How can you be a ghost?

"In here, we all have limited substance. That's what makes this situation complicated. If any of the dead Kensingtons decide to enter the inn and do more than interact with the Kent woman, they could pose a real, physical threat."

"Wonderful. Can things get any worse?"

"Ask them," said Owen.

They stood at the entrance to the dining room. It was packed with people, all of whom Peter knew. They were all focused on him which instantly made him self-conscious. The only sound was the crackling of the fire and the dull roar of the storm.

What struck Peter most of all was that, in every one of her incarnations, his lady love remained the most beautiful woman he had ever seen. His heart soared and his nether regions throbbed. Emmeline and Emelia blushed and looked down at the floor. Emily and Millie, more modern women, simply smiled.

I wonder which one it was that first night.

All four held up their hands. "We took turns," said Emily.

Oh crap, they can all read my mind.

"You silly man, what did you expect? We're all from inside your head anyway," said Millie

"But you're ghosts," said Peter. He nudged Owen. "A little help here."

"She's correct. Ghosts don't exist. We're all figments of your imagination. You're asleep in your bed at home."

"You're fucking with me, aren't you?"

"Of course he is," said Patrick. "Every O'Dale is a wisenheimer when he's not loaded."

"You should have seen how wallpapered he got the night we all died," said Philip.

"Applesauce," said Owen. "I was only a swigger when I was with you two."

"He did help save a lot of us when we were contraband," said Emmeline.

Emelia nodded, then said, "Killer on the piano, too."

"Don't use that word," said Emily. She rubbed her belly. "It still hurts."

"Please stop talking, all of you." Peter scratched an itch in the center of his chest. "This is ridiculous. Four stunning women, four identical O'Dales, and four of me." Waving to the crowd of Black people at the back, he added, "And I suppose all of you are the innocent families Kensington, or whoever he was at the time, slaughtered for the fun of it."

"Yes, sir," said one of the eight Black men. He must have been one of the fathers since he didn't look too old. "I am, sir."

A little girl popped her head from behind her mother's skirt. "He keeps eating my leg."

Another little girl added, "He put some of me in a stew."

Peter stood there staring at the multitude. All dead because of one evil family. A tear slid down his cheek. "There are more of you over at the pub. Another family. Oona and her cook."

Owen's face fell and Oliver gasped. "We suspected something like that might happen," said Oliver. "We hoped that maybe by starting early, all the pieces, like the Black family, wouldn't fall into place."

"It's a shame about Oona," said Owen. "She was Oliver's…niece, I think."

"That's right," said Oliver.

Peter watched as various people popped in and out of sight. One second Emmeline was there, then she was gone. At the moment, Owen was the only other person in the room with him.

"Why haven't I seen *all* of you—them—us— before? Only one or two?"

"Who you see depends on what you're holding or thinking about," said Owen. "Also, it's not like we have anything to keep us busy on this plane of existence. We're all restless, you know. Bodies all over the place while our spirits reside here waiting for whatever comes. Revenge, peace, that bitch Beverly being annihilated."

Emily popped back into the room. "When this is over, Peter, could you possibly get all our remains and bring them here? It might help calm things down."

"I'm in a grave at the bottom of the cliff," said Emelia.

"My bones are wedged amongst the rocks below the warehouse," said Patrick.

"A lot of us are in pauper's graves," said one of the older Black women.

Peter felt overwhelmed, but said, "We'll do what we can, everyone. I promise. Can you all help me and Emma against Beverly?"

Owen drew in a deep breath despite being an unbreathing ghost. "Not much, I'm afraid. We can move about, move a few small things here and there, carry the odd suitcase, but most of what you see us do isn't real even though you can see and feel it."

"We're a bit like a Greek chorus," said Oscar. "You know, making comments about what's happening, giving a bit of advice, perhaps guiding you in the right direction."

"So basically, you are useless in a fight," said Peter. He crossed his arms and stared at the returned throng. "Well, isn't that fucking marvelous."

"It's not quite so bad, Peter," said Emelia. "It also means the four Kensington's can't help this Beverly bitch either."

"Oh, bother," said Owen, looking over Peter's shoulder. "They're here."

The itch on Peter's chest grew in intensity. Before he could scratch it or see what Owen was on about, a shower of blood erupted from him followed by the blades of four sabres. The itch was replaced by the worst pain he'd ever experienced.

Looking at the bloody things sticking out of his chest, Peter said, "Shit, I can feel that. I thought you said they couldn't hurt us." The pain intensified.

Behind him, four people laughed. One said, "Die, sodomite."

Peter tried to grab the blades and push them back through his chest, but the just sliced up his fingers.

As everything grew dark, he said, "I've failed her again."

Beverly Kent, January 18, 2020

Beverly stood a few feet onto the walkway from her suite of rooms at the inn. Through the window, she could see down to the low wall that ran between the edge of the cliff and the warehouse. With a smile on her face, she watched Beau shove his sabre through Philip's chest then kick his victim over the wall and down to the sharp rocks below. A few moments later, she caught a glimpse of Patrick plummeting from the warehouse window to the frozen sea, blood spewing from his chest.

Straining her neck, she could just catch the edge of the path down to the pebble beach. Ben gave Paul a shove to slide him off the sabre. His victim reached for something in his coat pocket as he disappeared into the roaring waves. That incarnation had been a severe disappointment. Lacking the true bearing of a Kensington, the scum had been unable to control his urges and drawn unwanted attention. As a result, he'd missed out on the pleasures to be found in the secret room. But to make matters worse, that garbage had betrayed his country to a filthy enemy. That had been the single thing all the players in this game could agree upon: those Nazi swine had to die. He'd let the bitch do her worst, but had been too late to prevent her from removing Ben who might still have been of use. Small loss. What's a forty year wait to someone who is immortal?

Beverly shook her head. It was getting confusing, all these memories, and all as a man. Make that confusing and disgusting.

At last, the most painful of the lot. Off to Beverly's left, Buster crashed through the big window on the second-floor landing. His sabre pierced through Prescott's chest, but Prescott had his hands tightly wrapped around Buster's throat. That had been a bad one. Cheated of his pleasure with the animal bitch, then murdered by a simpering coward. At least Buster had the satisfaction of having slashed the throats of the two backstabbing O'Dales.

Always the O'Dales. Forever there to interfere with his plans or to cover things up after the deed was done and rob him of his glory. This time, though, she'd already taken care of the last O'Dale, disguised as a woman and pretending to know nothing about Beverly's history or destiny. The phantom O'Dales down in the lobby shouldn't prove to be a problem. Perhaps one of them had initiated the cycle early, but that only meant Beverly could experience the joy of killing that much sooner, and that much more. The cook had been a new kill this cycle.

She took a final bite from the young one's leg then tossed it aside. Beverly had had her fill at last. Thinking about the bitch waiting to die across the way, her stomach rumbled, and she decided she might like to try some older meat. It had been so fortunate that her cousin, long ago in New Orleans, had introduced her to the delicacy that is long pig. It was fortunate, too, that meat made itself available so freely and easily. Remembering Bart, she thought it was time for a hearty stew.

And then she watched it all happen one more time.

And again.

One more time.

How long had she been standing here watching the deaths and failures over and over and over? The last thing she remembered before the show was the ecstasy of blood and body parts flying around some rooms at the pub. She'd had something to eat then spotted her prey standing outside in the storm. She'd smiled at them, happy they were close by and ready to die.

Maybe she should saunter over to her secret room and

relive the passion she felt there in the past, playing with animals, gutting that bitch, bathing in blood and viscera. Well, not the last part. She wasn't Elizabeth Bathory trying to remain young.

After seeing Buster and Prescott exit the window one more time, Beverly crossed the rest of the walkway, all the time wondering when it had been rebuilt.

When she reached the far side, something made her stop. Beverly listened but only heard the wind outside.

The bitch is getting away!

Beverly descended the stairs as fast as she dared. It was dark and, though she had been this way many times in the past, none of those times had been as her. When she reached the bottom, she yanked open the door and stepped into the storm. At the end of the path between the buildings, she spotted someone passing. Lurching back into the door alcove, she waited for a few moments to allow whoever it was to go.

Peeking out, Beverly was relieved to see nothing but snow. She raced along the path until she got to the main road. Pausing for an instant to gather her thoughts, she knew where she had to go.

It was a difficult journey, running through the cold, wind, and snow, but her prey was up ahead. She was sure of it. Slowly, as Beverly got closer the vague movement in the snow ahead resolved into the form of that vicious bitch Ranahan. Beverly couldn't suppress the giggle when she was a few feet behind the animal. She reached out and tapped it on the shoulder.

The look of sheer horror on its face when it saw who was

there was marvelous. Beverly didn't have time to waste savouring the fear in the eyes of the prey. She lashed out with her fist and connected with the thing's belly. With a whoosh of exhaled air, it went down trying to breath. Beverly gave it a kick which sent it rolling onto the street.

Prodding her victim with the toe of her boot, Beverly was happy to see the thing was out cold. Grabbing one of its ankles, she dragged it back along the sidewalk to the library. At the front entrance, Beverly gave an almighty kick that sent the door crashing open. She dragged her burden into the library, heading straight for the stairs to the fourth floor. Unconcerned about the damage being done to the body she pulled up the stairs, Beverly smiled every time she heard the thump of its head hitting the edge of a step. By the time she reached the top and pulled open the door to the fourth-floor living area and her secret room, she had left a trail of bright blood in her wake.

When Beverly threw aside the door to her room, she was not the least bit surprised to see her four ancestors awaiting her arrival.

"Where were you idiots when I needed you?" Beverly waited for an answer.

"We're not allowed to go anywhere but here," said Ben. "It's a rule."

"Shut up, traitor! I don't want to hear another peep from you, or I'll find a way to destroy your spirit forever. I probably will anyway, you shameless piece of offal," she screamed.

"The others have gathered over at the inn," said Beau. "If we hurry and work together, we can take them all. I have a plan."

"Plan! You have a plan?" Beverly spat at him. "Remember the fiasco at Fort Fisher? That was your grand plan. All those other battles won because your men didn't follow your plans; they took the initiative and overcame your uselessness."

Beau stepped back. It was obvious no one had ever spoken to him like this before. Well, it was about time.

Dropping her victim's leg, she said, "Hang it up. You know where and how."

Beverly removed her greatcoat and tossed it aside. Removing the sabre scabbard, she gently placed it upon the table by the stove. There was a fire going that helped take the chill out of the room. Someone had been thinking ahead.

The sound of a pulley and chain indicated her prey was almost ready for play. She turned to see the animal lying on the floor while her four companions stood there looking like idiots. The chain swayed a little.

"What the almighty fuck are you doing, you fucking assholes. String her up, you useless cocksuckers."

Beverly looked at her ancestors in turn. She could tell Buster would be useless. He was all piss and vinegar until it mattered. The fool had let himself get murdered. Ben. Fucking traitor. He shouldn't even be here, tainting the good name of Kensington. Bart and Beau stood together by the wall. Evil and malice radiated off them. If looks could kill, the world would die a painful death.

She laughed. They all stared at her. She may have been the newest, and only a woman, but the power in her made the others seem like children. They feared her. Even Beau, clearly the worst of the lot, was wary of her.

"We can't do anything with her except feel her up," said Ben. He licked his wet lips and rubbed himself. Of all her ancestors, Ben was the most disgusting.

"Our interaction with the living is very limited," said Buster.

Beverly looked at Beau. "You possessed me, creep. Do something. Possess her and make her string herself up."

Beau shook his head. "I can only possess a direct relative. You." He grinned and Beverly immediately felt dirty. "I can do that again. I enjoyed being a woman. I could do things to myself."

She shuddered, remembering how it had been when Beau was inside her.

"So much promise and you end up being a waste of my time." She stepped over to her prisoner. When she saw it move, Beverly gave it a hard kick in the stomach. Crouching, Beverly stripped off the thing's coat then its cardigan. There was a spreading bloodstain on its blouse, probably from a wound caused by Beverly's hard boot.

"I have to admit, if it wasn't for your mongrel background, I'd find you quite attractive. Almost worth more than simply being murdered for my pleasure."

Grabbing some rope hanging from a hook on the wall, Beverly bound her captive's hands then looped the chain between her arms. She found getting the creature hanging a few inches off the floor easy thanks to the well-oiled pulley.

Standing in front of the hanging thing, Beverly had an idea. Turning to her ancestors, she said, "You four, see if you can be useful. Go find that Dawson asshole and bring him here. I don't care what you have to do to him, just get him here. And fast!" The four ghosts blinked out of sight.

"You know…was it Emma? Is that your name? No matter. You'll be dead soon enough and no one will care what you were called. You know, you can never have Dawson. He's mine to do with as I please. I am pleased to let him watch me gut you like the pig you are. Maybe I'll force him to devour some of you. A slice of thigh, maybe?"

The woman hanging from the chain didn't move. Her body swung slightly. The blood on her blouse had stopped spreading.

Feeling hungry, and curious, she held her captive steady and bit into its flank. As she tasted blood, Beverly wondered why none of her predecessors had ever done this.

Peter Dawson, January 18, 2020

The intensity of the pain in his chest was something he had never experienced before, even when his appendix burst mid-lecture several years ago. Opening his eyes, Peter realized he was still in the inn lobby, kneeling at the bottom of the stairs. Off to his left were some of the inn's ghosts—a couple of O'Dales, one of him, and a few Emmas.

Looking down at his chest, he was stunned to see nothing. There were no sabres protruding from his body, nor was there any blood from the horrendous wounds he had suffered.

Or thought he had suffered.

Peter stood on shaky legs. "What the fuck?"

"They can't really hurt you," said Owen. "But they can make you think they did."

He heard muttering behind him and turned to see four red-haired soldiers looking somewhat forlorn. Blood dripped from their sabres but disappeared before it hit the carpet.

"We were supposed to bring you to the dame," said the scrawniest one who seemed to be in a doughboy's uniform. "She's gonna be angry."

"Don't fawn, garbage," said a soldier wearing a Civil War officer's uniform. He looked like the meanest of the bunch and Peter guessed he was Beau, the one who had started this mess.

"What do you clowns want?" he asked, showing unexpected bravado while feeling scared out of his wits. "What dame? Beverly?"

"Yes." This must have been Buster since he was in a modern Marine's outfit. Something about him made Peter want to laugh, but he suppressed the urge. No point annoying these things any more than necessary.

"She's got that mongrel animal of yours up there. She's going to gut it and have it for dinner."

It dawned on Peter what they were talking about. "Shit! Emma! That lunatic's got Emma." He ran for the front door.

"No, Peter," said Oscar. "Take the walkway. It's faster."

"It's not there, remember. You blew it up in 1905."

"It's back for now. You can cross it safely. Go save her."

Peter nodded then went up the stairs three at a time. When he arrived at the fourth floor, his thighs ached, but he kept moving. At the end of the corridor, he saw the open door and the walkway beyond. When he reached it, he hesitated for a second then plunged ahead toward the library on the other side. The walkway felt and sounded solid.

The corridor in the library was pitch black. Beau appeared a few feet away carrying a lantern. He beckoned Peter to follow. Behind him, he could hear a lot of mumbling. Were the others coming as well? Peter didn't bother to check, but kept moving in the direction he hoped would lead to Emma.

Light shone through an open door. The secret room. Peter, or one of him, had been here a couple of times before. When he reached the door, the sight that awaited him almost forced him to recoil in abject horror.

Emma hung from a chain looped through a pulley on the ceiling. Blood from a small wound on her side had soaked into her pants. She was bruised, battered, and unconscious. He felt overwhelming relief when he saw her chest move. She was breathing, still alive.

Standing over by a window was his nemesis: Beverly. She leaned on a sabre, licked her blood-smeared lips, then smiled.

"About fucking time, loser."

"You won't get away with it this time, bitch," said Peter. Seeing the love of his life in danger brought out the bravado. This time, however, he believed in himself. "I won't let you hurt her again."

"How are you going to stop me, Dawson? I have the sabre…"—she waved it and made a few thrusts and slashes—"and you've got nothing."

Peter looked around for a weapon. Fuck. There was nothing close by except a wooden spoon and some pots on the table near the stove. "Doesn't matter, Bev. Your clowns couldn't hurt me downstairs. What makes you think you can now?"

"This," she said and leapt forward.

Peter tried to twist away but watched helpless as the sabre slid into his abdomen just below his ribs. The pain was excruciating. He fell to his knees. This time, the blood flowing from his wound was real. Gripping the edge of the table, Peter pulled himself to his feet. On shaky legs, he stared at Beverly, waiting for her next thrust.

"I can't fail her again," he said. As he spoke, he heard a distant rattle of chains.

"You! Can't fail her!" Beverly roared with laughter. Her ancestors laughed along with her. "Get the fuck out! This is *my* time." The four ghosts blinked out.

"What's so funny, bitch?" Peter tried to take a step closer. The pain when he moved almost made him vomit, but he knew he had to endure it if he was to save Emma. This time.

"Who do you think you are, you moron? *You* save *her*?" Beverly paced about in front of Peter. "It was never you who was supposed to save her. You never failed." Beverly pointed at Emma whose eyes were now open. She shook her head when she saw Peter was aware she was awake. "She did. She failed you, you useless piece of fucking scum. She was supposed to save you."

Now Peter felt confused. Had everything he learned in the last couple of days been a mistake?

"You're the one I kept wanting to kill, asshole. She was just a bit of fun. A mongrel to torture, slaughter, and eat. Except, thanks to those O'Dales, I never had the chance to partake."

Peter got closer to the window which caused Beverly to move into the center of the room. He had seen Emma struggling. Emma had pulled herself up the chain that held her. Now she grasped the pulley. He didn't know what Emma was trying to do, but Peter wanted to keep Beverly distracted.

Emma Ranahan, January 18, 2020

All she felt was anger. That was good because it dulled the pain, in her belly where a keloid must have split open, and from her stretched arms. She'd managed to pull herself up enough to get a grip on the pulley. Now, maybe she could get free and save Peter.

Save Peter? All along that was my job? Ah, Millie, we really fucked it up that time.

Good. Peter had seen her move and was smart enough not to acknowledge it. If he could keep that bitch distracted long enough, Emma could… What? She was hanging, battered, weaponless, in a freezing room with a psychopath threatening her man.

Her man.

That was all the motivation she needed.

Emma managed to raise her left leg enough to drop it over the section of chain that went from the pulley to the hook on the wall. The wall was only a few feet away. If she could reach it. She managed to kick off her boots. Her socks went with them. Emma didn't move in case the crazy bitch had heard her boots hit the floor. The chain was frigid and hurt her bare feet when she touched it. It didn't help that it was rusted and chipped, so it also cut into her flesh.

She crept her toes along the length of the chain until she touched the hook. With a quick look behind her, she saw that Peter was still keeping Beverly busy. Buster popped into sight next to Peter.

"Er, I think you'd better…"

Before he could finish, Beverly screamed, "I told you to get the fuck out of here. Go. Now. Leave me the fuck alone." Her voice broke. She was so angry, she had made herself cry. If she kept it up, she'd become hysterical. "Fucking go!"

Buster went away.

Peter looked relieved, but he kept up a running commentary with Beverly.

"How could you be so cruel, Beverly? I mean, sure, you're nasty to anyone who crosses you, but what you did to Oona and the others…"

She laughed. "They deserved it. Especially O'Dale. Always interfering. High and mighty. Holier than thou. Fuckers. And the mongrels? Who gives a fuck? They're trash."

"Your language has become quite ripe since we got here. Even when you were at your worst at the university, you never had a mouth like this." He winced. Peter's hand that had been on the side of his belly slipped down. There was a large, wet patch of blood. While she looked, Emma saw more blood ooze out of the wound. He fell against the table.

"You're going to die now, asshole," Beverly raised the sabre above her head, ready to bring it down on Peter's exposed neck.

Peter screamed and pushed the table over, sending the pots clanging to the floor. Emma took the opportunity to grab onto the pulley then kick out with her foot. She connected with the chain on the hook and managed to slip it free. The chain thudded to the floor, in the process hitting Emma in the stomach and ripping open another keloid.

She let go of the pulley and fell to the floor, immediately losing her balance and sprawling face-first into a rotten bale of cotton. Behind her, Peter and Beverly screamed at each other. Recovering her composure, she quickly pulled the chain from between her arms then used her teeth to loosen the rope that bound her wrists.

"Fucking animal."

Emma looked up in time to see the weirdest sight she had ever seen. Beverly ran at her with the sabre thrust ahead, aimed at Emma. Meanwhile, Peter had one arm around Beverly's waist attempting to pull her away, while with the other hand he beat her about the head with a…wooden spoon? Despite the danger, Emma couldn't stop herself from grinning. Trust Peter to protect her in the funniest way possible.

Beverly elbowed Peter in the face, sending him crashing into the overturned table then into the stove hard enough for it to shift and send a shower of soot down upon his head. The crazed woman whipped around, blindly swinging the sabre. It connected with the loosened stove pipe with a clang.

Emma lunged at Beverly, getting her legs around the woman's waist and her hands on the woman's neck. Beverly waved the sabre wildly, nowhere near to cutting Emma. Attempting to butt Emma in the face with the back of her head, but only succeeded in allowing Emma to get a tighter grip on her throat. Then she let go, keeping her legs around Beverly's waist, and grabbed two handfuls of flaming red hair.

Emma yanked the hair. Beverly howled and dropped the sabre, grasping for Emma's wrists.

"Peter. Get the sabre."

Beverly ran at the wall, turned quickly, and slammed Emma into the rough planking. Her back went numb for a moment, but Emma didn't relax her grip.

The whole time, Beverly screamed incoherently. Unable to dislodge Emma, she slammed into the wall again, this time next to the large window. It rattled on its hinges and its shutters burst open letting in a frigid Atlantic wind.

"I can't get her while you're riding her back, Emma," said Peter. He held the sabre out in front of him with a two-handed grip. It was clear none of his antecedents' military training had been passed down to him.

"Back off, Peter," said Emma.

While Beverly was in mid-maniacal scream, Emma let go and fell backward. She landed on her feet and waited for Beverly to turn and face her. She didn't know what she'd do against the crazy bitch, but she had to do something.

Spittle flew into the air as Beverly spun to face her. Before she could take a step closer, Emma punched her as hard as she could in the solar plexus knocking the wind out of her. While Beverly gasped for air, Emma gave her a hard side kick to the chest.

This sent Beverly hurtling back, losing her footing. She hit the windowsill and managed to grab hold of the frame. Emma kicked her again and sent her sailing out the window.

Beverly Kent, January 18, 2020

She couldn't breathe and could barely hold on to the window frame. She wanted to tell the fucking bitch that she'd get her but couldn't get the words out.

When the bitch kicked her the second time, some of Beverly's fingernails were ripped from her fingers as she went through the window. She stared down at the rough water of the bay as it rushed up to meet her.

For a moment, she wondered if this was how all those Peter's had felt as they plunged to their deaths.

Beverly hit the water hard. Finally able to breathe, she instead gulped in cold sea water.

Her head popped above the surface for an instant. She looked up to see her two worst enemies looking down at her.

She grinned. She'd be back.

Then everything went black.

Peter Dawson, January 18, 2020

He rushed to Emma's side, stunned by what he had just witnessed. The savagery on her face when she kicked Beverly through the window scared the hell out of him. Peter put his arm around Emma in a vain attempt to keep her warm. She was shivering for fuck's sake—whether from the cold or nerves, he didn't know. His arm would do diddly to help.

Emma seemed unconcerned by the cold. Her face now clear of any emotion, she leaned out of the window again and looked down. Peter followed her gaze.

There, a few feet from the edge of the cliff, Beverly's head shot out of the water once more. She glared back at them and grinned. A huge wave caught her and slammed her into the rock instantly pulping her head.

For a few seconds, there was a red stain on the water, then the waves washed it, and Beverly, away.

Coda

Emma Ranahan, January, a few days after

Emma stood at the edge of the cliff staring down at the spot where Beverly had gone under the water. After being crushed against the cliff, Beverly's body had disappeared. She doubted there would be a body washed up on the little pebble beach. Perhaps tomorrow, she and Peter would go down again and check to be sure. If they did find anything, would they simply bury it near Emelia's former grave, or dispose of it in some other, more permanent way? Burning and scattering the ashes? Or should Beverly join the other Kensington's in the family plot? That was unlikely as there appeared to be no more Kensingtons.

And how long would she and Peter wait before being satisfied that there would be no evidence?

For the cycle to end completely, there had to be no way for the spirit of Beau to return. Beverly had no living relatives, though there could be distant cousins scattered around the country. There had never been a direct line from Beau to Beverly anyway. It was the same with the others. Peter's relations were so far-flung they'd need twelve degrees of Kevin Bacon to even touch the periphery of each other's lives.

The O'Dale line had always been passed down through brothers and uncles. Besides, with the deaths of Owen and Oliver in 1985, that line had been destroyed. Except, where had Oona come from? As an O'Dale, she must have a relative somewhere. She had been a good friend to Emma and deserved to be remembered as more than just another victim of a timeless psychopath.

And Peter. There had been no hint anywhere in any of the official reports describing the past events. None of the extant letters or diaries had ever mentioned relatives.

Finally, there was Emma. She had known she was adopted, and there had been talk of mysterious distant relatives who never surfaced. Those snow globes had appeared, long-lost heirlooms, without warning or provenance. Would there be another in five years?

Five years. Emma could never allow herself, or Peter, to forget it had all happened for them five years early. Though dead, Owen had been able to influence events that Oona would not have known about in time. Could it start all over again in 2025? With luck and great care, no.

Now a new snow globe sat on Sol's dining room table. It was one of the surprises Peter had found when he finally entered the inn for real the other day, sitting on the shelf with the other broken globes. He said he hadn't spotted it any of the times he'd been at the inn. But since the events in the inn were not real, it was small wonder that detail had eluded him. Had the thing simply appeared conveniently so the survivors could contain the threat? The latest figures already showed in the windows: tiny reproductions of her, Peter, and Beverly. Peter had suggested encasing it in resin then perhaps concrete so it couldn't be broken. Where would they keep the concrete block so it would be safe and inaccessible to anyone who might, either deliberately or by accident, break it and free Beau?

The other surprise for Peter was that the interior of the inn looked nothing like he had described to her a few days before. There was no furniture. Carpets lay in rolls against the front desk, which was shoved up against a wall. The fireplaces were bricked up. Scaffolding stood everywhere, waiting for carpenters to get to work on the damage. Evidence of the 1985 fire was everywhere in the scorched woodwork and beams and the soot-stained ceilings.

Emma and Sol worked together to help Peter understand everything he experienced at the inn had been an illusion. He maintained that it had been real to him. Owen and Oliver were people with whom he had interacted. He'd slept in a soft bed and had…a wonderful experience.

Speaking of Sol, he had been able to nudge the police investigation into the disappearance of Beverly and the murders at the pub. The detectives were convinced Beverly had had a psychotic breakdown, slaughtered the people at the pub, then thrown herself into the bay in an act of remorse. Complete bullshit, of course, but more believable than the truth.

Peter had uncovered the grave of Emelia. Her bones had been unharmed, though it was possible to see where the sabre had done its worst. They found Patrick where he'd said he'd be, jammed between the rocks below the warehouse window. The water and small creatures had taken care of the flesh, but pebbles and shells must have been thrown up by the waves over time and covered the bones.

Though Emelia and Patrick were of different times, it seemed only fitting they be reinterred together. They were, after all, incarnations of the same two lovers who had been destined to be together. Sol would keep the bones in his attic until the summer when the ground would be workable. He'd also look into finding the remains of the other dead from the inn, including the anonymous Black families. They'd been considered collateral damage or fun for the killers. They deserved better. Peter promised he would help with the search and give them names.

Emma and Peter would return and bury them all somewhere near the inn grounds. The thought made Emma shiver. They'd be burying themselves. That would never feel normal.

As if anything that had happened in the last week had been normal.

A crunch on the frozen snow crust alerted Emma to the approach of someone. No, not just someone. It was Peter. She would always know when he was near. They were connected in so many ways, though the sharing of thoughts could be somewhat burdensome. If only he would think about something other than sex. Even now, despite the solemnity of the situation and the sex-dampening cold wind off the Atlantic, the man was aroused. Then again, Emma felt flattered that someone thought of her in that way at all. She had been on her own for so long, always self-conscious about the keloids and their possible return at the most inopportune time.

She scratched at the itch on her side where the crazy bitch had taken a bite. When the doctor had given Emma a tetanus shot, he hadn't asked how she got it. She was happy there was no hint of the keloids. Gone for good? *I hope.*

She felt Peter's arm around her waist and cuddled into him. He'd been able to twist his body enough when Beverly stabbed him with the sabre that she'd only sliced deeply into his side. Emma had almost vomited when he showed her the wound and she could see a couple of ribs.

At the moment, there was no shared physical warmth with Peter—it was too damned cold here—but it was what was inside that mattered. The second he came within a few feet of her, Emma knew she was safe, that he would lay down his life to protect her.

Ironic, then, that they had gotten everything so mixed up right from the start.

Killer. Victim. Hero. Friend.

Except they had the victim and hero reversed.

"Sol says we can have his car for as long as we need it. He doesn't plan to do any traveling anytime soon."

Emma smiled. "Isn't he too old to drive anyway?" She thought for a second. "Maybe not. He can still get randy when the mood takes him."

"Which seems to be every time you walk into the room," said Peter. "Hell, I just have to say your name and he gets like a horny Boy Scout who's snuck over to the Girl Scouts' showers for a peek."

"Are you *sure* you two aren't related?" She smacked his arm. "I am not going to dress up in a maid's uniform for your perverted pleasure."

"Will you stop doing that? Can't a guy have a dirty thought in private once in a while?"

She hugged him closer. "Never change, you wonderful man." She shivered. "Can we get out of here? I'm cold and hungry and, now that you've thought about it, just a little bit randy."

They set off along the sidewalk toward the inn next to Sol's place. There were no heartless maids, ghostly managers, or psychotic guests there. Just a warm bed and quiet.

"I can't wait to get the hell away from here, Emma. When can we leave?"

"A couple more days. I want to be sure there's nothing down there."

"You're the boss."

Peter Dawson, January, a few days after

He tried to suppress his memories about the inn. It was easy since all he had to do was think sexy thoughts and what he'd like to do with Emma and that's all she would see. When should he tell her?

"Why not now, Peter?" she asked.

"Shit."

Emma stopped walking, took hold of his arms, and looked deep into his eyes. "What is it? What are you not telling me? Please."

He sighed. It's not like it was bad news, necessarily. "Sol found some papers. He let me see them because he wasn't sure how you'd react."

"Fuck, Peter, get to the goddamn point."

"Okay. The new owners of the inn, and, by the way, of the library and pub, are really a trust fund. It had been set up by

Owen, the former owner, a few months before all the chaos went down in January, 1985. The trust was instructed to start renovations on the inn last year."

"So?"

"The trust was also behind you getting the librarian job."

Peter saw the light go on in Emma's eyes. "You mean Owen set this all in motion forty years ago?"

"Apparently. There's more. The terms of the trust also stipulated that, in the event of the demise of the O'Dale line, everything would be passed to the last living relative of the Ranahan clan. That's you."

Emma stared at him open-mouthed. She started walked toward Sol's place and pulled him along. "I own that dump?"

"Yep."

"And you were afraid to tell me. Why?"

He shrugged. "Given all that we've been through, I wasn't sure you'd want to know about owning the source of your centuries-long living hell."

"I wish we could talk to Owen about it."

That was one sad thing about the end of the murderous cycle: all the ghosts were gone. Peter had liked Owen. And the historian in him wanted to talk to all the others about their lives back in the past. He knew he was being selfish.

"Not really," said Emma, doing that mind-reader thing again. She stopped walking. "Look, Peter, can we go away somewhere for a while. Get the past few days out of our heads. Relax, enjoy some time together. Yes, do a lot of *that*, you pervert."

She's reading my mind again. "Then what?"

"Then maybe we come back to Wycliffe Point and run an inn. I can think of worse things to do. Wanna get married?"

Peter laughed. "A bit old-fashioned of you, isn't it?"

"Remember the others. We're both old-fashioned."

"I do like the idea, Emma."

Before they set off for Sol's again, Peter looked back at what might become his new home and glimpsed a shadow in one of the windows.

Owen waved from one of the second-floor windows and gave Peter Winston Churchill's World War II "V" for victory sign.

"Enough time"

(©2018 B Wozny)

Ain't it plain as January on your face
The love we had may never live again
I know strictly speaking I can be replaced
But I'd love to stay together, more than friends

but have we got enough time, have we got enough time,
have we got enough time?
(have we got) time, to make it happen, one more time?
have we got enough time, have we got enough time, have
we got enough time?
(have we got) time, to make it happen, one more time?

Here we are together in a lonesome place
Trying to make the best of who we are
I've seen disappointment on your pretty face but
I believe that we could still go far

Have we got enough time, have we got enough time, have
we got enough time?
(have we got) time, to make it happen, one more time?
have we got enough time, have we got enough time, have
we got enough time?
(have we got) time, to make it happen, one more time?

we've both made choices that were bad and good
made mistakes along the way

we've cleaned them up the very best we could
and it matters what we say, every second, every

Day, ain't it plain as January on your face
and I would not expect you to pretend
Speaking strictly as a member of the human race
I'd love to have the chance to start again

But have we got enough time, have we got enough time,
have we got enough time?
(have we got) time, to make it happen, one more time?
have we got enough time, have we got enough time, have
we got enough time?
(have we got) time, to make it happen, one more time?
 have we got time, to make it happen, one more time?

THE END?

Not if you want to dive into more of Crystal Lake Publishing's Tales from the Darkest Depths!

Check out our amazing website and online store or download our latest catalog: https://geni.us/CLPCatalog.

We always have great new projects and content on the website to dive into, as well as a newsletter, behind the scenes options, social media platforms, our own dark fiction shared-world series and our very own webstore. Our webstore even has categories specifically for KU books, non-fiction, anthologies, and of course more novels and novellas.

AUTHOR BIOGRAPHY

J. Edwin Buja has spent his life surrounded by books. He discovered early on that researching and writing hold the key to happiness. Who else would think scanning through decades of microfilm to index an old newspaper would be a dream job?

For more than forty years, he has been married to the most wonderful woman on the planet. Although he lives in a small village somewhere in Canada, his heart and second home reside with his horror family in New England.

His novels include *The King of the Wood* (2019) and *The Consort* (2022). He has also had more than twenty short stories published. He is currently working on the final novel of The Wood series, and another novel based on concerts he attended in Detroit in the 1970s.

He also writes Young Adult novels under the name John Buja. His latest release is *Coverdale* (2024). In 2000-2001, he published two middle-grade time travel/history books.

Readers…

Thank you for reading *Enough Time*. We hope you enjoyed this novel. If you have a moment, please review *Enough Time* at the store where you bought it.

Help other readers by telling them why you enjoyed this book. No need to write an in-depth discussion. Even a single sentence will be greatly appreciated. Reviews go a long way to helping a book sell, and is great for an author's career. It'll also help us to continue publishing quality books.

Thank you again for taking the time to journey with Crystal Lake's Torrid Waters.

You will find links to all our social media platforms on our Linktree page: https://linktr.ee/CrystalLakePublishing.

MISSION STATEMENT

Since its founding in August 2012, Crystal Lake has quickly become one of the world's leading publishers of Dark Fiction and Horror books. In 2023, Crystal Lake officially transitioned into an entertainment company, joining several other divisions, genres, and imprints, including Torrid Waters, Crystal Lake Comics, Crystal Lake Games, Crystal Lake Kids, and many more.

While we strive to present only the highest quality fiction and entertainment, we also endeavour to support authors along their writing journey. We offer our time and experience in non-fiction projects, as well as author mentoring and services, at competitive prices.

With several Bram Stoker Award wins and many other wins and nominations (including the HWA's Specialty Press Award), Crystal Lake Publishing puts integrity, honor, and respect at the forefront of our publishing operations.

We strive for each book and outreach program we spearhead to not only entertain and touch or comment on issues that affect our readers, but also to strengthen and support the Dark Fiction field and its authors.

Not only do we find and publish authors we believe are destined for greatness, but we strive to work with men and women who endeavour to be decent human beings who care more for others than themselves, while still being hard working, driven, and passionate artists and storytellers.

Crystal Lake Publishing is and will always be a beacon of what passion and dedication, combined with overwhelming teamwork and respect, can accomplish. We endeavour to know each and every one of our readers, while building personal relationships with our authors, reviewers, bloggers, podcasters, bookstores, and libraries.

We will be as trustworthy, forthright, and transparent as any business can be, while also keeping most of the headaches away from our authors, since it's our job to solve the problems so they can stay in a creative mind. Which of course also means paying our authors.

We do not just publish books, we present to you worlds within your world, doors within your mind, from talented authors who sacrifice so much for a moment of your time.

There are some amazing small presses out there, and through collaboration and open forums we will continue to support other presses in the goal of helping authors and showing the world what quality small presses are capable of accomplishing. No one wins when a small press goes down, so we will always be there to support hardworking, legitimate presses and their authors. We don't see Crystal Lake as the best press out there, but we will always strive to be the best, strive to be the most interactive and grateful, and even blessed press around. No matter what happens over time, we will also take our mission very seriously while appreciating where we are and enjoying the journey.

What do we offer our authors that they can't do for themselves through self-publishing?

We are big supporters of self-publishing (especially hybrid publishing), if done with care, patience, and planning. However, not every author has the time or inclination to do market research, advertise, and set up book launch strategies. Although a lot of authors are successful in doing it all, strong small presses will always be there for the authors who just want to do what they do best: write.

What we offer is experience, industry knowledge, contacts and trust built up over years. And due to our strong brand and trusting fanbase, every Crystal Lake Publishing book comes with weight of respect. In time our fans begin to trust our judgment and will try a new author purely based on our support of said author.

With each launch we strive to fine-tune our approach, learn from our mistakes, and increase our reach. We continue to assure our authors that we're here for them and that we'll carry the weight of the launch and dealing with third parties while they focus on their strengths—be it writing, interviews, blogs, signings, etc.

We also offer several mentoring packages to authors that include knowledge and skills they can use in both traditional and self-publishing endeavours.

We look forward to launching many new careers.

This is what we believe in. What we stand for. This will be our legacy.

Welcome to Crystal Lake Publishing—Where Stories Come Alive!

Also from Torrid Waters...

Harvest Time by Dan Fields, Chris Robinson, and Joe Filipas is a gripping novel that seamlessly blends elements of creature horror, American Gothic, and rural terror into an unforgettable road trip thriller.

Set against the backdrop of classic drive-in horror films like *The Texas Chainsaw Massacre* and *Pumpkinhead*, this story takes readers on a harrowing journey through the heart of America's dark, untamed landscapes.

For two young couples, a westward camping trip across the United States was meant to heal familial rifts and reconnect them with the natural world. The highway takes a fateful detour to a remote Nebraska town plagued by severe drought and besieged by unusually aggressive crows.

On a lone flourishing farm amidst the parched, forsaken land, the travelers encounter a malevolent force among the towering, neglected rows of corn. The sinister entity plans to force them into its twisted battle against the crow infestation. As night falls, they face a harrowing fight for survival that will challenge their very humanity.

Harvest Time is a masterful blend of suspense and supernatural terror, pushing its characters to unthinkable choices and aligning them with unlikely allies in a climactic battle to end the farm's cycle of destruction before dawn returns to light the last of the reaping. This novel is a thrilling exploration of the depths of human resilience and the dark secrets that lie buried in America's rural heartland.

Will you survive until the final harvest?

Also from Torrid Waters...

In *Fear of the Deep*, Julie Hiner plunges readers into the dark, uncharted waters of terror and suspense.

Bailey, a lifeguard with a heavy metal heart and a Jack Daniel's addiction, has long avoided the deep sea since a haunting accident. San Diego's sunny shores provide a façade of normalcy, where her nights are drowned in music and whiskey, and her days are spent keeping a safe distance from the ocean's grasp.

But the sea has a way of claiming what it wants. The discovery of a woman's body, marked by peculiar and familiar bite marks, washes up on her beach, forcing Bailey to confront the fears she's been running from. Deep beneath the waves, something sinister lurks, a nightmare born from genetic engineering gone awry. As Bailey delves deeper into the mystery, she finds herself entangled in a web of horror and science fiction, where sea creatures of the darkest depths become terrifyingly real.

With each tide, the line between reality and nightmare blurs, pulling Bailey into a psychological maelstrom. Her journey is not just a battle against the horrors emerging from the deep but a fight to overcome the demons within herself.

Fear of the Deep is not just a novel—it's a voyage into the heart of terror and the human psyche. It navigates the treacherous waters of horror suspense, sea stories, and genetic engineering science fiction, making it a perfect storm for fans of psychological thrillers and deep-sea adventures.

Are you brave enough to dive into the depths of *Fear of the Deep?* Hold your breath and plunge into this sea of suspense, where the darkest fears lie waiting beneath the surface.

Also from Torrid Waters...

A fast-paced story of survival, terror, family, and friendship.

The people of Wicker thought the mountain belonged to them—purchased with blood, sweat, and resilience. They forgot the deal their ancestors made. They forgot that their mountain belonged to something ancient, powerful, and hungry.

Charlotte Crowe and Rebecca Greenleigh grew up as best friends on the mountain, descendants of the original settlers of Wicker and inheritors of a terrible secret. They expected to grow old on their mountain. They did not expect the return of the wolves, the bone chimes appearing overnight in the trees, or their neighbors turning on one another. In a matter of days, everything they thought they knew is flipped upside down and they find themselves trapped in a place they once called home playing a dangerous game with a creature older than the mountain itself.

**THANK YOU FOR
PURCHASING THIS BOOK**

www.ingramcontent.com/pod-product-compliance
Lightning Source LLC
Chambersburg PA
CBHW070303310726
48976CB00005B/1553